JESSICA STOOD ON THE EDGE OF THE FOREST AND BREATHED THE COOL NIGHT AIR . . .

Suddenly, an arm went around her waist and a hand covered her mouth.

"Don't move, don't make any noise."

She knew his voice . . . It was the Raider!

"I'll take my hand away if you'll not scream. You could bring the English down on both of us if you scream."

He removed his hand and, in one motion, turned her around so that her back was hard against a tree, one of his legs wrapped securely around hers and one arm pinning her head and hair. His other hand was free to roam.

"What do you want?" she gasped.

"I came only to see you," the Raider said. "I watch you, Jessica. I see you. I think about you."

"I don't think about you," she said and tried to move away from him.

He leaned forward and kissed her neck just below her ear. "You never think of me?"

"No," she lied . . .

"Put your arms around my neck, Jessica," he commanded in a low voice.

She lifted her arms as he drew her closer to him. She could feel his body against hers, so warm and hard. Her breath was coming more quickly.

"You are mine, Jessica," the Raider whispered. "You are mine . . ."

Books by Jude Deveraux

The Velvet Promise
Highland Velvet
Velvet Song
Velvet Angel
Sweetbriar
Counterfeit Lady
Lost Lady
River Lady
Twin of Ice
Twin of Fire
The Temptress
The Raider
The Princess
The Awakening
The Maiden
The Taming
A Knight in Shining Armor
Wishes

Published by POCKET BOOKS

JUDE DEVERAUX
The Raider

POCKET BOOKS

New York   London   Toronto   Sydney   Tokyo   Singapore

This book is a work of historical fiction. Names, characters, places and incidents relating to non-historical figures are either the product of the author's imagination or are used fictitiously. Any resemblance of such non-historical incidents, places or figures to actual events or locales or persons, living or dead, is entirely coincidental.

An *Original* Publication of POCKET BOOKS

POCKET BOOKS, a division of Simon & Schuster Inc.
1230 Avenue of the Americas, New York, NY 10020

Copyright © 1987 by Deveraux Inc.
Cover art copyright © 1987 Lisa Falkenstern

ISBN: 0-671-70681-0

First Pocket Books printing June 1987

15 14 13 12 11 10 9 8 7

POCKET and colophon are registered trademarks of
Simon & Schuster Inc.

Printed in the U.S.A.

Author's Note

My fictional town of Warbrooke is set in what is now the state of Maine. During the 1760s, however, when *The Raider* takes place, that area was part of what was then called the Massachusetts Commonwealth. The land was later split off from Massachusetts, and entered the Union as Maine, the 23rd state, on March 15, 1820.

Chapter One

1766

ALEXANDER Montgomery leaned back in the chair and stretched his long, lean legs across the carpeted floor of the captain's quarters of *The Grand Duchess* and watched Nicholas Ivanovitch berate one of the servants. Alex had never seen anyone with quite as much arrogance as this Russian.

"I'll have your head if you misplace my buckles a second time," Nick said with his heavy accent and husky voice.

Alex wondered if in Russia grand dukes were still allowed to behead people who displeased them.

"Go now. Out of my sight," Nick said as he waved a lace-encased wrist toward the cowering servant. "You see what I have to bear," he said to Alex as soon as they were alone in the cabin.

"It's a great deal, yes, I can see that," Alex agreed.

Nicholas raised one eyebrow at his friend, then looked back at the charts spread across the table. "We'll be docking about a hundred and fifty miles south of this Warbrooke of yours. Think someone will be willing to take you north?"

"I'll manage," Alex said nonchalantly, putting his hands behind his head and stretching even more, his long body taking up most of the cabin space. Long ago he'd schooled his handsome face to conceal what he was thinking. Nicholas knew some of what his friend was feeling, but Alex didn't allow anyone to see the depth of his concern.

Months ago, while Alex was in Italy, he'd received a letter from his sister Marianna begging him to come home. She had said that he was desperately needed. She had told Alex what their father had forbidden her to tell: that he, Sayer Montgomery, had been badly injured in an accident aboard a ship and his legs had been crushed. They hadn't expected him to live, but he had and he was confined to his bed now, a cripple.

Marianna had gone on to say that she had married an Englishman, the customs inspector for the little town of Warbrooke, and he was . . . She hadn't gone into detail of what her husband was doing, probably because she was caught between loyalty to her husband and loyalty to her family and the townspeople she'd known all her life. But Alex could sense that there was much that she wasn't telling him.

She'd given the letter to one of the many seamen in Warbrooke and hoped that it would reach Alex and that he could come home. Alex had received the letter soon after he'd docked in Italy. The schooner he'd sailed out of Warbrooke on over four years ago had gone down three weeks before and he'd been waiting on Italy's sunny coast, not trying very hard to find another position as ship's officer.

It was in Italy that he'd met Nicholas Ivanovitch. Nick's family in Russia was first cousins with the tzarina, and Nick expected people the world over to be aware of this fact and to treat him with the awe and subservience that he thought his position gave him.

Alex had stepped in and saved Nick's thick neck from a gang of roving sailors who didn't like what Nick had said about them. Alex had pulled his sword, tossed it to Nick, and then drawn two knives, one for each hand, from his belt. Together the two men had fought back.

It had taken them an hour, and when they were finished, they were covered with blood, their clothes were in shreds, but they were friends. Alexander was treated to the Russian hospitality that was as generous as the Russian arrogance. Nick took Alex aboard his private ship, a lugger, a ship that was so fast that it was illegal in most countries since it could outrun anything on the seas. But no one bothered the Russian aristocracy since they followed no laws but their own.

Alex settled down on the opulent ship and for a couple of days enjoyed being waited on, his every wish anticipated, his every wish fulfilled by the army of cowering servants that Nick had brought with him from Russia.

"We're not like this in America," Alex had told Nick after his fifth mug of ale. He talked of the independence of Americans, of their ability to create their own country from a wilderness. "We've fought the French, the Indians, we've fought all the world and we've won!" The more he drank, the more he rhapsodized about the glories of America. After he and Nick had put away most of a keg of ale, Nick brought out a clear liquid he called vodka and they started on that. Say nothing else about the Russians, Alex thought, they can drink with the best of them.

It was the next morning, when Alex's head was splitting and his mouth tasted as if he'd just licked the bottom of a ship clean, that the letter arrived. Nick was topside, taking his bellyache out on his cringing servants, when Elias Downey asked permission to come aboard and talk to Alexander. Nick was diverted from his shouting and complaining long enough to escort the man downstairs—he was dying of curiosity to hear what this man's message of great importance was.

Alex merely rolled his eyes when Nick poured three glasses of vodka and set them on the table.

Alex ignored the roaring in his head as he listened to the tales Elias had to tell about what was happening in Warbrooke. He scanned the letter from his sister, but there was much that she'd not told him.

"That man she married is evil. He steals from all of us," Elias was saying. "He took Josiah's ship from him, said he thought there was contraband on it. He done it all legal and proper like, weren't nothin' any of us could do to stop him. If Josiah could come up with sixty pounds, he could sue your brother-in-law to get his ship back. That ship was all that Josiah had in the world and now he ain't even got that."

"What did my father do?" Alex asked, leaning forward. "I can't imagine him letting his son-in-law take a man's ship."

Elias's eyelids were beginning to droop with the effects of Nick's vodka. "Sayer ain't got no legs. They might as well have been cut off. He just stays in bed. Nobody expected him to live but he did—if you can call that livin'. He lays in bed, won't even hardly eat nothin'. Eleanor Taggert runs the place."

"Taggert!" Alex scoffed. "They still live in that backwater shack, still trying to control those damned kids of theirs?"

"James went down with his ship a couple of years ago and Nancy died havin' the last young one. A few of the boys shipped out, but there's enough of 'em left behind. Eleanor works for your father and Jess runs a boat around the harbor. They keep the family eatin'. Of course, you know the Taggerts, they won't take charity from nobody. That Jess, she's somethin'. She's the only one that'll stand up to your brother-in-law. 'Course it ain't as if the Taggerts have anything to lose by standin' up to him. They don't own nothin' that anybody'd want."

Alex exchanged smiles with Elias. The Taggerts were the town joke. They were used as contrast to everyone's bad luck. No matter what happened to you, you could always look at the Taggerts and see somebody worse off than you were. They were poorer than anyone else, and dirtier—and they covered their misery with pride.

"Is Jessica still as hot tempered as she always was?" Alex murmured, smiling at the memory of a scrawny, dirty-faced brat who, for some reason he had never understood, had singled him out to make his life miserable. "She must be about twenty now, right?"

"There abouts." Elias's eyes were beginning to close.

"And still not married?"

"Nobody wants them kids," Elias said, his voice beginning to slur. "You ain't seen Jess in a long time. She's changed."

"Somehow I doubt that," Alex said just as Elias's head slumped forward onto his chest and he fell asleep. Alex looked up at Nick. "I'll have to go back and see what this is about. Marianna asks me to come home and help them. I doubt if it's as bad as they make it seem. My father has always believed the town of Warbrooke to be his personal little fiefdom and

5

now he's having to share the authority with someone else and he doesn't like it. And if one of those Taggerts is sticking his nose in it and stirring up trouble, it's no wonder there's a commotion. I'll go back and see what it is. I heard of a ship leaving for America in about six weeks' time. Maybe the captain doesn't have his crew yet."

Nick tossed back the last of the vodka. "I'll take you. My parents wanted me to see America and I have cousins there. I'll take you to this town of yours and you can see what is going on. A son should obey his father."

Alex smiled at Nick and didn't show how concerned he was about his father's injury. He couldn't imagine his big, loud, demanding father being an invalid confined to bed. "All right," Alex said. "I'll be happy to go with you."

That had been weeks ago, and now they were within hours of docking and Alex was looking forward to seeing his homeland again.

The town of New Sussex was booming with business. There was the noise of the ships docking, of people shouting and hawking wares, of arguments. And there were the odors of dead fish and unwashed people, mixed with clean, pure sea air.

Nick stretched his big body and yawned, the sun reflecting off the gold embroidery of his jacket. "You are welcome to stay with my cousin. He has nothing much to do and he will be glad of the diversion of you."

"Thanks just the same but I think I'll start home," Alex answered. "I'm anxious to see my father again and to see what mischief my sister has gotten herself into."

They parted at the dock, Alex carrying only one bag

across his shoulder. First he planned to purchase a horse and then a new suit of clothes. Everything he owned had gone down in Italy and after he'd met Nick, he'd worn nothing but the comfortable, baggy pants and shirt of seaman's gear.

"Here! Watch that!" a British soldier, one of a group of six, yelled at Alex. "Scum like you should look out for your betters."

Alex had no time to defend himself before one of the men pushed him from behind. The bag Alex carried fell forward just as the soldier pushed him again. Alex fell face down into the dirt, his ears ringing with laughter as he spit out dirt and debris.

He was on his feet in seconds and starting for the group of soldiers who'd already turned their backs when a strong hand stopped him. "I wouldn't if I were you."

Alex was so angry that at first he couldn't focus on the sailor beside him.

"They have the right, and you'll only get into more trouble if you go after them."

"What do you mean they have the right?" Alex said through his teeth. Now that he was upright, his senses were returning to him. There were six of them and one of him.

"They're soldiers of His Majesty and they have every right to do what they want. You'll get yourself thrown in jail if you fool with the likes of them." When Alex made no reply, the sailor shrugged and kept on walking.

Alex, after a moment of glaring at the soldiers' backs, reshouldered his bag and kept walking. He tried to return his thoughts to clean clothes and a good horse between his legs.

As he passed a tavern, he caught a whiff of fish chowder and realized he was hungry. Within minutes,

7

he was seated at a dirty table and eating savory stew from a deep wooden bowl, remembering meals with Nick. They had eaten with gold utensils off porcelain plates so thin they were transparent.

He wasn't prepared when he felt the sharp tip of a sword at his throat. He looked up to see the same soldier who'd pushed him into the dirt moments before.

"So here is our little sailor again," the man taunted. "I thought you'd be long gone by now." The young soldier's face changed from teasing to serious. "Get up. This is our table."

Alex's hands moved slowly toward the underside of the table. He didn't have a weapon on him, but he had skill and speed. Before the soldiers knew what was happening, Alex sent the table toward them, knocking the first man down and landing so heavily on his leg that he screamed in pain. The other five attacked Alex at once.

He managed to knock two of them out, then grabbed the handle of the heavy pot hanging over the fire. It burned his hands, but it also burned the entire midsection of the man he tossed it to. He was just about to bring a chair down on the head of the fifth man when the innkeeper hit Alex over the head with a tankard.

Alex sank to the floor gracefully.

A bucket of cold, dirty water was splashed on Alex's face, and he came to painfully. His head was roaring and it was difficult to open his eyes. Based upon the smell of the place, he was sure he was in hell.

"Get up. You're free," came a gruff voice as Alex tried to sit up. He managed to open one eye but closed it again against the dazzle.

"Alex," came a voice he recognized as being Nick's. "I came to get you out of this filthy place, but I'll be damned if I'm going to carry you. Get up and follow me."

The dazzle had been the several pounds of gold embroidery on Nick's uniform. Alex realized his friend was wearing one of the several uniforms he used whenever he wanted something from someone. Nick had said that people the world over were impressed with the gaudiness of the Russian uniforms and it got him what he wanted. Alex also knew that Nick wasn't about to dirty that uniform by giving his friend a hand.

In spite of the fact that Alex's head was about to fall off his shoulders, he managed to hold it on and stand up. He was beginning to see that he was in a jail, a filthy place with ancient straw on the stone floor and heaven knew what in the corners. The wall he touched was cold and slimy and the slime coated his hands.

Somehow, he managed to follow Nick's perfectly straight back out of the building and into the fading daylight. A magnificent carriage and equally magnificent horses awaited them. One of Nick's servants helped Alex into the carriage.

Alex was hardly seated when Nick began raging at him.

"Did you know that they planned to hang you in the morning?" he growled. "I only heard about you by chance. Some old sailor saw you get off my ship and then get knocked around by those soldiers. He saw you kick the table over on one of them. Did you know you broke his leg? He may lose it. And you burned one of them and a third one *still* hasn't waked up after you bashed him. Alex, a person in your station in life can't do that sort of thing."

Alex raised an eyebrow at that statement. No doubt Nick, in his station in life, would have every right to do what he pleased.

Alex leaned back against the seat and looked out the window while Nick continued to tell him that he couldn't do what he'd done. While Nick was talking, Alex saw an English soldier grab a young girl's arm and pull her behind a building.

"Stop here," Alex said.

Nick, who had seen what Alex had, refused to have the driver stop the carriage and when Alex tried to get out anyway, Nick pushed him forcefully against the seat. Alex grabbed his head in pain.

"They're only peasants," Nick said, his voice full of disbelief.

"But they are *my* peasants," Alex whispered.

"Ah, yes, now I begin to understand. But there are always more peasants. They breed rapidly."

Alex didn't bother to answer Nick's absurdities. His head was hurting as much from what he'd seen as from the blow he'd received. He'd heard rumors of horrors that were going on in America, but he hadn't really believed them. In England there was talk of the ungrateful Colonists, how they were like delinquent children who needed a firm hand to rule them. He'd even seen American ships being unloaded and inspected before they could return to America. But, somehow, he hadn't really believed what he'd heard.

He lay quietly against the padded seat and didn't bother to look out the window again.

They arrived at a large house on the outskirts of town and Nick jumped out, leaving Alex to find his own way. He was obviously very angry with his friend and had no intention of helping him further.

Alex climbed out and followed Nick's valet into a room where a bathtub full of hot water was waiting.

Alex stripped and washed, the hot water helping his sore head. But with the clearing away of pain, he began to wonder about his sister's letter. He'd dismissed it as the emotional reaction of a woman, but now he wondered if what was going on here was what she meant when she had said that Warbrooke needed help. Elias had said that Josiah's ship had been taken because he was suspected of selling contraband. If the soldiers felt so superior that they could attack a harmless seaman on the street and molest a young girl without fear of punishment, what were the officers, the men in power, capable of?

"I see you're still thinking of what happened today," Nick said as he entered the room. "What do you expect when you walk about the wharf dressed as you are?"

"A man has a right to dress how he wants and he should be safe."

"That is the doctrine of all peasants," Nick said with a sigh. He motioned to a servant to begin unpacking his many bags and trunks. "Tonight you may wear my cousin's clothes and tomorrow we will see that you are dressed properly. Then you may travel to your father's home without fear."

As usual, Nick made it a command rather than a suggestion. He had been giving orders all his life and they had been obeyed.

After Nick left, Alex dismissed the servant who held one of Nick's monogrammed bath towels ready, took the towel and wrapped it about the lower half of his body. It was dark outside now, but the lamplighter had lit the lamps and Alex could see the soldiers roaming about the streets. They were quartered with the citizens and came and went at their leisure. Not far away he heard raucous laughter and the sound of glass breaking.

These men were afraid of nothing. They had the protection of the King of England on their side. If someone fought them, as Alex had today, they had every right to hang him. They were English and the Americans were English, too—but the Americans were considered to be a savage, ignorant lot that had to be disciplined.

Turning away from the window in disgust, Alex glanced at the half-open trunk of Nick's. There was a black shirt lying across the top.

What if someone gave them some of their own terror back? he thought. What if a man, dressed in black, came out of the night and let these arrogant soldiers know that they couldn't hurt the Colonists without fear of punishment?

He rummaged in Nick's trunk until he found a pair of black breeches.

"May I ask what you are doing?" Nick asked from the doorway. "If it is jewels you are looking for, I can assure you they are safely hidden."

"Be quiet, Nick, and help me find a black handkerchief."

Nick walked across the room and put his hand on Alex's arm. "I want to know what you are doing."

"I just thought that I might give those Englishmen something to worry about. A black ghost coming out of the night perhaps."

"Ah, yes, I am beginning to see." Nick's eyes began to shine. This was an idea that appealed to his Russian blood. He opened a second trunk. "Did I ever tell you about my cousin who rode his horse down the steps of our country house? The horse broke both its front legs of course, but it was a magnificent moment."

Alex looked up from the shirt he was holding. "What happened to your cousin?"

"He died. All the good ones die young. Another time he was drunk and decided to ride his horse out of a second story window. Both he and the horse died. He was a good man."

Alex kept his comments about Nick's cousin to himself as he pulled on the tight black breeches. Nick was shorter and heavier than he was, but Alex's legs were thick from years of fighting for balance on board ships so the breeches, made to be snug, were like skin on Alex. The shirt, cut full in the arms and gathered across the bodice, flowed above the breeches.

"And these," Nick said, holding up tall, knee-high boots. "And here is a handkerchief." He opened the door. "Bring me a black plume!" he bellowed down the hallway.

"You don't have to spread the word to everyone," Alex said as he pulled on the boots.

Nick shrugged. "There is no one here but my cousin and his wife."

"And a hundred or so servants."

"What do they matter?" He looked up from the trunk to a servant who held out a large, black-dyed ostrich plume.

"The countess sends her regards," the servant said before leaving the room.

Within minutes Nick had Alex dressed in black. He cut holes in the handkerchief and tied it about the lower half of his friend's face, then set a large tricorn hat on his head. The plume curled about the brim, a few tendrils hanging over Alex's forehead.

"Yes," Nick said, standing back and admiring his work. "Now, what do you plan? To ride about the streets and frighten the men and kiss the girls?"

"Something of the sort." Now that he was dressed, Alex wasn't sure what he'd originally planned.

"There is a horse in the stables, a beautiful black.

It's in the end stall. When you return, we will drink to . . . the Raider. Yes, we will drink to the Raider. Now go and have your fun and return soon. I am hungry."

Alex smiled and then followed Nick's directions down to the stables. Under the cover of darkness, he faded into nothing in the black clothing, and as he moved about, he began to have a sense of purpose. He thought of the soldiers pulling the girl into the alley and he thought of Josiah losing his ship. Josiah had taught the three Montgomery boys to tie their first knots.

The horse Nick recommended was an angry devil that had no desire for any man to ride it. Alex pulled it around, then mounted, fought for—and won—control of the beast. They shot out of the stables and headed toward the streets.

Alex moved the horse quietly along the outskirts of the main street and watched for a place where he might be useful. It didn't take him long to find it. Outside a tavern, a pretty young woman, her arms full of small kegs of beer, was being surrounded by seven drunken soldiers.

"Give us a kiss," one man said. "Just one little kiss."

Alex didn't waste time before spurring his mount from the shadows and into the group. The horse, its feet flying, was nervous enough to make the men stop and take notice, but the man clad in black on top, his head silhouetted by the lamplight made them step back in fear.

Alex hadn't considered how he would disguise his voice, but when he spoke, he spoke with the accent of an upperclass Englishman, not with the flat voweled English that had developed in America over the last hundred years.

"Try someone your own size," Alex said and drew his sword as he advanced on two of the men who were stepping backward, away from the apparition and the angry black horse.

Deftly, Alex removed the buttons off the uniform of first one man, then the other. The buttons clattered on the cobblestone street and the horse crushed one under its iron-clad hoof.

Alex backed the horse away, already moving into the shadows. He knew that he had surprise on his side and that as soon as these men recovered their senses, they'd attack or call for help.

He swung his sword through the air with a loud whoosh and brought it to rest under the chin of another soldier. "Think before you harass an American again or the Raider may find you." He pulled his sword tip down the man's uniform, carefully laying it open to his skin, but not so much as scratching the man.

With that, Alex laughed, a laugh of pure pleasure, a feeling of triumph surging through him that he had the upper hand with these overbearing louts who traveled only in packs. Still smiling beneath his mask, he turned his horse and headed down the street at a breakneck pace.

But no matter how fast he was going, he couldn't outrun the bullet that was fired at his back. He felt something hot tearing through his shoulder. His head flew backward and the horse reared, but he managed to hang on.

He turned back to the woman and soldiers still standing there, one of the men holding a smoking pistol in his hand. "You'll never catch the Raider," he said with triumph in his voice. "He'll haunt you day and night. You'll never be free of him."

He was wise enough not to press his luck any longer

but turned the horse and tore down the street. Shutters on the houses were beginning to open and people were looking out just in time to see a man in black fly past their windows. Behind him, Alex could hear a woman, probably the barmaid he'd rescued, shouting something, but he was too concerned about his bleeding shoulder to hear what she was saying.

He rode the horse to the edge of town and knew that he had to get rid of the animal. As he was, he was too conspicuous atop the black devil. Near the docks, in the shelter of the confusion of the ships and ropes, he dismounted, slapped the horse on the rump and watched it head back toward its stables.

Alex couldn't see his shoulder, but he could feel that he was losing a great deal of blood and he knew that he was losing strength rapidly. The nearest point of safety was Nick's ship, docked not far away and guarded by Nick's crew.

Weaving between the ships and keeping himself hidden, he listened to the increasing pitch of the people in the streets. It seemed that the entire town was coming out of their houses and joining in the search. When he reached Nick's lugger, he prayed that the Russian crew would allow him on board. The Russians could be as fierce as they were loving.

But Alex need not have feared, for one of the crewmen saw him and swung down to the dock to help him aboard. Maybe they were used to their master's friends arriving in the middle of the night wearing blood soaked shirts. Alex didn't remember much after the sailors helped him aboard the ship and half carried him into the hold.

Alex opened his eyes to see the familiar swing of a lamp as it swayed to the rhythm of the sea.

"Well, it looks like you may live after all."

Alex moved his head just a bit to see Nick sitting beside him, his coat off, his shirt dirty with blood on the front. "What time is it?" Alex asked as he started to sit up but was dizzy with the effort so he lay back down.

"It's almost dawn," Nick said, getting up to move to a basin of water and wash his hands. "You almost died last night. It took a while to get the bullet out."

Alex closed his eyes for a moment and thought about his foolish stunt of being the Raider. "I hope you don't mind my imposing on your hospitality a while longer, but I think it will be a day or so before I can travel to Warbrooke."

Nick dried his hands on a towel. "I don't think either of us had any idea of the consequences of what you did last night. It seems that this town was looking for a hero and you've been elected. You can't step onto the street without hearing about the exploits of the Raider. It seems that he's responsible for every deed that's been perpetrated against the English in the last ten years."

Alex gave a groan of disgust.

"That's the least of it. The English have sent every soldier at their disposal to look for you. There are already posters out for your arrest. You are to be shot on sight. They've been here twice this morning and demanded to search my ship."

"I'll go then," Alex said, moving to sit up, but he was very weak from the loss of blood and his shoulder hurt abominably.

"I've kept them away by threatening them with war with my country. Alex, if you stepped onto that gangplank, you'd be shot within minutes. They are looking for someone tall and slim, with black hair."

17

Nick's eyes burned into Alex's. "And they know you're wounded."

"I see," Alex said, still sitting on the edge of the bed, and he did see. He knew that he was facing the end of his life, but he could not stay here and risk getting his friend involved. He tried to stand, leaning heavily on the chair in front of him.

"I have a plan," Nick said. "I have no wish to be pursued by the English navy, so I'd like to allow them to search."

"Yes, of course. At least that way I won't have to walk down the gangplank. I was dreading that." Alex tried to smile.

Nicholas ignored his attempt at levity. "I have sent for some clothes of my cousin. He is a fat man and a gaudy dresser."

Alex raised an eyebrow at that. To his taste, Nick's clothes put even peacocks to shame, so what must this cousin's be like?

Nick continued. "I think that if we pad you to fill the clothes, fortify you with a little whiskey, put a powdered wig on over that mass of black hair, you'll pass the soldiers' inspection."

"Why don't I put on the disguise and just walk off the ship?"

"And then do what? You will need help and whoever gives it to you will be putting his life in danger. And how many of your poor Americans could resist the five-hundred-pounds reward that is being offered for your head? No, you will stay here on my ship with me and we will sail for this town of yours. Will there be someone there to take care of you?"

Alex leaned back against the wall, feeling even weaker than when he woke. He thought of the town of Warbrooke, the town his grandfather had settled and most of which his father now owned. There were people there who were his friends, people he'd known all his life—and he was a product of those people. If he was brave, then they were twice as brave. No English soldiers were going to frighten the town of Warbrooke.

"Yes, there are people there who will help me," Alex said at last.

"Then let's get you dressed." Nick threw open the cabin door and called for a servant to bring the clothes he needed.

"Alex," Nick said gently. "We're here." He looked at his friend with sympathy. For the last week Alex had been running a high fever and now he looked as if he'd been on a week long drunk: his eyes were sunken, his skin dry and red, his muscles weak and rubbery.

"Alex, we're going to have to dress you in my cousin's clothes again. The soldiers are still searching for the Raider and I'm afraid they've come this far north. Do you understand me?"

"Yes," Alex mumbled. "They'll take care of me in Warbrooke. You'll see."

"I hope you're right," Nick said. "I'm afraid that they may believe what they see." He was referring to the ridiculous sight Alex made in his fat padding and brocade coat and powdered wig. He certainly didn't look like the handsome young man come home to save a town from a dastardly brother-in-law.

"You'll see," Alex slurred, since Nick had been giving him brandy to help him face the coming exertion. "They know me. They'll laugh when they see me like this. They'll know that something has happened. They'll take care of me until this damned shoulder heals. I just pray they don't give me away in front of the soldiers. You'll see, they'll know that no Montgomery ever dressed like a peacock. They'll know there's a reason for this."

"Yes, Alexander," Nicholas said soothingly. "I hope you are right."

"I am. You'll see. I know these people."

Chapter Two

"I DON'T know why *I* have to be there to meet him," Jessica Taggert said for the thousandth time to her sister, Eleanor. "Alexander was never anything to me—nothing good, that is."

Eleanor tightened her sister's corset strings. Eleanor, by herself, was considered a pretty woman, but when Jessica was present, she was overshadowed —as was every other woman in town. "You have to go because the Montgomery family has been very good to us. Get down from there, Sally!" she said to her four-year-old sister.

The Taggert house was little more than a shack, small and only as clean as two women with full-time employment and the responsibility of taking care of seven young brothers and sisters could make it. The house was on the edge of town, set back in a tiny cove, with no close neighbors; not because the family chose to be so isolated, but because eighteen years ago when the fifth loud, dirty Taggert had entered the world and there didn't seem to be an end to their numbers in sight, people stopped building near them.

"Nathaniel!" Jessica shouted to her nine-year-old brother who was dangling three, fat, angry spiders on a string in front of his little sister's face. "If I have to come over there you'll be sorry."

"At least you wouldn't have to see Alexander," Nathaniel taunted before wisely scurrying from the house just after he tossed the spiders onto his sister.

"Hold still, Jess," Eleanor said. "How do you expect me to lace you into this dress if you're wiggling about?"

"I don't particularly want you to lace me into it. I really don't see why I have to go. We don't need charity from the likes of Alexander Montgomery."

Eleanor gave a heartfelt sigh. "You haven't seen him since you were both children. Maybe he's changed."

"Hah!" Jess said, moving away from her sister and lifting the infant, Samuel, off the floor where he was trying to eat some unidentifiable substance. She saw he had one of Nathaniel's spiders in his fat, dirty little hand. "No one as bad as Alexander changes. He was a pompous know-it-all ten years ago and I'm sure he hasn't changed. If Marianna was going to get one of her brothers to come and help her get away from that man she was fool enough to marry, why couldn't she have asked one of the older boys? One of the *good* Montgomerys?"

"I think she wrote each of them and Alex received his letter first. Sit still while I get some of the tangles out of your hair." Eleanor took her sister's hair in her hands and couldn't help feeling a little jealous. Other women spent many hours trying to do what they could with their hair to make it look good, while Jessica exposed hers to sun, salt air, sea water and her own sweat—and it was more beautiful than anyone else's. It was a thick, soft blonde that shone in the sunlight.

"Oh, Jess, if you just tried, you could get any man—"

Her sister cut her off. "Please don't start on me again. Why don't *you* get a husband? A rich one who'll support us and all the kids?"

"From this town?" Eleanor sniffed. "From a town that's afraid of one man? From a town that lets a man like Pitman run it?"

Jessica stood and pulled her hair back from her face. There were few women pretty enough to be able to scrape their hair back that tightly and still be beautiful, but Jessica succeeded. "I don't want one of those cowards any more than you do." She put baby Samuel down on the floor again. "But at least I'm not fool enough to think that one man, especially somebody like Alexander, is going to save us. I think all of you remember the Montgomerys as a group, not as individuals. I couldn't agree more that there was never a more magnificent group of men than Sayer and his two oldest sons and I cried as hard as any of you when the boys went off to sea—but I didn't cry when Alexander left."

"Jessica, I don't think you're being fair. What in the world did Alex do to you that's made you dislike him so much? And you can't count the schoolboy pranks he pulled. If they counted, Nathaniel would have been hanged four years ago."

"It's his attitude. He always thought he was so much better than anyone else. His brothers and father would work with everyone else, but Alexander

23

thought of himself as too good. His family was the richest one in town, but he was the only one who was aware of it."

"Are you talking about the charity? The time you threw the lobsters he'd brought us in his face? I never understood that since the whole town was always giving us things."

"Well, they don't now!" Jessica spat in anger. "Yes, I mean the charity, living from hand to mouth every day, never having anything, always wanting. And Pa coming home every nine months, just in time to get Mother—" She paused to calm down. "Alexander was the worst. The way he smirked every time he brought a bag of cornmeal. The superior way he looked at all of us each time he saw us. He used to wipe his breeches every time a Taggert baby got near him."

Eleanor smiled. "Jess, it was necessary to wipe your breeches—or your skirt or your hair—every time a Taggert baby got near you. I don't think you're being fair. Alexander was no better or worse than the other men in his family. It's just that you two are only two years apart in age and therefore you felt more kinship with him."

"I'd rather be kin to a shark than to him."

Eleanor rolled her eyes. "He did help Patrick get the post as cabin boy on the *Fair Maiden.*"

"He would have done anything to get rid of one more Taggert. Are you ready to go?"

"I have been for some time. I'll make a deal with you. If Alexander turns out to be the pompous spend-thrift you seem to think he is, I'll bake you three apple pies next week."

"I'll win this without trying. With his arrogance, he'll probably be expecting us to kiss his hand. I hear he was in Italy. Probably met the Pope and learned some things from him. Think he'll wear scented lace underwear?"

Eleanor ignored her sister. "If I win, you have to wear a dress all week and be nice to Mr. Clymer."

"That old fish-breath? Oh, well, it doesn't matter. I'm going to win. This town's going to see that, when Alexander is alone and not surrounded by his brothers and father, he's a lazy, vain, condescending, pompous—" She stopped because Eleanor was pushing her out the door.

"And, Nathaniel, if you don't watch after those kids, you'll hear from me," Eleanor called over her shoulder.

By the time they got to the dock, Eleanor was having to drag Jessica. Jess kept enumerating all the things that needed doing: the fishing nets that needed repairing, the sails that had to be mended.

"Well, Jessica," said Abigail Wentworth as the Taggert sisters stepped onto the dock, "I see that you couldn't wait to see Alexander again."

Jessica was torn between wanting to smack the woman and turning to leave the dock. Abigail was the second prettiest girl in town, and she hated being second to Jessica's first. Therefore, she loved to remind Jessica that she was a ripe and ready sixteen while Jess was drying on the vine at the grand old age of twenty-two.

Jessica gave Abby her sweetest smile and prepared to tell her what she thought of her when Eleanor grabbed her arm and pulled her away.

"I don't want you two to get into a fight today. I want this to be a good day for the Montgomerys without Sayer having to get you out of the stocks. Good morning, Mistress Goody," she said sweetly. "There it is, that's the ship Alex is on."

Jessica's jaw dropped at the sight of the ship. "But

that beam is too narrow. I'm sure that's against statutes. Has Pitman seen that yet? He'll probably confiscate the ship and then where will your precious Alexander be?"

"He's not mine. If he were anybody's, Abigail wouldn't be here waiting for him."

"How true," Jess sighed. "Wouldn't she just love to get her hands on the Montgomerys' eight thousand feet of dock space? What are those people looking at?"

Eleanor turned to see a group of townspeople standing stock still and gaping. The crowd began to part, their mouths open, but no sound came forth.

As Jessica and Eleanor waited, a man came toward them. He was wearing a jacket of canary yellow, with a wide border of embroidered flowers and leaves about the edge and hem. The jacket covered an enormous belly, and sunlight flashed off the many colors of the silk embroidery. The breeches covering his fat legs were emerald green, and he wore a full wig that hung down in curls past his shoulders. He walked across the dock, stumbling now and then from what was obviously too much drink.

The townspeople seemed to think he was another official from England, but Jessica recognized him right away. No amount of weight or wig could completely cover that imperious Montgomery expression. In spite of his extra hundred pounds, she could still see those cheekbones that Alexander had inherited from his grandfather.

Jessica walked forward, swishing her skirts and letting everyone see her. She'd always known that Alexander Montgomery was rotten to the core and here was proof. The minute he was out from under his father's rule, this is what happened to him.

"Good morning, Alexander," she said loudly and

with laughter in her voice. "Welcome home. You haven't changed a bit."

He stood there and looked at her, blinking uncomprehendingly. His eyes were red from drink, and once he swayed so badly that a dark, burly man had to catch him.

Jessica stepped back, looked Alex up and down, then put her hands on her hips and started to laugh. Moments later the townspeople began to join her.

They couldn't stop even when Marianna Montgomery came running onto the dock. She halted when she saw Alex.

"Hello, Mary, my sweet," Alex said with an off-center smile and again the man in the dirty shirt had to steady him.

The crowd stopped laughing while Marianna looked at her brother in disbelief.

As Alex kept smiling, Marianna's mouth kept falling farther open. At last, she put her apron over her face and began crying. She ran from the docks, her heels showing beneath her skirts, her sobs carrying on the wind.

That sobered the crowd. They gave Alex and his peacock coat a few contemptuous looks and began to go back to their work. The wind echoed with the words "Poor Sayer" and "But his brothers are such men!"

Within a few minutes, there were only four of them on the dock: Jessica, enjoying it all enormously because she'd always told everyone that Alex was no good, a frowning Eleanor, a bewildered Alexander, and the big man in a dirty shirt.

Jessica just stood there with a triumphant grin on her face while Alex's eyes began to clear and he turned to look at her. "This is all *your* fault," Alex whispered.

Jess's smile grew broader. "Oh, no, Alexander, this

is your fault for at last showing your true self. You had them all fooled for years, but not me. You must tell me who your tailor is." She turned to her sister. "Wouldn't you love to have a petticoat that color?"

Eleanor squinted her eyes at her younger sister. "You've said enough, Jessica."

Jess widened her eyes innocently. "I have no idea what you mean. I was merely admiring his clothing—and his wig. No one in Warbrooke has worn a wig for years." She smiled her sweetest smile at Alexander. "But here I am keeping you and you must be hungry." She looked pointedly at his enormous belly. "Something like that must take constant work."

Alexander made a lunge for her throat, but Nick caught him.

"My goodness," Jessica mocked. "The piglet has claws."

"I'll get you for this, Jessica Taggert," Alexander said beneath his breath.

"With what? Cream cakes?"

Eleanor stepped in before Alex could say another word. "All right, Alexander, let's get you home. You there," she said to Nicholas, "get his baggage and bring it. You can take care of your master in his home. And you, Jessica, we need something to eat for dinner. Go fetch it."

"Yes, ma'am," Jess said. "I'm just grateful I'm not part of the Montgomery family. I can feed half a dozen kids, but that . . ." She looked at Alex's big belly.

"Go!" Eleanor ordered and Jessica left the dock, whistling happily and talking about the pies Eleanor owed her. Eleanor took Alex's arm, not saying a word about the fact that he was obviously too drunk to walk by himself. The man she thought was Alex's servant stayed behind on the dock.

"What's his name?" Eleanor asked Alex.

"Nicholas," Alex said through clenched teeth, his anger making his face red and his eyes black.

Eleanor stopped, still holding Alex's arm. "Nicholas, you are to do what I say. Get your master's belongings and come with me. And I mean for you to do it now."

Nick stood where he was for a moment, then gave Eleanor a lusty look up and down. He smiled just slightly and turned away to get the small bag of clothing that he'd borrowed from his cousin for Alex's use. "Yes ma'am," he said softly when he joined them, and walked behind them, watching the sway of Eleanor's skirts.

"Two hundred and fifty pounds if he's an ounce," Jessica was laughing. She was sitting at one end of the Taggert table, Eleanor at the other end. In between were seven Taggert children in assorted sizes and ages and varying degrees of dirt. Each person had a wooden bowl full of steaming fish chowder and a wooden spoon. They were precious utensils and treated with the courtesy of fine silver. The stew was quite plain, with no seasoning to speak of, nothing but fish cooked for a long time in water. The few vegetables from last summer had been eaten and the new garden had not borne fruit yet.

"What did Sayer say?" Jessica asked, still laughing into her stew.

Eleanor gave her sister a glare. She had worked at the Montgomery house for four years now, and after Alex's mother had died two years ago, she'd taken over as housekeeper. Marianna, the oldest of the Montgomery children, a spinster who either because of her size or her domineering manner had never had a husband, had been given the responsibility of taking care of her invalid father and the big, rambling house. But when the new customs officer, John Pitman, had arrived and begun to pursue her, Marianna had forgotten about everything else. Of course half the town had tried to explain to her that the Englishman wanted her father's wealth, but Marianna had arrogantly refused to listen to them. It didn't take Marianna two weeks after the wedding to realize the people were right and now she carried the burden of knowledge that she was responsible for many of Warbrooke's problems. She turned over her household duties to Eleanor and now spent most of her time in her room completing one piece of embroidery after another. If she could not cure the disease she had caused, she planned to disassociate herself from it.

"I don't think we should discuss this now." Eleanor gave a meaningful look to the children who were studiously looking into their bowls of stew, but were truthfully listening so intently that their ears were beginning to wiggle.

"Mr. Montgomery said that Mrs. Montgomery had always spoiled her youngest son and that he'd warned her that something like this would happen," Nathaniel said. "I guess he meant Mr. Alex's clothes and how fat he is. Miss Marianna cried a lot. Eleanor, who is that man Nicholas?"

Eleanor glared at the young Taggert. "Nathaniel, how many times have I told you not to eavesdrop? And you were supposed to be taking care of Sally."

"I went, too," Sally said. "We hid in the—"

Nathaniel put his hand over his little sister's mouth. "I was taking care of her, but I did want to know. Who is the man Nicholas?"

"He's Alex's bondsman, I assume," Eleanor said, "and don't you try to change the subject. I've told you a hundred times—"

"Isn't there an apple pie around here somewhere?" Jessica asked. "I've heard all I can bear about Alexander Montgomery. He's a fat old whale that's been beached and he's at last showing his true colors. Nate, tomorrow I want you to take a bag down into the cove and gather lobsters."

"Not again," he groaned.

"And you, Henry," she said to the twelve-year-old, "go see if the blackberries are out yet, and you'll have to take Sam with you. Philip and Israel, you'll have to go with me tomorrow while I make a lumber run down the coast."

"Lumber?" Eleanor said. "Do you think you should? The *Mary Catherine* can't handle that much weight."

Jessica stiffened her back as she always did when someone said something about her boat. It wasn't much and maybe it was true what Jahleel Simpson had said, "The *Mary Catherine* can float but she sure don't like to," but it was her boat, the only thing her father had given her except brothers and sisters to take care of and she was proud of it. "We can sail it and, besides, we need the money. Someone has to pay for these apples."

Eleanor looked down at her bowl that now contained a slice of apple pie. Sometimes she "borrowed" food from Sayer Montgomery's kitchen. Not often and not very much and she always paid it back, but she felt terrible about it just the same. If Sayer or Marianna had thought of it, she was sure that they would have told her to take what leftovers she needed, but Sayer was too busy feeling sorry for himself and Marianna was too busy crying that she'd brought all the evils of the world onto the town's shoulders when she'd married the customs officer to think of anyone else.

Two-year-old Samuel decided to wrap his sticky spoon in his sister Molly's hair and pull. That stopped all adult conversation.

Alexander woke the next morning with a pain in his jaw from having ground his teeth all night. Even asleep he felt his anger. Standing there on the dock yesterday, worried about whether his shoulder would start bleeding again, looking out across the people and seeing the English soldiers on their lathered horses—soldiers who were obviously looking for someone—and then having to see that brat Jessica Taggert laughing at him was almost more than he could bear. How easily the townspeople had believed him to be the coward Jessica said he was. How quickly they forgot what he'd been.

He'd gone to his father's house and already word of him had spread. Marianna had her head on her father's bed and was crying noisily. Sayer merely looked at his son and waved his arm to dismiss Alexander, as if the sight of his youngest child disgusted him too much to speak.

Alexander was too weak from the loss of blood, too angry about what had happened on the dock to attempt to defend himself. He followed Nicholas out of the room and went to his own where he fell onto the bed.

Even the sight of Nicholas Ivanovitch, Grand Duke of Russia, carrying in his luggage didn't cheer him. He drifted into a half sleep in which he dreamed of strangling Jessica Taggert. But then part of the dream had him making mad love to her. When had she grown so damned pretty? The horror of being taunted by a beautiful woman gave him very little peace.

Now, his head hurting, his shoulder throbbing, he

lay in bed and stared at the ceiling. Part of his brain, the tiny part that wasn't absolutely furious, was beginning to function. Maybe the fact that they all believed his disguise was to his advantage. He'd seen what was going on in New Sussex, the way the English soldiers ruled the town. He'd heard of the atrocities committed against the Americans as they were treated like bad children. He'd even seen the prices for goods that in England sold for half as much—yet they were goods shipped on American ships.

Perhaps some of that was going on in Warbrooke.

On first wakening, he'd wanted to call Marianna and show her his wound and tell her about his being the Raider. He knew his sister would help him while he recovered, would protect him from the wrath of the English. And how he'd like to see her face when she saw that he wasn't the fat drunkard she thought him to be! But now he realized that he'd be putting her life in danger.

He turned when a sleepy-eyed Nick came into the room and sat down heavily in a chair. "That woman got me up before daylight and had me cutting wood," he said morosely and with some wonder in his voice. "It was due only to my keen observation of my own workers that I had any idea of what to do. That woman is not very tolerant of even the slightest hesitation, though."

"Jessica?" Alexander questioned, his voice little more than a sneer. Just the thought of that woman made his hands ache to put them around her pretty white throat.

"The other one. Eleanor." Nick hung his head in his hands.

Alex had seen examples of Nick's moods before and he knew that the best thing was to not allow him to continue feeling sorry for himself. He managed to sit up in bed, the sheet falling away from his strong broad shoulders, exposing the bandage.

"I don't think I should let anyone know that I'm not as I appear," Alex began. "I think I'll remain in my peacock clothes until my shoulder has healed and until the interest in the Raider has died down. Could you spare me a servant? Someone discreet who isn't afraid of a little danger?"

Nick's head came up sharply. "All my men are Russians and no Russian is afraid of anything. Are you planning to be the Raider again?"

"Possibly." The only thought he had in his head right now was of paying Jessica back for laughing at him. He had a vision of being dressed in black and climbing in her bedroom window and tying her lovely white hands to the bedposts and . . .

"Are you listening to me?" Nick demanded. "Never have I found a more insolent people than you Americans. I should sail for my homeland now, before I meet another one of you. But this Raider appeals to me. I will send my ship south to fetch more of my cousin's clothing and a new wig."

"And leave me one of those servants you abuse, I hope."

"No," Nick said thoughtfully. "This game amuses me. I will stay here and continue to pose as your bondsman. I will keep the secret of what you are." His eyes narrowed. "And I will make this Eleanor Taggert sorry she said such things about me as she did this morning."

"It's a bargain then," Alex said. "We'll stay together. I shall be the most delicate example of young manhood in America. And you will show us Americans how to work."

Nick frowned at that. "If someone sends me to the fields, I will quit. Ah, but I will have some tales to tell my family."

"I hope your family believes you more than mine does. Shall we start getting me dressed? I'm already beginning to hate that wig."

Chapter Three

ALEXANDER allowed himself plenty of time to dress. After checking his wound, he and Nick began carefully padding his thighs until they filled the satin breeches, wrapping layers around his mid section until his belly stuck out almost a foot, then setting the heavy powdered wig on over his black hair. When they were through, he was so bundled that sweat was already beginning to form on his brow.

"I don't know if they're worth this," Alex said bitterly.

"They are your people." Nicholas shrugged.

"Who have turned against me." Alex had a vision of Jessica Taggert as she laughed at him on the dock. If she hadn't been there, would the townspeople have believed his disguise?

It was eleven o'clock when he waddled into the

common room of the Montgomery house, and many people were waiting there for him. They pretended that they had genuine business with the Montgomery household, but Alex could see by their eyes that they were waiting for him. For just a moment, he held his breath, sure that someone would laugh and tell him to abandon his disguise now that he was home and among friends.

But, one by one, they looked back at the drinks they were nursing.

Alex glanced at Eleanor as she directed two women in cooking over the open fireplace. The common room was a combination kitchen, parlor and meeting room. Since the Montgomery family owned most of Warbrooke, they did the most business, and during the day nearly everyone in town came through this room for one reason or another. Sayer Montgomery had always seen that drink and food were waiting for those who came to his house.

Two men in a corner of the room, sitting at the end of one of the two tables, began to speak quite loudly.

"My son-in-law grew that wheat himself but before I could take it to Spain, I had to stop in England and unload it for them to inspect."

"And I had to take cocoa from Brazil to England to be inspected before I could bring it to Boston."

The men looked over their drinks to Alexander, but he was pretending not to hear them. They weren't bothering to pay him the courtesy of speaking to him directly, so why should he show them his concern? And what did they expect him to do about English law? It was as if they still believed these were the days of medieval law and he was the lord who could go to the king personally and complain.

"And I lost my ship because of sixty pounds," Josiah Greene said.

Alexander looked at the enormous plate of food that Eleanor set before him. He felt as if he were the only person in the audience of a play he'd already seen. As he ate, he listened to Josiah's tale. No doubt he'd told it a thousand times, but the men here were replaying it for Alexander's benefit.

They told how Josiah had had a beautiful ship, one he'd been very proud of—but he'd angered John Pitman. Something about a piece of land Josiah owned and wouldn't sell. Pitman said that he was sure Josiah had a hold full of green paint—a contraband article. Pitman seized Josiah's ship but found no paint, so he brought a dozen soldiers and searched Josiah's house in the middle of the night. In the course of the "search" a cellar full of food was destroyed, linens were ripped apart, furniture broken and his daughters terrorized. Josiah tried to get his ship back, but he was told that he'd have to put up a bond of sixty pounds. Since all his money was invested in the bond he had to give Pitman each time he sailed out of Warbrooke, he couldn't afford another sixty pounds. His friends collected the money for him, but the burden of the proof of innocence was on Josiah's shoulders. Pitman said there had been green paint on board; Josiah said there never had been. They stated their cases before the Colonial Admiralty Court—a judge, no jury—and the ship was given to Pitman and his officers since Josiah could not prove that he'd never had green paint aboard his ship.

Alexander soon forgot his own misery as he glanced at Josiah, a man broken, all quite legally, by a greedy Englishman. Pitman wanted land Josiah owned and had not only gotten the land but had come to own everything else that had belonged to the Greene family.

Alex kept his head bent over his food because he didn't want them to see the anger that was boiling in him. If he was to keep his disguise, he could not allow them to see how their words affected him. He felt their eyes on him, watching him and waiting to see if he was the man they thought he was. They were like children who thought someone with the Montgomery name could fix their problems and make everything right once again.

Alex was saved from showing his feelings because the door opened and in walked Jessica Taggert with a couple of big baskets full of oysters.

Jessica took one look at the people, all of them standing completely still and looking as if they were expecting a storm to break, and knew immediately what was going on.

"Still got your hopes up?" she laughed, glancing from one man to the other. "Still think this Montgomery is going to help you? God only made three Montgomerys: Sayer, Adam and Kit. This one doesn't deserve the name. Here, Eleanor," she said, handing the baskets to her sister. "It looks as if you'll be needing these, what with a parade going through here all day." She gave Alex a smirking look, although he hadn't raised his head from the plate. "It looks like they'll all get something to see with that one here."

Very slowly, Alex raised his head and looked at her. He tried to keep the fury out of his eyes, but he was only partially successful. "Good morning, Mistress Jessica," he said in a low voice. "Are you selling those? Have you no husband to support you?"

The men at the table across the room began to snicker. With Jessica so pretty, there wasn't a man who hadn't had contact with her in some way. Either they'd asked her to marry them after they'd worn out

39

a wife with bearing babies, or they had a son who'd tried for her hand, or a cousin—or else the men just dreamed of having her. But now, here was a man who was insinuating that maybe nobody wanted her.

"I can take care of myself," Jessica said, drawing herself up to stand straighter. "I want no man under my feet; no man to tell me what to do and how to do it."

Alexander smiled at her. "I see." He gave her a look up and down. Long ago, Jess had learned that she couldn't run her little boat while wearing long skirts so she had adapted a sailor's garment for her own use. She wore tall boots beneath baggy pants that reached her knees, topped by a loose blouse and an unbuttoned waistcoat. Except that her waist was very small and she had to belt the pants tightly to hold them up, she was dressed like most of the men in Warbrooke. "Tell me," Alex said smoothly, "do you still want the name of my tailor?"

The men began to laugh with more gusto than the joke warranted. So many of them had watched Jessica saunter down the dock, her hips moving in a way that made them gape. Even in her men's clothing, she obviously had all the curves every woman wished she had.

Eleanor stepped in before another jibe could be made. "Thank you for the oysters. Maybe you could bring us some cod this afternoon."

Jessica nodded mutely, still angry at the way Alexander had made the men laugh at her. She glared at Alex for a moment, not even bothering to look at the men around her who were laughing and so thoroughly enjoying her humiliation, then turned on her heel and left the house.

Eleanor grabbed Alexander's plate, still half-full of

the food he couldn't eat, and gave him a hard look, but she didn't say a word. After all, he was her employer's son. Instead, she turned to Nicholas, who was lounging against the door jamb. "Take this out to the hogs. And do it now!"

Nick opened his mouth to say something and then closed it, his eyes sparkling. "Yes, ma'am," he said. *"I* don't contradict women."

At that, more laughter erupted, and for a moment Alex felt a part of the town again, not like the stranger he'd been forced to become.

But their laughter stopped a moment later when Alex stood—or, rather, attempted to stand. He wasn't used to the protrusion that was his padded belly and it caught on the lip of the table. At the same time, he twisted his shoulder, pulling on the partially healed gunshot wound. Between the pain and his confusion over what was holding him in his seat, it took a moment to get untangled.

To him, it was almost humorous—but to the townspeople it was pathetic.

Alex looked up to see pity in their eyes. Turning away to hide his anger, he left the room. It was time to meet John Pitman.

He was just where Alex thought he'd be, in the office that had served the Montgomerys for three generations. He was a short, stocky man, balding back to midway on his head. Alex couldn't see his face because he was bent intently over ledgers spread across the desk. Before Pitman looked up, Alex scanned the room and saw that two portraits of Montgomery ancestors had been taken from the walls and there was a heavy lock on a cabinet that had belonged to Alex's mother. It looked as if the man meant to stay.

"Ah hem," Alex said, clearing his throat.

Pitman looked up.

Alex's first impression was of eyes that pierced a man: big, intense, glittering like black diamonds. This man could do anything, Alex thought, maybe good, maybe bad.

John Pitman looked Alex up and down, his hard eyes measuring him, seeming to remember what he'd heard of Alexander Montgomery and comparing it with what he now saw.

Alex thought that if he wanted to fool this man, he was going to have to work at it. He withdrew a lace-edged white silk handkerchief. "So warm today, isn't it? I feel fairly faint with the heat." He minced his way, letting his hips lead him, toward the window and lounged against the jamb, the handkerchief delicately dabbing at the sweat on his neck.

Pitman leaned back in his chair and silently appraised Alex.

Alex gazed out the window, letting his eyelids droop lazily as he watched Nicholas throw feed toward the chickens and doing it in such a way that the breeze caught half the seed and carried it away. Eleanor came running toward him, her apron flapping and two of the Taggert brats on her heels.

Alex looked back to Pitman. "I take it you're my new brother-in-law."

Pitman took a moment to answer. "I am."

Alex moved away from the window toward a chair. He sat in it primly, crossing his legs as best he could considering the padding on his legs and belly. "And what is this I hear about your stealing from the people of Warbrooke?" He waited a while before looking up at Pitman. The man's eyes reflected his soul. Alex could almost see him doing calculations in his head.

"I do nothing illegal." Pitman's voice was restrained.

Alex picked imaginary lint from the lace at his sleeve, then held the lace up to the light. "I do so love good lace," he said wistfully and then looked back at Pitman. "I imagine you married my spinster sister to obtain access to the eight thousand feet of wharf we Montgomerys own."

Pitman said nothing, but his eyes glittered and his hand moved toward a drawer. A pistol? Alex wondered.

Alex used his tiredest voice. "Perhaps we should try to understand one another. You see, I have never fit in with the Montgomerys, such a loud, overbearing, brutish lot. I favored music, culture, the art of the table rather than standing on the deck of a lurching ship, swearing at a pack of smelly sailors." He shuddered slightly. "But my father decided, as he said, 'to make a man' of me and sent me away. The money he gave me ran out quickly so I was forced to return."

Alex smiled at Pitman but the man said nothing. "If I were one of my brothers, I believe I'd have every right to evict you from this office." He nodded toward the locked cabinet. "I imagine that is full of papers, perhaps even some deeds of ownership. And it would be my guess that you used Montgomery funds to purchase what goods you own, thereby making them, legally, Montgomery deeds."

Pitman's eyes were like two coals on fire and he looked as if he were about to spring at any moment.

"Let us make a bargain. I have no desire to spend my life in this room juggling pieces of paper, nor do I want to be confined on a boat where I am expected to do heroic deeds such as my revered brothers accomplish on an hourly basis. You do not touch the

Montgomery lands—we *never* sell the land—and pay me, say, twenty-five percent of your profits and I will not interfere with you."

Pitman gaped for a moment, his eyes going from dangerous to wary. "Why?" was all he said.

"Why not? Why should I put myself out for anyone in this town? My own sister has not extended a welcome to me, merely because I do not live up to the expected ideal of the Montgomery name. And, too, it's easier for me to allow you to do the work while all I do is collect part of the profits."

Pitman began to relax and his hand moved away from the desk drawer, but there was still caution in his eyes. "Why did you return?"

Alex gave a laugh. "Because, my dear fellow, they expect me to do something about *you.*"

Pitman almost returned Alex's smile and relaxed even more. "Perhaps we can work together."

"Oh yes, I believe we can." Alex began to talk to Pitman in a lazy style that he hoped would convey the impression that he wasn't really interested, but he wanted to know to what extent Pitman had put the Montgomery holdings in debt and, if possible, to find out what he was planning. Pitman's appointment as Customs Officer gave him a massive amount of power. It was left up to his integrity whether he abused that power or not.

It was while Alex was attempting to get information from Pitman that he saw a head appear at the top of the window—an upside-down head of one of the Taggert kids. The head disappeared almost in the same instant, but Alex knew that the child had been listening.

Alex waved his hand at Pitman. "I'm tired now. You may tell me more later. I think I shall take a stroll, then nap before supper." He yawned behind his handkerchief and then rose and left the room without a further word to Pitman.

"If I get my hands on that kid, I'll wrap his ears about his throat," Alex muttered. He couldn't hurry through the corridors of the house because if someone saw him, his image would be shattered. It wasn't easy to act languid and still hurry. He had to catch that child and find out what he'd heard.

Once outside, he stood still, trying to figure where a child would have run to if he'd been caught doing what he shouldn't. Alex remembered how many times he'd escaped to the woods when he was a boy.

Following an old Indian trail, he walked into the quiet darkness of the forest that ran behind the Montgomery house. About half a mile in was a cliff that led down to a little rocky beach called Farrier's Cove. Alex headed for it now.

Agilely, he made his way down the bank and came face to face with the Taggert boy he'd caught eavesdropping and Jessica.

"You may go, Nathaniel," Jessica said haughtily, her eyes on Alexander, every bit of her hatred showing in them.

"But, Jess, I didn't tell you—"

"Nathaniel!" she said sharply, and the boy clambered up the embankment and they could hear his footsteps retreating.

Alex didn't say a word to her, since he wanted to find out how much the boy had told her.

"So now we know why you came back to Warbrooke. Those poor fools thought you were going to help them. Twenty-five percent should keep you in laces."

Alex tried to keep his face from showing his emotion. It looked as if the brat had told her everything. Amazing memory—not to mention hearing—the child had. He turned his back to her so that she couldn't see his face. He had to find a way to keep her from talking. If this got back to the townspeople or . . . He thought of his father, already an invalid: this would kill him.

He turned back to her, smiling. "So how much do I pay you to keep your mouth shut?"

"I don't sell myself for money."

He gave her a sneering look up and down, then put his handkerchief to his nose as if to get away from her fish-stinking clothes. "I can see that."

She advanced on him. He was taller than she, but with his s-curved slouch, they were almost equal. "There are no words low enough to describe you. You'd take money from a man who ruins people just so you can have those silk clothes."

As she moved closer to him, Alex forgot all about what she'd heard and that he wanted to keep her from repeating it. All he was aware of was her eyes flashing with fire and passion and her breasts inches from his chest and heaving. She kept yelling at him and calling him names that no lady had ever called him before, but he didn't hear a word of it. When her lips were very close to his, she stopped abruptly and moved back. Alex's breath was coming from deep within his chest.

Jessica stood back and looked at him, her eyes blinking rapidly, as if in confusion.

Alex recovered himself and looked with longing at the sea. He considered jumping into the water to cool off.

"And who do you plan to tell about this?" he asked at last, no longer looking at her. He was too aware of the privacy of where they were to trust himself too far.

"The people of Warbrooke are afraid of Pitman

because he represents the king—not to mention the English navy. But you, they aren't afraid of you. If they knew what Nate heard this morning, they'd tar and feather you and then hang you. You wouldn't be allowed to live. They want someone to blame for what happened to Josiah."

"So what do you plan to do with your information?"

"It would kill your father if he knew." She looked down at the rocky beach. Not far from her was a basket half-full of clams which she'd obviously been digging before he came.

"Perhaps I can make your decision easier for you." He tried to keep his easy stance, tried not to let her see the energy and desire that was running through his body at the moment. "If you let other people know, even so much as your sister, your family will suffer. Now you have a roof over your head and food to eat." He studied his fingernails. "And all those brats of yours are alive." He looked back at her.

Something inside him tightened when he saw that she believed his threats. Was there no one who had known him all his life who'd stand up and say, "Alexander Montgomery wouldn't do such a thing"?

"You . . . you wouldn't."

He merely looked at her, not bothering to comment.

"You make Pitman look like one of the Lord's angels. At least some of what he is doing is for his country. For you, it's just greed." She turned on her heel as if to leave, then on impulse spun and slapped Alex across the face. A cloud of powder flew up from his full wig.

Alex had seen the slap coming but he didn't stop her. Anyone who'd heard all she had that morning had a right to slap the cause of her pain. He dug his hands into the padding on his thighs. He wanted to pull her into his arms and kiss her.

"I pity you," she whispered. "I pity us." She turned, her slim little body straight, and walked up the bank to the forest.

Chapter Four

"BEN Sampson's going to lose everything he owns. You mark my words," Eleanor was saying. She and Jessica were in the Taggert kitchen, Jess finishing a meal, Eleanor cleaning.

"Possibly," Jessica said mildly. "But then again he may make a profit." Last night she'd docked her little ship next to Ben's big one that had just returned from a voyage to Jamaica. While she'd been welcoming Ben home, one of his crew dropped a crate. The false bottom had been full of contraband tea. "All he has to do is store it twenty-four hours, then he can sneak it down to Boston."

"If you saw the crate break, how many others did, too?"

"No one." She gripped her wooden mug in her hand. "Not even your precious Alexander saw it."

"What's that supposed to mean? All I said was that

he certainly doesn't eat much for a fat man and that he's extremely polite and considerate. He never causes me nor anyone else the least bit of extra work," Eleanor said as she chopped the head off a big haddock.

"You don't know anything about him," Jess said, thinking of what Nate had overheard. If Ben were caught and his property confiscated, Alexander would profit. "I just wish Adam or Kit would come home. They'd kick Pitman out of the house."

"Their brother-in-law? A man appointed by the king? Be realistic, Jessica. Are you going to sit there and dawdle all night? I have to get back to the Montgomerys' and you need to take these fish to Mrs. Wentworth."

Jess glanced at the basket of cleaned fish. "Lazy bunch of women," she sneered. "Mistress Abigail is afraid the men won't like the smell of fish on her pure white hands."

Eleanor slammed the basket on the table. "It wouldn't hurt *you* to think a little more about how you smell. Now, go on, take this and don't start a fight with Abigail."

Jessica started to defend herself, but Eleanor didn't bother to listen before leaving the little house. Reluctantly, Jess took the basket of fish and started toward the Wentworths' big house.

She'd delivered the fish to Mrs. Wentworth and thought she was going to escape without having to see Abigail, but her luck ran out just as she opened the back door and stepped onto the porch.

"Jessica!" Abigail said. "How good to see you."

Jess knew Abigail was lying through her teeth. "Good evening. Fine clear night it's going to be, isn't it?"

Abby leaned forward in conspiracy. "Did you hear about Mr. Sampson? He brought in tea today and he didn't go through England. Do you think Mr. Pitman will find out?"

Jessica couldn't speak she was so astonished. If Abigail had heard of the tea, then of course Pitman had. "I have to warn Ben," was all Jess was able to say at last. She started toward the porch stairs with Abby, who had no intention of missing out on the excitement, close on her heels, when they were nearly run down by a man dressed in black riding a big black horse.

Both women came to a halt, Jess with her arm across Abby's chest in a protective gesture.

"Jess," Abby said breathlessly, "was that man wearing a mask?"

Jessica didn't answer but took off running, following the masked man's trail of dust. Abigail pulled her skirts to her knees, praying that her mother or the church deacons wouldn't see her, then followed Jessica.

They stopped at Ben Sampson's house. There were six British soldiers holding muskets on Ben.

"I don't know what you're talking about," Ben lied, and the sweat pouring off his face in spite of the cool evening air gave him away.

"Open up in the name of John Pitman, the king's agent," one of the soldiers said, raising his musket higher.

"Where's the man in black?" Abigail whispered.

Jessica listened to the sounds of the town and the evening. "There," she whispered, directing her glance toward the trees behind Ben's house. She saw a movement then grabbed Abby's plump arm and pulled her to the safety of the porch of the house across the street. They had just reached safety when all hell broke loose.

The masked man rode toward the soldiers, a weighted fishing net spreading behind him. The element of surprise was on his side, for the soldiers and Ben all stopped to gawk at him. The masked rider flung the net over four of the soldiers, then pulled a pistol on the other two. About the rider's belt was an arsenal of weapons. Instinctively, the men who weren't ensnared in the net dropped their muskets. The trapped ones still had their guns, but their hands were struggling with the net rather than with triggers.

"No man from Warbrooke has tea that hasn't been declared," the man on the horse said. He spoke with an odd accent, not quite English, not quite like the people whose families had been in America for generations.

Abigail looked at Jess and started to say something in protest, but Jess shook her head.

"Go back to your master and tell him that if he falsely accuses again, he'll have to answer to the Raider." He tossed the lead line of the net to one of the soldiers. "Take them back."

The man who called himself the Raider rode past Ben and the soldiers, the horse's hoofs striking very close to their legs.

As he rode past Abigail and Jessica standing on their high perch of the porch, he reined his horse sharply and looked at them.

Even with the mask covering the upper half of his face and the tricorn pulled low, he was a handsome man. Piercing black eyes were fiercely alive behind the silk mask and below it was a sensual, full mouth with finely chiseled lips. His black silk shirt, black pants and boots clung to his broad-shouldered, muscular body.

Abigail gave a heartfelt sigh and nearly swooned under the Raider's gaze. She would have fallen if Jess hadn't caught her beneath the arm and held her upright.

The Raider's lips stretched into a smile, not a grin, but a smile of such sweetness and knowing that Jess had to hold onto Abby with added strength.

Still smiling, the Raider leaned forward, put his big hand behind Abby's neck and kissed her long and sensually.

By now the soldiers and Ben had almost forgotten the reason for the Raider's appearance. He appealed to their sense of romance and, besides, it meant nothing to the homesick soldiers whether or not they found tea in Ben Sampson's cellar. Here was a masked man dressed in black, charging about the country and kissing the pretty girls.

They applauded when the Raider kissed Mistress Abigail, then held their breath when he turned to Mistress Jessica—the woman who'd haunted every man's dreams but had laughed in the faces of all of them.

Jessica was astonished at the look in the eye of this man who called himself the Raider when he released Abigail. Did he think *she* was as foolish as Abigail, who drooled over every man who paid her a compliment?

As the Raider leaned forward, as if he meant to kiss her also, Jessica leaned backward. She couldn't move too far as she was still holding Abby upright. "Don't you touch me," she hissed at the man.

She wasn't prepared for the change in his eyes. It was almost as if he hated her.

One minute she was standing on the porch, supporting a half-fainting Abigail, and the next she was being pulled across the Raider's saddle. The pommel hit her in the stomach painfully just as she heard Abigail hit the floor of the porch. She also heard the deafening sound of laughter from the soldiers and Ben. Doors up and down the street began slamming as people came outside, leaving their dinner tables, to see what the commotion was.

They were greeted by the sight of a man dressed in black with a black face mask, on a black horse, riding down the street with what had to be Mistress Jessica, bottom end up, across the saddle. He was followed by a parade of four soldiers with a net half over their bodies and making no attempt to escape, their net being pulled by two more soldiers, and all of whom were laughing heartily. The soldiers were followed by Ben Sampson, who was supporting a limp-limbed Abigail Wentworth. Down the road, the townspeople saw Mrs. Sampson and her two oldest boys removing crates from their cellar.

No one had any idea what was going on, but they joined the laughter when the masked man dumped Jessica Taggert in a tub of dirty washwater that Mistress Coffin had slovenly left overnight.

Jessica looked up, blinking from the washwater in her face.

"Please apologize for me to Mistress Coffin for ruining her wash," the Raider called over his shoulder before kicking his horse and disappearing down the street.

Jessica's ears were ringing with the people's laughter as she struggled to get out of the tub. She tried to keep her head up but it wasn't easy. She was sure every person in Warbrooke was in the street now and watching her.

With as much dignity as she could muster, she lifted herself out of the tub, knowing that her sailor's clothes clung to her body and gave the people all around her more reason to laugh.

Out of nowhere, Nathaniel appeared and took her hand. Dear, sweet Nathaniel, she thought and regretted all the times she'd threatened to kill him for his mischief.

"You stop laughing at my sister," he yelled, but no one obeyed him.

"Take me to Eleanor," Jessica managed to say. She would *not* cry. Under no circumstances in this world would she cry. She kept her back straight, her chin high and didn't look right or left.

Nathaniel, for reasons of his own, led Jessica not to Eleanor but to Sayer Montgomery.

Jessica, all her energy expended on trying not to cry, just stood there rather stupidly and stared at the old man who'd lost the use of his legs. In her childhood, he'd seemed formidable to her and she hadn't seen him except in quick glimpses since he'd been injured.

Vaguely, she was aware of Nate telling the old man what had happened, explaining why Jessica was soaking wet and her fishy clothes were smelling to high heaven, and why her face was fat and puffy with unshed tears.

Sayer's eyes widened, then he held out his arms. "I may be useless as a man nowadays, but I still have shoulders for pretty girls to cry on."

Jessica didn't think twice but almost fell on him and cried as if her heart were breaking. "I didn't do anything to him," she wailed. "I've never met him, so why should I let him kiss me?"

"Ah, but he was the Raider," Sayer said, holding her and stroking her back. He didn't mind her fish odor in the least. "Most girls would have acted as Abigail did."

"Abigail is an idiot," she said, sitting up slightly, but still in his arms.

"True." Sayer smiled. "But an awful pretty one. Quite kissable."

"But I'm . . . I mean . . ." Jessica started crying again. "The boys don't like me and I don't like them."

"Yes they do like you. They're just afraid of you. Hardly any of them can do half of what you can do. They see you captain that leaky tug of yours and haul anchors and"—he paused to smile—"and keep young Nathaniel in line and they know you're a better man than they are."

"Man?" she gasped. "Do they think I'm a *man?*"

He pulled her back to him, burying his hands in her hair that was hanging down about her waist. "Far from it. They all know you're the prettiest girl they've ever seen."

"Not as pretty as Abigail," she said, glancing out of the corner of her eye at him.

"Abigail is pretty today, when she's sixteen, but she won't be pretty tomorrow. You, my dear, will be pretty when you're a hundred."

"Well, I wish I were a hundred today. How can I face the townspeople tomorrow?"

He put his fingertips under her chin. "You did nothing wrong. Now think about it this way: while everyone was watching you, Ben's wife was able to get the tea out."

"But all Pitman has to do is *accuse* Ben."

Sayer's once handsome face turned hard. "Yes, my son-in-law has only to accuse. Perhaps Alexander—"

"Alexander!" Jessica said, sitting up. "How could you have two glorious sons and then the third one be so . . . so . . ."

"That's a question I've been asking myself," Sayer

said thoughtfully, then looked at Jessica. "I want you to think about what this Raider did for Ben. Try to think of what happened to you as part of the whole picture." He smiled. "And next time, when you see this Raider, run the opposite way."

"Next time! He wouldn't have the courage to appear again. Pitman will have his soldiers tearing the countryside apart looking for him."

Sayer pushed her off the bed. "Go now and get cleaned up. Really, Jessica, you should wear a dress now and then."

She smiled at him, feeling much better. "Aye, Captain." She bent and kissed his cheek. "Thank you." She left the room.

Sayer waited a few moments and then bellowed, "Nathaniel!" Within moments the boy appeared, holding his little brother Samuel's hand. "I want you to find out what you can about this Raider."

"I can't do nothin'. Eleanor gave me the baby to take care of. He can't even climb a tree." The boy's lip stuck out several inches.

Sayer frowned in thought a moment. "Look in that drawer yonder and bring me that ball of string and that brass ring and my knife. When my boys were babies and Lily was young and sailed with me, I knotted her a bag to tie the babies onto her back. We'll see if we can make a carrier for Samuel. Think you can climb a tree with that hefty young 'un on your back?"

"I could climb to the stars," Nathaniel said. "You got any peppermint? It keeps him quiet."

"You find out who this Raider is and I'll buy you a barrelful of peppermint."

"Sam likes peppermint, not me," Nate said, his jaw set in a line that looked remarkably like his sister's.

"And what does Nathaniel like?" Sayer asked as he began to knot lengths of heavy string onto a brass ring.

"My own dory so I can catch and sell fish."

Sayer smiled. "All right. And we'll name it *The Raider*. Now hold this end. Sam, go look in that box and see what you find."

Nathaniel and Sayer smiled at each other.

Jessica wiped away tears with the back of her sleeve and started walking through the woods toward the Taggert house.

She gasped when John Pitman stepped out of the trees. Usually, he was perfectly dressed, never a button undone, as if he wanted to show the Americans how to dress. But tonight he was dishevelled, his coat gone, his waistcoat unbuttoned. And his eyes were wild and he smelled of rum.

"Mistress Jessica," he said in a slurred voice, "the only other person to turn him down."

Jessica had never been too close to the customs officer and didn't want to be now. She gave him a weak smile and tried to get by him. The last thing she wanted was to be alone with this drunken man who was used to having his own way.

"Ah, Mistress Jessica," Pitman said softly, blocking her way and looking at the ties on her shirt. "Have you dried by now? Has his hated memory gone from you?"

She took a step backward. "You came out here and got drunk because of this glory-seeking villain, this Raider?" She was incredulous.

He moved closer to her. "Can't you see the hour? What would a man with a warm and pretty wife waiting at home be doing in the woods with a bottle at this hour? I come here every night." He moved so he was almost touching her, then took the string that tied her blouse shut in his hand. "I come here and dream of you Mistress Jessica, of Jessica with the saucy hips, of Jessica—"

With eyes wide, Jess pushed him and began to run. He was so drunk that it took him a moment to regain his balance and by then Jessica was gone. She ran through the woods, staying off any path, until she reached the Taggert house and slammed the door. She dropped the oak board that bolted the door.

Eleanor came into the room wearing her nightgown and cap. "Where have you been?" she asked. "We were worried about you."

When Jessica didn't answer, Eleanor put her arms around her sister. "You've had a rough day, haven't you? I heard about what happened earlier."

Jess didn't want to remember the Raider, or the wash tub, or drunken John Pitman's hands on her. "Go back to bed," she said to Eleanor. "I'm going to wash some of the filth off of me then I'll be there."

Eleanor nodded sleepily and padded back to bed.

After a sponge bath throughout which she cursed all men everywhere, Jess climbed the ladder to the loft. All the Taggerts were in one bed, the taller ones heading north, the smaller ones with their heads pointing south. She tucked the quilt around them more securely and kissed the nearest heads.

Nathaniel lifted himself on one elbow. "Why were you running?"

The child never missed anything. "I may tell you tomorrow. Go to sleep now."

Nate lay back down between two brothers. "I'll find him for you, Jess. I'll find the Raider and you can hang him."

Jess smiled at the thought. "I'll use Mrs. Coffin's

clothesline for the noose. Now go to sleep." She was still smiling as she climbed into bed with baby Samuel and Eleanor.

Jessica slammed her shovel into the rocky beach, grabbed a clam, then threw it at the basket.

"They aren't your enemy, you know."

She looked up to see Alexander Montgomery standing there, the yellow silk of his coat flashing in the sunlight.

"Have you come to laugh at me, too?" She glared at him with great hostility. "This morning wasn't enough for all of you? You have to sneak up on me so you can *privately* laugh at me?" She pulled another clam from its hiding place in the sand. She'd done her best to survive the morning but it hadn't been easy. As soon as she walked into the common room at the Montgomery house, everyone had doubled over with laughter. The men were a storehouse of wash day jokes, with Mr. Coffin laughing the loudest.

A sleepy-looking Alexander had come into the room and they'd all rushed to tell him of the fabulous exploits of this courageous hero, this Raider. According to the townsmen, the Raider was extremely tall (over six feet), handsome ("he certainly made little Abigail Wentworth swoon") and an excellent swordsman. Jessica could, of course, have kept her mouth shut, but she couldn't resist pointing out the fact that the Raider had never so much as drawn his sword, much less demonstrated his skill with it. That had returned their attention to her. They had said she didn't appreciate the fact that this man was risking his life to help others.

Jessica had grabbed the basket and shovel Eleanor used for digging clams and run to her private beach. Now Alexander had come here to ruin her solitude.

"I don't need you to laugh at me," she said, hands on hips.

Alex sat down on a tree that had fallen across the beach. "I didn't come to laugh. I just wanted to say I don't think you deserved what happened to you yesterday. I think the Raider was wrong."

Jessica kept glaring for a moment, then closed her mouth and attacked another clam hole. "You came down here and risked getting your pretty clothes dirty to tell me that? Why? What do you want from me? Twenty-five percent of what *I* earn?"

Alex's voice was very calm when he answered. "I know what it's like to have the whole town laugh at you for something you can't help."

Jess looked at him and remembered all too well how she'd made the town laugh at him when he'd returned to Warbrooke. Her cheeks flushed red and she dug for another clam. "I'm sorry about that. Maybe I was a little too zealous. But everyone said that one of the Montgomery boys was going to come back and fix everything. I thought it was a ridiculous idea and when I saw you—" She stopped as she looked at his face. "I'm sorry I laughed."

She continued digging clams but without as much anger.

"Do you *really* like my tailor?" Alex asked. "I could have him run something up for you. Maybe something in blue to go with your hair."

Jess started to make a sharp retort but as she looked at his smiling face, she began to smile, too. "How many clams would I have to dig to pay for a blue silk dress?"

"It would cost you more than clams. It would cost you friendship. All you have to do is stop inciting the town to ridicule me and I'll buy you the dress."

"Oh." A wave of guilt washed over Jessica. She

hadn't thought how Alexander felt being the butt of all the jokes—but now she knew the feeling all too well. "Please don't buy me a dress," she said, looking down toward her shovel.

"Then we can be friends?"

"I . . . I guess so."

There was a pause and she glanced at Alexander to see that he was smiling. He wasn't a bad-looking man, although much of his face was hidden beneath the big powdered wig. No doubt that snobby servant of his shaved Alex's head every morning. Of course his clothing and that belly of his were preposterous. Even Abigail, who liked almost any man and especially rich single men, ignored Alexander.

Alex, with a smile of contentment, removed his satin jacket, stretched out on the log, his big belly standing up like a piece of whale fat floating on the sea. "Tell me what you thought of the Raider."

Jessica was thoughtful a moment. "He likes glory. Why else would he ride through the middle of town for everyone to see him?"

"Perhaps that was the idea. Maybe he wanted everyone's attention on him so Ben could remove the tea. You heard, didn't you, that they're gone? Ben, his wife and all four kids left in the middle of the night. Don't you think the Raider gave them that chance to escape Pitman?"

"Don't mention that man's name to me! You who take money from him!"

As she walked by him, he caught her wrist, encircling it with his fingers but not squeezing. "Did it ever occur to you that if I take twenty-five percent of my esteemed brother-in-law's profits, then I will know how much he's earning? And as a partner of sorts, I can look over his books. I might, if he begins to trust

me, find out whose ship he's planning to take next."
He released her wrist.

"No, I never thought of that."

Alex put his hands under his head. "Do think about it."

Jess put clams in the basket and looked up at him out of the corner of her eye. His fat thighs were straining against the yellow satin breeches and his belly was about to pop two buttons.

"It doesn't matter about this Raider, he won't have courage enough to reappear. Pitman's on to him."

"And of course you're sure Pitman's smarter than the Raider."

It was difficult for her to consider the Raider in any terms but hatred after what he'd done to her. "He's a glory-seeking braggart and I hope I never see him again."

"You have no idea who he is? After all, you were very close to him."

"No idea at all, but I'm sure I'd recognize him if I saw him again. He has a very cruel-looking mouth. Oh no!" she gasped, looking out to sea. She had spread one of her two precious fishing nets on a rock to dry and now one of the many lobsters that the tide had lifted out was carrying it away. She made a grab, missed, then ran into the sea.

Alex was off his log in seconds. He caught himself just as he started after her. He had to remain in character. "Jessica, are you planning to swim to China after that net?"

She stopped, waist deep in the icy water, and watched the net float away from land. "I think I can get it if I could get down that rock ledge." She gave Alex an appraising look. "Could you hold my feet so I can hang over the side?"

Alex nodded, keeping his eyes raised, not looking down at her dampened shirt clinging to her breasts. "I think I could manage."

"I'm awfully heavy."

He wiped his sweating palms on his padded thighs. "Let's try it."

Jess stretched out on the grass, using her arms to support her half way over the rock ledge.

Alex stood over her. The baggy sailor's pants were clinging to her thighs and showing every curve of her lovely little fanny.

"Alex!" Jess said impatiently. "Are you going to hold me or not?"

"I will," Alex said in a subdued voice, then took her ankles and lifted her so she could hang over the side of the ledge.

"Just a little more," Jess said, stretching to reach the net. "Got it. You can pull me up now."

Quite easily, Alex pulled her up, being careful not to let her body touch the rough rocks. He dropped her feet when her head was on flat land.

Jess lay still for a moment while she examined the net. "No new tears, I'm thankful for that." Lithely, she got to her feet. "Alex, you look a little pale. I think I was too heavy for you. Sit down and rest."

Alex did as she bid.

"I'll get the clams and walk you back. A man of your . . . physique shouldn't have exerted himself like that." She ran down the little bank and picked up the basket of clams and when she returned, Alex was still sitting on the rock, his face white, his forehead sweaty. Poor man, she thought, he isn't used to exercise. She extended her arm to him. "Lean on me, I'll help you. We'll go back to your father's house and Eleanor will brew you a cup of tea—legal, expensive tea," she added, smiling and patting his hand that was on her arm. "Eleanor will help you recover."

"She thinks I'm ninety years old!" Alexander said to Nicholas, through his clenched teeth as he brushed the big stallion.

They were on a piece of land off the coast of the Warbrooke harbor, a tiny rocky island good for nothing but the breeding of mosquitoes and black flies. Eighteen years ago a ship had gone aground on the island's south coast during a hideous winter storm and all hands had died. One man had been found the next morning frozen to the top of the main mast, a lantern in his hand. People said that for days a light could be seen wandering about the island, but upon investigation, no one was to be found. Someone called it Ghost Island and everyone kept away from it. It was the perfect place to hide the Raider's horse and gear.

"She stands in front of me wearing wet clothes that stick to her heavenly little body, then lies down on the ground and crawls around so that her backside—sorry," he said to the horse when he brushed too hard. "What does she think I'm made of?"

"About two hundred and fifty pounds of fat."

"Fat doesn't make me less of a *man*," Alex said. He was wearing only breeches that clung to his big, muscular thighs. The sun was warming and browning the skin of his broad back.

"Then maybe it's the wig," Nick said, his eyes smiling. "Or maybe the satin. Or perhaps it's the lazy way you walk or the fact that you do nothing all day except read and eat. Or it could be the slightly whining tone in your voice."

Alex opened his mouth to speak but closed it again

as he brushed the horse even harder. "I'm not *that* good of an actor. She should see that I . . . that I . . ."

"That you lust after her?"

"Jessica Taggert? Not on your life! Why should I expect anything from any of the Taggerts? There isn't a brain in any of them except Eleanor."

"But it wasn't Jessica's brain you were lusting after, was it?"

"I only brought this up to show you the stupidity of the woman. She said she'd recognize the Raider, that he had a cruel-looking mouth, but there I was right in front of her. Let's not talk about her. Did you see that little Abigail Wentworth when I kissed her? Now *she's* a woman a man could spend some time with."

"If a man wanted to be bored to death two years after the marriage," Nick said, yawning. "You'd have to create entertainments for her. What would you do when she got bored with the Raider? Dress as a devil for two years? Then what?"

"Abigail recognized what the Raider was doing. He was risking his life to save someone else. Jessica didn't see that at all."

"Perhaps she had too much dirty water in her eyes to see much."

Alex winced. "I apologized to her for that. At least I did the best I could. I certainly wouldn't have sought out a brainless, aggressive woman like Jessica if I hadn't had a reason."

"Makes perfect sense to me. Check his right foreleg," Nick said, lazily giving Alex orders in the way only a Russian grand duke could. "Maybe Alex should seek out Mistress Wentworth and leave Mistress Taggert alone."

"Good idea," Alex said, returning to his brushing.

Chapter Five

Sweat was trickling down the back of Alexander's neck, mixing with the thick powder of the wig and making an itchy paste. He longed to pull the thing off and scratch, but he kept his languid position of sprawling across the hard sofa in Abigail Wentworth's parlor.

"And he's tall and very handsome," Abby was saying as she sat dreamily looking out the window, her big brown eyes almost turning to liquid.

"I thought he wore a mask." Alex was playing with the plume from his hat. Yesterday morning he'd taken the opportunity, while Pitman was at breakfast, to search the man's office. He'd found a letter from an admiral of His Majesty's navy thanking Pitman for confiscating the *Mermaid*, Josiah Greene's ship, and saying that Pitman's share of the profits from the sale would be arriving on the *Golden Hind*. This morning Alex had heard that the *Golden Hind* had been sighted and would be in Warbrooke tonight.

"Well, of course he wore a mask," Abigail was saying. "But a woman knows these things. He was extraordinarily handsome."

"Not like anyone in Warbrooke?" Alex asked, looking at her over the feather. All he had to do was figure out how to hide on the ship, take the money away from the king's representative and escape without shedding any blood—particularly his own.

"Of course there's no one in Warbrooke like the Raider. I've lived here all my life and there's no one as graceful as the Raider, no one as tall, no one as brave. He's the most—"

Alex didn't listen to the rest. In the week since the raid, Abigail had set herself up as the authority on the Raider—and her big mouth was making it more difficult for Alex to appear as the Raider again. Pitman didn't like that he had lost a battle to a cocky masked man and no one in town dared remind him of his loss—except Abigail that is. It seemed all she was capable of talking about. For two days after the raid she was the town's center of attention, since everyone wanted to hear her impressions of this man. But by the fourth day, people were thinking once again about putting food on the table and clothes on their backs. Everyone except Abigail, that is. She still talked of nothing except the Raider.

Alex had decided to take Nick's advice and spend some time with pretty little Abigail, but as far as he could tell, Abby hadn't yet noticed him. The only man she thought of was the Raider.

"Believe me, I know what he looks like."

"Jessica Taggert said he had a cruel-looking mouth."

Abigail stood, her plump bosom heaving in anger. "What does the likes of a Taggert know? You saw what the Raider thought of her, didn't you? I've always thought she needed a bath."

Alex opened his mouth to say that maybe the Raider had been angered because he'd wanted so much to kiss Jessica and she'd refused him. But he wasn't really interested in Abigail's answer enough to bother to comment. What he most wanted to do was go to Ghost Island, shed his hot clothes and dive into the cold saltwater of the sea. And he needed to plan how he was going to relieve Pitman of his ill-gotten money.

Politely, he excused himself from Mistress Abigail and went outside to the busy main street of Warbrooke. He felt drawn to the cool breezes from the ocean and started walking that way. A couple of strangers in town stopped to gawk at him. Today he was wearing his royal blue satin outfit, the waistcoat embroidered with green and yellow silk flowers. Nick had sent his entourage of servants to New Sussex to bring back more of his fat cousin's clothes, so now Alex had several gaudily-colored garments as well as four enormous, and hated, wigs from which to choose.

The first thing he saw was Jessica's old tub, the *Mary Catherine*, tied at the wharf. Warbrooke had the deepest harbor on the American coast and even large ships could sail in quite close.

"Ahoy, Alex!" Jessica called down to him. She was in the rigging of the boat's tallest sail, trying her best to patch rotten and broken ropes. "Been courting?"

A couple of sailors behind him laughed as they looked Alex up and down.

"And who have you been courting?" Alex called back, referring to her male garments. He was pleased to hear the sailors laugh even harder before they moved on.

Jessica grinned and clambered down the rigging. "Come on board," she called, "but mind your pretty clothes, there's tar and nails about."

The boat Jess owned was even more derelict when seen at close view than from afar. It was a tiny thing with only two sails, but even at that, he wondered how she sailed it alone. The anchor must weigh two hundred pounds at least.

Below, down the narrow stairs and corridor and into the single cabin, he smelled every fish the boat had ever taken on. For the first time, he used his scented handkerchief for real.

"Too much for you?" Jessica asked, grinning.

He tested one of the two chairs for sturdiness, then sat in it. "How do you stand this tub?"

Some of the light went out of her eyes. "I'm a Taggert, remember?"

"True, and no doubt that means you can't smell anything."

Jessica laughed. "Maybe it is a little difficult to take. I have some rum. Would you like a tot?"

"After an afternoon with Mistress Abigail, I need a hogshead."

"The town's prettiest girl? The love of the Raider's life?"

Alex groaned. "Don't mention that man to me. After all Abby had to say, I hope I never hear of him again."

Jessica poured two wooden mugs half full of rum. "Don't tell Eleanor," she said, smiling.

Alex took a drink and then grimaced. "I see why the

smell doesn't bother you. A few swigs of this and your nose falls off."

Jess sat down, one foot in the chair, the other propped on the knob of a cabinet door. It was a masculine stance, but Jessica's body made it very unmasculine. Her breasts were outlined by the full shirt, and the pants wrapped themselves about her thighs—just exactly what Alex imagined his hands doing. He leaned back in his chair.

"So what is Pitman up to?" Jess asked, cradling her mug of rum, letting the liquid seep into her bones. A moment of rest like this and someone to share her precious rum with was pure pleasure. None of the women would have anything to do with her, and the men either treated her like a disease or they thought she lacked virtue and attacked her. Sitting with Alex who had no physical interest in her was a rare treat, rather like having a special friend.

"Jess, how would you get in touch with this Raider?"

"Why do you want to know?"

"I have some information he might be interested in." He proceeded to tell her of the money arriving for Pitman. If the Raider appeared with this knowledge that could only have been obtained by searching Pitman's private papers, Alex was afraid Jessica might guess who had found that information.

"I guess you could always tell Abigail," Jessica said, smiling maliciously. "I'm sure the Raider slips into her bedchamber at night."

"Are you jealous?" Alex raised one eyebrow.

"Of a sneak thief? The Raider is no better than a highwayman. If he had any courage, he'd stand up and denounce Pitman."

And hang for it, Alex thought. "So you have no idea

how the Raider heard of Ben Sampson's smuggling tea in?"

"Everyone in town knew about Ben and the tea. Even Abigail had heard of it." She put her mug down and leaned forward. Her eyes were bright and the color in her cheeks heightened.

Alex began to sweat again.

"What if we start passing this information around? What if we tell a few people that the *Golden Hind* is delivering money to Pitman from the sale of Josiah's ship? If the rumor starts at the wharf, maybe Pitman will think it came from a sailor of His Majesty's ship."

Alex sipped his rum and thought that maybe there was more than one Taggert who had some brains.

Jessica stayed on deck even when the sailors from the *Golden Hind* made lewd remarks to her. They'd been out to sea for months and the sight of so pretty a woman on the little relic docked next to them was more than their imaginations could handle. Usually, Jess took precautions and stayed away from newly arrived ships, but last evening she had made every effort to put her little ship next to the big one. It loomed over her like some fat old lady, the leering eyes of the sailors like rats at her beltline. Jess did her best to ignore them.

After Alex's visit yesterday morning, they'd separated and started casually spreading their rumors about Pitman's money arriving on the *Hind*. It hadn't taken many tellings to irritate the people. The money was from the sale of a ship belonging to one of their own and they directed their anger at the newly arrived English sailors. Already, four fights had started and three men were in the stocks in the town square.

After starting the rumors, Jessica had sailed out of

the harbor and gone shrimping. She'd trawled close to the northeastern shore where she could see the arrival of the *Golden Hind,* and all afternoon she'd cast and recast her net—and waited. She wasn't sure what she planned to do, but if the Raider appeared and he needed help, she planned to help him.

A couple of times her mind rebelled at the idea of helping the man who'd so publicly humiliated her, but her desire to repay Pitman made her forget her own personal anger. If the American people didn't start protesting the English treatment, there wouldn't be any end to their tyranny.

The hold was half-full of squiggling shrimp before the *Golden Hind* had arrived and Jessica had tried her best to act nonchalant as she pushed her way into the harbor and tied up next to the big ship. She'd no more than dropped her sails before Nathaniel was there to catch her rope and tie her ship next to the square-rigger.

Nate scurried up the rope Jess tossed over the side. "You're out late. Eleanor made me wait for you."

Jess didn't answer him but started watching the activity on the English ship as best she could considering her much lower position.

"Gor . . ." Nate said, looking at the amount of shrimp in the hold.

"Get the other kids and bag it, then take it around and sell it," Jess snapped.

Nathaniel gave her a shrewd look. The boy saw much too much for someone of his few years.

"Don't give me any trouble, just do it!" Jess was annoyed because she couldn't see what was happening on the *Golden Hind.*

She stayed on board her stinking ship all night. When Eleanor came to the dock, Jessica barely answered her questions about why she wasn't coming home. She slept very little, not allowing herself to go downstairs to the relative luxury of her berth, instead staying on deck, leaning against the side of the ship, a bailing pin nearby in case one of the sailors decided to do what all of them threatened.

At dawn she rose, stiff, a kink in her back, and heard the soft whinny of a horse nearby. Hanging over the side of her ship, she looked below to see a saddled horse ready and waiting.

She came fully awake. The horse had streaks of gray on its coat, but nothing could hide the sleek lines and the nervous prancing of the animal. It was the Raider's horse.

A head appeared on the other side of the *Mary Catherine.* It was George Greene, Josiah's oldest son, an angry young man of twenty-six who'd been cheated of his inheritance.

Jessica turned to him.

"You saw it, too," George said softly, then louder, "I hear you have shrimp to sell, Mistress Jessica." His eyes told her that they were being watched.

"Aye, George, that I do. Let me get you a bag." Jess tore down the steps below and pulled out a burlap bag, stuffed a length of frayed rope inside and ran back up the stairs. "Will that be enough?" She stepped close to George. "Do you know anything?"

"Nothing. Father is afraid to hope. He wants Pitman dead."

"I'd like to sail under her," came a voice from above them.

"You'd better go," Jess whispered. "I wish you enjoyment of the shrimp," she said for the sailor's benefit.

"I'll stay with his horse. He may need me."

Jess nodded and turned away.

Suddenly, above them came a shout and then the sounds of unfamiliar ruckus.

"It's him!" George said and the hope in his voice was what would usually be reserved for the second coming.

"Go to his horse," Jess commanded. "He may need help." She ran up the short ladder to the upper deck, put her foot in the rigging as if to climb but never got the chance.

From the high ship rail of the *Golden Hind,* the Raider swung down on a rope tied to the top of the mainmast. The sunlight flashing off this man, a bound chest under his left arm, effectively stopped all movement in the vicinity.

For a moment everything seemed to stop moving. The tall Raider lithely swung across the ship, slipped down the rope and came to land in front of Jessica on the upper deck.

His eyes caught hers.

"You got the money," she breathed, her eyes happy and alive.

He caught her to him with one strong arm and kissed her half-open mouth.

Jessica was too startled to be able to move away from him, but stood there while he kissed her. But when he pulled away from her as quickly as he'd come to her, she no longer thought of why they were there. She was aware only that this stranger had dared to kiss her. She drew back her hand to strike him, but he caught her wrist and boldly kissed her palm. "Good morning, Mistress Jessica," he said, his lips smiling in a knowing way.

The next minute he was gone, heading toward the rope slung over the side of the ship.

But she had no precious time to waste on anger. She had to help the Raider escape. If the *Golden Hind*'s sailors were dumbfounded, her captain was not. Jess could hear orders being shouted and above her was movement as four men prepared to board her ship.

She wasn't fool enough to try to stop His Majesty's sailors, but perhaps she could delay them. She grabbed a coil of rope at her feet, rope as big around as her arm, and tossed an end to George who'd reboarded at the first sound of excitement. The Raider disappeared over the side of the ship.

Four sailors came scurrying across the deck of Jessica's ship, close on the heels of the Raider.

George pulled his end of the rope, Jess half-hitched hers to the railing and all four sailors went sprawling just as they heard the sound of hoofbeats on the wharf.

"Take them!" she heard the captain shout from the ship above them and the next moment rough hands eagerly clutched her body. The men grinned when their hands brushed against her breasts and buttocks.

She was pulled off her ship, onto the wharf and across the gangplank of the *Golden Hind,* then shoved to her knees before the English captain, with George beside her.

The captain, a short, heavyset man in his fifties, looked down his nose at her. "So this is how the ladies dress in the Colonies?" he sneered. "Take them below."

Jess was separated from George and thrown into a filthy little room in the hold of the ship. There were two inches of slimy water on the floor and she was sure the room had once been a repository for pig manure.

Within five minutes, she felt as if she had always

been in this dank, dark place. She couldn't move without kicking up the sediment on the hold floor. There was no bench to sit on, no way to get out of the filth.

She stood there, the water quickly seeping through the leather of her boots, and waited. She didn't regret helping the Raider but now she thought of the consequences of her actions.

Hours later, when the door to the cell was opened, Jessica was prepared to meet a hangman.

Instead, standing on deck was Alexander, resplendent in yellow satin, the sunlight hitting his big belly and reflecting into her eyes. She put her hand up against the glare.

She couldn't see Alexander very well, but she could feel his anger all around her.

"Come!" was all he commanded, in a low, seething voice.

"I—" Jess began, but he shoved her shoulder and pushed her toward the gangplank.

Jess tried to keep her head up as she passed the crowd that had gathered on both sides of the wharf.

Alex climbed onto a wagon seat without so much as looking at Jessica. As she weakly climbed up beside him, he flicked the reins to the horses and they started down the street.

"What are you so mad about?" she shouted over the noise of the wagon, but he didn't answer her.

He drove her across a dirt road to the back of the forest, then up a hill. She knew there was a spring nearby.

"Get down," he commanded when he'd stopped.

"Not until you tell me what's going on," she answered.

Alex, fighting his way around his belly, walked to

her side of the wagon. "I had to bribe your way out of a hangman's noose, that's what. You were playing with the English navy when you helped the Raider. That captain planned to use you and George as examples and hang you. He figured that'd stop the Raider."

"Oh," Jessica said, getting down. "I thought they might want to do that. Why are we here?"

Alex calmed his voice. "Eleanor sent you clean clothes and there's soap and towels. You smell worse than you did before you went into that cell." He put his handkerchief to his nose. "And Eleanor thought you should stay out of sight for a few days."

"Why didn't she come with you?" Jess picked up the bundle from the back of the wagon.

"It seems she had a little collision with a bucket of washwater. I think she told Nick something to the effect that he wasn't too good to do some washing. I believe Nick thought otherwise."

Jessica gaped at him. "So that overgrown boy tossed dirty water on my sister?"

"I believe so, yes."

"I'll give him a piece of my mind," she said, getting back on the wagon.

Alex caught her arm. "Eleanor has already told him what she thought of him and I'm sure he need not hear anymore. The problem now is you. You badly need a bath."

Reluctantly, Jessica followed him up the hill to the spring and its little pool.

Alex seated himself, his back to Jessica, while she began to disrobe. She couldn't see the way the sweat began trickling down his neck or how clammy his palms grew. "Tell me what happened," he said, managing to make his voice sound somewhat normal.

As unemotionally as she could, Jessica began to tell how she'd spent yesterday shrimping and watching for the *Golden Hind*. Only part of her mind was on her story, the other part was wondering why Eleanor had sent this man with instructions to take her to bathe. In other circumstances it would have been unthinkable to remove her clothing with a man nearby—but to her, Alexander Montgomery was so far removed from being a man that it seemed quite natural. Now, if instead that awful Raider were here . . .

"Go on," Alex prompted, wiping his palms on a relatively dry patch of grass. "What happened after the Raider appeared?"

Jessica soaped her toes. "I *hate* that man! I hate him! There I was, risking my neck to save his and once again he makes a fool of me."

"I heard that he kissed you."

"If you can call it that. He tried to anyway. And after what I'd done for him. My arms are sore from hauling shrimp nets and he treats me like that. I ought to have snatched the mask from his face and shown everyone who he was. He deserved that."

"But you didn't," Alex said quietly. "Instead, you threw a rope and stopped the pursuit of the king's men. He wouldn't have escaped if it hadn't been for you."

"And look how he repays me. I didn't do it for him, I can assure you. I did it for Josiah Greene."

"Did you hear that the Raider gave the money to Josiah? And Josiah left town immediately."

"With George?"

"No." Alex hesitated. "Tomorrow George is to be given twenty lashes with a lead-tipped cat-o'-nine-tails."

Jess didn't breathe for a moment. "That could kill

him," she whispered. Quickly, she began to rinse the soap from her hair. "Alex, we have to do something to help him."

"No, 'we' don't and especially not you. You already have a black mark against you after today. Whatever you do, Jess, you can't help the Raider again."

"Don't worry, the only help he'll get from me is to lead him up the hangman's steps."

"Really angry at him, are you? Did you ever think that maybe he thought his kiss was a way to say 'thank you'?"

"No," Jess said, moving to stand before him, tying the front of her dress. It was a faded, worn, green cotton and the ties were fragile with age. The dress had belonged to her mother, then to Eleanor before Jess acquired it. "I think he believes himself to be what every woman wants."

She sat down in front of him and began to use a wooden comb Alex had brought to pull the tangles from her hair.

"And he's not what you want? Here, turn around and let me do that. You won't have any hair left in a minute." Alex began to gently comb her long hair.

"Most certainly not." She leaned her head back, enjoying the feel of his combing.

"Wouldn't you like to have a home and kids of your own, Jess?"

"And who'll marry a Taggert? All the men are afraid they'll have to raise Nathaniel. You know what this town needs?" She turned to look at him. "Adam. Or Kit. Yes, Kit could do it."

"My brothers?" Alex asked, aghast. "What exactly do you think my brothers could do?"

"Save us. I mean, save the town. They wouldn't allow Pitman to run the Montgomery house. They'd throw him out on his ear."

"And risk the wrath of the king?" Alex was incredulous.

"They'd find a way around it. Somehow they'd manage to save Warbrooke, free your sister and get rid of Pitman. There are other customs officers, you know."

Alex leaned back against the grass, picked a daisy and held it to his nose. "So, you think my brothers could do all that?" He used the flower to conceal the way his mouth was tightening.

"Adam or Kit could, I'm sure. When I was a little girl, I used to . . ."

"What?" Alex asked lazily.

Jess smiled dreamily. "I used to imagine being married to Adam. He was always such a handsome man, so proud, so intelligent—and he had eyes like an eagle's. You don't know where he is now, do you?"

"Hell," he said, then added quickly, "I'm sorry, I pricked my finger. The last I heard, Adam was on his way to Cathay and Kit was fighting in a war somewhere."

"I don't guess Marianna's letters requesting help will reach them then."

"No, I'm the only one who's coming."

"Oh," Jess said, suddenly realizing how she must be making Alex feel. He didn't seem able to help the way he was. "Alex, have you ever thought of getting some exercise? Maybe if you helped me haul shrimp for a few days, maybe you'd lose some weight."

Alexander shuddered delicately. "No, thank you. Are you ready to leave? It's getting chilly here."

"We haven't talked about what we're going to do about George."

"There's nothing we can do. George will heal. I had to put some money in that captain's hands to keep him from hanging George. Better to lose a little skin from his back than to lose his life. Tomorrow you're to remain home during the flogging." He gave her a sideways look. "Maybe the Raider will save George."

She snorted. "And who will save the Raider? He's incompetent at best. His arrogance is going to get someone killed."

Maybe me, Alex thought.

Chapter Six

Alexander looked about him cautiously. It had been difficult rescuing George Greene from under the whip. Nicholas had helped by setting up his servants at the back of the crowd and, just as Alex, dressed as the Raider, was ready to ride from his hiding place, Nick gave the order to fire. In the ensuing confusion, Alex was able to gallop through the people, pull George into the saddle behind him and escape unharmed. It'd taken him a lot longer to escape the English soldiers, but they didn't know the area and it had been a child's game of hide-and-seek to evade them.

Josiah Greene was waiting at the edge of the forest with horses and passage on a ship traveling south. "I knew you'd come," Josiah said. "I knew you'd not let my boy be whipped for saving you."

Alex was a little disconcerted that Josiah had so easily predicted the Raider's actions and where he would enter the forest, because if Josiah guessed, perhaps next time an army would be waiting for him. Without speaking, the Raider released George and disappeared into the trees.

It was amazing how soon he'd become a symbol of hope to these people, Alex thought. Already, they were depending on the Raider to save them from any injustices. All except Jessica Taggert, that is.

Adam could save the town, Alex thought, remembering Jessica's words. Or Kit could. Have you ever thought of losing weight, Alex? He'd like to show her just exactly how much he weighed. Eleanor sent him out with clean clothes for Jessica and orders to see that she bathed. Neither of those women seemed to have any idea he was a man. Jessica disrobed when he was standing but a few feet away from her. And that time he had held her by the legs so she could reach that rotten old net of hers! That time he hadn't thought he was going to live through it.

He adjusted the mask on his face, making sure it was tight. There were times when he wanted to grab Jessica, grab her and show her he was a man.

"Ooohhh."

He heard a cry that was half swoon, half plea and instantly realized he'd been so involved in thinking about what he'd to do to Mistress Jessica that he hadn't been keeping watch.

He reined his horse in, stood still and listened as someone came thrashing toward him. He drew his sword and waited.

Mistress Abigail Wentworth, her pretty face flushed from the exertion, came bursting through the trees. She took one look at the Raider atop the black stallion, put her hand to her breast and began to sink to the ground.

Alex was off his horse in seconds and caught her before she hit the floor of the forest.

"Will you use that on me?" she gasped, lying in his arms and rolling her eyes toward his sword. "Will you slice the clothing from my body before you have your way with me?"

"Why no, I . . ." He wasn't sure what to answer her but the sight of her heaving bosom so exposed to his view—she'd removed her scarf so a great deal of young, pink flesh was showing—made him think about her offer. "Are you all right?"

She threw her arms about his neck, pressing her bosom to his chest. "I am your slave, your captive. Do with me what you will."

Alex raised his eyebrows, but never a man to question extreme good luck, the next minute he was kissing her. She returned his kiss with such passion that before he knew what he was doing, he was halfway to the ground with her.

She was eager, warm, willing—and the daughter of one of his father's oldest friends.

"Abby," he said, trying to disentangle himself from her arms. Her hair had come loose and it was soft against his cheek. "Abby." Her name came out like a groan.

"I love to hear you say my name. My own Raider. My own true love." She moved her hips against his, trying to kiss him again, but he pulled away.

"Go home to your mother," he said and found his voice a little shaky. Why did he have to be the Raider in his own hometown? Anywhere else and he'd take this eager young filly without a thought. "Go home, Abby. Please go home."

She flung herself against a tree, her face flushed, her breasts about to come out of the tight dress. "How noble you are," she whispered.

"Or how stupid," Alex mumbled, looking at her. If he didn't get out of here soon, he'd lose his resolve. With half of his mind calling him a fool, he jumped into the saddle of his horse. "Goodbye, Mistress Abigail," he whispered as he urged his horse forward.

"Damn all women!" he cursed. Jessica thought he wasn't a man at all and Abigail thought he was more man than a herd of stallions. He shifted in the saddle, feeling like only half the man Abby thought him to be. Now all he had to do was make it to Ghost Island— and he prayed he would encounter no more women.

Jessica looked at the big basket full of blackberries and grimaced. She owned her own ship, had sailed, by herself, as far south as New Sussex, yet today she'd been relegated to picking blackberries like a naughty child.

And it was all the Raider's fault!

When it had been announced that George Greene was to be whipped, everyone had said the Raider was going to save him. They had said the Raider *had* to save the boy, as if it were a matter of honor.

As if they knew anything about the Raider's sense of honor or anything else for that matter, she thought. Everyone in town seemed to have endowed this Raider with magical skills, talents that no human had ever possessed. They expected this masked man to right all wrongs, to single-handedly fight the British laws.

But not everyone had believed the Raider to be perfectly good. Jess had delivered twenty pounds of haddock to the Montgomery house and had been told Sayer wanted to see her. She hadn't seen him since the evening the Raider had thrown her in the washwater and she'd cried in his arms. She had been smiling when she entered Sayer's room but not when she left.

Sayer had demanded that she stay away from town the next day. It had been on the tip of her tongue to ask him what gave him the right to make such a demand, but she hadn't said what she thought. The Montgomery family had been good to hers over the years and, besides, she couldn't very well be disrespectful to an old and crippled man who was only concerned for her well-being. Reluctantly, she had agreed to stay in the forest for the entire day. Sayer hadn't even wanted her on the wharf or near her own ship.

So now, here she was, doing children's work, all because of that man who called himself the Raider.

Near the blackberry patch, under some trees, was a bed of moss that looked very inviting. It might do Eleanor some good to have her sister come back very late and give her a little something to worry about. Smiling somewhat smugly, she stretched out on the moss and was asleep in minutes. Unfortunately, she began to dream about the masked man who was upsetting her life so badly. She was reliving the time he had humiliated her and the time he had kissed her when she'd been helping him to escape.

"Jessica! Jessica, are you all right?"

Jess awoke with difficulty, clutching at the strong arms that held her. "I was dreaming," she said. "He—" She stopped because the person holding her was the man who was causing all her problems: the Raider.

"You!" she gasped. "You!" Without another thought, she drew back her fist and hit him on the jaw.

"Why you little brat!" he seethed at her, grabbing her shoulders and pushing her to the ground. The worn-out fabric of her dress front split open, exposing a thin line of soft, white fabric from neck to waist. The pink of her skin showed beneath the fabric.

Jessica felt the dress split, then saw the look in the eyes behind the black mask. "If you touch me, I'll—"

"Feel rewarded," he said angrily, keeping her pinned to the ground while his lips came down on hers.

Jessica felt his lips for the second time and began to fight. She'd die before she let this man force himself on her. She kicked out at him, catching him once on the shins. She felt him suck his stomach in at the pain, but he kept his lips glued to hers.

He threw his leg over hers to keep it still. Jess tried to wiggle out from under him. She flung her head sharply to one side, away from his torturous kiss.

The Raider pinned both her hands above her head with one of his, then took her chin in his other hand and forced her mouth back under his. To keep her hips still, he put his full body weight on her.

For a moment, Jessica was still. There were emotions shooting through her that she'd never felt before. Was this what the newly married women giggled about? Was this the emotion that made engaged girls starry-eyed?

The Raider pulled away from her lips, but kept his face close to hers. It was evening and the starlight made his face darker, his eyes more brilliant than ever.

"Jessica," he said, and there was some wonder in his voice.

She blinked at him a couple of times, then in one violent motion pushed him off her and stood.

The Raider, that finely chiseled mouth of his smiling, looked up at her. "Well, Jessica, for all your men's airs, you are a woman after all."

Jess grabbed a handful of blackberries from her basket and prepared to throw them at him.

Like a big cat, he leapt to his feet and grabbed her hand. He closed his hand over her little one and squeezed until the berries oozed out between her fingers. Looking into her eyes, he began to lick the juice from between her fingers. For some reason, the sight of his tongue made Jessica's heart beat a little faster.

He easily pulled her hand behind her back and moved so his body was touching hers. "I believe I missed a few berries," he whispered, then bent and pressed his face to her chest and began kissing the top of her heaving breast.

He looked back at her.

Jessica was staring at him in wide-eyed astonishment, not understanding at all what she was feeling. She couldn't move but just stood there stupidly, allowing this man to touch her.

"Good-bye, my sweet Jessica. I'm sure we'll meet again."

As he mounted his horse, Jessica just stood there, hands to her side, crushed blackberries running down her skirt, and watched.

He raised his fingertips to his lips.

It was his smile, that knowing, smug smile, that made Jessica come out of her stupor. She grabbed another handful of berries and sent them flying at his head. But he was already gone and all that was left was the sound of his laughter echoing through the trees.

"I hate him! I hate him! I hate him!" she said, stamping her foot and snatching the two baskets of berries she'd picked. "I really, truly, honestly, absolutely hate him." She started down the path toward town, but on impulse looked back at the bed of moss where she'd lain with the Raider. Without thinking about what she was doing, she plucked a little yellow flower from the edge of the moss and tucked it into the torn bodice of her dress.

"Have to fix that," she murmured as she ran her hand along the edge of her dress.

"I hate him, I really do," she repeated, as if she hadn't really believed herself the first time, then started home.

"Punishing the horse again?" Nicholas asked as he walked up behind Alexander. "That could only be caused by your lady Jessica."

Alex kept brushing the horse with vigor, making the stallion's black coat shine. Absently, he swatted at mosquitoes as they sought his sweaty, bare skin. "The last I heard, you weren't faring too well yourself. Did you wash the kitchen floor?"

Nick grunted in response as he eased his big body onto the driest spot of ground he could find on the marshy island. "That woman will find herself being used as a mop."

"I know what you mean. Jessica is going to be the death of me. One minute she's as cold as winter; she has frost on her lashes. The next minute I'm getting sunburned."

"Eleanor wanted me to clean the fireplace. I told her I put things in the fireplace but I take nothing out."

"Of course Jess did risk her life to help the Raider. He would have been caught if it hadn't been for her. And then for the Raider to treat her with so little respect! It wasn't right."

Nick rubbed his hand on his jaw. "I've always been told that I have the bearing of royalty. Many women have told me that they would know that I was the czar's cousin even if I were wearing nothing. Or perhaps especially then. So why does this Eleanor Taggert not know that I'm Russian royalty? How can she dare treat me as . . . as a scullery maid?"

Alex began to comb the coarse mane of his horse. "She's really very courageous. Did you know that everyone in town was laughing at her for getting herself thrown in the hold? George Greene was a hero, the Raider was a hero, but Jessica Taggert was a foolish girl."

"Eleanor must be blind. She has the bluest, clearest eyes ever made by God but they are useless."

"They laugh at her for her clothes, and for that old boat of hers, and for all those kids, but she's doing the best she can. Little Molly told me Jess has the trousers she wears and that single ugly old green dress." He stopped brushing. "And the Raider tore that."

"Eleanor said—" Nick broke off. "I thought *you* were the Raider. Did *you* tear her dress?"

Alex frowned. "Yes, I guess I did. I didn't mean to, it was all Abigail's fault. 'Do with me what you will'," he mocked. "And then there was Jessica, lying on the ground. She was asleep, but at first I thought she'd been hurt and the Raider—I mean me—I grabbed her and she hit me and . . ."

"Her dress was torn. I understand. Did you tear it completely off?"

"Of course not! Even the Raider, blowhard that he is, wouldn't hurt a virtuous woman."

"You should have used your sword. The women like that. I once sliced a gypsy's dress off, layer by layer, while she danced. And later—"

Alex threw down his brush and started toward Nick. "She's not like that! She's brave and generous and intelligent and—"

"But the Raider took advantage of her. Perhaps you

should challenge him to a duel." Nick's eyes were laughing, his mouth twitching.

Alex stood over Nick, his muscles straining with anger, and he began to see the absurdity of what he was saying. He turned back to his horse. "I may be the Raider but I am Alexander also."

"Ah, the dilemma, whether a woman loves the man himself or what she thinks he is. Or perhaps she is torn between a man's mind and his kisses. Which do you think she'll choose?"

Alexander didn't answer his friend because, at the moment, he wasn't sure which man he wanted her to choose.

He laughed aloud at his thought. "What do I care what Jessica Taggert does? I'm grateful she helped the Raider. Helped me, I mean. She's pretty and desirable, but so are half the other single women in the world. My father informed me last night that it was time I married and produced an heir or two. He says he doesn't want to die without grandchildren. I think he's spending too much time with young Nathaniel."

"Don't mention that boy's name to me!" Nick said. "He never leaves Eleanor's side. Yesterday I—" Nick stopped, smiling at some memory he seemed to want to keep to himself. "I would not have so much trouble if I did not have that boy around." His head came up. "Why don't you marry your Jessica?"

"As who? The Raider or Alexander who she thinks is fat and lazy? The Raider would marry her while leaping from one yardarm to the next so the soldiers couldn't catch him, and Alex would never be able to make up his mind which coat to wear. I doubt if she'd have either man."

"Ah," Nick said.

"And what does that mean?"

"Ah. Nothing more, nothing less."

Alex gave a final brushing to the horse. "Tomorrow Alexander Montgomery shall go courting. There are other women in this town besides Mistress Jessica. Sweet, docile, lovely women, women who judge a man by what's inside him. I may not look so good when I'm padded and wigged but there is a *man* underneath. Jessica will see that when she knows there are women who can see beyond a few yards of satin."

"You have more faith in women than I do."

"I have faith only in Jessica. She has more sense than most women."

"As has her sister. Except now and then—"

"Now and then Jessica can be an idiot. Why doesn't she see that I am—"

The men continued with the lament of all men.

Eleanor tried to prepare dinner on the same table where Jessica was doing her accounts.

"Would you be more careful with that?" Jess snapped when Eleanor splashed batter on a precious piece of paper. "I don't think old man Clymer will like cornmeal on his ledger."

"He won't care what's on it. All he wants is an excuse to see you. He's only pretending that his hand is injured. Yesterday I saw him using an axe."

"Whatever the reason, we can use the leather from his tannery. The children need shoes for winter."

Eleanor kept stirring the batter in the big wooden bowl. "Jess, have you seen Alexander lately?"

"Not in about a week," she replied, adding numbers in her head.

"You didn't have a quarrel, did you?"

Jess looked at her sister as if she'd lost her mind. "What are you talking about? What would we quarrel about?"

Eleanor poured the batter into a cast-iron spider by

the tiny fireplace. "I don't know. You two seemed to be such good friends for a while and now you never see him. You aren't laughing at him again, are you?"

Jess gritted her teeth. "No, I didn't laugh at him. I didn't shake my finger at him. I didn't jump around a corner and yell 'boo' at him either. You ought to know why I haven't seen him or anyone else." She glared at Eleanor over the table. After she'd been taken prisoner for helping the Raider escape and Alex had obtained her release, Jessica had been given a blistering lecture by Sayer Montgomery, with Eleanor sitting nearby and crying juicily into half a dozen of her employer's clean handkerchiefs. It had been bad enough that Jessica had been banished to the forest the day George Greene was to be whipped, but when she'd returned with her dress torn and a bruise on her throat, Eleanor had been nearly hysterical. Jess had lied about her dress, but Eleanor had seen through it and Jess had given herself away by blushing when the Raider's name was mentioned.

Now, a week after the raid, Jess was still more or less housebound. She hadn't been on her boat, she hadn't been in town. Instead, she'd been left with the full care of all seven children. As if that weren't enough to drive her out of her mind, old man Clymer had asked her to balance the accounts of his leather-tanning business in exchange for several tanned hides.

So for a week Jess had recorded sales (Clymer was two years behind in his bookwork), pulled a child away from the fire, added a column of figures, prevented one child from killing another, re-added the column, yelled at Nathaniel to stop tormenting his sister and go dig clams, re-added the column, then swatted Sam because he was pulling the cat's tail, then . . . On and on for seven whole days.

And now Eleanor was asking her if perhaps she'd

angered Alexander. "I haven't angered anyone. I have been the perfect young lady. I have dipped candles, I have washed clothes, I have washed faces and bottoms. I have—"

"And you have avoided the customs officer. You know the man suspects you, Jessica. Only Mr. Montgomery—"

"Yes, I know," Jess sighed. "I am very grateful. I really am glad of all he's done and I am very sorry I ever was such a fool as to help the Raider." She caught her sister's eye. "Any news yet?"

"There are reward handbills posted everywhere. Mr. Pitman means to have this Raider of yours."

"Not mine!" Jessica said. "Not mine at all! I merely happened to be in the wrong place at the wrong time."

Eleanor opened her mouth to speak, but a knock on the door stopped her. It took her a moment to make her way through the children who'd run to the door, but she opened it to see Alexander standing there, resplendent in pink twilled silk. His wig of powdered curls was tied loosely at the nape of his neck with a pink satin bow. In his hands was a carved wooden chest. He patted a child's head while he greeted Eleanor, then looked at his hand that had touched the child.

Eleanor handed him a damp cloth. "Good evening, Alexander. What brings you out on this fine evening?"

"I wonder if I might talk to Jessica?" he said rather shyly. "Outside. I mean, I thought we might walk down to the mill."

"Sam! Stop that. I don't know, I need to work on these ledgers," Jess said. "Is it important?"

"She'll be right there," Eleanor said, pushing Alex out the door and taking the wet cloth from him. "Jessica," she said sternly, "take my cloak and go with him."

"There's too much danger for me to leave the house, but a Montgomery arrives and suddenly I'm safe. Who'll protect me from the hummingbirds that attack that coat of his?"

"Jessica . . ." Eleanor warned. "Go! He's been courting young women all week."

Jess's eyes widened. "And you think I'm next? Oh heavens, Nathaniel, go get me a bucket of war paint, Master Alex is on the hunt."

Eleanor just stood there, glaring at her sister.

"All right, I'll go. Nate, if you hear me call, come get me."

"And the hummingbirds?" Molly said.

Eleanor pushed Jess, wearing her sailing garb, out the door without a cloak. "Be nice to him," she whispered before closing the door.

"Hello, Alexander, been working?" Jess asked, smiling at him as they began to walk. She would have been glad to see him—anything for a diversion—if she hadn't been so anxious to get Clymer's accounts done.

"I hear you've been seeing Mr. Clymer this week," Alex said, clutching a wooden chest that was propped on his protruding belly.

"More than I wanted to. He says he hurt his hand and can't do his accounts. Four times a day he finds a reason to visit me."

"Has he asked you to marry him yet?" Alex asked.

"I'd put it at every twelve minutes. The last time he did, Sam wet on his leg. Ol' fish-face Clymer didn't move a muscle, just stood there and waited for my answer."

"Which was?"

"'No thank you, Mr. Clymer, but it was very kind of you to ask.' Same as it has been for years."

"Why don't you marry him? He's rich and he could

give you and Eleanor and the kids a nice place to live, nice clothes, all the things women want."

"Not *all* women. Eleanor and I made a vow after our parents died that we'd only marry if we wanted to, and we'd wait for the right men. We won't settle for second-best."

"And Clymer is second?"

She stopped walking and looked at him. "Alex, what is this all about? And what have you got in that box? Eleanor says you've been courting this week. Has something gone wrong?"

"Could we sit down? These shoes pinch my feet," he said honestly. He sat on a flat rock just off the road. "Truthfully, Jess, I came to you for advice. My father wants me to get married." He was watching her face intently for expressions of emotion.

"And?" Jess asked. She sat on the grass near him, a weed in her teeth. "There are lots of women around here. None of them to your liking?"

"A few. Cynthia Coffin is awfully pretty."

"She sure is, and she bakes great bread. Your father would like her. So, did you ask her?" She didn't see the look of disgust on Alex's face.

"I haven't asked anyone yet. I'm just searching. The Coffins loved the idea of me for a son-in-law."

"Mr. Coffin would love to get his hands on your father's wharf space. He probably thinks you're incompetent as well as . . ." She stopped and gave him a quick look up and down. "New coat?"

His face brightened around a steely look in his eyes. "Like it?"

"Alex, why don't you—"

"And Ellen Makepeace invited me to supper," Alex said, cutting her off.

"Ellen is a sneak. I wouldn't marry her if I were you."

Alex's jaw clenched. "Cathryn Wheatbury didn't seem interested in me at all."

Jess yawned. "That's because she's in love with Ethan Ledbetter. But then so are a lot of women. Ethan's going to give you some trouble. You have the money and the Montgomery name, but then Ethan has . . ." She smiled.

"Ethan has what?"

"Looks, charm, intelligence. He's very much a gentleman. The last time he was on the *Mary Catherine* we—"

"On the *Mary Catherine!* What were you doing alone with him?" Alex demanded.

Jessica sat up and looked at him in surprise. "Now don't you go ordering me around, too. I've had more than my share from both your father and my sister. It so happens that Ethan came to buy some haddock— and he came with his mother. Ethan had to carry the fish for her."

Alex relaxed his body. "It's a wonder he could lift them."

"With those arms?" Jess said, smiling dreamily in memory. "That man could carry the hindquarters of a whale home. You know, Alex," she said, sitting up straight, "a couple of times it's crossed my mind that maybe Ethan is the Raider. They're built alike, both tall, strong, both very good-looking, and I doubt that Ethan's afraid of anything. Only last year he—"

Alex was sitting upright on the rock, his back as rigid as a sword blade. "How do you know what the Raider looks like? The last time I saw you, you were saying you hated him."

"I do, but that doesn't make me blind. Ethan has the strength to swing on a rope like the Raider did."

"So do half the sailors on the dock. Maybe any one

of them could be this Raider you seem to think so highly of."

"That I . . ." She looked at him in the fading light. "Alex, are you jealous?"

"Of the Raider?" he gasped.

"No, of Ethan. A lot of young women in town watch Ethan wherever he goes. You have to understand that when you court a woman, you may be competing with Ethan and, well, Ethan doesn't . . . I mean he's . . ." She was trying to be tactful but it was difficult. She looked pointedly at Alex's belly and hair.

For a moment Alex glared at her, then he lowered his eyes. "I want to tell you something, Jessica, something I've told no one else in Warbrooke, not even my father . . . Only my body servant, Nicholas, knows this. You see, after the ship I was on went down off the coast of Italy, I had a fever, a very high fever. I nearly died."

He looked at her through his lashes. "As a result of my illness, some of the muscles of my body were affected." He put his hand on his stomach. "You see, because of the fever, I can't lose weight. I can't control the muscles, they were too weakened."

Jess couldn't speak for a moment. Waves of guilt washed over her as she remembered all the times she'd laughed at him. "And your hair?" she asked.

"My hair? Oh yes, I lost that, too. The wigs cover my bald scalp."

"Alex," she whispered, "I'm really sorry. I had no idea. I guess your illness made you weak, too. That's why you can't ride or work or even walk very well."

"Yes," he said.

"But your clothes," she said. "Perhaps if you wore—"

"It's the only thing I have left," he said. "Take away

my silk clothes and all you have is a fat, bald, weak-muscled former sailor."

"I . . . I guess so. Alex, I'm so sorry. If only those idiot women knew."

"Women?"

"The ones you're trying to get to marry you. If they knew, surely one of them wouldn't mind being a nurse rather than a wife. Have you tried Nelba Mason?"

"Nelba Mason!" he gasped. "She makes toads look pretty. Does she have a mouth under that nose of hers?"

"Yes, a small one, but no lips. Alex, her father has two hundred acres of good farmland. All right, forget Nelba. Surely one of the girls must like your money."

"Not compared to Ethan's arms," Alex muttered.

"That's a good point. But surely, there is someone who'll have you."

"Here," Alex said abruptly. "This is for you."

Jess took the wooden chest from him, then opened it to see a blue cotton dress inside.

"It was my mother's," Alex said. "Hardly worn at all."

"But, Alex, I can't accept this."

"My sister married Pitman and gave him power in the town and Pitman's the reason the Raider appeared and the Raider tore your dress—Eleanor told me—so I owe you a dress."

"But Alex—"

He put his hand on hers. "Please take it, Jess. And I brought oranges for the children. They're there in the chest under the dress."

"Oranges?" Jess whispered and she remembered something that had happened when she was a little girl. She'd always thought Adam Montgomery was the most fascinating of men. Even when he was just a tall, long-legged boy, she used to follow him. Once, when she'd been hurrying after him across the wharf, she'd fallen and scraped her knee. She had had no idea Adam even knew her name, much less that he knew she was toddling after him. But he'd turned, picked her up, set her on a post, examined her knee, then smiled at her and said, "I'll walk slower." That night he'd sent Alex over to deliver a precious pineapple just for her.

"Jess?" Alex asked. "Are you all right?"

She looked up at him and smiled. "You might make a Montgomery after all."

"Might?" he asked, his eyes widening. "I see, as compared to one of my illustrious brothers."

"Now, Alex . . ." she began, seeing that she'd managed to make him angry again. "I'll accept the dress and the oranges. Thank you for them."

"Shall we return?" he said stiffly.

Jessica hadn't meant to hurt his feelings and, as compensation, she took his arm while they walked.

He turned to smile at her and put his hand over hers for just a moment.

"Don't worry, Alex, you'll get someone. You'll see. I'll talk to Eleanor and we'll see who we can find. I'm sure that between your father's wharf space and that big house of his we'll find a pretty young woman who doesn't mind fat, bald men. Of course we may have to search in the south, since we don't have a chance with the women who've met Adam and Kit. But we'll find someone. Don't you worry." She smiled up at him in the darkness, but he had his head turned away and he didn't say another word all the way back to the house. He handed Jess the wooden chest and politely, and rather coolly, Jess thought, took his leave.

The next day, Eleanor insisted Jessica remain at home again. The talk of the Raider was still strong and there was much speculation as to who he was.

101

Jessica's name was mentioned frequently. Eleanor didn't tell her sister that Jessica's name was always accompanied by laughter. The pretty girl had become a source of amusement.

By nightfall, Jessica was anxious to get out of the house. She kept imagining the bottom rotting off her boat or English soldiers being ordered to seize it. Eleanor said she was flattering the boat, that only the rats seemed to want the vessel.

Jessica left the house to empty a trough of dirty water and for a moment stood on the edge of the forest and breathed the cool night air.

Suddenly, an arm went around her waist and a hand covered her mouth.

"Don't move, don't make any noise."

She'd have known that accented voice anywhere. She shook her head and tried to get rid of his hand.

"I'll take my hand away if you'll not scream. You could bring the English down on both of us if you scream."

Jessica didn't like to agree to his blackmail, but his big hand was cutting off her breath. She nodded.

He removed his hand, she took a deep breath and, in one motion, he turned her around so that her back was hard against a tree, one of his legs wrapped securely around hers and one arm pinning her head and hair against the tree. His other hand was free to roam.

"What do you want?" she gasped, looking into his eyes behind the mask. "Why are you here? What have the English done now?"

"I came only to see you," the Raider said, moving his body so that it touched hers. His free hand was on her waist, his fingers and thumb caressing her ribs. "I watch you, Jessie. I see you. I think about you."

"I don't think about you," she said and tried to

move away from him, but she was pinned too securely.

He leaned forward and kissed her neck just below her ear. "You never think of me? You don't remember the time we were in the blackberry patch?"

"No," she lied, feeling herself sinking into the tree as his warm lips roamed all over her neck.

His hand encircled her neck, his thumb touching just under her chin, then his long, sensitive fingers traveled downward, his fingertips moving under the scarf that filled the low, square neck of the dress.

"Is this a dress to replace the one I tore?" he asked, his fingers lightly caressing the round, soft tops of her breasts.

"Yes." Her voice was hoarse and shallow as she felt his hand beginning to massage the back of her head.

"Where did you get it?"

"Alexander," she whispered. His lips were traveling downward.

The Raider lifted his head to look at her. "I saw you two together in the dark. What is he to you?"

"My friend."

"Put your arms around my neck, Jessica," he commanded in a low voice.

Jessica was too weak to disobey him. She lifted her arms and put them about his neck as he drew her closer to him, no longer needing to pin her to the tree. She could feel his body against hers, so warm and hard. Her breath was coming more quickly.

"You are mine, Jessica," the Raider whispered. "You are mine."

She could feel the silk of his mask as it caressed her skin just above her lips. She wanted him to kiss her, wanted his lips on hers, but he was denying her that touch.

"I belong to no man," she managed to say.

He caught her hair again, pulled her head back, and then took her mouth with his.

Jessica responded in spite of her intentions. This man had no right to touch her, no right to say that she was his, but as his lips touched hers, she didn't give another thought to right and wrong. Her arms were strong around his neck and when he pulled her to him, she responded in kind, wanting her body closer and closer to his.

"Jessie," he whispered, pulling her head into his shoulder until she couldn't breathe. "I can't bear to see you with other men."

"Who are you?" she whispered. "Tell me that. I'll keep your secret."

"No, my darling, I'll not risk your life."

She tried to push him away but he didn't budge. "You can't keep appearing in my life, ridiculing me, holding me against trees, mauling me in blackberry patches and expecting me to . . . to . . . I don't know what you expect from me. I don't know who you are, nor do I want to know. I wish you'd go away and never come back. The English are going to catch you and they'll hang you on the spot."

"Would you care?"

Her hands tightened on him, her cheek buried in the silk of his shirt, feeling his heart beat in her ear. "Why should I care?" she lied. "I don't even know who you are. Choose some other woman for your attentions."

He put his finger under her chin and lifted her face. "Do you really mean that? I came tonight only to see you. I know you're being hidden because you helped me and I wanted to thank you for it."

"You humiliated me before everyone, making all of them laugh at me."

That mouth of his, with lips of finely sculptured

flesh, slid into a smile, a slow, secret, knowing smile. "A kiss is a humiliation?" He briefly, sweetly, touched his lips to hers. "A kiss isn't a reward?" His teeth playfully caught her lower lip, the tip of his tongue running over the fullness of it. "I couldn't resist kissing you that day, in spite of the danger. If I hadn't stopped to kiss you, I wouldn't have needed your help."

"Then you were a fool. To risk hanging merely to kiss a girl . . ."

He kissed her four times. These short, quick kisses were somehow more intimate than a longer one. "It depends on the girl."

"Jessica!" they heard Eleanor call.

Involuntarily, Jess clutched at the Raider, and since she was looking toward the house, she didn't see him smile. "You must go."

He put his hands on both sides of her face. "Promise me you'll stay out of what I do. I can't bear to see you taken again. Don't risk your pretty neck for me. If I hang, I mean to hang alone."

Her hands slipped down to touch his neck. She could feel the wariness in him and she guessed that he was alert to the possibility of her trying to remove his mask, but she was only interested in touching his neck, so warm and alive. She truly hated the idea of a rope about that neck.

"Jessica," Eleanor called again, this time closer.

"Go," Jess whispered. "Go before someone sees you."

He smiled at her again, quickly kissed her and then was gone. Jessica stood there for a moment, missing his warmth. Her mind told her she should be glad he was gone, but her body wanted more of him. She straightened the scarf tucked in her dress and was refastening her hair as Eleanor appeared.

"Where have you been?" Eleanor demanded.

"Right here," Jess said dreamily. "Not far."

All evening Jessica was only half with her family. How could a man she didn't even know mean anything to her? How could she mean anything to him? But the Raider talked as if he cared about her.

She didn't, of course, care about him. Just because he was more courageous than a hundred men together, because he risked his life to help others, because he kissed her until she couldn't breathe, because he'd chosen her out of all the women in Warbrooke—no, that was no reason to give him a second thought.

"Jessica," Eleanor said sternly, "if you aren't going to eat those turnips, give them to someone who will."

"Yes," Jess mumbled. "I'm eating." But she didn't eat and Nathaniel gave her plate to Molly and Sarah. Jess didn't even notice.

Chapter Seven

"You are to come with me," the young English soldier said, staring straight at Jessica.

"She hasn't done anything," Eleanor protested, three children clinging to her skirts. "She was an innocent bystander to the raids."

"That will be determined by His Majesty's appointee, John Pitman."

"It's all right, Eleanor," Jessica said, determined to not allow her voice to shake. Pitman had only to accuse her and it would be as good as being convicted. She gave a quick look of encouragement to her family and then followed the four soldiers sent to fetch her.

Nathaniel walked beside her. "I'll protect you, Jess," Nate said, his young eyes looking very old.

She gave him a weak smile and kept her head aloft. The soldiers led her to the sprawling Montgomery house, not going through the door to the common room but through a side door she'd never entered before. It led to the office that had for years belonged to Montgomery men. She'd often seen Adam there, sitting by his father, quietly learning how to manage the extensive Montgomery holdings.

John Pitman sat behind the desk that had serviced generations of Montgomerys.

One of the soldiers pushed Jessica's shoulder, so that she sat heavily in a chair before him.

"Mistress Jessica," Pitman said after he waved the soldiers away. They were alone in the room. "I have been told that you have knowledge of this criminal who calls himself the Raider."

"I know nothing about him. Neither who he is, where he lives, nor anything else."

"Yet he kissed you."

Jessica moved uncomfortably in her chair. Too vividly she remembered the night she'd stumbled across Pitman in the woods. He'd told her that he didn't sleep with his wife, and he'd tried to kiss her. "Many men try to kiss me," she said in a low voice, looking him in the eye. "I don't invite such attention."

His eyelids lowered a fraction, showing that he remembered what she was referring to, but then his eyes strayed to the front of her dress.

Jessica suddenly realized that this man had never paid her the least bit of attention until the Raider had noticed her. "I know nothing of the Raider," she said again, this time louder.

Pitman stood and walked around the desk toward her. "I don't know whether I believe you or not. You saved him the last time he appeared."

"I merely tossed a rope to George Greene. How was I to know your English soldiers would be so clumsy?"

He looked at her for a long moment. "Yes, that is what I was given to believe."

Jessica wondered if Alex had paid his brother-in-law to get her released.

Pitman moved closer to her, put his hand on her shoulder. "I never realized until recently how pretty you are, Mistress Jessica."

"Not until the Raider pointed it out to you?"

He moved his hand away. "You have a sharp tongue on you. Perhaps too sharp. If you continue helping this brigand—"

"You'll what? Punish me because you can't catch him?"

Pitman drew his breath in sharply and Jessica wished she hadn't spoken. He opened his mouth to reply but the door burst open.

"What is the meaning of this?" Alexander demanded, slamming the door open against the wall. His heavy wig was flying out behind him. "I was told you've been arresting women."

Pitman moved behind the desk. His face wore an expression of boredom. "I did not arrest them, I merely had them brought here for questioning."

"I'll not have it," Alex said, his voice becoming higher by the second. "Do you understand me, I'll not have it. Come along, Jessica." He held out his hand for her as if she were a child.

Jessica took it, never looking back at Pitman, and followed Alex out of the room. "Who else did he talk to?"

Alex didn't answer but began pulling her down the corridors of the house.

"Alex, where are we going? Who else did he question?"

At last Alex opened a door, pulled her inside and shut it behind them. He let out a heavy sigh of relief.

"Alex," she said again. It was a large room with furniture covered with yards of muslin to protect it from the dust.

Alex sat down in a chair, a cloud of dust and powder from his wig wafting about him. He lifted a sheet behind him, opened a drawer and withdrew an embroidered fan that perfectly matched his green satin vest. "All right, Jess, tell me everything."

"There's not much to tell. He wanted to know if I knew anything about the Raider."

"And you don't, of course."

Only his kisses, Jess thought.

"Do you?" Alex persisted.

"Not anything that will help Pitman execute him, I don't. I really should go home and tell Eleanor that I'm all right."

"Eleanor knows; I sent Nate. What *do* you know about the Raider? Sit down and quit wandering about."

Jessica removed a dust cover and sat on a small, pink tapestry-covered chair. "I don't know who he is or how to contact him. I know nothing about him." Except his hands on my body, she thought and she wasn't about to tell Alex or anyone else about that.

"Have you seen him again?" Alex asked softly, his gentle eyes suddenly turning intense.

"I . . . Alex, why are you interrogating me, too?"

"I told you, I feel responsible for you. I don't want this Raider around you. I don't trust him. There's too much of the braggart about him."

"He's all right," she snapped. "At least he's trying to help. Everyone else in town sat on their backsides and did nothing while Josiah's ship was stolen out from under him."

"I thought you considered this Raider a coward, too frightened to stand on his own without hiding behind a mask."

"He'd be shot if he protested openly." She wanted to change the subject. "Isn't that a picture of your mother?"

Alex seemed to want to ask more questions, but instead he fanned himself awhile longer and then stood. "This was my mother's room. I wanted to show you something." He went to a large painted chest against one wall and opened it. Inside, carefully folded, were many dresses.

"These were my mother's and they're just lying here rotting. I thought maybe you and Eleanor would like to have them."

Instinctively, she pulled back from him. "Charity to the Taggerts? Just because I took one dress from you doesn't mean I'll accept this. I don't want your pity, Alexander Montgomery. You always did think we were nothing but dirt."

"No, Jess, I didn't mean—"

"What is going on here!"

Both of them turned to see Marianna Montgomery Pitman standing in the doorway. It was a formidable sight. The Montgomerys' tall, broad-shouldered physique looked great on the men, but it left something to be desired on a woman. Marianna stood six feet tall, wide-shouldered, deep-bosomed, slim-hipped—she had a body any man would envy. With her big body went a personality that was a cross between a typhoon and a newborn baby. No one ever knew whether Marianna was going to be domineering or try to snuggle in your lap.

"Alexander, I asked you a question."

It looked like it was Marianna's day to be stormy

111

and Alex was beginning to cower before his sister. Jess stepped forward. "I was brought here for questioning by . . . by your husband and Alexander so kindly brought me in here to show me your mother's lovely things. We were just leaving."

"Oh," Marianna said and sat down heavily as the wind seemed to leave her sails. "My husband. I did make a mess of that. I didn't know he was like this before I married him. I don't want anyone hurt because of me. I sent for Adam and Kit, but I guess they never received my letters. I'm sure they'd come if they could."

Jess patted her on the shoulder. Marianna made her feel so small and light. "They'll be here when they can. In the meantime we have the Raider."

"Yes," Marianna said. "He has been a help, but John means to kill him."

"Marianna," Jess said, "if you hear of anything the Raider should know, tell me, I may have a way to reach him. I might be able to—"

Alex, whom she'd almost forgotten, grabbed her elbow and half pushed her from the room.

"I will," Marianna called. "I'll tell you, Jess."

"Of all the foolhardy things," Alex said as soon as they were out of the house. "She's *married* to Pitman, don't you realize that? What if she let him know what you said? What if Pitman thought you could contact the Raider? *Can* you contact him? Why haven't you told me of this?"

"Alex, you're hurting my arm. For somebody whose muscles are weakened, you can certainly grip." She rubbed her bruised arm. "I think Marianna hates Pitman more than anyone and I'm not sure I can contact the Raider, but I might . . . I might see him again. Could we walk to the stream, Alex? I'm thirsty."

He caught her arm again but without so much force. "When did you see the Raider again?"

"Last night. I don't know why I'm telling you this."

"What did he want?"

"It was a purely social visit."

"Social?" Alex gasped, stopping at the stream edge. Jess cupped her hands and drank, then removed her shoes and began to bathe her feet in the cool water.

"Yes, social. Alex, aren't you warm in all that clothing? There's no one here, take off that wig. I don't mind seeing a bald head."

"But you'd rather see the Raider's black hair, wouldn't you?"

She had her skirt to her knees. "What is wrong with you today? Did you get turned down in marriage again? First you treat me with pity, then you yell at me."

"Put your skirt down. You may not think I look like one, but I am a man."

"Ah," she said, smiling, smoothing her skirt. "Too long at sea. We'd better get you married. Have you tried Sally Bledman? She lives about ten miles south of—"

"I know where Sally Bledman lives. If you're through, I'll walk you home. I don't trust you to stay out of trouble on your own."

She stood and started walking beside him, bemused by his kittenish fit. When they reached the road, she saw Ethan Ledbetter approaching, a fifty-pound sack of grain on each shoulder. Her heart started beating faster. Was this man the Raider? Was this the man who held her in his arms at night?

"Wait," she said to Alex as she smoothed her hair and tucked her scarf in neatly. It was the same scarf the Raider liked to remove, she thought, and her hand began to tremble.

113

"Good morning," she said as Ethan passed.

He slowed and smiled at her, obviously somewhat astonished at her unusual display of attention. He almost dropped one of the grain bags. "Good morning, Mistress Jessica." He walked backward for a ways, until he stumbled over a rock and nearly fell. He watched her until she was out of sight.

Alex clamped down on her elbow again. "Utterly disgraceful. You should be locked away somewhere."

"Who asked you to be my father?" she snapped.

"Father? Father!" he gasped, then pushed her arm away so hard that she nearly lost balance. "Walk yourself home and if you get into any trouble, I hope your Raider saves you."

"So do I," she called after him as she watched him waddle down the road. "So do I."

"Jessica!" Eleanor said for the fourth time. "Are you listening to me at all?"

"She's listening to the outside," Nathaniel said.

That brought Jessica out of her lethargy. She turned and gave Nathaniel a quelling look, but the boy ignored her.

"What does that mean, Jessica? For two days now you've been acting strangely, as if all of your mind weren't here."

"I'm just trying to finish these ledgers and stay out of trouble. Just what I'm supposed to be doing." She glared at Nathaniel who was giving her an adult look, as if he knew what was on her mind.

It had been two days since she'd left the cove where the Taggert house was set, and her imprisonment was voluntary. Since the day Pitman had questioned her, she had felt the Raider nearby. There were nights when she lay in bed and knew he was close. She'd even heard a low-pitched whistle outside and known it was him—but she refused to go to him.

Eleanor told her that the talk of the Raider had begun to die down. The consensus was that Pitman had frightened the man away and that the Raider had returned to wherever he had come from. Eleanor said the townspeople were beginning to believe that the Raider was a sailor and his ship had left port.

Jessica didn't make any reply, since she knew all too well that the Raider was still in Warbrooke. She wanted to deny her attraction to him and so she ignored his calls to her, ignored his presence in the forest that ran behind their house. She never stepped outside without one or more of the children with her, hoping the Raider would keep hidden from the children. How in the world Nathaniel knew about the Raider waiting outside for her, she didn't know, but she'd long ago given up trying to second-guess Nate.

"Jessica, take these slops out for me," Eleanor said. "It'll do you good to get some air."

Jessica looked out the south window of the little house and saw the dark sky and the stars. "No, thank you, have one of the children do it."

"I need to go to the privy and I'm scared of the dark," Sarah said.

"Jess, go with her." Eleanor gave her sister a threatening look. "Just what is wrong with you?"

"Nothing. I'll take you, Sarah," Jess said reluctantly. "Anyone else need to go?"

The other children were more interested in something Nate was drawing in the ashes on the hearth, so Jess took Sarah's hand and led her to the privy. The child seemed to take forever and Jess kept glancing about nervously, but there was no sign of a masked man lurking behind a tree.

By the time she was returning with Sarah, her heart had begun to lighten. Of course if she did see him again, all she had to do was tell him to go away. She didn't have to put up with his mauling of her. If he appeared again, she'd be strong and decisive and tell him to get away from her.

Her walk was almost jaunty as she reached the house. Sarah went inside, Jess following. But as Jessica had her hand on the latch, something—no, someone—grabbed it. There was no doubt who the hand belonged to.

"Jessica, close the door. You're letting the night air in," Eleanor said.

Jess gave her hand a jerk, but he held it firmly and then he began to—oh heavens—he began to kiss her palm, then the inside of her wrist.

"Jessica! What is *wrong* with you?" There was a great deal of exasperation in Eleanor's voice.

The Raider was nibbling at her fingertips. "I thought I . . . I'd take those slops now. Would you hand them to me?"

Eleanor had a lap full of mending and now she began to look at Jessica curiously.

Suddenly, Nathaniel jumped up and ran to hand Jessica the bowl of kitchen slops, but when he tried to look out the door, Jess managed to block his view.

The next moment, the Raider pulled her outside, shut the door, then clasped her in one motion. The bowl of slops went tumbling as he drew her to him in a kiss. It was as if he were starving, as if his life depended on this kiss.

In spite of her good intentions, Jessica responded in kind.

"Go away," she said breathlessly when at last they broke apart.

He put his finger to her lips to silence her, nodding

toward the house. Then he grabbed her hand and went running up the hill and into the forest. When he stopped, she was out of breath, but he immediately began kissing her neck and shoulders as he pushed her dress to one side.

"I've missed you, Jessie," he whispered. "I called for you night after night, but you didn't come to me. Why?"

She tried to push him away but she had no strength. "I don't want to see you. I wish I'd never met you. Everyone in town thinks you've left. Why don't you go somewhere else? You've helped Josiah, now go away."

"Do you want me to leave? Do you *really* want me to leave?"

"Yes, I do. My life has become miserable because of you. First you toss me in dirty water, then you kiss me, then I'm imprisoned because of you, then I'm arrested and questioned. Oh, Ethan, please leave."

He stopped kissing her. "Ethan?"

"I didn't mean to say that. No," she whispered, "don't tell me if I'm right or not. I don't want to know who you are. I don't know why you've chosen me." She looked up at him. "Or have you? How many other women are you seeing secretly, pulling them out of their houses during the night? Whistling to them while they try to sleep?"

"So you *did* hear me. As for other women, I don't have the time for courting more women. You are all a man can handle. Of course, your own loyalties are not as clear. You lust after Ethan Ledbetter, spend half your life with Alexander Montgomery and even encourage old man Clymer."

She pushed away from him. "What right do you have to talk to me about other men? Abigail Wentworth said you climbed in her bedroom window."

"Who told you that?"

"Ah ha! You admit it."

He caught her to him, but Jessica wouldn't look at him and kept her hands tightly to her side. "Jessie, she's a liar. She pops from behind trees at me. She brags with no reason to boast. A lot of the talk about me would die down if it weren't for her. She keeps my life in danger."

Jess softened toward him and when he kissed her hair and held her so closely, she slipped her arms about his waist. "Please leave Warbrooke. Pitman and his soldiers will catch you sooner or later. Your only chance is to leave now."

"I can't. There's work to be done."

"Work?" She clasped him tighter. "Not another raid? You can't go."

"Ah, Jessica, it means a lot to me that you don't want me caught. Would you care very much to see me hanged?"

"Why should I care?" she said angrily. "What are you to me? I don't know who you are. I've never had a conversation with you. You've done nothing but—"

He put his hand under her chin and made her face him. "I've done nothing but love you. No other man has been able to chisel through the shell of Mistress Jessica. Other men think you need no one, but I know better. You just need a man who is as strong as you are."

"I hate you," she murmured as she buried her face in his silk-clad shoulder.

"Yes, I can see that you do. Now, give me a kiss because I have to go."

She kissed him lingeringly.

"Stay home tomorrow or go fishing. I hope I see you tomorrow night."

"Hope? What do you mean?"

"Ssssh," he whispered, kissing her softly to silence. "Eleanor will be out here in a minute." He kissed her again, then pulled her arms away, kissed her palms and was gone.

For a moment, Jess stood there under the trees, rubbing her arms against the cold night air, then went inside. Eleanor didn't say a word to her but gave her disarranged hair and clothes a keen look. Jessica didn't offer a word of explanation.

That night, as she was tucking the children in, she leaned over Nathaniel. "What are the English doing that might interest the Raider?"

"Gunpowder," Nate answered at once, not showing the least surprise at Jessica's question. "Two wagon-loads of gunpowder are being brought from New Sussex tomorrow."

Jessica nodded and left the room. The Raider meant to take that powder from the English. And do what with it? she wondered. She knew right away that he meant to destroy it so the English couldn't use it against the Colonists. But all he had to do was make one error and he could go up with the powder.

It was a long time before she was able to go to sleep.

Chapter Eight

J ESSICA was relieved that Eleanor didn't ask a single question when, at five the next morning, she walked with her sister to the Montgomery house. Jess mumbled something about wanting to see Marianna but guessed that Eleanor was at the point where she didn't want to know exactly what her sister was doing.

Jessica waited until Eleanor had set all the children to a task, then disappeared into the corridors of the big house.

"Jessica!" she heard Sayer Montgomery call and, reluctantly, she went into his room. Sayer didn't waste any words. "Nathaniel tells me you're up to something and he thinks you're seeing the Raider at night."

Jessica made a vow to kill her little brother the next time she saw him.

"I'll admit that your temper is lovely for your

complexion, but come over here and tell me what is going on. And close that door."

Obediently, Jessica did as he bid and in just a few sentences, she told him all she knew, ignoring his comment about the Raider's nightly visits.

"So," Sayer said, "you think the Raider is going to try to relieve the English of their gunpowder." He didn't wait for Jess to answer. "Nothing will happen before tonight. I want you to go fishing today. Stay out all day and come back about sunset. I'll know something then. Go on now. Bring me fresh fish tonight."

Jessica left him alone and decided to do as he commanded, but it wasn't easy. All day she had difficulty keeping her mind on her work. She hauled nets until her arms ached and didn't even mind when they came up empty. By sunset she was more than ready to return to port.

Marianna Pitman was waiting for her.

Jessica tossed a rope to a dockhand while Marianna came aboard. "I have to talk to you."

As soon as the ship was secured, Jess followed Marianna below.

"How can you stand this place, Jessica? It really needs a good cleaning."

"I've never had a rich father to feed me," Jess said stiffly. "What do you want of me?"

"I didn't know who to turn to," Marianna said, looking up at Jess with big eyes as she sat down. Jess realized that today was Marianna's day to be little-girlish. "You're the only one the Raider seems to talk to—except Abigail of course—so I came to you."

"Go on," Jess encouraged.

"Quite by accident I found out something this afternoon. My husband has no idea that I know it. You see, the gunpowder is a trap."

"A trap?"

"Yes, like a hunting trap. Didn't you think it was odd that everyone in town knew about the arrival of the gunpowder?"

"No, I've been staying away from the town for a few days."

"Well, everyone did know and it's because my"—she swallowed—"my husband *wanted* everyone to know. He plans to put the gunpowder in a storage shed, put two guards on it, then walk away. But the *truth* is that not only is there gunpowder in the shed, but there are boxes of it hidden in the bushes around the shed. And, also, there'll be soldiers hidden. When the soldiers see the Raider, they're to light the gunpowder."

Jessica sat down. "And the Raider will be caught in the middle of a circle of explosions."

"Yes," Marianna said. "I'm afraid so."

"How much time do we have?"

"It depends on when the Raider attacks, but the gunpowder is being unloaded now."

"Now," Jess said. "Now." So any time between now and tomorrow morning, the Raider might be blown to bits. "Marianna, did your mother have a black cape? Something with a hood on it?"

"Yes."

"May I borrow it?"

"Of course. How are you going to get word to the Raider?"

"I don't think I'll be able to. All I can do is try to be there tonight and warn him."

Marianna looked at Jess with one eyebrow raised. "Don't be the fool that I was. I fell for a man's sweet words and all he wanted was my father's money."

"I'm sure the Raider secretly covets my fishing

boat. Let's go get the cloak and I'll try to work out a plan."

Jess lay on the cold, damp ground and waited. It had been hours now that she'd lain in one spot and waited and watched. By now she had an idea where each of the British soldiers were hidden in the trees, ready to set their piles of gunpowder off as soon as the signal was given.

But there was no sign of the Raider. As the night grew darker, Jess grew more alert. Something would happen soon now. Her muscles ached from remaining so still so long and her eyes hurt as she stared so intently at the shed in the middle of the secret circle.

The two guards around the shed began to laugh, then one of them walked away as if to relieve himself in the bushes. Minutes passed and the guard did not return.

Jessica tensed. Whatever was going to happen, now was the time. She had no doubt that the Raider had incapacitated the guard. The second guard went looking for the first but he didn't return either. Even listening as hard as she was, Jessica heard not a sound.

She kept her eyes on the shed. The Raider would appear there. But she saw nothing, heard nothing. Just when she was beginning to think she was wrong, she saw a movement to the right and heard the cry of a dove. It was a signal and the soldier was about to light the trail of gunpowder that led to one of the dumps surrounding the shed. She hadn't seen anything but someone somewhere had.

Without a conscious thought of what she was doing, she leaped from her hiding place and started running straight toward the shed. She had enough sense not to yell because if she ever got out of this alive, she didn't want her voice recognized.

The Raider appeared out of the shadows surrounding the shed. "Jessica," he gasped.

"It's a trap. You're surrounded by gunpowder."

He didn't waste a second but grabbed her hand and started running. All around them could be heard the hiss of gunpowder as it burned its way to the hidden crates of the explosive.

They were almost to the forest edge when he slammed her to the ground and threw his body over hers.

The sound of the explosions was deafening, blocking out all thoughts as she buried herself under the Raider's big body.

The explosions seemed to be still going on in her head when the Raider leaped off her, grabbed her hand and pulled her into the forest. She followed him with difficulty, stumbling over roots and rocks, obviously not able to see as well in the dark as he could.

He half pushed, half pulled her down a steep bank, dragging her under the roots of a tree. He held her head against his chest and she listened to his heart beating wildly. Above them came the tramping of feet and then shouting. The Raider held her to him.

Something was wet on her hands and although she couldn't move to see, she knew it was blood. "You're hurt," she whispered.

In answer, he kissed her very hard. There was thankfulness in that kiss.

The soldiers had gone by. "I have to get you home. They'll be looking for a woman. Get into your nightclothes as soon as you can. Oh God, Jess, you shouldn't have done it. Pitman will suspect you. Come on."

He gave her no time to reply but pulled her along the edge of the stream. They traveled quickly, under branches, through thorny bushes, up a hill and then down again, through the water for a while. They did not take a direct path to her house. "They'll have dogs out," he whispered once but said no more. She tried to see where he was hurt, but it was too dark.

At the Taggert house he stopped long enough to take the cloak from her. "They'll search for this. Go." She turned but he caught her arm. "Thank you, Jessica" He didn't kiss her as she wanted him to before he disappeared into the darkness.

Eleanor was waiting for her. "Jess, oh Jess, what have you done now?" she asked, looking at her sister's wild appearance.

"I'll tell you tomorrow. I've been in bed all evening. We know nothing. Help me undress."

"There's blood all over your arms. Jess, what happened?"

"It's his blood," Jess said, grabbing a cloth as Eleanor put the nightgown over her sister's head. "He was hurt protecting me."

A loud knock sounded at the door. "I was home," Jess repeated. "Wait a minute," she bellowed toward the door.

She was rubbing her head and yawning by the time she got to the door. "Who is it?" One by one, the children were coming into the room.

"Open up in the name of the king."

Jess opened the door and eight soldiers burst inside, John Pitman behind them.

"Where were you tonight?" Pitman demanded, glaring at Jessica.

"Sleeping until I was so rudely awakened," she said, her eyes red. "What's happened?"

"Search the place," Pitman commanded. "Bring anything suspicious to me. And especially look for a black cloak."

"I'm afraid my wardrobe doesn't include a black

cloak," Jess said. "Could you please tell me what this is about?"

He gave her a look of contempt. "Gunpowder was blown up tonight and it would have taken that Raider with it, but some woman helped him escape."

"And you think *I* did it? After the way the man has treated me? I'd think I'd be the last woman you'd suspect."

"These are all the clothes in the house, sir," a soldier said, tossing a pile of children's and the two women's clothing on the table.

Pitman stared at Eleanor and the children looking bewildered, then at Jessica sitting in a chair and yawning as if she were very bored by all the commotion and couldn't wait to get back to bed. He asked a soldier for his bayonet, then, smiling at Jessica, he cut the garments into shreds.

"She was here!" Nathaniel yelled. "I had a toothache and she was with me."

Jessica pulled Nate to her, holding his hands to keep the angry boy from attacking Pitman.

"Let's see if we can set an example to anyone else helping the Raider," Pitman said. "Take them outside."

Roughly, the women and children were pulled outside and they stood huddled together while the sounds of destruction came from within the house. The children buried their faces in the women's nightgowns. Only Jessica and Nate watched through the open door, their faces identical masks of anger and hatred.

The soldiers and Pitman came outside. "Torch it," Pitman ordered.

"It'll be the last move you make," came a voice behind them. Alexander Montgomery, sitting side-saddle atop a gray mule, a blue-and-white striped banyan on over his nightclothes, a wig askew on his head, was aiming a set of dueling pistols at Pitman's head. Except for the weapons, he was a ridiculous sight.

Nathaniel ran to Alex and held the mule's reins.

"This is king's business, Montgomery, not yours," Pitman said. "You touch a king's officer and you swing."

"Destroying the homes of women and children has nothing to do with the king. If you want your Raider, why aren't you out chasing him instead of taking your anger out on these helpless creatures?"

"This one"—Pitman pointed at Jessica— "knows something. A woman helped the Raider."

"And she's probably still with him, nursing his wound. I heard there was blood on the leaves. Why aren't you searching the houses to see who is missing?"

Pitman narrowed his eyes at Alexander. "This isn't finished, Montgomery. I'll see you tomorrow."

Alex kept his pistols aimed at Pitman while the man and his soldiers mounted their horses and left the cove.

When they were gone, Eleanor ran to Alex. "Oh, Alexander, you were wonderful."

"Help me off this foul animal, will you?"

"Yes, of course. Jessica, wasn't he wonderful?" Eleanor asked as she helped Alex maneuver around his stomach and fat legs and dismount. She turned to look at Jess, but Jessica was slowly ushering the children inside the house.

Alex waved Eleanor's protests away and followed Jessica into the house. The place was a shambles; nothing in the interior had been left whole.

Jessica was standing by the fireplace, holding what was left of a music box that had belonged to her mother.

"Oh, Jess," Eleanor said, putting her arm around her sister.

Sally began to cry.

Alex stepped forward. "Let's get the children and get out of here. You can stay at my house for the time being."

"No!" Jessica fairly shouted, making Sally pause in her crying. "We're Taggerts and we stay on Taggert soil. We've not taken charity before now and this won't make us start."

Alex looked at her for a long while. "All right," he said softly. "Eleanor, see if you can repair the beds enough for the night. We'll get the children down, then talk about what needs to be done."

Jessica didn't say a word but picked up Sam and began to hug him until he also began to cry.

"Here," Alex said, taking the baby from her. "Who wants to hear a story about pirates?"

The children, scared, tired, wanting anything to make their world seem safe again, agreed eagerly.

Jessica, looking numb, walked out the front door.

"Stay by her," Alex told Nathaniel. "Don't let her go far."

Nate nodded and followed his sister outside.

An hour later, Alex had all the children in bed and, he hoped, asleep. Jessica had returned, and she and Eleanor had repaired the mattresses enough that they all could sleep for the few hours left of the night.

"Jessica," Eleanor said, "we have to accept help from someone. Look at us. All the clothes we have are our nightclothes."

"We'll repair them."

"We have no cooking utensils, no table, no chairs. They destroyed the flour. We have *nothing.*"

"We'll manage," Jessica said. "We'll repair the clothes and eat off clam shells."

Alex entered the room. "Eleanor," he said softly, "why don't you go to bed? Jess, how about a walk outside?" He didn't give her a chance to refuse but took her arm and led her through the doorway. There was a hint of dawn in the sky. He stopped at the edge of the cove by the water.

"It *was* you with the Raider, wasn't it?" Alex asked.

Jessica stood still and looked at the water.

Alex turned her to face him and gave her a little shake. "How could you do such a damnably stupid thing? Do you realize that you risked not only your life but your brothers' and sisters' lives as well?"

What had happened in the last few hours was beginning to penetrate Jessica's brain. What they had lost, what they could have lost—all because of her. She lowered her head and nodded.

"From what I heard, you ran into the midst of a circle of gunpowder that was about to explode. And for what? To save the life of a man you don't even know."

Slowly at first, tears began to roll down Jessica's cheeks. She could taste the salt in her mouth but she didn't wipe them away. "I know," she whispered. "The children could have been hurt."

"Do you always plan to do this, to act first and think later? Oh God, Jessica, you could have been killed." He wanted to pull her into his arms but he didn't dare. He was torn between wanting to thank her and wanting to strangle her.

"I'm sorry," she whispered, her throat nearly closed with unshed tears. "I couldn't let him be killed.

Marianna told me it was a trap and I *had* to warn him. There was nothing else I could do. I didn't mean for the children to be hurt. I didn't mean—"

"Ssssh," he said, taking her hands in his. He didn't dare allow himself to touch her in any other way.

"He was hurt." She pushed up the sleeves of her nightgown to show him the dried blood. She'd only had time to wash it off her hands before Pitman had burst into the house. "He threw his body over mine when the powder went off and he was hurt. He may be lying in a ditch bleeding to death. Pitman's soldiers will find him and kill him."

He tightened his grip on her hands. "If Pitman searches the houses, your Raider will have time to escape. I don't think he's bleeding to death."

"How would you know?" she snapped.

"That's better." He smiled and drew a handkerchief from his pocket. His voice changed. "Now, Jess, we've got to talk business. You may be willing to eat your pride and try to clothe yourself with it, but those children deserve better. There are three trunks of clothes at my house that belonged to my mother and heaven knows Marianna couldn't fit more than her left leg in any of those dresses. It's time my father quit enshrining everything my mother touched. And there are trunks of children's clothes in the attics. They were to be used for our children, but Marianna doesn't look like she'll have any, Adam and Kit are too busy doing glorious deeds to settle down, and no woman will have me, so you may as well take those clothes, too. No! Not one word of protest. In a way, this has been caused by a Montgomery and Pitman's atrocities will be righted, as best they can be, by a Montgomery. Tomorrow we'll look into finding you some furniture and something to eat. Now, I want you to go to bed and get what sleep you can."

Jessica managed a small smile through her tears. "You really were wonderful tonight, Alex. Thank you for saving the house from being burned." She stood on tiptoe and kissed his cheek. "Thank you," she repeated and went inside the house. She tried not to look at the debris around her, but just as she was turning toward the mattress where Eleanor was sleeping, she heard one of the children crying.

She mounted the stairs to the loft. At first glance, all the children seemed to be asleep—but Nathaniel had his eyes too tightly shut. She knelt beside the bed and pulled the boy into her arms. He tried to do the manly thing and control his tears, but Jess rubbed the back of his neck and rocked him and he cried until he didn't have any more tears left. Nate acted so grown up that sometimes she forgot that he was just a little boy.

"Is he going to burn our house down?"

"I don't know," Jess answered truthfully. Pitman had been thwarted tonight, but she didn't know what would happen when Alex or someone else wasn't around to stop him.

"I'm scared, Jessie. Mr. Pitman hates us. Why?"

"I'm not sure. I think he hates the Raider and he thinks we're connected with him."

"But you *are* connected with the Raider, Jessie. You see him at night and you saved him from the gunpowder, didn't you? You're the only woman brave enough to walk into gunpowder. Maybe Mr. Pitman knows that about you."

"I'm not sure it's bravery as much as stupidity. Someone had to save him. When Marianna told me—"

Nate drew away from her. "Why didn't *she* save the Raider? She came to you because you're brave and she isn't. And Mr. Alex is brave, too."

"That he is. Now you go to sleep. It'll be morning soon and we have lots of work to do." When he started to speak, she smoothed his hair. "I don't know the answers to your questions. Maybe someday you'll be like me and act before you think. But from now on, I'll think of my family first. All right?"

"Yes, Jess. Good night."

"Good night, Nate."

Nick was awake by the time Alex returned from the Taggert house—as was everyone in the Montgomery house.

"What have you done now?" Nick growled. "A man can't get any sleep with you roaming about the country. Your father wants to see you."

"He can wait," Alex said. Now that he was home and with someone who knew his secret, he didn't have to hide his pain. "Help me undress. The blood's stuck my clothes to me."

"Ah, I'd heard the Raider was wounded. Your brother-in-law has dogs looking for you and the woman." Nick helped Alex ease out of his banyan, then his nightshirt. Under the garments was wrapped the padding and under that his tattered Raider costume. "It looks as if some of the gunpowder hit you."

"Just the debris. It removed some skin on my back."

Nick gave a low whistle as he pulled away the blood-soaked padding. Great furrows of skin were gouged from Alex's back and embedded in the gashes were pieces of black silk. "I'm going to soak this with water. It'll loosen the blood. I take it the woman was Mistress Jessica."

"Of course. Only she'd be fool enough to walk into a circle of gunpowder that was ready to explode."

"But she saved your miserable life, didn't she? I'm

going to have to use a knife to remove the cloth. My father would disown me if he saw me playing nursemaid."

"Stop bragging and get on with it."

"Where did you go after the explosion?"

"To save Jessica's hide. Pitman ran right to her, just as I thought he would."

"So now Mr. Pitman has another enemy: Alexander Montgomery. How are you going to smooth this one over?"

Alex gritted his teeth against the pain as Nick pulled shreds of silk from the raw places on his back. If he could have had treatment soon after the explosion, it wouldn't have been this painful because the blood would not have dried with bits of the fabric inside the wounds. But he didn't regret his actions. He had been right in going to Jessica before having his own wounds seen to. As it was, he had barely made it to her in time. "I don't know. I just want to sleep for a few days. Tell Pitman I am indisposed after my ordeal at the Taggerts."

"And let him suspect you may have injuries besides exhaustion?"

"Then I'll tell him I'm in love with Jessica and I couldn't bear to see her come so close to harm."

"You're in love with her? Or is the Raider?"

Alex was quiet for a moment. "She risked her life to save a man she says she hates. She's as bad as Abigail, in love with a dashing figure on a black horse."

"Sit up and I'll bandage your ribs."

Alex struggled to sit up. "Alexander rides up and holds two pistols at the head of the king's man and all he gets is a kiss on the cheek. Yet the Raider stupidly walks into a trap and he gets tears shed over his welfare. She was scared the bastard was bleeding to death in some ditch. And when *I*, Alexander, assured her he was safe, she bit my head off. Damned stupid woman! Why can't she see who is the real hero in her life? Do *all* women fall in love with a pretty face and broad shoulders?"

Nick poured a tumbler full of rum. "Tell me, if Nelba Mason had been standing on the porch that day of the first raid, would you have tried to kiss her? Would you have dumped her in washwater if she'd refused you?"

Alex downed the rum and shivered at the thought. "I'd have celebrated," he said a moment later. "It's not the same thing at all. Nelba can't remove that nose of hers and besides, she didn't risk her life to save the Raider."

"Maybe she would if the Raider courted her in the middle of the night."

Alex refused to comment. "Get out of here and let me sleep. And take those bloody rags and burn them."

"Yes, master," Nick mocked before leaving.

Chapter Nine

A<small>ND</small> now the Montgomerys seem to have adopted the Taggerts," Mrs. Wentworth said. "I think that if they wanted to exercise their Christian charity, they could have chosen a more worthy cause."

Mr. and Mrs. Wentworth were at breakfast with their only child, Abigail. There was nothing on the table, in the room or on their bodies that wasn't of the finest quality, all of it imported from England. They wanted nothing to do with any crude American products.

"Eleanor has worked for the Montgomerys for years—she practically runs that house—and of course there is the fact that if Marianna hadn't married Mr. Pitman, the Taggerts might still have their belongings," Mr. Wentworth said.

"The Raider!" Mrs. Wentworth declared. "Don't

mention that highwayman to me. It's people like him who are going to get us in trouble with England. We lose England's support and *then* where will we be? What kind of government could we have without England to guide us?"

Abigail was concentrating on a buttered roll. "What did you hear about last night's explosion?"

"Everyone thinks that Jessica Taggert was involved. Mr. Pitman had every right to search their house, although I didn't appreciate his waking us up to make sure we were all here. As if *we'd* be involved with a ruffian like that Raider," Mrs. Wentworth said, giving her daughter a fierce look. "No one in my family would ever have anything to do with such as him."

"Do you think Jessica Taggert was that brave?" Abigail asked. "Do you think the Raider is in love with her?"

"Love? Ha!" Mrs. Wentworth snapped.

"The town is saying she's a heroine," Mr. Wentworth offered. "I was out this morning and that's all anyone could talk of, how Jessica had saved his life, and how much this town owes her. Not to mention the Raider. He'd be dead now if it weren't for Mistress Jessica."

Abby stood up so quickly, her chair nearly fell. "No one knows for *sure* that it was Jessica Taggert who saved him!" she cried. "The soldiers said she looked as if she'd been asleep and there was no evidence that *she* was the one who helped the Raider. If Alexander Montgomery hadn't—"

"Now there's a young man you ought to encourage," Mr. Wentworth said. "Alex had many fine qualities as a boy and I'm sure—"

"Now he wears them on the outside," Abigail interrupted. "He's fat and ugly and lazy and he follows Jessica Taggert around like her lapdog."

"Yes, but his father owns—"

"I don't care what his father owns. I'd much rather have a *man* like the Raider than a hundred rich, fat toads like Alexander Montgomery." She ran from the room.

Upstairs in the privacy of her own room, she was boiling angry at the entire town. Why was it assumed that a bit of riffraff like Jessica Taggert would risk her life to save the Raider? After all, wasn't it she, Abigail, who he'd first kissed? He'd shown his disapproval of Jessica by throwing her in the washwater, but he'd obviously very much liked Abigail. So why did they think Jessica was the one who'd saved him? Why not Abigail?

She leaned forward and looked into her mirror. That mirror had come all the way from France. Wouldn't someone as brave and gentlemanly as the Raider choose a woman from a family who could afford French mirrors? Why would anyone believe he'd want one of the Taggerts?

She heard the front door open and close as her parents left, her father going to the big ship's chandlery he owned and her mother to the market. Not that her mother *had* to do her own shopping, but one can never trust servants.

Abigail kept looking at herself in the mirror and wondered what the town would think if they knew someone else had saved the Raider. Abby wondered if even the Raider knew who the woman had been. After all, it had been very dark and everyone said she had been covered from head to foot with a black cape and hood.

She stood up straighter, admiring her shape in the glass. If the Raider didn't see the woman and he thought Abigail had saved him, then wouldn't he be . . . grateful?

Of course she'd need some proof—just in case people didn't believe her. With a smile, she thought of the flames in the fireplace downstairs.

As the *Mary Catherine* sailed into dock, the first thing Jessica saw was Alex glistening in the sun, looking like a small, oddly shaped lighthouse. If he was waiting for her, then he must have news she had to know.

"Permission to come aboard, Captain?" he called, smiling.

Jess frowned but she hoped his smile meant there was no tragic news he had to tell her. "Aye, sailor," she called as she threw down the gangplank. "Did you bring your scented handkerchief?"

"That I did," he called back. "And a pomander," he said, holding up an orange studded with cloves.

He started up the gangplank, but halfway up, he seemed to have an attack of sorts. He put his hand to his head and began to sway as if he might fall. Jessica ran to him and put her arms about his waist to steady him.

"Are you all right, Alex?"

"Much better now, thank you. Just let me stand here and get my balance. No, don't move your arms. I need your strength." He rested his cheek against the top of her head a moment. "Ah, I think I can move now. If you'll just help me inside."

"Of course, Alex," she said, holding on to him as he leaned heavily against her. She had to help him every step of the way into her cabin. She helped him into a chair. "Could I get you some rum?"

Alex sighed as he leaned back in the chair. "No, I raided the larder. Here." Slowly, he began pulling things from his pockets: a little bottle of French cognac, half a loaf of bread, a quarter pound of cheese and a jar of mustard.

Jess laughed. "And I thought you had news." Since Alex seemed to be so weak, she sliced the bread and cheese, applied mustard liberally and handed it to him.

"I do. Abigail Wentworth has been arrested for helping the Raider escape the gunpowder."

"What?!" Jessica gasped, choking on a mouthful of bread. "But she couldn't have. Didn't Pitman search the houses and wasn't she home sleeping?"

"So were you, Jessica," Alex said calmly, sipping his cognac.

"All right, give me the details. What did that idiot girl do to get herself thrown in jail?"

"She started telling people that she was the one who saved the Raider. And as proof she showed where her hair had been singed off by the explosion."

"Didn't she realize that when Pitman heard, she'd be arrested?"

"I don't think she thought that far ahead."

"Probably not," Jess said. "She probably only thought of getting the Raider's attention. But surely she knew the Raider'd know she wasn't the one who saved him?"

Alex shrugged. "Who knows what she thought? You haven't said much about that night. Was the Raider very grateful to you?"

She ignored his question. "So, what's to be done about Abigail? We can't just let her rot in prison. What will Pitman do to her?"

"Maybe we should let the Raider save her since he's the one she wants."

"Alex, don't start being jealous again. I'm sorry Abby is in love with the Raider and I know you courted her for a while, but you wouldn't really want her. She doesn't have a brain in her head. As this episode proves. Now, what are we going to do?"

"I don't think *we* should do anything," he said sternly. "Jess, haven't you learned your lesson *yet?* You nearly destroyed your family's home by running off to help the Raider. Abby has gotten herself in trouble and it's not your responsibility or problem to get her out."

"The only way she'll be released is if I step forward and confess that I was the one who helped the Raider."

"Over my dead body," Alex said with feeling. "And maybe over your own dead body if that's what it takes."

"I will do as I see fit!" she snapped.

"No, you won't," Alex said calmly. "I'll get you out of this as I always have."

"You? What have you ever saved me from?"

Alex looked at his cognac. "So soon they forget. The hangman's noose after you threw the rope and saved the Raider when he stole Pitman's money. Then I saved your house from being burned after you saved the Raider from the gunpowder. Did it ever occur to you, Jess, that this Raider you care so much about, is a particularly incompetent fellow?"

"How can you say that after what he's done to help this town? At least he's *doing* something to stand up against Pitman. He's making a stand when no one else is."

"It's a stand that usually seems to catch fire—and you're always there with a bucket of water to douse the flames."

Jess tried to control her anger. "I resent your saying these things, Alex. The Raider, I'm sure, meant well when he went into the gunpowder, it just happened to be a trap. Do you realize that right now he could be dying somewhere? I don't know how badly he was hurt and he couldn't go to someone for medical help or they'd know who he was. The man deserves more respect than you're giving him."

"Or maybe not as much as you give him. Jess, let's not fight. Abigail is the problem here. I did have an idea of how I might be able to save her from being hanged."

She was still smarting from his words against the Raider. "All right, let's hear it."

"If we got someone, a man, to admit that he was with Abby that night, we could—"

"You mean the Raider?" she gasped. "Have the Raider come forward and say he spent the night with her? He was with *me* that night."

Alex's eyes turned angry. "Can't you get that man off your mind for even a few minutes? I meant *any* man. A sailor. A store clerk. A male pelican for all I care. Just so he can talk. If he came forward and told the court that he was with Abby that night and it was a secret because he didn't want her parents to know, she might be excused."

"But what about her hair? Stupid girl! The Raider protected me with his own body. Not a hair of mine was singed. Of course he—"

"Jess!" Alex stopped her. "Her hair was singed when they rolled too close to the campfire."

Jess smiled. "Alex, that's awful. Abby will never be able to hold her head up again in this town."

"As angry as Pitman is, the way Pitman is angry, she should be grateful to have a head still on her shoulders."

Jess took a deep drink of her cognac. "But where are you going to find a man foolish enough to get up in front of the town and take the blame for something like that? Especially when he didn't do it?" Her head came up. "What will be their punishment? Surely they'll *both* be punished."

Alex looked at the last bite of cheese. "Oh, probably nothing more than the stocks," he said. "But I do have the perfect man in mind."

"Who?"

"I think I'll surprise you. Leave it to me. I'll settle this like I've settled your other problems."

"I can take care of myself, but if by some chance you do get Abigail free, I'll do something for you. I'll help you find a wife. By this time next year, the Montgomery house will be crawling with babies." She put down her drink. "Oh, Alex, I just thought—your weakened muscles don't extend to . . . I mean . . ." Her face turned red. "*Can* there be babies? Your babies, I mean."

He gave her a long look, then turned away and sighed. "I haven't tried being with a woman since my fever, but I think I could do all right if I were propped up and she gave me a great deal of help." He turned back and gave her a weak smile.

"Oh," she said, gulping the last of the brandy. "Perhaps we'd better not tell anyone that or we'll never get you a bride. I can't imagine a woman—" She stopped before she hurt Alex's feelings again, but she thought of the Raider, smiling broadly at the idea of his needing any help.

She recovered herself. "You work on a man for Abigail and I'll do my best to find you a bride."

"It seems that I have the easier job. Here," he said, tossing her an orange, "eat this and then we'll both set to work."

Ethan Ledbetter stood in the box before the judges. All the women in the courtroom were leaning for-

142

ward, eager to hear anything this beautiful young man said.

The judge, in his full, long wig, asked Ethan to repeat himself.

"Mistress Abigail didn't want anyone to know we were lovers, so she said she was with the Raider. She barely made it back before the soldiers came searching. If she'd been a few minutes later, she'd have been caught."

"That's a lie!" Abigail shouted. "I don't even know this man. I told the truth: I made the whole thing up and I singed my hair in the fireplace. I've never—"

"Bailiff, if you don't quiet this woman, I'll have her removed. Now, Mr. Ledbetter, what about the hair?"

"We rolled too close to the campfire," he said, with some pride in his voice.

For a moment, the courtroom was too shocked to reply, but then they let out a sound half between laughter and a roar of outrage.

The bailiff restored order while the judges conferred.

"We have reached a decision," one judge said. "The defendant, Abigail Wentworth, and the witness, Ethan Ledbetter, are to be taken from here and—" The audience waited. "And married before sundown."

Abigail fainted and Ethan looked as if he were about to.

"I lied," Ethan cried. "I only wanted to help the Raider. I lied."

The judges, looking utterly disgusted with the whole case, waved their hands in dismissal.

Alex took Jessica's elbow and escorted her from the courtroom, but Jess pulled away from him and waited until the prisoners were brought out. Abigail was crying, as was her mother, but Ethan had his handsome jaw set, his head high. He looked proud in spite of the people gaping at him. When he passed Alex, he stopped, looked at Alex with hatred, then spit in his face.

Very calmly, Alex took his handkerchief and wiped away the spittle as Ethan was shoved forward.

"Shall we go, Jess?" Alex asked.

Jessica went with him but she didn't allow him to touch her. Nor did she speak to him until they were away from the crowd.

"Of all the hideous things to do to a person," she gasped, so angry she could barely speak. "You *knew* the court would force them to marry, didn't you?"

"I had an idea it might happen."

"How did you get Ethan to agree to say he'd been with Abigail?"

"I don't see why you're so angry. I merely appealed to Ethan's patriotism. I told him he'd be helping his country and, especially, his town."

"And he believed you." Her hands were fists at her sides. "Just because you have the Montgomery name, people believe they can trust you. Oh, you've done a terrible thing, Alexander Montgomery. You've betrayed your name." She turned on her heel and stormed away.

"Wait just a minute, young lady," he said, grabbing her arms and pulling her off the road a few feet into the forest. "I told you what I was planning to do and you had no objections. What's made you so angry? The fact that I chose Ethan Ledbetter to dupe? Or the fact that your handsome young man fell for it so easily?"

"He's not mine and release me!"

Alex still held her upper arms tightly. "Why are you so angry at *me?* I got Abigail free, not that she deserved it with all her lies, and Ethan, a mere blacksmith, is marrying into one of the richest families in Warbrooke. I don't see anything so bad about what I've done."

"Except that Ethan now has to spend the rest of his life with an idiot like Abigail."

He released her arms. "Just days ago you were suggesting Abigail to *me* as a bride but now she isn't good enough for your precious Ethan."

"Don't you understand?" she said softly. "Ethan might be the Raider."

"I see," he said in a cold, flat voice. "And you wanted the Raider for yourself, is that it? *You* were planning to ensnare Ethan yourself."

"No!" She put her hands over her ears. "You're confusing me. I just hated seeing anyone so unhappy, that's all. You should have told Ethan he might have to marry her."

"If he wasn't smart enough to figure out that if he got up in front of the entire town and admitted he'd slept with Abigail then he would have to marry her, then he deserved what he got. He's lucky he got off so easily. If the town wasn't in such an uproar over the Raider, he'd not have gotten off so lightly. And Abigail! It's a wonder she's not being stoned."

"You risked *both* their lives! You couldn't be sure the judge wouldn't sentence them both to death."

"The judge owes the Montgomerys too much money. I had a nice talk with him before the trial. Of course I didn't know how the townspeople would react. I was afraid Abigail might come in for some abuse."

"Too many mothers are glad to get her married so their daughters will have a chance."

Alex smiled at her. "There, that's better. Jess, do you really care about this Raider that much?"

She turned away from him. "I don't know what I

feel. I just worry that he's injured. All that blood last time made me—"

"Yes, I know, you worry if he's dead or not. Maybe he has sense enough to know he's not very good at being a Raider and he's given it up."

She gave him a hard look. "I hope Nelba Mason *does* marry you. Her character is as pleasant as her face. Now, would you mind staying away from my family and me and giving us a little peace?" With that, she turned and left him.

"Damn, damn, damn," Alex said after she left. He thought he was being so clever when he'd persuaded Ethan to say he'd slept with Abigail. "The Raider's not nearly as intelligent as you think he is," he said aloud before turning toward home. As far as he could see, the Raider had done far more damage than good.

Chapter Ten

⟊

THE arrival of the English admiral in Warbrooke nearly brought the town to a halt.

Admiral Westmoreland was a big man, and in his brilliantly colored uniform, with his stiff back, his voice that could be heard over a tempest at sea, and his entourage of lesser officers that surrounded him at all times, he was formidable. He was piped onto land and the gathering crowd parted to let the parade of men, led by the admiral, a head taller than the others, pass.

The admiral started up the hill, going straight toward the Montgomery house as if he knew exactly where it was.

John Pitman, adjusting the wig he was wearing for this formal occasion, met him a hundred yards in front of the Montgomery house. Behind him, strolling languidly, was Alexander, yawning with the boredom of it all.

"Sir," Pitman said, almost bowing before Westmoreland.

The admiral looked Pitman up and down, glanced at Alex, then strode ahead toward the house. "I assume you are Pitman. Are these your quarters?" he boomed out while one of his men opened the door for him. He walked into the common room and effectively halted everyone there. The children stopped their chores, while Eleanor stopped with her spoon above the stew pot.

The admiral didn't bother to ask any questions but waited with obvious impatience while Pitman hurried forward. "This way, sir," he said, leading the big man to the Montgomery office.

Alexander, following the circus of men, gave Eleanor a shrug as he passed her, indicating that he had no idea what was going on.

In the office, the Admiral stood, looked about until he saw Alex, then stopped. "Out," was all he said and two men moved forward to remove Alexander.

Alex managed to sidestep them. "I'm afraid you'll have to accept me since I own the building," he said, looking down at his nails as he leaned against the wall.

The admiral's voice made the rafters creak. "I don't take insolence from subordinates, and especially not from popinjays like you. Remove him."

As Alex allowed himself to be removed from the room, he cursed the fact that he couldn't do anything to defend himself without raising suspicions. So he stayed outside and continued cursing—this time directed toward the thick-walled house that his ancestors had built that didn't allow him to hear very much. Once he heard Westmoreland's voice boom that if you spare the rod you spoil the child—and he knew the child was America.

Alex's worst fears began to come true, as he realized that the admiral was there to retaliate for what the Raider had done. When he heard the name Taggert in the admiral's loud voice, Alex came alive. He went to the common room, where everyone was moving in slow motion, their ears inclined toward the hall that led to the office.

"Keep the children with you," Alex said to Eleanor. "No matter what happens, keep the children with you." He didn't pause or say anything else as he left the house and made his way, as hurriedly as his disguise would allow him, toward the wharf.

Jessica was on the deck of her ship, slinging salt-water about with a mop.

"Jess, I need to talk to you," Alex called and he tried to keep the urgency out of his voice but it was difficult.

"I have nothing to say to you," she said, moving out of his line of vision.

Alex glanced over his shoulder to see if the admiral and his men were in sight yet. "Jess, come down here! I have to talk to you."

"Hey, Montgomery, your girl won't talk to you?" someone called.

Alex started up the gangplank. "Jess," he hissed, purposefully making his voice whine, "if I fall off here because of you . . ."

With a look of disgust, she went down the gang-plank to meet him. "It would serve you right." She started to help him onto the ship, but he caught her about the waist and, with some force, led her down to the wharf. "Alex, I have work to do. We can't all spend our days being lazy like you can. I have a family to feed."

Alex could see the admiral and his men coming toward them. "I told you that I have to talk to you." He put his arm through hers and began pulling.

"What is *wrong* with you? I don't want to talk to you. I don't even want to see you. Now, let me go." She turned her head. "Who are they?"

Alex caught her by the upper arms and made her face him. "Listen to me, Jess, what I say may save your life. We are English subjects. The English think of us as their children. Legally, they have rights. Maybe someday we can change that, but for now they have every right."

"Alex, you are crazy. And I don't have time for a lecture on politics; I have work to do."

He didn't release her arms but held her so that she was looking at him.

A man behind them began to speak to the crowd that had gathered around the admiral. "By the order of His Majesty, King George III, Admiral Westmoreland has been sent to put a stop to this man who calls himself the Raider. The admiral will remain in the Colonies until this man is dead. Anyone found harboring the Raider will be executed on the spot, with no trial. It has come to the attention of the admiral that one Jessica Taggert has given aid to the enemy."

Jess stopped struggling in Alex's grasp and went dead still.

"By the decree of the admiral and the king, the ship belonging to this Taggert woman, the *Mary Catherine*, will be taken from this dock and burned at sea."

"No!" Jess managed to scream once before Alex got his hand over her mouth and silenced her. He put his big, padded arms around her and pulled her back against his belly.

"I'm going to take you to the house now, Jess," he whispered. "I don't want you to see this."

She fought him every step of the way, struggling against his hold on her, kicking at him, trying to bite his hand, doing anything to get him to release her, but he held fast. He managed to get her through the doorway to the Montgomery house. Except for the children and Eleanor, the common room was empty.

"What is it?" Eleanor whispered, seeing her struggling sister with Alex's hand over her mouth.

"The admiral was sent to kill the Raider. Pitman said Jess had something to do with the Raider, so the admiral is setting an example by burning the *Mary Catherine.*"

Eleanor was too stunned to react.

"Get me a bottle of whiskey," Alex ordered. "I'll take her to my room."

Jess renewed her struggles as Alex hauled her down the corridor. He passed his father's open door, but only glanced at Sayer, neither of them saying a word. By the time Alex reached his bedroom with Jess, Eleanor was there with the whiskey. "I don't want to see anyone," he said, grabbed the bottle, then shut the door with his foot, the latch falling into place. He released Jessica.

"You bloody coward," she screamed. "Let me out of here. I can stop him."

Alex leaned against the door so she couldn't open it. "No, you couldn't. That man has a look of hate in his eye. He plans to have your Raider—and if he can't have him now, he'll take anyone connected with him. He means to make an example of you."

"He can make an example of someone else. Get your big, fat body away from this door and let me out."

"You can say whatever you want to me, but you're

151

not leaving here. That Englishman would love to have a reason to string someone up. I've seen his type before. He'd love to hang you from the crow's nest and *then* set the ship afire. All I want is to keep you alive, whether your ship burns or not."

"It's none of your concern. It's *my* ship that man means to burn. Open this door." She began to push at him, using all her strength, digging her heels into the floor, her back against his side, but she couldn't move him.

"Jess," he said in a gentler voice. "If you go out there and try to fight that man, you'll end up dead. I'm not going to allow that."

"Allow it!" she screamed at him. "Who are you to allow or disallow anything to me?" She pushed and pushed at him until her energy began to sag—and she began to remember what the admiral's man had said. They were going to *burn* her ship.

She slid down Alex and hit the floor. "My father gave me that ship," she whispered. "It was the only thing he ever gave me except brothers and sisters to raise. None of the boys wanted it. They wanted to sail the oceans on a big ship; they wouldn't have anything to do with the smelly *Mary Catherine,* but Eleanor and I saw it as a way to feed Mother and the kids. Do you know how hard it was to get anyone to teach a *girl* how to sail?"

She sat there, leaning against Alex's leg and began to think about what it would mean to have no ship. "Kit helped me some. And Adam was always there to teach me a new knot or two, but mostly it was old Samuel Hutchins. Remember him? He died a few years ago."

Alex slid down beside her, so that she leaned against his shoulder, and handed her the whiskey bottle. "I used to laugh at you. I was so jealous that you were younger than I was but you had your own ship."

Jess took a healthy swallow of the whiskey. "You said no girl should be allowed on a ship, much less to own one, and you said the *Mary Catherine* didn't deserve the name of a ship."

"True, I said that, but I would have traded everything I owned for your ship or any other. My mother didn't want to let me go to sea. She said she'd lost two sons to the sea and she wasn't going to lose her baby."

Jess took another deep drink. "She was right. Look what happened to you. You lost your manhood and she died before she saw her best sons again."

She didn't see the look on Alex's face. "The *Mary Catherine* may have had problems, but she was good to me. Oh, God, Alex, how am I going to feed the children?"

Alex put his arm around her so that her head rested against his shoulder. "I'll help you, Jess. I'll be there to help you."

She pushed away from him. "Like you were today? Is your idea of help to run from danger?"

"I believe I have the sense to run when the odds are stacked against me," he said stiffly. "What could you have done against the admiral and his soldiers? I tell you, that man would have loved to hang someone. And he has every right."

"At least the Raider isn't afraid of his own shadow like the rest of you in this town are."

Abruptly, Alexander stood and glared down at her. "You and your Raider! It's that idiot who got the town into this mess. If he'd kept his nose out of it and hadn't gone seeking glory, your ship wouldn't have been burned and several lives including your own wouldn't be threatened now. If anything, you ought to be hating the man, not praising him."

Jess stood, hands on hips, and glared at him. "Don't you realize that something has to be done about the way the English treat us? The Raider realizes that. We don't have nearly the rights that the English have. How can that man burn my ship just because he wants to? What course of action do I have?"

She didn't bother to give him time to answer. "Let me tell you this, Alexander, *you* may be a coward, but that doesn't mean that *all* of us are."

"What is that supposed to mean?"

"I've heard of things that are happening in the south. There have been pamphlets written, speeches made. Maybe something like that can be done in Warbrooke."

Alex leaned against the door. "Jess, you're talking treason," he whispered, looking at her pretty neck.

"It's not treason if we are free of England and we're our own country. Then it's patriotism."

He held out the bottle of whiskey. "Drink this and let's talk."

"Ha! I'm to trust you? A coward like you?"

He leaned forward until he was nose to nose with her. "I'd like to remind you that *I* saved you from Pitman, that *I* saved Abigail's neck, and today I probably saved you from hanging. That doesn't sound very cowardly to me."

She rubbed her bruised arms. "I don't like your methods."

"We can't all be your romantic Raider. Besides, I thought you were convinced he was dead."

"Don't say that! Let's go to my house and—"

"Not on your life. You aren't stepping foot out of

this door today. I don't trust you not to go directly to this admiral and challenge him to a fistfight. I plan to keep you alive day by day. Now, tell me what you have in mind when you talk of patriotism."

But no matter how much he coaxed, Jessica wouldn't tell him anything.

Jessica awoke with a sick stomach, an aching head and a tongue made of hide glue. Her first thought was that she would never trust Alexander. He had no intention of talking to her about patriotism. He'd only wanted to get her drunk so that she was too befuddled to fight what had been done to her.

Slowly, keeping her head steady, she threw back the covers of Alexander's bed. It's a wonder he doesn't sleep under pink satin, she thought.

"Good morning," Alex called from the doorway.

"It's not good. Alex, I *hate* that coat," she groaned.

He grinned. "It's new. They're lovers' knots and pineapples. I rather like it. Want something to eat?"

"Where are my boots?"

"Here. Jess, I think you should rest today."

"Of course I should. Just sleep the afternoon away. How are the children?"

"Eleanor is coping fine. She and I raided the larder and there's more than enough food for them."

"Taggerts don't—"

"Accept charity, I know. You want some help?"

Jess pulled on the second boot. "I have to go fishing. I have to—" She stopped suddenly because she remembered her ship was no more. "Did they burn her?"

Alex sat beside her on the bed and took one of her hands. "Yes, Jess, they did. I met Admiral Westmoreland—he's quartered himself and ten of his men at the Wentworths'—and I think I've persuaded him that you were never really involved."

She jerked away from him. "That won't bring back my ship."

"No, but if you stay away from the Raider, it might help."

She stood, grabbed her head and stomach to steady them, then glared at him. "What do you understand? All you know is . . . is lovers' knots and pineapples. For all anyone knows the Raider is dead. He's dead, my ship is burned and I—" She stopped and turned away, but she'd break before she cried before this man who looked like a nest of fireflies.

"Jess . . ." Alex began, moving closer to her.

"Don't you touch me." She moved away from him, unlatched the door and left the room. She didn't pause in the common room either, just called, "Come with me, Nathaniel," as she passed and kept going. She refused to look at the townspeople who stopped and gawked at her. They were afraid of her now, afraid some of the trouble she was in would touch them.

She paused for a moment by the blacksmith shop. Ethan Ledbetter, bare forearms glistening with sweat, his sweaty shirt plastered to his back muscles, was hammering on a hot horseshoe—and Abigail was standing in the shadows, looking at him as a hungry child looked at a Christmas feast.

Hot tears came to Jessica's eyes. Was the reason the Raider hadn't appeared because Ethan now had Abigail?

"Jessie?" Nate said from beside her. "Mr. Alexander is coming."

"Then we are going," Jess said angrily and started walking quickly.

She worked herself without stopping for four days. At the end of the first day, Eleanor had given her a piece of her mind.

"You may try to kill yourself if you want, but you're not going to kill Nathaniel." Eleanor had carried the exhausted child upstairs.

So Jess went out alone. She threw nets into the sea and pulled them back. She nailed together an old pushcart and hawked the fish she caught about town. Many of the people were afraid to buy from her. Her name was tainted now and everyone was afraid of the admiral and his soldiers.

The admiral walked the streets of Warbrooke from early until late. His soldiers jumped at every sound. One of them shot a little girl's puppy when it ran in front of him unexpectedly. The taverns by the wharf were closed.

Warbrooke was a town under military rule.

Three times Jess tried to talk to men about freedom, about protesting what was happening, but no one would listen to her.

At the end of the fourth day, she was at the little cove north of her house. Her hands were raw and blistered; she was cold; she was hungry. She thought of the children at home and she gathered her net for one last cast.

"Jessie."

At first she thought it was only the wind saying her name.

"Jessie."

She turned on her heel and looked into the darkness where the land formed a little cliff on one side of the cove. She saw nothing at first, but then out of the darkness came a hand, a hand extended toward her, palm up.

She ran to him.

The Raider held her in his arms so tightly her ribs nearly cracked. "Jessie, Jessie, Jessie," he whispered over and over, clutching her, his face in her hair.

"You're here. You're all right," Jess gasped, tears in her eyes and in her voice. "Let me see. Let me see where you were hurt." Frantically, she began pulling his shirt from his pants, eager to see that he was indeed unharmed.

"Let me help you," the Raider chuckled as he unbuttoned his shirt.

"I can't see. It's too dark." She was so near to bursting into tears. She hadn't cried when they'd burned her boat and she hadn't cried when the people had ostracized her, but now she didn't know if she could hold back any longer.

"Then use your hands," the Raider said softly. "Here, Jessie, I'm not worth crying over." He pulled away from her long enough to turn his back to her. "The gunpowder sent some rocks flying. Feel the ridges? They're healed now."

She ran her hands over his strong back, feeling the scars. She remembered all too well that he had received those while protecting her. The flood of tears could not be held back any longer. She buried her face in the skin of his back, mashing her nose against his spine, her mouth open, tears coming in a deluge. Her hands dug into his skin at his waist.

"Jessie, my darling," he whispered, turning and pulling her to him. "You have more to cry about than anyone. Go ahead and cry."

"I thought you were dead. Or married."

"Neither," he said as he picked her up, then sat

with her in his arms, holding her close, her tears wetting his neck, his chest, his back. "I wouldn't marry a silly nit like Abigail. I want only the *best.*"

Jessica began to cry harder.

He stroked her hair, caressed her back, then his hand moved down her hip and onto her thighs. "And I certainly wouldn't be stupid enough to let someone talk me into saying I'd slept with her when I hadn't."

"She loves him," Jess gasped. "I saw her."

"You saw Abigail and Ethan, not me." He began to unbutton her shirt.

"There was blood on my hands. Everyone said you were dead. Alex said you *should* be dead." Her tears came harder.

"What does he know?" He pulled her shirttail from her pants, then unbuckled her belt. "Why do you spend so much time around him anyway? That coat he had on today isn't good for your eyes. It'll give you squints."

"It's lovers' knots," she sobbed. "Did you know they burned my ship?"

"Ah yes, my darling." He drew her to him and lifted her up as he began sliding the loose, baggy pants over her hips. "There was nothing I could do to stop them. It happened too quickly. I hear you spent the night with Montgomery."

She pulled away from him, looking into his eyes glistening behind the mask.

"*Not* the way you mean. What in the world?!" She gasped in horror as she looked down at herself clad in her chemise, her trousers down to her ankles, and her boots still on her feet.

The Raider practically dropped her upper body on the rocky shore, then in one lightening movement, went to her feet and pulled off her boots and her trousers.

Jessica, sniffing, blinking to clear her eyes, was too astonished to move.

The bare-chested Raider began moving toward her like a panther, on all fours, silkily moving his body over hers.

"Why you—" she gasped, then hit him in the jaw with her right fist. She wasted no time rolling out from under him.

But he caught her ankle and pulled her back to him, pinning her beneath him. "What do you think you're doing?"

"Me?" she gasped. "If you think I'm going to let you touch me you're crazy. You—"

He kissed her.

"If you think I'm—"

He kissed her.

"I never planned—" she said more softly before he kissed her again.

"Jessie," the Raider whispered against her lips. "You're driving me crazy. I think about you all the time. I love you, don't you know that? I've been in love with you for a long time and I'd make my declarations to you if I could. But I can't go any longer without making love to you."

"No, I—"

He kissed her again. "You have a choice. We make love tonight on the soft, cool sand or I rape you tonight on the sharp rocks."

Her eyes widened. "You wouldn't."

He grinned at her. "I'll love it either way. It's your choice."

"But . . . but that's no choice at all."

"Maybe I'll start with one and end with the other.

Although I've heard rape—especially on a virgin, if you are one—is painful. For a woman, that is. Some men, though, find that all that kicking and clawing and scratching spurs them on."

"Of course I'm a virgin," she snapped.

"I thought so," he murmured as he moved his head down to her neck and began to nibble her skin. "Make up your mind yet?"

"A woman should only sleep with the man she's to marry." Her eyes were closed as his lips began moving down her body.

"Maybe you'll marry me when I'm no longer the Raider."

"And live where?"

He chuckled as he put his face between her breasts. He untied the laces with his teeth since his hands were holding hers above her head. "You'll live wherever I am. Jessie, Jessie, how beautiful you are." His tongue was running along the roundness of her breasts. "Have you decided yet?"

"Decided?" Her voice sounded far away. "Yes, I'll live where you do."

His tongue encircled her nipple. "Is it to be rape or lovemaking?"

She couldn't concentrate. "The church says I must save myself."

"Ah, then, consider yourself forced." He released her hands. "Jessie, how much I love you."

Jessica didn't think anymore as his hands slid inside her underwear and deftly began to remove it. The night air on her skin was an added caress as he removed all her clothing. His hands seemed to be everywhere, running up and down her body, inside her thighs, on her calves. Then her feet were moving on his body, and she found her soft soles touching his bare legs. She could feel the hair on his legs and the coarseness of it felt wonderful, exciting and so different from her own body.

His hands cupped her breasts, kissed her body, his tongue moving down to her navel.

Jessica groaned as he moved on top of her.

When he first entered her, she felt the pain and began to fight him. He held her body and his still, and began to kiss her slowly and lingeringly until she relaxed under him. And when she relaxed, her legs began to open.

"Don't fight me, Jessie, love me." He nibbled her ear and when he entered her fully, there wasn't as much pain. "I . . . Jessie, I need you."

"Yes," she whispered. "I am here."

After a few swift strokes, trying not to hurt her, he collapsed on top of her, sweaty, limp, sated.

"I love you, Jessie," he whispered as she caressed his dark hair, feeling the knot of his mask.

For some reason, she did not repeat his words back to him but was silent as she clasped him to her, her legs tightly by his.

As Jessica began to come to her senses, she thought of the enormity of what they had just done. Now she was linked to this stranger for all eternity. She moved her head so that she could look at him and what she saw was a man in a mask. She didn't even know what this man who'd made love to her looked like.

"Mmmm," he said, studying her look. "Angry at me for having my way with you?"

"Who are you?" she whispered throatily.

"I can't tell you that, sweetheart. I would if I could. Did I hurt you?"

"You're hurting me now," she said and felt tears welling in her eyes.

He moved off her, then gathered her in his arms and rocked her. "You've been talking to people all week. What about?"

Her tears began to dry as anger replaced her other emotions. "Cowardice."

"Whose? Theirs or yours or mine?"

"Theirs, of course. I don't believe I'm a coward and I know you aren't."

He was caressing her bare skin. "Jessie, I want you to put your clothes on. A few more minutes of this and I'll be having you on the rocks again."

Jessica hesitated.

"No, no." He smiled. "Virgins need rest between bouts."

She moved away from him and reached for her clothes. In spite of the lack of light and his mask, she could see his eyes' brightness as he watched. Her first impulse was to cover herself but then she began to feel powerful, as if only she could bring this magnificent man low. She arched her back as she pulled on her undergarments.

"Jessie . . ." the Raider warned.

She gave him a sly smile while looking at him through her lashes.

With a low growl, he sprang for her. Oh, what a delicious sight, she thought, this muscular, tawny-skinned, masked man moving through the night toward her. She opened her arms to him. He began kissing her neck hungrily.

"I may not know your face when I see it, but there are other parts I'll recognize. You'd better keep your clothes on in town."

He laughed against her neck. "Get up, you little temptress, and get dressed. I want you to tell me what cowardice you were talking about."

She wanted him back in her arms, but no matter how she moved her body, he didn't touch her again. While he dressed—and watched her, she was sure—she thought she heard a few groans coming from him, but he seemed to have infinite control.

When they were both dressed, he pulled her into his arms again and when he held her tightly to his chest, she could feel how much sweat was on his body. She smiled contentedly and rubbed her cheek against the damp silk of his shirt.

"Now tell me what you've been doing."

She told him just about everything that had happened since she had seen him last. Her throat closed as she started talking of the loss of her ship, but the Raider gave her a little shake.

"No more feeling sorry for yourself," he commanded.

Surprisingly, his harsh words made her feel better and she was able to continue without tears.

"So," he said slowly, "you want to stir up more trouble."

She pulled away to look at him. "I want to fight. That man had no right to burn my ship. Just because England is our mother country doesn't give her the right to treat us like . . . like . . ."

"Children?" he supplied.

"We really aren't children, you know," she said quietly. "We're adults and we have the intelligence to govern ourselves."

"Jessie, you are talking treason."

"Maybe, but I've heard rumors about things that are being said and written in the south. I thought that maybe if I could get hold of a few pamphlets, I could make the people of Warbrooke realize we're not alone."

"And how are you going to get these pamphlets? How do you distribute them without getting caught? How do you protect your family while you're saving the country?"

"I don't know," she said angrily. "It's just an idea. I haven't worked out the details yet."

"Maybe I could help," he said softly.

As usual, Jess didn't think before she spoke. "No, I get in more trouble helping you than I do alone. Maybe someone will give me a ride on a ship leaving port. I can—"

It had taken a while for the Raider's temper to reach the boiling point, but now it spilled over. He grabbed her shoulders. First he cursed her in a few words of Italian, then in Spanish. He caught his breath and then spoke between teeth clamped together. "*I* will get your pamphlets. *I* will distribute them and *you* will stay home where women belong."

Her eyes flashed angrily. "If I'd stayed home until now, you'd be dead."

For a moment they glared at each other.

"Who have you been talking to?" he asked.

"No one," she said, beginning to back down. "Alexander merely pointed out a few facts to me."

"That fat sea walrus? Why is he always around you? What do you want from him?"

"Are you telling me who to see?" She started to rise. "You don't own me because of what we just did. And you have yet to prove that you can do anything without a great deal of help. Some Raider you are! The only successful raid you've ever made is under a woman's skirt."

Jess put her knuckle to her mouth. She knew she'd gone too far.

The Raider stood, his eyes hot with anger.

"Wait, I didn't mean that," she began. "It was just that you shouldn't have told me to stay home."

He didn't say another word to her but turned on his heel and disappeared into the night.

For a while, Jess stood there, straining her eyes and ears for a sight or sound of him, but she heard and saw nothing. Turning, she gathered her nets and fish and started home.

Chapter Eleven

WEARILY, Jessica threw down a load of fish and lobsters on the big table in the Montgomery common room. Eleanor snapped at Molly to watch what she was doing, then slammed a corn muffin pan into the brick oven. She hissed at the scrawny dog in the cage turning the spit, then gave Nathaniel a dirty look because he wasn't already at work cleaning the fish.

"What's going on?" Jess asked.

"Him." The word was as much seethed as spoken by Eleanor.

Jess looked in question to Nate as he retrieved a lobster from where it had fallen to the floor.

Nick, Nate mouthed, motioning his head toward the doorway.

"What has your Nicholas done now?" Jess asked, taking a corn muffin hot from a pan.

Eleanor turned on her sister with angry eyes. "He's not mine." She calmed herself. "Alexander is ill. He may be dying, for all I know, and that great, hulking, arrogant monster won't let me in to see him. He says Alex wants to see no one."

"That's probably true," Jess said, her mouth full. "He probably doesn't want anyone to see him without one of his rainbow coats." She dusted off her hands. "But he'll see me." She went down the hall and had her hand on the latch to Alex's room before Nick came from another room and saw her.

"He doesn't want to see anyone."

Jess knocked on the door. "Alex, it's me, Jessica. Eleanor is worried about you. Unlock the door and let me in." There was no answer. She looked at Nick. He was a big, thick, dark man who was now looking down his nose at her in a particularly haughty way.

"I want to see him," Jess said, her jaw set.

"He is not receiving callers."

Jessica started to say more but then smiled and shrugged. "Just make sure he eats well," she said cheerfully, then turned and went back to the common room. Eleanor looked at her askance and Jess shook her head before leaving the house.

She had no intention of allowing that man to tell her what she couldn't do. She skirted the house, through the weeds and bushes, making her way to Alex's bedroom. She stopped short as she passed Sayer's window. Very calmly, the elder Montgomery looked up from his book.

Jess swallowed hard, but as the older man merely kept looking at her, she gave him a weak, tentative smile and continued on. He was watching her intently when she passed the second window, but he didn't call to her or question what she was doing skulking about his house.

When she reached Alex's window, she was pleased to see the shutters were open. She put one foot inside before someone grabbed her belt and pulled her back out. She looked up at Nicholas Ivanovitch.

"Mistress Jessica," he said in a shaming voice. "I wouldn't have believed this of you. Now run along and don't be sneaking into a gentleman's bedchamber."

Jess's hands made fists at her sides, but she turned on her heel and left. What did she care what had happened to Alexander? All he did was give her trouble anyway. It was *his* fault she'd made the Raider so angry. If Alex hadn't planted those nasty doubts in her head about the Raider's usefulness, she'd never have questioned him.

She could feel tears gathering in her eyes, but she sniffed them back. Maybe the Raider had told her he loved her, and maybe he did hate her now, but she'd survive.

She sniffed some more and headed back to the cove. The Wentworths wanted fifty pounds of clams for dinner for the admiral and his officers. The thought of the last time she'd seen snobbish Mrs. Wentworth made Jess smile. The woman had had to take on some of the cooking for the English officers. The Wentworths were expected to feed and house the Englishmen and all their wealth was going into the men's bellies.

"That'll teach her," Jess said, smiling and swinging her clam shovel.

That night Eleanor was tearful. The children were used to Jessica's emotions and rages, but Eleanor was a different matter. Usually, she was their rock, someone who was steady and unshakable.

"Something is wrong with Alexander. I know it," Eleanor said. She was sitting at the table, seeming to have completely forgotten her role of serving food. The children looked at their empty crockery plates, then up at Eleanor and they seemed to understand the depth of her concern.

Jess motioned to Nick and the two of them brought the stew and cornbread to the table, silently dishing it out while Eleanor voiced her worry about Alex.

"The food I send in to him is barely touched and never a sound comes from the room. The door is locked; the shutters are bolted over the windows. I think something is wrong."

"What's the worry?" Jess asked. "So the man has a cold. He's so vain he probably doesn't want anyone to see him with a red nose."

Eleanor came out of her seat in fury, pointing her wooden spoon at Jessica's face. "We owe our very *lives* to that man," she yelled. "You're so busy dreaming over your glamorous Raider that you don't see how much that dear man has done for us. He saved our house from being burned. He kept you from being hanged. When Pitman destroyed everything we owned, Alex replaced it. When the *Mary Catherine* was burned—because of your Raider—Alex saved your neck by keeping you from making a fool of yourself. *Alexander* is the one who's helped us. The clothes we're wearing, the dishes, the furniture, the food—everything we owe to Alex. And you can't even be so much as courteous to him. So help me, Jessica, if you ever again say one word against him again, I'll . . . I'll . . ."

Jess was aghast. Eleanor was always bossy, but she'd never dared yell at her sister before. "Make me wear a coat like his?" Jess said meekly, trying to lighten the moment.

One moment Eleanor was standing utterly still and

the next, Jessica had a bowl of hot stew pouring down her face. The door slammed on Eleanor's way out.

Jess threw the bowl aside and plunged her head into a bucket of drinking water. When she came up for air, all the children were standing around her, their eyes wide in fear.

"Will Eleanor die and leave us, too?" Phillip whispered.

"Not unless I kill her," Jess muttered, then looked at the children's faces and sighed. "No, she's just angry. Just like I get sometimes."

"All the time," Nate said, making Jessica glare at him.

"You stay here and eat and I'll go get Eleanor."

It wasn't easy making good her promise to the children. First, Jessica had to chase her sister for a quarter of a mile through the forest, but as Eleanor wasn't used to moving about outdoors at night, Jess found her just as she became entangled in a blackberry bramble. Jess had to listen to more of Alexander Montgomery's many virtues—and when Eleanor ran out of those, she started in on how the bondservant Nicholas was above himself.

Jess just worked at freeing her sister's hair from the thorns and listened. She wasn't about to comment on Eleanor's belief that one man was a saint and the other a devil.

At home Jessica swore that she'd get in to see Alex the next day, no matter what she had to do, and that she'd be very kind to him and thank him for all his help and not make one comment about what he was wearing.

"Even if the light blinds me, I'll not say a word," Jess promised.

Eleanor woke her at four the next morning and told

her to go then, while Nicholas was asleep. Jess grumbled but she obeyed. She didn't want a repeat of Eleanor's temper. Yawning, Jess left the house and went up the hill toward the sprawling Montgomery house.

Alex climbed in the window of his dark bedroom, stretching his shoulders in weariness and rolling his head, trying to ease the kinks in his neck. He tripped over the end of the bedstead.

"Taggert!" Nick's voice came from the bed.

Alex stood still. "Is Jess here?" he whispered.

Nick sat up and rubbed his eyes. "Oh, it's you. What time is it?"

"Three in the morning." Alex sat on the edge of the bed and removed his boots. It had been wonderful to wear his own clothes in Boston. It had been nice not to be sneered at, and to have ladies look at him from over their fans. No one pointed at him or laughed at him or ridiculed him. "Why are you in my bed and why did you call out 'Taggert'?"

"Those women!" Nick growled, getting out of bed slowly. "Eleanor was sure you were dying and demanded to see you. Then she sent the other one, your Jessica, to sneak in the window. I caught her by the seat of her pants."

"If you hurt her, I'll—"

"What?" Nick challenged.

"Thank you, most likely," Alex muttered.

"Did you get your pamphlets?"

Alex stretched his back. "I've been on a horse for three days. No sleep, very little food, but I got the damned things. As soon as I've slept a day or so, I'll distribute them." He smiled. "So Jessica tried to sneak in the window. She didn't see that the room was empty, did she?"

"No, I got her out in time. Take your bed and I'll go to my own. Tomorrow the women can come in."

"Not unless I'm warned. I'll need to put on a"—he sighed—"a wig and my fat suit."

"That's your problem. Tomorrow I'm going to lie on my boat and let my servants wait on me. You can take care of yourself."

Alex was too tired to protest. He pulled off the rest of his clothes and slipped naked into bed, asleep before the covers settled.

He was awakened by small hands on his wrist and traveling up his arm.

"Alex," came Jessica's voice. "Alex, are you all right?"

Somewhere in his tired brain, Alex sensed danger—and lust. He took Jess's hand in his own and had it halfway to his lips before the danger won out. "Jess?" he said thickly.

"Yes," she whispered. "I came to see that you're all right. Eleanor is frantic about you."

Alex's mind was slowly beginning to function. Right now he was neither the fat Alex nor the masked Raider. He opened his eyes, thankfully, to a dark room. "Hand me one of those wigs," he said, moving down under the covers. The last thing he needed was for Jess to see his full head of hair. The last time he'd seen her, she'd been running her fingers through that hair.

"Alex, I told you that I can well stand the sight of a bald head."

"Please, Jessica," he whined.

His eyes were beginning to adjust to the darkness. When she thrust the smallest wig at him, he peeped at her from beneath the covers. "Turn your back."

She groaned but obeyed and, surprisingly, didn't say a word.

Usually when he wore the small wig she had handed him, he had to tie his hair down tightly to conceal it and now he had difficulty getting his thick hair under the wig. He hoped no black tendrils were straying for Jess's sharp eyes to see.

"Would you hand me a coat?" he asked petulantly. Maybe a bright satin coat would keep her from looking at him too closely.

Jess spun around on her heel to look at him. "I promised Eleanor I wouldn't say a word about your clothes, but I think the only way for me to keep my promise is if you don't wear one of those things. Now sit up so I can look at you. Eleanor is convinced you're at death's door and, by your voice, you aren't far away."

Alex stayed under the covers and, after a few silent curses directed at nosy women, he looked up at Jess. "I can't sit up. I don't have anything on." He almost lost his resolve when he saw Jess shudder at the prospect of seeing his nude body. Too quickly, he thought, she opened a chest at the foot of the bed, withdrew a clean shirt and tossed it to him as she turned her back. He sat up, the covers falling away and revealing his strong, powerful body. As he slipped the shirt on, he thought he ought to make her pay for what she had said to him when he was the Raider.

He moved down in the bed, put a pillow over his stomach, and covered his arms so only his hands could be seen. "All right," he said tiredly. "I'm decent now."

Jess lit a candle and studied his face. "You don't look so bad. What's been wrong with you?"

"Just a flare up of my old illness. Did I tell you, Jess, that one doctor said I might not live very long?"

She frowned, then put the candle down. "You don't *seem* to be ill most of the time. Except that you *look* awful, you don't act especially decrepit." Her eyes widened. "I'm sorry, I promised Eleanor I wouldn't insult you. Well, now that I've seen you're all right, I'll go. I have fish to deliver. Now, you eat something and stop making my sister yell at me. Maybe I'll see you in a couple of days." She turned to leave,

By a lightening quick motion, he caught her wrist. "Jess, couldn't you stay a moment? It's so lonely here."

She tried to shake his hand away but couldn't. "That's your fault, Alex. You post that sea bull outside and he lets no one in."

"I know," Alex said wistfully. "It's just that I don't want anyone to see me like this."

"You look a sight better like that than in those—" She broke off. "All right, I'll stay for a minute or two. What do you want to talk about?"

She started to take a chair, but Alex kept holding her wrist and pulled her to sit on the bed beside him.

"What have you been doing while I've been ill?"

"Fishing."

"Nothing else?" he asked.

"What else *can* I do? It takes three times as long to gather half my catch now that I don't have a ship."

He still didn't release her hand but held it. "No problem selling them?"

At that she smiled. "Admiral Westmoreland and his men are eating every penny of the Wentworths' profits from the chandlery. Mrs. Wentworth was frying clams yesterday."

"How's Abigail?"

Jessica's mouth twisted in disgust. "The gossip is that she and Ethan retire directly after supper."

Alex coughed to cover a laugh. "And how's your Raider?"

175

"Mad," she said before she thought, then closed her mouth.

"Mad as in angry or as in insane?"

"That's none of your business." She tried to move away from him but he held her hand firmly.

"Lovers' quarrel?" he teased.

"We're not—" she said, then broke off and looked down.

"You can tell me," he coaxed. "I take it you saw him again. Glad he wasn't making a raid. I've been too sick to save you."

She pulled away from him that time, grabbed a pillow and slammed it on his head, powder filling the air. "You ass!" she yelled. "You pompous, lazy ass! What happened is all your fault. *You* make me doubt him. He's *hope* to this town, while all you are is something to laugh at. You're nothing but a—" She broke off because, when she raised the pillow, Alex didn't move. His head lay to one side at a sharp angle.

"Alex!" she gasped and half fell across him, her face close to his. "Alex, I didn't mean to hurt you. I forgot that you're so fragile. Oh, Alex, I didn't mean it. Please don't be dead. I really am grateful for all you've done to help us." She picked up his head and pressed it to her breast while stroking his cheek. "Alex, I'm sorry," she said softly. "I won't hit you again."

Alex smiled against her breast, enjoying her for several long moments, and then his hands came up to her back as he groaned.

She started to pull away, but he held her fast.

"Jess, your strength feels so good. Hold me a minute. Let me feel your strength flowing into me."

She clutched his head closer to her, her hands gripping him. "I didn't mean to hurt you. You say such awful things that I forget you're so breakable."

"Would . . . would you be sorry if I weren't here any longer?"

She hesitated. "Why yes, I believe I would be. You've caused me a lot of problems, but you've really been a friend to me and my family. I was pretty mad but, when I look back on it, you really did save me the day they burned the *Mary Catherine*. I might have done something that could have been somewhat foolish."

Alex raised one eyebrow. "Somewhat. Yes."

"Are you feeling stronger?"

"Much," he sighed, snuggling his head against her breast.

"Alex, ah . . . I'm not sure this is what Eleanor had in mind. I need to go to work."

"Yes, of course," he said weakly, releasing her. "I understand. I'll just stay here alone until someone remembers me and brings me food."

"I'll tell Eleanor as I leave," she said, straightening her clothes.

"She won't be here this early."

"I guess not. I'll tell her at home. I have to get my nets."

"What do a few more hours of hunger make to one so close to death?" He rolled his head to one side.

Jessica sighed. "Maybe there's something left over in the kitchen. I'll see."

She brought back cold chicken and bread and cheese, watered wine, and hard-boiled eggs. She put the platter beside Alex and started to leave, but he couldn't seem to reach anything by himself. Minutes later she found herself sitting cross-legged beside him and eating as heartily as he was. She began to tell him of her ideas for distributing handbills to the people of Warbrooke.

"We can't let this oppression continue," she said adamantly.

"And your Raider refuses to help? I assume you asked him."

Jess found herself telling him about everything except their lovemaking.

"You said he was angry. Why?"

Her eyes flashed. "I listen to you too much. I told him he was incompetent."

"In those words?"

"More or less," she said, blushing at the memory of her actual words. "He's not happy with me now. I may never see him again."

Alex squeezed her hand for a moment. "If he's smart, he'll come back."

She smiled at him, then glanced at the sun coming through the shutters. "I have to go. I'll miss all the fish." She set the crumb-covered platter on Alex's desk, then paused and, on impulse, kissed his forehead. "Thanks for all you've done and thanks for listening to me. I'll tell Eleanor to let you rest."

He smiled at her in such a way that she stared at him for a moment.

"You know, Alex, you don't look half-bad like that. When we find you a bride, we'll have to let her see you in bed. Rest now," she said and left the room.

Alex leaned back on the pillows and laughed. "Jealous, Raider?" he said aloud. "You ought to be. She never talked to you like that." He tossed the wig on the floor and settled down to sleep, a smile still on his lips.

Chapter Twelve

WHEN there was no sign of the Raider immediately after Admiral Westmoreland's arrival, and the town cowed so easily at the sight of the English troops, the admiral began to relax. He enjoyed the sight of the people looking at their feet, their eyes angry but not daring to contradict him. He even began to brag. He told anyone within hearing distance that all that was needed was an iron fist.

Thus, he was unprepared for the Raider's next appearance.

The townspeople were wakened at dawn by the ringing of the big bell on the end of the Montgomery house that signaled danger. The bell had once been used to warn of Indians but now heralded fires and other disasters.

Men and woman, in various states of dress, came running from their houses. They called to each other, "What is it? What's happened?"

One by one, they began to see the handbills tacked onto their doors. With eyes that widened with every word they read, they gaped at the posters. The bills stated that Americans had rights, that English rule was going to come to an end. They said the English had no right to search without warrants or to house troops in American homes. There were words against the customs laws, saying Americans had the right to import and export goods without going through England.

"Seize them!" Admiral Westmoreland bellowed, standing on the Wentworth porch, wearing his uniform jacket over his long nightshirt. After a look of disgust at Mrs. Wentworth, he tore the handbill from her hands. "Back to the kitchen where you belong, woman."

He turned on his heel to return to the house, but then the bell at the lighthouse on the south end of the peninsula began to ring. People stopped to look.

There, standing precariously on the top of the lighthouse was a figure dressed in black.

"It's the Raider," someone whispered and the word "Raider" seemed to spread like a typhoon throughout the crowd.

As the town watched, he loosened a sheaf of handbills and let them float to the ground. Then he was gone.

"After him!" the admiral shouted to his half-clad soldiers. Two men had shaving lather on their faces.

"And seize these filthy things," the admiral shouted, crumpling a handbill and throwing it to the ground. "Anyone found with one of these will be hanged." With that he went back into the house and so didn't see Mrs. Wentworth step on the wadded handbill and slide it under a flowerpot.

That afternoon, Alex looked up from a tankard of ale in the Montgomery common room to see Jessica enter, a smile on her lips. She threw down a net of fish. She smiled even more broadly when she saw Alex.

"Did you see him?" she breathed. "I didn't. I couldn't get here in time, but everyone says he was wonderful."

"I assume you mean the Raider?" Alex looked down at his ledger. He was trying to see just what Pitman was doing with the Montgomery books. "Damned foolish if you ask me. Now the town'll have serious problems from the admiral."

"I agree," Eleanor said as she held her hand in the oven, counting off seconds to judge its temperature. "We'll all be punished for what he did."

"Yes, but did you read the handbills? I didn't see one." Her face fell. "He didn't leave one on our door."

"First sensible thing I've heard," Alex said. "Now, Jess, could you please stop interrupting me with your fairy tales of that overdressed rabble-rouser? I'm trying to add these figures."

Jess glared at the top of his powdered wig, then jerked the ledger around to face her. "Two hundred thirty-eight pounds and twenty-nine shillings," she said almost immediately. She glanced up at Alex, then took his pen from him, ran her finger down the other five columns and wrote the total at the bottom of each one. She turned the ledger to face him. *"Some* of us can do things. Not *all* of us sit on our behinds and watch."

With that she turned and left the house, ignoring Eleanor's demand that she return and apologize to Alex.

But Alex's words, unfortunately, turned out to be true. Admiral Westmoreland was enraged that the Raider would dare appear while he was in command. Three cargoes were seized immediately and put under guard. He said the shipmasters were suspected of carrying contraband, but everyone knew the three men had been in the street the morning of the Raider's appearance and the admiral had seen them reading the Raider's handbills.

Two men were jailed after English soldiers appeared in the middle of the night, searched their houses, and found the illegal documents.

But the admiral didn't dare hang the men, because even he could see how the townspeople were reacting. The Raider had done just what Jessica had wanted him to do—he'd given the people hope.

The admiral didn't want to push the rabble over the edge—as he thought a double hanging might—he just wanted to let them know who was in command. He whipped a young man for impertinence when the man was heard to mutter something about "independence."

Jessica was returning one evening from gathering fish when she saw someone in the stocks in the town square. She almost tripped over Abigail who was hiding and sniveling in the shadows.

"What are you doing?" Jess demanded. "I almost ran into you."

Abigail began to cry harder.

With a sigh, Jess put the bag of clams down. "What's wrong, Abby?" she asked, trying to make her voice sympathetic. "Have a fight with Ethan?"

Abigail blew her nose, then pointed toward the stocks.

Lately, the stocks had always been full, but now

Jess's eyes widened. "Is that . . . your mother?" She was aghast.

Abby nodded and began crying again.

Jess put her hand against a tree to steady herself. It had been amusing to see Mrs. Wentworth frying clams, but now to see that proud lady like this was not amusing. "The admiral?" she asked.

Abby nodded. "He said her attitude wasn't properly subservient to the English." Her voice rose. "He dropped cigar ash on her brocade chair and she complained." Abigail began to cry harder.

"How long has she been in there?"

"Four hours. She has to stay three more, in the dark."

"With no water, I guess."

Abby looked appalled. "Oh no, the admiral's orders—" Jessica said something that made Abby's eyes widen. "I think I agree with you," Abby whispered, "but he said no one was to speak to her."

"I won't say a word," Jessica said firmly, then went to the public well, withdrew a dipper full of water and carried it to Mrs. Wentworth. The woman was pathetic, her eyes dull, lifeless, her neatly arranged hair scraggling.

The woman looked up in surprise as Jess held the water to her lips.

"Your maid is probably stealing you blind," Jess said softly. "And I hear Mr. Wentworth is allowing the dogs in the front parlor. And Abigail and Ethan are fighting."

Mrs. Wentworth's head came up as far as it could, considering the yoke about her neck. "If she thinks she can come home after the way she embarrassed me, she'd better think again. And I'll have James's hide. And that maid—" She broke off, a smile beginning to form on her lips. "Thank you, Jessica," she whispered. "I don't deserve your kindness after all the things—"

"Sssssh," Jess said, smoothing back Mrs. Wentworth's hair. "You're my best customer. Shall I bring you a cartload of oysters tomorrow?"

"Yes, and could you get Eleanor to bake me half a dozen of those wonderful oyster loaves of hers? That is, if Sayer doesn't mind. And I'll need—" She stopped abruptly. "Oh, Jess, run!"

Behind Jessica, on horseback, appearing suddenly out of an alleyway, as if he wanted to catch evildoers, was the admiral. He held Jessica where she was with his swordtip.

"Who are you?" he roared down at her.

"Jessica Taggert, former captain of the *Mary Catherine*," she said loudly.

He pulled the sword up, making her face him. "Ah yes," he said softly, "the one the Raider wanted. I can see why now." He dropped his sword. "I gave orders that no one was to speak to this woman."

"She didn't say a word," Mrs. Wentworth declared. "She was just passing."

The admiral looked from one woman to another, not sure what to believe.

"Mistress Jessica delivers the clams you like so much, sir," Mrs. Wentworth said, a pleading tone in her voice.

Jessica just glared at the man.

He looked Jess up and down. "You're too pretty a lady to dress like that. Wear women's clothes or you'll find yourself in the stocks." He smiled. "Or perhaps I shall let my soldiers dress you. Good evening . . . ladies." He turned his horse and left them.

"Go!" Mrs. Wentworth cried. "Go, and thank you, Jessica."

Jessica ran, through the square, past Abigail who was staring at her as if she were half fool, half saint, grabbed her clams on the run and then headed toward the Montgomery house.

The common room was empty. As she was trying to catch her breath, Alex sauntered into the room.

"I saw you running," he said, concern on his face. "Is everything all right?"

"Has Eleanor gone?"

"One of the kids was sick. Marianna sent her home."

"Which one?"

"One of the smaller ones." He shrugged. "Why were you running?"

Quickly, she told him about Mrs. Wentworth and the admiral. "I have to go home. These clams are for tomorrow."

Alex grabbed her arm before she could leave. "Jess, I wish you'd stay out of the admiral's way. Did you ever think that maybe the reason the Raider didn't leave a handbill on your door was because he wanted you to stay out of this?"

She turned on him. "I am *sick* of your cowardice. Are we sheep that we are to go meekly to the slaughter? We have to *fight*."

"Let the *men* fight," he said angrily. "This is not a place for women and children."

"Poor Mrs. Wentworth is sitting out there in the stocks merely because she was protecting the covers on her furniture and you say we women aren't involved in this? Release my arm, I have to see to my family."

"You won't have any family left if you keep antagonizing the admiral," he called after her. "Damn the Raider!" he said under his breath and when Marianna walked into the room, he thought, damn her too because she'd married Pitman and started it all.

"What a look, Alexander," Marianna said. "Have I done something?"

He swallowed his anger. "You can help me find some dresses for Jessica Taggert."

Marianna opened and closed her mouth a couple of times. "I'm afraid to hear what that young woman has gotten herself into now. Come along to Mother's room and talk to me while we search for things Jessica can wear."

It was hours later that Alex was on his way to his bed and his father called to him. Immediately, Alex's spine stiffened. It seemed he could forgive everyone for believing his disguise—except his father. The way the man had greeted him when he'd returned home, so coolly, still made Alex angry when he thought of it. What was it Jessica had said? Something about Kit and Adam being the "best" sons.

"You wanted to see me, sir?" Alex asked stiffly from the doorway. At least, his voice was stiff. Whenever he saw his father, he exaggerated the languid laziness of his body that he affected.

"Did I hear Jessica's voice raised in anger?"

"You did." Alex yawned, allowing the lace at his sleeve to flutter. "She was angry because I did not agree that the Raider is our savior."

"You don't agree that he's helping the town?"

Alex bent his knees so he could see himself in the mirror across his father's bedroom. He adjusted a curl on his shoulder. "I think the man is merely stirring up trouble. If he didn't appear, perhaps the admiral would go back to England."

"You told Jessica this?"

Alex looked at his father. "Of course. Shouldn't I have?"

"Everyone has his opinion. By the way, did she find you the afternoon she was thrashing through the weeds?"

Alex didn't allow his surprise to show. "She came the next morning. Was there anything else? I am quite tired after my recent illness."

"Go," Sayer said with a grimace. "Go get your sleep."

Alex's fists were clenched at his sides as he went down the corridor to his bedroom.

Jessica was still angry at Eleanor the next morning as she gathered her nets and started toward town. She'd left her clam shovel at the Montgomery house and, besides, Eleanor had insisted she go to Marianna and thank her for the four dresses she'd sent last night.

"That woman is getting altogether above herself," Jess muttered, referring to her older sister. Eleanor had wasted precious early morning moments fussing with Jessica's hair, tying her corset and worrying over how her sister looked.

"How am I to fish wearing these skirts?" Jess had wailed.

"You can't fish if you're in jail," Eleanor had said. "And that's where you'll be if you don't obey the admiral."

So now she was dressed up like a dressmaker's doll and on her way to the Montgomery house.

She was so angry that she didn't see what was happening around her. One man, on horseback, was so taken aback by the sight of her that he ran his horse into a carriage. The carriage horses shied, but the driver couldn't control them because his attention was focused on the beautiful Jessica Taggert. His horses leaped, and the driver fell forward and landed in a horse trough. The carriage horses panicked and began running with old Mrs. Duncan inside screaming—but no one paid her any attention. Two men, gaping at Jessica, walked into a woman carrying six dozen eggs. The eggs fell, some broke, some started rolling. A man carrying a cage of geese and watching Jess, slipped on three of the eggs. The geese ran out of the cage and under the blacksmith's legs. The blacksmith dropped a hot horseshoe—he was watching Jess and not paying attention to what he was doing—the horseshoe grazed the leg of a horse and the horse kicked out the side of the building, which felled a post that was supporting an anvil, which hit another post. The building collapsed just as the black-smith and the horse escaped.

Unfortunately, the admiral, standing next to Alex-ander at the top of the hill, saw it all.

Alex's eyes were full of tears from suppressed laughter by the time Jessica reached them.

"I came to thank you for the dresses," Jessica said belligerently, not looking at the admiral.

The admiral looked down the hill at the chaos: men and women yelling, animals screaming, everyone run-ning about, then looked down at Jessica. His face turned red.

He raised his finger to point at her. "Married!" he roared. "Married in a fortnight and heaven help the man." He stormed past her, went down the hill and began to shout orders to try to organize the chaos.

Jessica turned to look after him. "What in the world?" she gasped. "What happened down there?"

Alexander's laughter exploded as he pulled her inside the house.

"What jellyfish got you?" she asked, thinking Alex had lost his mind.

Alex was going to tell her except that Amos Coffin

turned around, took one look at Jess and hit his mug against the stone fireplace. It shattered, but Amos just stood there gaping and holding the handle.

"You see a sea monster?" Jessica snapped at Amos. Alex began to laugh again. "Men!" she sneered, got her clam shovel and started out the door.

"Don't go through town again," Alex called, choking on his laughter. "Warbrooke can't afford your walking through town again."

She gave him a look of disgust, then slammed the door behind her. Of course she wasn't going through town again. She always took the forest path; he knew that.

Chapter Thirteen

JESSICA had difficulty figuring out how to fish while wearing a dress. Since she was alone in the private little cove that she was beginning to consider hers—hers and the Raider's, she thought with a smile—she removed the scarf from the deep, square neck of the dress and used it to tie the hem of the skirt to her waist. The removal of her scarf left her breasts rather fully exposed, but she was too busy to consider that. She took off her hose and shoes and, bare-legged to the knee, she cast her nets.

It was nearly sundown when Eleanor appeared, clumsily making her way down the cliff side into the cove.

Immediately, Jessica was alert. "Someone's hurt," she said, nearly dropping her net.

"No," Eleanor answered. "I hoped you might be here. Alex is watching the children so I could come talk to you." She looked her sister up and down, eyeing the way both the top and bottom halves of her were exposed. "I certainly hope none of the men followed me."

"What men?" Jess asked, pulling in a net full of fish, lobsters hanging onto the edges.

"I told Alexander you'd have no idea what was going on. Jessica, didn't you hear the admiral? He said you had to marry someone within the next two weeks."

"Oh, that. Did you make the oyster loaves for Mrs. Wentworth?"

"Jessica!" Eleanor shouted. "*Listen* to me. You have to pick a husband."

"Eleanor, I am not going to let that man bully me. I have no intention of marrying anyone—at least not now."

Eleanor moved to stand in front of her sister. "A lot of people heard the admiral this morning and he has to stand behind what he said or look like a fool. Oh, Jessica, how do you get yourself in these muddles?"

"I don't know anything about this. Let Alex talk to the man. They seem to be friends," she said nastily.

Eleanor sat down on a fallen tree. "What can I do to make you listen? The admiral has his reputation at stake. Twenty people within my hearing have told him you'll *never* marry and every time anyone says that, the admiral gets angrier. Now he's saying you'll marry an American in two weeks or on the fifteenth day, you'll marry an Englishman."

Jessica was beginning to actually hear Eleanor's words. "All this has happened in one short day?"

Eleanor raised one eyebrow at her sister. Jessica

had no idea of the havoc she'd caused this morning. "Jess, there have been fourteen eligible and two ineligible men come to the Montgomery house today, most of them bearing gifts for you."

Jess began to smile. "What sort of gifts? We could use a pig. Anybody brings a pregnant sow, I'm his."

"Jess, this is *serious.*"

Jessica sat down by her sister. "The admiral was sent here to find the Raider and that's all. He doesn't have the power to force a marriage."

Eleanor took her sister's hand. "He burned your boat; he can burn our house. I think he spoke without thinking this morning, but now he has to stand behind what he said. And, besides, I don't think the men of this town will allow him to back down. Too many of them want a chance to be your husband."

"Really?" Jess said, smiling. "Anyone interesting? What about Mr. Lawrence's youngest boy?"

"He's seventeen years old!"

"Get them young and they're easier to train. All right," she said when Eleanor started to yell again. "We'll straighten this out. I still think Alexander is the one to fix this."

"He certainly does rescue you often enough."

"He's just a nosy old maid, that's all. He can't do anything else, so at least he can talk. Here, help me with these fish and let's go home. We'll worry about this tomorrow."

"When there are only thirteen days left," Eleanor said heavily.

Jess, bending over the nets, looked at her sister. "I guess I could marry that big Russian of Alex's."

"Over my dead body," Eleanor snapped then put her hand to her mouth. "I mean . . . Of course . . ."

Jessica started whistling as she emptied her nets.

It was later, as they neared the path to their leaky little house, that Jessica began to understand what Eleanor was talking about. Men lined the path home, some holding wilted flowers, some molded maple sugar candy, some just standing there, their caps in their hands.

"I own six acres of good farmland, Mistress Jessica, and I'd be pleased to have you for a wife."

"I own the *Molly D* and you could sail with me. I'll hang you a clothesline wherever you want."

"I own the depot twenty miles north of New Sussex and I'll buy you a mule for plowing."

"I own six mules, three oxen and eight cooking pots. I'd like to marry you, Mistress Jessica."

Her mouth open, Jessica stared at the men as Eleanor pulled her through the gauntlet. She jerked hard on Jessica's arm when she nearly stopped in front of a man holding a fat pig by a string.

"You're no help at all," Eleanor hissed as she slammed the door behind them.

"I had no idea I was so popular," Jess said, smiling. "Maybe I should just stand on the wharf and let them bid for me. Although that man with the pig was very good-looking."

Eleanor slammed a bag of corn meal on the table. "I ought to sell you, just outright *sell* you. Then maybe the kids and I could have some peace."

"No food, but peace," Jess said complaisantly. "Eleanor, don't be so upset. This will blow over. I have no intention of marrying anyone right now. You'll see, Alex will use his silver tongue to reason with the admiral and the old man will forget all about me. You'll see." She leaned back in the chair and thought that she had no intention of marrying any man except the Raider. All she had to do was wait

193

until he could reveal himself to her and then she'd proudly walk down the aisle to him.

Jessica was trying to concentrate on her fishing but she kept looking over her shoulder. The last week and a half of her life could only be described as hell. There seemed to be men everywhere: men reaching for her, men with bowed heads, men offering her their worldly goods. They came from as far south as Boston and there was one French fur trader who had come in from the northern woods. He'd heard there was a shipload of beautiful women for sale. He seemed rather disappointed to find only one woman. He thought Jessica was "real pretty," but there just wasn't enough of her.

Jess had had an awful time escaping the men to make her way to her private little cove.

It had taken most of the first week, but Eleanor and Alex had just about persuaded her that the admiral meant what he said when he'd commanded Jessica to get married. He'd made some threats against her home, her family and her way of earning a living if she didn't obey him—and keep him from looking like a fool. He'd even introduced her to the man he said he'd force her to marry if she disobeyed him: a big dullard with a heavy lower lip that was constantly wet. The admiral had laughed at Jess's involuntary shudder.

But now, doing something familiar like hauling nets made Jess think of how her life would change if she married. So far, no man in his proposal had even mentioned her young brothers and sisters. And some of them had taken an active dislike to Nathaniel.

Jess smiled. Of course Nate didn't help any. He loved making the men look like fools. He asked one old man how old he was, then laughed uproariously at the answer. He insisted one scrawny chicken farmer show his bicep, then told Jess the man wasn't strong enough for her. He swatted a man's head, saying he saw lice in the ancient wig the man wore. Nate weeded out the worst of them.

But even the best of them didn't interest Jessica. There was only one man who interested her and he was the Raider. She had only to close her eyes and she could feel his hands on her body. Why didn't he come forward? Why didn't he ask to marry her? Why wasn't he rescuing her from these lecherous men?

At the sound of a falling rock, she opened her eyes and turned sharply to see old man Clymer inches away from her, his grubby little hands outstretched and reaching for her. She took a step backward and almost tripped over her net.

His eyes were on her nearly bare bosom, then his gaze moved down to her bare legs. Up and down, his eyes couldn't rest.

Jess put her hands up to cover herself. "Mr. Clymer, you shouldn't be here." She was backing away from him.

"Why not?" he rasped, advancing on her. "You are here. Jessica, I have loved you for years. Marry me. I'll give you *anything.*"

She was looking about for a weapon but saw only fish at her feet. She bent, grabbed a twenty-pound haddock by the tail and hit Mr. Clymer on the side of the head.

He was stunned only momentarily before he grabbed her, pulled her to him and tried to kiss her mouth.

Jess pushed at his face while turning away. He was amazingly strong for a man his age.

"Jessica," he murmured and buried his face in her breasts.

"Let go of me, you old piece of fish bait!" she yelled, but he ignored her.

"I mean to make you my wife! To have you always! Mine, Jessica, mine for all eternity."

Twisting about, she saw Alexander standing on the cliff above the cove. "Help me!" she screamed. "Get this squid off of me. Mr. Clymer," she begged, "remember yourself."

Alexander took an infuriatingly long time getting down into the cove. Jess struggled while the fat old man slathered her breasts with his wet kisses. She thought she might be sick.

Alex minced his way across the rocks, making sure his shoes didn't get wet. Delicately, he kicked a fish aside as he made his way to Jess. He tapped Mr. Clymer on the shoulder.

At first the man didn't respond. Alex had to tap him three times before he looked up. His red, glazed eyes bugged when he saw Alex. He straightened and pulled away from Jessica.

"Might I suggest that you'll find your own home more comfortable?"

"Why yes . . . I was just . . . Yes, I'll . . ." Mr. Clymer released Jessica, then scrambled up the cliff bank. They could hear him running through the forest.

"Well!" Jess said, straightening her dress and then looking around for her fish that had flopped all over the cove. "Some rescuer you are!"

"I got rid of him, didn't I?"

"Not until after he'd . . . You should have hit him." She broke off to look down at herself with a sneer. "He slobbered all over me." She went to the water and began to wash her exposed bosom. She was unaware of the increasing heat in Alex's face as he watched her.

Alex turned away and sat on the fallen tree. "Have you made up your mind yet?"

"About what?" she asked, tossing a couple of codfish in a bag. "Oh, you mean about marriage. Yes and no."

He dusted an imaginary bit off his coat. "Let me guess. You want to marry the Raider, but he hasn't come forward to ask for your hand."

Jess dropped a fish, then retrieved it. "What do you know?"

"Every unmarried woman in town wants to marry the Raider. They all seem to think he's taller than life. It's like marrying a handsome prince from a child's fairy tale."

"He's flesh and blood, I know that for a fact," she said smugly.

"A flesh-and-blood who isn't here. How do you know he isn't one of your many suitors?"

"I'd know him, believe me. Alex, put your foot on that fish's tail and hold it there."

With a sigh, he put his toe on the big fish's tail. "Jess, you have four days in which to decide. You have to make up your mind."

She tossed the last fish in the bag and then sat down on the tree by Alex. "Can I be honest with you?"

"Of course," he said softly, his eyes intent.

"I don't like *any* of them." She looked down at her hands. "I don't want to let Eleanor know, but I'm getting a little worried. I know you've guessed how I feel about the Raider. He and I are . . . we've been closer than most people think." Her head came up. "I don't want to marry any other man. I want to wait until this is all over, then the Raider can reveal himself to me and I'll be more than happy to marry him."

"But, Jess, our problems with England won't be solved overnight. What if they go on for years? What if England sends more men to pursue the Raider? What if he can *never* reveal himself to you?"

"I'll wait. He'll come to me someday, unmasked, and I'll be waiting for him."

"But you don't have until 'someday.' You have four days and you have to marry someone."

"I'll wait."

He rolled his eyes upward in frustration. "What do you plan to do? Wait until midnight four days from now? If he hasn't arrived by then, will you close your eyes and choose one of your other suitors?"

"I don't want any of them!" she said with force. "All they want from me is . . . is what Mr. Clymer wants. I can't go off and leave the children. Who will support Eleanor and the babies? All those men want me alone, not the kids. They want their own children, not someone else's."

"I'll take the kids," Alex said softly. "I have room for them at my house."

She paused, smiled at him and squeezed his hand. "That's kind of you, but I couldn't do that. What if the Raider is the captain of a ship? I'd be sailing with him and you'd have the care of all those children. I couldn't even help support them."

He held her hand in his tightly. "I want you to come with the children."

She gave him a blank look. "The Raider and me *and* the kids to live with you? That's real generous of you, Alex, but—" She stopped, her eyes wide. "You couldn't mean . . ."

"You could marry me, Jess," he said solemnly. "I'll take care of you and Eleanor and the children."

Jess began to smile, then her laughter bubbled out.

"You!" she gasped. "Oh, Alex, what a joke. I want the Raider, and I get offered a weak-spined, blue-and-orange piece of seaweed. You've certainly lightened my day. And old Mr. Clymer thought—" She stopped when she saw Alex's face. *Never* had she seen such anger on a human face before.

He rose from the log.

"Alex," she said, "you were kidding, weren't you?"

He turned his back on her and made his way up the steep hill.

"Alex," she called after him, but he didn't look back. She kicked at the rocks and shells on the beach, sending many snails flying. She hadn't meant to hurt Alex's feelings—again, she thought. Eleanor was right, he'd been good to her and her family and they owed him a great deal. She should have turned him down gently, or at least without calling him a . . . She didn't like to remember what she'd called him. She put her scarf back in the top of her dress, gathered her nets and catch and started home.

Jessica had no sooner made her way through the tidal wave of suitors—accepting gifts of food along the way, for she was nobody's fool—than Eleanor started in on her.

"Mr. Clymer came by here and he was very angry."

"I think this is ham," Jess said, inspecting her bundles. "And here's candy for all of you."

"I hope they always want to marry you, Jessica," Molly said, putting the maple sugar man in her mouth.

"But you don't *have* always," Eleanor said. "Oh, Jess, you have to make up your mind."

"I know which man I want."

Eleanor ignored that remark. They'd already had a long discussion about the Raider, with Eleanor saying

Jess had to be practical rather than romantic. "There's that man who owns the *Molly D,*" Eleanor said.

"How many of the kids will he take with him when he sails?" Jess asked as she sat down and began sucking on a piece of candy. "And, besides, he has a wart on his chin."

Eleanor named several men, but Jessica found fault with each of them.

Eleanor sat down at the table, her head in her hands. "That's all of them. You've refused every man I know."

"Even Alex," Jess said, remembering his anger.

"Alex?" Eleanor's head came up. "Alex asked you to marry him?"

"I think so. He offered to take on all the kids but he wanted me to go with them."

"What did you say to him, Jessica?" Eleanor asked, her voice very, very calm.

Jess grimaced. "I didn't know he was serious. I'm afraid I laughed at him. Tomorrow I'll apologize. I'll turn him down in a much nicer way and I'll—"

Eleanor leaped up from the table and leaned over Jess. "You what?!" she yelled. "You turned down Alexander Montgomery? You *laughed* at his proposal of marriage?"

"I told you I thought he was kidding. I had no idea he was serious until I saw his face."

Eleanor grabbed Jess's arm and pulled her up from the table. "Watch the kids, Nate," she called. Jess protested as Eleanor dragged her through the men camped outside their house, through the town and then up the hill to the Montgomery house.

Alex was in his bedroom, a book open in front of him. He didn't rise when Eleanor burst into the room, nor did he look at Jessica.

"I've just heard what a fool my sister has made of herself," Eleanor said, breathless. "She was just so overwhelmed at the generosity of your offer that she was giddy."

Alex glanced down at his book. "Eleanor, I have no idea what you mean. I merely happened to rescue Mistress Jessica from one of her suitors. I remember we talked of marriage in general, but nothing specific."

"Let's get out of here," Jess said, turning away, but Eleanor was leaning against the door.

"Alexander, I know she was rude but then she often is. Still, she'll make a fine wife. She's strong and sometimes she's intelligent, a little proud, I admit, and sometimes she opens her mouth when it should be kept closed, but she's a hard worker and she'll help put food on the table and—"

"I am not a mule! Eleanor, I'm going."

Alex leaned back in his chair as Eleanor threw her body across the door. Jess was pulling on the latch.

"I've seen her start work before sunup and not stop till she dropped and—"

Alex put his book aside, his index fingers together and contemplated Jessica. "I could buy a team of oxen for what you're talking about, and an ox doesn't talk back. What else do I get out of this besides a fieldworker?"

Jess glared from one to the other and tried harder to push Eleanor out of the way.

"She comes with six free little workers. Think what you could do with all those eager little bodies to help you. You could expand and—"

"I could go bankrupt trying to feed them. Any other enticements? How about a dowry?"

"Dowry?" Jess gasped. "If you think—"

Eleanor poked her in the ribs. "On your marriage

will come one-half interest in a beautiful little cove that's alive with oysters and sundry other sea creatures."

"Hmmm." Alex slowly got up, walked toward Jess, then looked her up and down.

Aghast, Jess let go of the door and scowled at him.

He took her chin and lifted her face. "She isn't unpleasant to look at."

"The prettiest girl in town, in the whole area, and you know it. Some of the sailors have said she's prettier than any of the girls they've seen all over the world."

He dropped her chin, and stepped back. "I don't know what came over me when I asked her to marry me, purely sympathy I assure you. I felt sorry for her after seeing that fat old man pawing her." He adjusted the lace at his sleeve.

"Yes, of course, Alexander, but you *did* ask her to marry you and we wouldn't want the words 'breach of promise' whispered in connection with the illustrious Montgomery name, would we?"

"I wouldn't marry you—"

Eleanor clamped her hand over Jess's mouth.

Alex turned away, stifling a yawn. "One woman is as good as any, I guess. And it would be more convenient to have a wife than these bond servants moving in and out. By the time you get one trained, she leaves. I imagine you'll be marrying soon and leaving us, Eleanor. What will we do then? Shall we set the wedding for three days hence?" He sat down and lifted his book. "You can move in tonight. Put the boys in Adam's room and you and the girls in Kit's room. And feed everybody."

Jess pushed away from Eleanor. "We Taggerts don't take charity."

"But it won't be charity, my dear, it will be all in the family."

Eleanor was pulling Jess from the room. "Thank you, Alexander. God will seat you at his right hand for this act of generosity."

"And, Eleanor, clothes for everyone. I don't want children in my care dressed in rags."

"Yes, Alexander. Bless you, Alexander." Eleanor closed the door behind them.

Chapter Fourteen

J ESSICA sat on the floor of the Taggert house, facing the fireplace, roasting a fish stuck on a long stick over the little fire. The house seemed oddly silent with the children gone. No one was laughing or crying; no child was jumping on her back or begging her to give him a ride. She should have been enjoying the quiet but, instead, she missed the children—she even missed Eleanor. Or at least the old Eleanor who wasn't always shouting at her.

Two days ago, the very evening of Alexander's proposal, Eleanor had packed what little they owned and moved into the Montgomery house.

Jessica had refused to go with her. She had said she had no intention of marrying Alexander and therefore she was not going to move into his house. Eleanor had screamed some things that surprised Jessica; she wondered where her sister had learned such words. Eleanor had said she'd have to come to her senses sooner or later and that she and the kids would be waiting for her by Alexander's side.

So, Jess had remained alone since then. Alexander —the presumptuous ass—had sent a town crier about to announce his engagement to Jessica. When some of her more persistent suitors refused to leave, that arrogant Russian of Alex's had played a few tricks with the men's clothing with the tip of his sword. Jessica came back from fishing to see a suitor—the one who'd offered the pig for her—running away as he clutched his trousers on.

She barely glanced at Nicholas before slamming into her house. Alexander—the coward—was nowhere to be seen.

So here she sat for a second night alone, the wind whistling through the cracks in the walls, with nothing to eat but roasted fish, since it was the only thing she knew how to cook.

A crack of thunder outside and the ensuing downpour of rain made her feel even more lonely and isolated. She didn't hear the door open.

"Jessica?"

She glanced about to see Alexander standing there, his bright yellow coat shimmering in the darkened room. "Go away."

"I brought some food," he said, holding out a basket. "Some of Eleanor's pasties. With beef. Not a fish in it." He put the basket down, then removed his yellow coat and carefully spread it on the floor to dry.

She didn't answer him, just kept her eyes on her fish.

"And cheese and bread and a bottle of wine and . . ." He hesitated. "A piece of chocolate."

The chocolate did it. She dropped her fish in the fire

and held out her hand to him and he put a piece of real chocolate in it. She began licking it. "What do I have to do to pay for this?"

"Marry me," he said, sitting down and then clamping his hand on her shoulder to keep her from leaping up. "Jessica, we have to talk about this. You can't remain in this house sulking. Two more days and Westmoreland will be here to get you."

"He'll not find me," she said, her jaw stiff.

Alex began unloading the food from the basket, his eyes downcast. "Do you hate the idea of marriage to me so much?" he asked softly.

She turned to look at him. Without his coat, he didn't look so preposterous. His big white shirt was gathered and the dampness made it cling to his shoulders. Although she knew him to be fat, from this angle, he looked almost slim.

"I don't like to be forced into anything," she said. "Women don't have too many choices given to them in life, but who they marry should be one of them."

He unwrapped a pastie—meat and vegetables in a crust—and handed it to her. "I guess desperate times call for desperate measures. Jess, you have to be practical. Either you get married within the next couple of days or you'll have a half-wit forced on you. I may not be much to look at but I do have all my wits about me."

"Alex, you don't look so bad, especially when you're not wearing one of those hideous coats." She nodded her head toward the shimmering pile of satin behind him.

Alex turned and grinned at her. "Have some wine, Jess," he said jovially. "I stole it from my father's private stock. He brought it from Spain ten years ago."

She smiled back at him and accepted the mug of wine, loving the clean, sharp taste of it.

"To business," he said. He was roasting cheese over the fire, removing it just before it dripped. "You don't want to marry me, your Raider hasn't even shown up and you have two days left. What do you plan to do?"

"I can't go off and leave the children," she said, "or else I'd leave town. Someone has to support them. Eleanor can't do it alone. And no other men seem to consider the idea of taking me and the children."

"I see. Maybe I'm to win you by default." He put a piece of cheese on bread for her.

"Alex," she said pleadingly. "It's not you so much as it is that I don't want to marry but one man."

"Your elusive Raider."

"Yes." She finished her wine. "Besides, there are things about me you don't know. You wouldn't *want* to marry me if you knew them."

"All right," he said, refilling her mug. "I'm prepared for the worst. Tell me what horrible secrets I don't know."

"I . . . I'm not a virgin," she whispered, her head down.

"Neither am I. What else?"

"Alex! Didn't you hear me? I said I'd been with another man. I can only marry him."

"Would you like more cheese? Stop looking at me like I'm an idiot. I know what you're saying. I also know you've lived all your life in this little town. There are some places where it's not unusual for a woman to be married and have two or three lovers at the same time."

"Really?" Jess asked, interested. "Tell me."

He smiled at her. "I don't think a man should tell his wife-to-be about adultery. All right, you've told me you're not a virgin. I assume it's this Raider."

"Yes, he and I—"

Alex put up his hand. "I'd prefer not to hear the details. I'm sure it was a moonlit night and you found his black mask fascinating. Here, eat this. I don't like skinny women."

She accepted the cheese. "Alex," she said softly, "how did you lose . . . I mean, who was the woman who was . . . your first, you know?"

He leaned back on his arms. By a trick of the light, she could barely see the mound of his big belly surrounded by the lemon yellow satin of his vest. "Remember Sally Henderson?"

"The seamstress?" Her head came up. "But she was my mother's age. She left town when we were children. Alex, you're lying."

He turned and grinned at her in a way that made her relax her muscles. She sprawled on the floor a few feet from him. "Sally Henderson," she murmured. "You must have been a boy."

"Old enough, I guess."

"And no one since then?" she asked, eyeing him. He certainly did look different in this light. He didn't have on that wig with all the curls, but, instead, wore the small one tied by a black ribbon at the nape of his neck. She'd never noticed before how the whiteness of the wig contrasted with the black of his brows.

"A few here and there," he said, grinning at her over his shoulder. He turned onto his belly and looked at her. "I was pretty rotten to you when you came to my room with Eleanor, Jess," he said. "I never met anyone with the ability to make me angrier than you. A man doesn't like to be called a piece of seaweed when he's just asked a woman to marry him."

"For the kids' sake."

"What kids?" he asked.

"You *did* ask me to marry you because of the

children, didn't you? And also because your father wants you to marry. Isn't that why?"

He took a while to answer as he sat up and looked into the fire. "Of course. I *need* seven kids hanging on me, their sticky hands on my expensive coats. Yesterday Molly used my best wig to cradle a bird with a broken wing. And Samuel sat on Marianna's silk embroidery wearing a wet diaper. And Philip climbed in bed with me at two this morning because he heard a noise and the other kids were afraid to sleep alone so, by three, they were all in bed with me. Yes, I'd say they were a real joy to have around, something of yours I've always coveted."

Jess looked at the fire. She was afraid to say a word. She wanted to ask him why he'd asked her to marry him, but she couldn't bring herself to do it. Could he possibly *want* to marry her? She looked at him while he had his head turned. She hadn't been exactly kind to him since he'd been home, but they had spent a lot of time together and she felt, well, almost attached to him. The first man she'd ever noticed was a Montgomery and she'd been selling fish to the Montgomerys since she could hold a net. She remembered Alex's mother sitting her down beside Alex, feeding them both milk and cookies.

"Alex," she said softly. "What about children?"

"I'll keep them," he said firmly. "No matter what they do. Father spends a lot of time with Nate, and Marianna may take on the girls, so that leaves me with the rest of the boys. Sam follows me like a fat Christmas goose and Philip—"

"No, I mean *our* children."

He kept his back to her. "We'll have to postpone our children, Jess," he said softly and there was great sadness in his voice. "I can't . . . not yet. We'll have to wait."

Jess's heart went out to him as she looked at the back of him. Silhouetted as he was by the firelight, all she saw was his broad shoulders, his lean jaw, and his kindness to her. She remembered all the things he'd done to help her—and all the times she'd been ill-tempered with him.

She sat up and put her hand on his shoulder, her lips next to his cheek. He put his hand over hers. "Alex, thank you for all you've done for me, thank you for putting up with the kids, and for tolerating my temper."

She leaned forward so that she was facing him. He really did have a handsome face she thought and, on impulse, she bent forward to kiss his lips.

He turned and her kiss landed on the corner of his mouth.

His reaction made her feel very sorry for him. No doubt she reminded him of times before his fever.

She patted his hand. "That's all right, Alex, I don't mind. I understand. And I'll marry you. If the Raider doesn't come forward to claim me by Tuesday night, I'll marry you on Wednesday morning."

For a man so fat, Alexander certainly reacted quickly. He was on his feet before Jess could blink.

"If he doesn't what?" he shouted. "I'm to wait until the night before my wedding to see if I have a bride or not? Jessica, you go too far! You may think you're the most desirable woman in the world, but there are other women."

She stood, hands on hips. "Women who'll marry you for your money? Why else would they marry you? Your looks? The way you make love to them? Even with your money you can't get anyone else. I've never lied to you. I want the Raider. If he comes for me, I mean to take him."

"But I'm second choice, is that it?"

"I didn't have any choice at all, Alex," she said, softening, walking toward him.

He was putting on his damp coat. "How can you be so stupid as to love a man who only appears now and then? A man who won't show you his face or tell you his name?"

"I didn't say I loved him."

Alex stopped and stared at her. "If it isn't love, then what is it? Lust?"

"No, I . . . I don't know. He's like me. We think alike. I've never met a man like him before. I think I could love him."

Alex went to the door, then turned back. "You can damned well love me, too," he said and went out into the rain.

For an astonished moment, Jess stared at the door. "Love?" she whispered. Was Alexander in love with her? For some reason, the thought pleased her very much. Whistling, she went upstairs to her lonely, cold bed.

Alex was shoveling hay for the Raider's big black stallion.

"I thought I'd find you here," Nick said, laughter in his voice, a smirk on his lips. "I hear shouting and you run away to your private island."

Alex didn't answer him. "Doesn't Eleanor give you enough to do?"

"I gave her something to contemplate this morning," he said smugly. "She was too busy to even remember her sister's name. So, you're going to marry your Mistress Jessica tomorrow morning."

"Someone is," Alex said, filling the horse's water trough. As usual, he was stripped to the waist. Whenever he didn't have to wear the padded clothes, he wore as little as possible.

"The wedding night with that little cat should be memorable."

Alex gave Nick a malevolent look. "I can't sleep with her and you know it. She'd know I wasn't fat and she'd know the reason for the disguise in a minute."

"Perhaps you could tell her the truth."

"Jessica?" Alex spat. "Tell *Jessica* the truth? That woman has no sense at all. She'd probably borrow my mask and challenge the admiral to a duel. Besides,"— he grinned—"it's better for my disguise if she doesn't like me. If we spent a few nights together, she'd look at me, well, differently. People might guess I wasn't the weakling I appear to be."

Nick groaned. "So, you'll marry her but not sleep with her."

"Oh, I'll sleep with her all right—as the Raider. Alex will support her and put up with those damn kids, and the Raider will enjoy her."

"So Jessica will think she's an adulteress."

"It's only for a while. Until I think it's safe to tell her. Or maybe I'll go to Boston and get cured of my disease. Alex will lose weight and the Raider will be no more."

"I hope it works out as well as you plan. Are you ready to return? I don't like this place at night."

"The Raider will protect you," Alex said in a deepened voice, making Nick laugh.

Together, they rowed back to the mainland.

All evening, Alex kept hoping Jessica might come to him, might apologize for her remarks, but she didn't appear.

Eleanor walked into the common room. "They're all in bed at last. She hasn't shown up yet?"

"No," Alex said, looking down at his empty mug.

"I guess everything's ready for the wedding tomorrow," she said.

Alex nodded glumly.

Eleanor patted his hand. "Alex, it'll be all right. Jessica really does have some brains and someday she'll see what a good man you are. You just have to wait for her to come to her senses."

"I don't think I'll live that long. Do you think she's with the Raider?"

"I think she's at home sulking and hoping the Raider will come to her."

Alex slammed his fist on the table. "I don't want her to see him. If she sees him tonight, she'll *never* marry me tomorrow."

Eleanor clasped his hand. "I wouldn't be too sure of that. There are more things to life than . . . babymaking." Her face turned red.

Alex grinned at her. "Not to a young, healthy woman like Jessica."

"A woman who has helped me clothe, feed and house seven children for several years," Eleanor reminded him. "You underestimate Jess." She looked around the room. "Do you know where Nate is? He should be in bed."

"I sent him over to see if Jess needed anything."

"Oh no," Eleanor breathed. "You sent Nate to Jessica? Don't you know how much Nate *adores* Jessica? She sheds one tear and—" Eleanor stopped at the puzzled look on Alex's face. "If Jess does something really stupid like decide to run away, Nate will help her. Alex," she said, standing, "you have to go find Nathaniel and see what's going on."

Alex stood rather abruptly, then remembered his disguise. "I don't want to go out in the cold. I think it's going to rain again. You know how wet I got last night. Can't you send someone else? Someone healthy like Nick."

"Nicholas is *too* healthy. No, Alex, you have to go.

213

Take your father's horse. It hasn't been ridden in months."

"That brute?"

"Then take Adam's stallion, whatever, but *go.*"

Alex started to protest but the urgency in Eleanor's voice spurred him on. He turned and left the house. There was, fortunately, no one in the stable to see the supposedly feeble Alexander saddle his father's horse with lightning speed. He skirted town and rode hard, through the rain, to the Taggert house.

Nathaniel was asleep on the floor, the fire almost dead, a half-eaten apple by his hand.

"Nate, where's Jessica?"

"Hello, Mr. Alex," Nate said, blinking and sitting up and starting to eat his apple.

"Where's Jessica?" Alex repeated.

"She was crying about the Raider, so I told her."

"Told her what?"

"Told her that the Raider's camp is on Ghost Island and he keeps his horse there."

Alex was speechless, his mouth open.

"But I didn't tell her you were the Raider."

Alex sat down on a stool hard. "Who else knows?" he whispered.

Nate swallowed, then crossed his fingers behind his back. "Just me. And Sam. We followed you. I mean, I followed you. Sam just slept. I think that's why Sam likes you so much, but, don't worry, he can't talk."

"But you can, you little spy." Alex pulled Nate to him. "I ought to raise a few welts on your backside. How long have you known?"

"Since the second raid."

Alex leaned back against the stones of the fireplace. "You've known all this time and not told anyone?"

"I told Jessica," Nate said, skirting a direct answer.

Alex was looking at the boy with new respect. "So,"

214

he said slowly, "you told her the Raider camped on Ghost Island?"

Nate's dilemma showed in his eyes. "She was so sad. She wanted to see you before she married you."

Alex was amazed that this boy could keep these characters straight and keep this information to himself. "All right, she shall see the Raider tonight. I want you to go home and see Eleanor, she's worried about you. Tell her I've gone looking for Jessica."

The boy nodded solemnly.

"And, Nate, don't mention to Eleanor about Ghost Island."

"Of course not," he said with dignity. "If too many people know, you could be captured and killed."

Alex found the idea of his life being in a nine-year-old's hands a sobering thought. But Nate had only broken the trust for his beloved sister. "Go on, go home," he said gently. "And, Nate, tell Eleanor to give you a piece of apple pie." Alex smiled. "And a flagon of ale. If any man deserves a drink, you do."

Nate grinned fit to crack his face in two. "Aye, aye, sir," he said and went out into the rain.

"Jessie," she heard him call. "Jessie."

Jessica brushed her tears away and then began running, blindly, knowing only that she was running toward *him*. Her foot caught in a broken branch. She tugged at it frantically.

"No, Jessie, be careful," she heard him say and then she was in his arms. He was kissing her hungrily, his lips all over her face and neck, while she just clutched at him, holding him to her, afraid to let him go. Her fingers dug into the flesh over his ribs.

"Jessie," he said, his voice full of wonder and laughter. "Did you miss me?"

She was too glad to see him to mind his laughing at

her. "I didn't mean it. You *are* a successful Raider. You were magnificent when you delivered the handbills. You gave the people hope. You—"

He kissed her to silence, and when she was breathless, he knelt and unfastened her ankle, then lifted and carried her to the shack that sheltered his horse.

"Promise me you'll not come here again."

"How did you know I was here? Did Nate tell you?"

He put his fingertips to her lips. "Don't you know that I watch you, that I see you wherever you go?"

"Then you've seen all the men? You know about the marriage? You must—"

He kissed her again as he began untying the laces of her dress. His long, lean fingers slipped under the edges of her scarf and slowly pulled it away. "Such beauty so lightly covered," he murmured as he put his face against her breasts.

Jessica leaned back against the pile of hay, feeling his hands and lips on her flesh. He quickly unfastened the front of her dress, exposing her breasts to his touch, his hot hands running over her cool skin.

He lifted her in his arms to kiss her while he slid the dress off her shoulders, then removed her underwear until she was bare to the waist, exposed to his sight and touch.

Only this man did she trust, no one else in the world. Only here in this man's arms did she feel safe, as if she could give control to someone else.

Her hands began touching his body, pulling at the silk shirt until she could feel his skin. He shed the piece of cloth easily, as if his natural state were one without clothing.

He laid her down on the hay and easily slipped the skirt over her smooth, round hips, his lips moving downward, following his hands, pausing to nip lightly at the soft curve of her buttocks. He kissed her knees, her calves, then the arch of her foot and when he returned to her lips, he wore no clothing except the black mask.

Jessica gasped at the feel of his skin against hers, his long legs rubbing against hers.

There was no pain when he entered her, only joyous passion. She was eager for him and she was willing to show it.

He laughed with pleasure at her exuberance and rolled with her until she was on top, smiling as he watched the pleasure and surprise on her face. He guided her for a few moments, then rolled again until she was underneath, but this time he lifted her legs about his waist, holding her bottom up as he plunged deeper and deeper.

He forgot about watching her but thought only of his own pleasure. He pushed down and she clung to him, arching to meet his final, frantic thrusts.

She gave a quick, short, sharp scream at the end but then buried her open mouth in the smooth, hot skin of his shoulder.

"Jessie, my love," he whispered, his sweaty body holding hers very tightly.

It was a long time before Jessica felt the cramping in her legs and moved to ease her body. But the Raider held her close.

"Cold, my love?" he whispered.

"No," she said, smiling, kissing his arm thrown across her, almost as if he thought she might try to leave him. "I thought I wasn't going to find you," she murmured, relaxed and drowsy. "I didn't think it was going to happen. Alexander will be hurt, but I'll soothe him."

He didn't say anything as he nuzzled his face against her hair. "Alexander?"

"Yes," she said, smiling in the dim light. "I'll have to tell Alex that I can't marry him."

"Marry?" the Raider said, sounding rather stupid.

"I thought you said you watched me. Surely you know about the admiral's decree. I'm to marry someone tomorrow. I waited for you as long as I could, but then Alex offered and for a while I thought I was going to have to marry him. You *are* willing to take the children, aren't you?"

The Raider didn't loosen the hold he had on her. "Jessie, I can't marry you."

"Well, of course I know you can't very well stand before the congregation wearing a mask. I'll tell people I met you while I was fishing and you've been away at sea. That way no one will suspect that you're—"

"Jessie, I can't marry you."

"Because of Alex? He knows about you. Alex is very understanding. I'll explain—"

"Jessie, please don't make this worse. I cannot marry you."

When what he was saying finally began to penetrate her brain, she tried to pull away from him but he held her fast. "Release me," she said through her teeth.

"Jessie, you have to understand that there are reasons why I can't marry you."

"One," she said, trying to get away from him. "All I need is one intelligent reason."

"You'll have to trust me."

"Ha!" She pulled her head away enough to look at him. "Now I understand what I am to you. Are you married? Do you have children of your own? What do I know about you? How easy I must seem to you. Do you laugh about me with your friends? How many other women do you—"

He kissed her mouth and held the kiss until she

stopped struggling. "Jessie, you have every right to your anger. I deserve everything you say. But please believe me that I love you and only you."

"Then don't let me marry someone else," she whispered.

"Montgomery can't make love to you."

It took Jess a moment to understand what he was saying. "You bastard," she said under her breath. "You'll let me marry Alex because he can't do the only thing you *can* do?"

"I couldn't bear another man touching you. Jessie, I love you."

She pushed hard at him, but he held her in the hay. She glared at him. "Alexander was right about you. He said you weren't much of a Raider and, now, I don't think you're much of a man."

"You didn't doubt my manhood a moment ago," he said indignantly. "Jessie, let's not fight." He began to kiss her neck.

"So," she said quietly, "tomorrow you'll let me marry another man."

"I have no choice. Westmoreland made his ultimatum and I can't marry you, so, if it must be someone, Montgomery is the best choice. At least he won't be touching you."

She relaxed her body, and when she felt his grip loosen, she rolled away from him. "And neither will you be touching me."

"Jessie," he said, reaching out his hands for her.

She grabbed her clothes and almost returned to him when she saw a shaft of moonlight touch his nude body, but she thought of what he'd said and her anger surged. She began pulling on her clothes.

"Did you think I was going to marry someone else and come sneaking away in the night to you?"

"Jessie, you don't love Montgomery."

"Maybe I don't, but he's been good to me in a way you with all your bravura will never understand." She stood still in the moonlight in her underwear. "Let me make this clear to you: tonight is your one chance. One, no more. If I marry another man tomorrow, there'll never again be any more of this."

The Raider was on his feet in a moment, his nude body pressing against hers. "You to live like a nun? How will you feel a week from now when I slip into your bedroom?"

"Our bedroom. My husband's and mine."

He smiled at her. "Would you like to wager that Montgomery won't sleep with you? You might roll on him and crush him."

"Alexander is a good man and you leave his name out of this. Is that your final word? You won't marry me?"

"I can't. If there were any way I could, I would. Jessica, I'll visit you. You can visit me here."

She angrily pulled on her dress. "No, I take vows tomorrow and I plan to honor them."

He smiled knowingly. "You'll never be able to do it."

"You have never met a Taggert before."

Chapter Fifteen

HER wedding day was a rainy one, bleak and drizzling, the world looking as unhappy as Jessica felt. She kept her chin high and refused to think of the Raider's words to her. But she wasn't going to be some tragic heroine who loved one man while married to another. From this day forward, she was going to put the Raider out of her mind. Even as she thought this, part of her mind was laughing in disbelief.

Eleanor had helped her dress in a navy blue silk dress that had belonged to Alex's mother and then commanded her to sit perfectly still while she saw to all the preparations for the wedding breakfast.

Eleanor didn't try to talk to her sister about the forthcoming marriage and Jessica was sure she was too disgusted with her to speak.

But as Jess sat there, alone in Adam's room, she became fidgety and thought she'd like to talk to Alex. She looked out the window, saw that no one was in sight, then made her way along the edge of the house, through the weeds, to Alex's room. When she passed Sayer's room, she glanced in to see Nate helping the old man get dressed. Nate started toward Jess, but Sayer caught her brother's arm and nodded at her. She nodded back to him and continued on to Alex's room.

As politely as circumstances allowed, Jess knocked on Alex's window. When he didn't answer, she climbed into the room. "Alex," she called but heard no reply, so she sat down on a chair and waited. He entered through a door leading to another room. He wore a brilliant scarlet coat embroidered with darker red flowers and tendrils that put her plain dress to shame.

When he saw her, there was an immediate look of pleasure on his face but then it changed to one of annoyance. "You shouldn't be here. Haven't you heard that it's bad luck to see each other before the wedding?"

"I wanted you to know that I saw the Raider last night."

Alex was primping before a mirror. "I'm sure it was a strenuous meeting. I'm surprised you're here today. Didn't he sweep you away on his black horse? Carry you to his golden castle?"

"Alex, I came to talk to you, not to fight. I want to tell you that I'll honor my vows to you. I won't—" She had to swallow hard. "I won't be seeing him again."

Alex just stood there, staring at her for a moment, and she couldn't read what he was thinking. "Come with me, Jess," he said and led her through a door.

"My room was once the nursery, but one by one my

older sister and brothers left and I stayed in it. My mother used this room for sleeping when one of us was ill. I've had it furnished for you. You have your own bedroom."

Jessica looked at the little room, prettily done for her with a small bed, a wardrobe, a chest and a chair. It was the first time in her life that she was to have a space that was entirely hers alone.

"Alex, you're very good to me. Better than I deserve. I swear that I'll be a good wife to you."

"Fresh fish every day?" he asked, his eyes laughing.

She smiled at him. "And a child in every room. Alex, could I try on that coat? I like red."

He laughed then and removed his coat.

The coat was much too big for her, but the red brought out the lights in her hair and made her cheeks pinker. He stood behind her as she looked at herself in the mirror and put his hands on her shoulders.

"Jess," he said softly, "I'm going to buy you a wardrobe fit for a princess." He paused. "A wardrobe fit for my wife. I'll be a good husband to you, the best that I know how to be."

All Jess could see in the mirror was his face, a shadow darkening his wig and no shining coat to take away from the handsomeness of his face. Quite naturally, she turned toward him, and, just as naturally, his face lowered toward hers.

His lips were almost on hers when they were interrupted by Nicholas's chuckle.

Alex pulled away from Jess as if she were poisonous. Nick was smiling patronizingly at her appearance in Alex's scarlet coat.

"Your sister believes you've run away," Nick said to Jess.

Jess removed Alex's coat but Alex wouldn't come close enough to her to take it, so she folded it carefully and put it on the bed. Of all things, she thought, she'd almost kissed Alexander Montgomery. The Raider had said she'd never be able to live like a nun. But *Alexander?* Smiling at the absurdity of her thoughts, she left the room.

Eleanor met her in the hall, her face white with anger. "I thought you'd decided not to go through with it."

"Do I have a choice? You give me an alternative and I'll take it."

"Hmph!" Eleanor sniffed. "You have the best of the bargain. You're just too stubborn to see it."

"Maybe when Alex is sleeping I can try on *all* his coats."

Eleanor grabbed her sister's arm and pulled her into the front parlor where the ceremony was to be held. The wedding ceremony began and was over quickly. Jess put her cheek up for Alex to kiss and thought he smelled like cinnamon. One of the children again, she thought.

In spite of the fact that the wedding had been forced by the hated Admiral Westmoreland, it was a Montgomery wedding and the food and drink were plentiful, so the guests enjoyed themselves. There were whispers about how awful it was that a beautiful young woman like Jessica was being sacrificed to a fat, effeminate, decrepit man like Alexander. The men murmured things about the power of Montgomery money, while the women said gold was a poor bedmate.

A couple of men, trying to alleviate Jessica's misery, whispered to her that they'd be happy to supply what she obviously wasn't going to get from Alexander.

Admiral Westmoreland came by the house and

congratulated the bride and groom, just as if he'd not been the one to cause this unwanted marriage. Jessica opened her mouth to say something, but Alex clamped his hand on her arm painfully and then thanked the admiral.

"Coward," Jess hissed at Alex, then turned away and smiled at two good-looking young men.

"Jess . . ." Alex began, but she took the arms of the two men and left him alone.

When night came, Eleanor pulled Jessica out of an energetic reel with a handsome blond man and led her down the hall and toward Alex's bedroom.

"I was having such a good time," Jess protested.

"You can have a good time alone with your husband."

"By counting the number of flowers on his new coat? Ouch, Eleanor, that hurt. Lately, your temper hasn't been at all pleasant."

Eleanor didn't speak until they reached Alex's room. "This is a gift from Marianna," she said, holding up a white cotton nightgown edged with deep eyelet flounce.

"It'll take more than that to get a rise out of Alexander," Jessica said, rolling her eyes.

"Now, you stop that!" Eleanor snapped. "There's nothing wrong with Alexander. He might do a lot better if he got a little encouragement from you."

"Encourage him to do what?" Jess asked, aghast. "Look, Alex and I have this worked out. We married each other for convenience. You heard him. He needs someone to put this house into order. Someone other than that big, snooping Russian of his—ouch! Eleanor, I want to take the corset off, not tighten the strings."

"Jess, you'd help matters if you thought of Alexan-

225

der as a *man*. He's your husband now and you should treat him as such. Here, lift your arms and put this on. Now, get into bed and I'll brush your hair."

"Alex set up a bed for me in that room."

"But not for tonight. Jessica, you listen to me. All Alex needs is a little encouragement. You have to use a few feminine arts on him." She glared at her sister. "Don't tell him he's fat or that you can outsail him or that you hate his clothes. Be *nice* to him. He's your husband now."

Jessica was yawning. "All right, I'll sleep here. I don't like sleeping alone anyway."

Eleanor kissed her sister's cheek. "You won't regret this," she said and left the room.

Jess was asleep in moments but woke when Alex entered the room. She watched him move about, his fat belly silhouetted in the dim light. He lit a candle, then drew in his breath when he saw Jessica.

"What are you doing here?" he said, his eyes widening at the sight of her.

She was not going to get angry. "We got married, remember?"

"I thought you'd be asleep now—in your own bed," he said pointedly.

She clutched her hands together and gave him a sweet smile. She didn't like the way he was treating her, as if she were an intruder. "Alexander, this is our wedding night."

"I know," he snapped, "but I'm tired and I have a headache and I want to sleep."

He did look tired. His eyes were red-rimmed and his face was beginning to sweat. She tossed back the covers, then stood on the bed, putting her hands on his shoulders. "I can rub your head until it feels better. Come to bed and I'll—"

She stopped because Alex pushed her down in the bed.

"Go to your room," he said angrily. "I told you that I want to sleep. Alone. Do you understand me?"

"Yes," she said, as much puzzled by his anger as anything. "I wasn't planning to remind you of the past. I mean, remind you of when you could still—"

Alex had his back to her and didn't turn around. "Just go, Jessica. Just go," he said hoarsely.

Frowning, she went to her own room and snuggled down under the covers. She was asleep instantly, but something woke her. She sat up. "Alex?" she said, when she heard a noise.

"It's me," said a deep, accented voice that she'd come to know well.

The Raider was all over her at once, pulling at her clothes, burying his hands in her hair, kissing her face and neck. He was a starving animal, wanting her, needing her.

For a moment, Jessica clutched at him, as eager for him as he was for her.

But then, when he had her gown half off, she remembered who she was.

"No, no, no," she chanted, pushing at him. "I'm married now. Get away from me."

"Jessie," he whispered, yearning in his voice. "I came to give you your wedding night."

She pushed at him with all her strength. "You didn't participate in the ceremony and you can't participate now. I *told* you that. Didn't you believe me? Now get out of here before you wake Alex."

"He's snoring too loudly to hear anything. Jessie, please."

"Get out of here!" she said much too loudly, but she knew she was close to giving in to him. "I'll scream until everyone hears me. They catch you, it'll be your neck."

"Jessie, you can't mean this. That fool Montgomery is never going to sleep with you. Do you mean to spend your life alone in this bed?"

"If I must. But I'll certainly not spend it cuckolding my husband. If you're not out of here in thirty seconds, I'll scream."

He stood to his full height, towering over her, his black clothes making him almost disappear in the shadows. "I want to see how you feel in a week or so. Will you be able to resist me after that muscleless husband of yours has ignored you night after night?"

"I'll resist you even if it turns into year after year."

He laughed at that and Jess realized how little conviction she'd been able to put in her voice. After a quick caress to her cheek, he slipped out the window and was gone. It was almost dawn before she stopped tossing about in the bed and went to sleep.

Alex was awakened by Nick's big hand on his shoulder. "Your father just sent for me. He wants me to carry him into the common room, and your sister says he plans to visit you in your bedroom. He wants to see the newlyweds together."

Sleepily, Alex nodded, getting out of bed before Nick shut the door behind him. He stretched his nude body, his fingertips touching the ceiling, before getting a long nightshirt from a chest and putting it on. He chose his largest, gaudiest wig.

He stopped as he remembered the harrowing experiences of the previous day. First, he'd almost kissed Jess, thereby giving everything away, but, thankfully, Nick had interrupted them. After the wedding, he'd been conscious only of the fact that now Jessica was to be his forever. He'd never experienced such a feeling of possession in his life. He wanted to take her away from the house; he wanted to veil her and keep her completely to himself. He didn't want others to see or speak to her.

He was afraid that if he got too near her, he just might abduct her, so he'd stayed away from her, not even letting himself stand close enough to smell the fragrance of her hair.

But he'd had to stand there and watch while she danced with man after man. She was his wife but she wasn't. He couldn't hold her, couldn't touch her, had to act tired and uncaring when he wanted to show her how truly energetic he felt.

He'd breathed a sigh of relief when Eleanor took her away, but then his imagination nearly killed him as he thought of what they were doing. Jessica was being prepared for his bed.

He had stayed for hours after Jessica had gone. Everyone else had gone to bed, but Alex had stayed alone in the common room. He had been afraid to have even one drink, one mug of ale, because he had known it might weaken his resolve. He'd told himself that what he was doing was for the good of America and worth his personal agony.

But when he had walked into his bedroom and seen a sleepy-looking, gentle-eyed Jessica in his bed, he'd almost turned traitor. He had known he had to get her out quickly or he'd never be able to control himself.

He had meant to make up to her for his rudeness when he'd come to her as the Raider, but the little she-cat was damned hardheaded. She'd thrown him out without too much misery on her part.

So here he was now, facing another agony. His father wanted to see the newlyweds in Alex's room. Of course he wanted to see them in bed together. Alex grimaced as he adjusted his wig. His father wanted to make sure his weak-spined son had done his duty by his wife. Alex jammed his fist through the sleeve of the nightshirt. Sayer wouldn't visit Adam or Kit to see what they had done with their brides. Not his *best* sons.

Angrily, he opened the door to Jessica's room.

The sight of her head, just barely visible above the covers, made him forget his father and his country.

Jess turned over and looked up at him. "Alex, what . . . what are you doing in here?"

The fear in her voice dampened his ardor considerably. He slouched and made his voice whine. "Nick just told me my father is going to visit the newlyweds in their bedchamber. My father wants grandchildren of his own and I'd not like to make him think there was no possibility of them. Would you join me in my bed?" With that he spun about on his bare heel and went back to his own room.

Jessica lay in the bed, blinking after him. For a moment, she'd thought he'd known about the Raider's visit last night. She was relieved to see that he knew nothing.

She lay still and thought of Alex standing over her. He always looked so much better when he wasn't wearing one of those absurd coats of his. In fact, watching him walk in that long gown, she couldn't see his fat legs or his big belly. Odd, but she'd never noticed before what broad shoulders he had.

She jumped out of bed, started toward his room, then on impulse looked at herself in the mirror. She picked up her comb to smooth her hair but then didn't. Her hair was billowed out about her head and right now her eyes looked bright with anticipation.

She went into Alex's room.

He was lying there, his belly making a mound under the covers, and looking up at her. She'd never before noticed what thick eyelashes he had.

She smiled at him. "Aren't you going to invite me in?" she asked with a lowered voice.

Alex seemed to hesitate before he pulled back the covers and she climbed in beside him. He stayed on his side of the bed, as far away from her as possible.

She moved around in the bed some. "Alex, I think your bed is much more comfortable than mine." She turned toward him, but he was lying as stiff as a ship's mast, his eyes on the ceiling.

"I guess we should pretend to be the loving couple." She moved her body next to his, but if anything, Alex grew stiffer. She raised on one elbow. "Alex, you aren't a bad-looking man at all." She put her finger to his cheek. "Remember the time you held the pistols on Pitman and saved our house from being burned? You were very brave that night."

Alex kept his arms to his sides and didn't look at her.

She moved near him so her body was pressed against his. "Alex," she said softly, running her finger along his chin, "you've been awfully good to me and my family. You know, it's amazing, but in this light you look almost as handsome as your brothers."

He looked at her out of the corner of his eye. "I knew that would get some reaction from you," she laughed and then listened as she heard voices outside the door. Alex didn't move.

"Here," she cried, "put your arm around me. At least *pretend* that we're married."

Woodenly, Alex obeyed her. Jess curved herself into his body, putting her knee across his stomach. She snuggled against him and thought how solid he felt, how big his shoulders were, how hard his thighs and soft his stomach. She sighed contentedly.

When the knock came on the door, she didn't hear it and when Alex answered it, his voice cracked.

Nick entered the room carrying the emaciated Sayer. Alex's father had aged many years in the short time since his accident.

"Father," Alex said, his voice sounding strained. He tried to sit up but found Jessica clinging to him like a barnacle.

She opened her eyes only enough to smile at Sayer.

"Jess!" Alex hissed.

Sayer waved his hand. "Let her sleep. I didn't mean to disturb you. I had no idea you'd still be in bed," he lied. "Nicholas, take me in to breakfast."

Nick carried the old man out of the room, giving Alex a wink before he shut the door.

Alex was half sitting up, Jessica wrapped around him. There was sweat on his brow.

"Alex," she whispered and turned her face up toward his in a way that meant that she wanted to be kissed.

He drew back from her. "Jessica, it seems to me that you'd be amenable to copulation. I believe it could happen. If you whisper vulgar words to me and—oh yes, tell me dirty stories, and dance, naked of course, the more suggestive the better, then in an hour or so, I might be able to perform. Of course you'll have to get on top and be very, very quick. I tend to find procreation rather dull—and messy. But if you are determined to use my body, you may do so."

It took Jessica a moment to recover herself, then she began to laugh. "Oh, Alex, what an imagination you have." She rolled away from him and got out of bed. "Someday, I'll have to tell you about *real* men. Poor Sally Henderson." She looked back as she heard a thud behind her. It almost looked as if Alex had fallen out of bed, as if he'd made a grab for something and missed.

She started to help him up, but he looked up at her in fury. "Touch me and you'll regret it."

She drew back. "Alex, you get the vapors more often than a woman," she said before leaving the room.

"What have you been doing to Alexander?" Eleanor hissed an hour later.

"Absolutely nothing. He is as untouched as when I found him," Jess said, her mouth full of breakfast.

"If I didn't know better, I'd think he looks like he's been crying."

"It couldn't have been anything I did. Eleanor, where are the household accounts? I'd like to look at them."

Chapter Sixteen

BY noon of the day after the marriage, the Montgomery household was well aware that they had a new mistress. Jessica treated the rambling old house as she would have a ship, and the overfed, underworked bondsmen and women as her crew. Ceilings and floors were washed, as well as everything in between. She set Nicholas to hauling barrels out of the cellar so she could take inventory of supplies as well as send the ratcatcher in to do his work.

John Pitman boarded himself inside his office, Marianna decided to visit the sick people of Warbrooke, while Sayer had himself carried to the common room where he could help Jessica bellow orders. Everyone said he'd never looked happier.

Alexander disappeared right after breakfast and by

sundown he still hadn't returned. By then most of the men of Warbrooke were telling themselves they were glad they'd not won Jessica's hand. There was much sympathy for poor Alexander who was run from his own house so soon after their marriage.

"If she'd spent a night with me, she wouldn't have so much energy this mornin'," was what one man after another said.

They all chuckled smugly.

"Sit down!" Eleanor commanded her sister. "You've worn everyone—including me—out. It's time to rest. Where's your husband?"

"Husband? Oh, Alex."

"Yes, Alex. Where is he?"

"I have no idea." As Jess looked out the window, she saw John Pitman walking down the hill toward town. "Where's he going?"

"To a meeting with the admiral. He'll be back later."

"You mean he'll be away through dinner?"

"Jess!" Eleanor called, but Jessica was already on her way down the hall.

"Could you bring me something to eat in Alex's room?" Jess called over her shoulder.

An hour later she looked up to see Alex opening the door of his bedroom. She was sitting cross-legged on his bed, the household ledgers that Pitman kept so closely guarded, all about. Also about her were scattered bread crumbs, half a piece of apple pie, a wedge of cheese, three plums and a mug of ale.

"Hello, Alex. Where have you been?"

Alex stood in the doorway staring at her. Her hair was disarrayed, her clothes were half unfastened, as if she'd started to undress and stopped in the middle of the process, and there were crumbs on her chin. She was beautiful—and he was all too aware that he couldn't touch her.

"What do you think you're doing?" he asked crossly.

"Taking care of your house, what does it look like? Want something to eat?" She held out about half a pound of cheese. "Sit down and quit scowling. Take off your coat; take off your wig; take off your shoes. Make yourself comfortable."

"Because you run about in various states of undress, doesn't mean I plan to," he said primly, handing her a hand mirror.

She brushed the crumbs off her face. "All right, have it your way," she said, looking back at a ledger. "Another one! Your brother-in-law cannot add. Nearly every column is misadded."

Alex sat on the end of the bed, as far from Jess as possible. "Here, let me see that." It took Alex only minutes to figure out what Pitman was doing. "Jess, how many pairs of shoes have you bought for yourself since our engagement?"

"None, of course. What do I need with new shoes? I have a pair of shoes. Only patched once."

Alex winced. "We'll fix that tomorrow, but according to this, you've bought three pair of expensive satin shoes in the last week."

"Satin? What a waste they'd be. Step once onto the rocks and they're gone."

"Didn't you read these columns?"

"I'm better at adding than I am at reading. Look at this, Alex. It says here that Eleanor bought the kids three pair of shoes each." She looked up at him. "Why's he lying?"

"Because he presents these accounts to my father

each week and my father authorizes his steward to release the money. And the totals are wrong as well?"

"The actual totals are less than his figures. Not much but some. The money adds up after a couple of ledgers. It looks like your brother-in-law is embezzling money." She shoved the ledgers off her lap and stood. "Alex, you'd better eat something." She gathered all the food remnants and set them on a table by him. "If you'd like, I'll get you something hot."

"No, thank you. Jess! What are you doing?"

"Undressing. I'm going to bed."

"But you can't do that."

"Alex, I promise not to roll over on you in my sleep. I don't snore, I don't grind my teeth and I don't even take up very much room. And since I don't plan to do any naked dances, you'll not be expected to perform any husbandly duties. But I do plan to sleep in here with you tonight. I don't want to be alone in that other room tonight."

"You can't sleep with me, Jessica," Alex said.

"I don't think your back is strong enough to carry me out of this room."

"What's wrong with that room?"

"I don't like the window." She moved ledgers and stacked them on the floor.

Alex caught her hand as she started to push her dress down over her shoulders. "It's the Raider, isn't it? He comes through the window. You're staying with me because you can't resist him."

Jessica groaned. "Alex, I'm staying with you so I can get a full night's sleep and also because I don't like sleeping alone. Now, please get undressed. I'll never be able to sleep with that coat flashing at me."

Alex sat there and watched as she removed her dress, but turned away when she started on the laces of her underwear.

She put a cool hand to his forehead. "Alex, are you well? You're sweating. It isn't that fever returning, is it? Now go get undressed. I promise I won't look."

It was a long, long night for Alex. He lay in bed, Jess curled up beside him and sleeping like a child, and he couldn't allow himself to touch her. He felt every movement of her breasts against his side. Her night-gown rode up and her long, lean legs touched his. He'd gone into another room and put on a nightgown, leaving his wig on and returned to her. She was already asleep and as soon as he put his weight on the bed, she had groped for him, her hands seeking his body, and pulled him to her as if he were a child's comfort toy.

As she clung to him, he tried to reason out what he was doing. He couldn't tell her he was the Raider. Look at how she was snooping into what Pitman considered his private territory. She'd never be content to let Alex continue raiding when he needed to and keep her pretty little nose out of it. Jessica would involve herself in every aspect of whatever the Raider was doing—and she'd get herself in trouble—or worse.

Jess pulled her knee over Alex's maleness and he reacted instantly. So much for dirty stories and naked dances, he thought.

He didn't sleep until just before dawn. He held her, looked at her in the darkness, caressed her hair, ran his hand down the length of her until he knew he'd have to stop while he still could. He started thinking of all the most awful things he'd ever seen in his years at sea. He tried anything he could to keep from thinking of the delicious bundle in his arms.

An hour before dawn, exhausted after two sleepless nights, he fell asleep.

At dawn, six of the seven Taggert children jumped

onto his stomach. As usual, Samuel's bottom half was juicily wet.

Jessica rolled out of the line of fire while Alex said a few words meant to discipline sailors.

"Gor . . ." Philip said, impressed.

Sam laughed and jumped on Alex's belly.

"Jessica, get him off of me. He's wet me through to my backbone. Can't you control these brats?"

Jess had already picked up Sam but at Alex's last words, she dropped him so that his diaper made a splat sound. But Alex didn't notice because when Jess leaned over, he could see all the way down her nightgown.

"Ah, here they are," Eleanor said, opening the door. "Out!" she commanded. "Let them have some privacy. Alex, did you sleep in that wig?"

"Privacy!" Alex grumbled. "No one in this house knows the meaning of the word."

Eleanor closed the door and while Alex watched in open-mouthed astonishment, Jess stripped off her nightgown and pulled on underwear and her dress. "Alex, you look awful. Have you been sleeping well? Stay there, I'll bring you some milquetoast. On second thought, you don't smell so very good. I could bring you a bath. Wash your hair and back for you. And your feet. I don't guess you can reach your feet over that belly too well."

"Get out of here, Jessica," Alex said through clenched teeth.

"Are you always in a bad mood in the morning?"

"Out," was all he could manage to say.

Jess gathered the ledgers on the floor and left him alone.

By the end of the second day of their marriage, Jessica was ready to call it quits. She was trying her best to be a good wife to Alex, just as she'd promised, but everything she did displeased him. First of all she'd brought him a tray of food, all of it carefully chosen so he didn't have to chew very much.

But when she'd tried to feed him, he'd pushed her halfway across the room. He said she was not to treat him as an invalid. Jess said she thought he was an invalid. It had been her experience that he couldn't even walk a few feet that she didn't have to put her arms around him and support him. She said she had gone into marriage with him with her eyes open and she had known she would have to be a nurse and was willing. He'd growled at her to bring him two pounds of beef or anything that he could chew.

He'd left the house after that and returned when Jess was scrubbing Samuel down in a tub set before the fire in Alex's room. Sam had decided to play with the new piglets and the sow had chased the terrified boy through several feet of mud and manure until Nick had pulled the boy out by his collar. Nick had comforted a crying Eleanor while Jess dumped buckets of water over Sam before taking him inside and giving him a proper bath.

Alex stood in the doorway and gaped at her for a moment, then turned his back. "Jessica, you are indecent."

She glanced down at her wet, clinging underwear. "I didn't want to get my dress wet. Alex, you have to get over your shyness. We did get married, you know. Sam, stand still so I can dry you. Alex, do I remind you of when you were a man?"

He whirled to face her. "I'm a man now. God, Jess, you look—" Sam launched himself into Alex's arms, his damp arms hugging Alex with all his might. Alex smiled and hugged the nude little boy back, nuzzling his damp neck. "For once, Sam, you smell good. You want me to read to you?"

Sam laughed in answer.

Jess took the boy. "I'll put him down before he has an accident on your fine coat."

"Jess, please cover up. There are men about the house."

"Ah yes. Sorry. I'm not used to a house full of men."

Minutes later she was back, bending over, cleaning out the tub.

"Jess," Alex asked. "What would you do if you'd married your Raider?"

She paused in scrubbing. "Help him. I'd know where he was going to be when and I'd be there to cover his back. I'd ride with him."

"What if he refused to let you know where he was going to be?"

She grinned. "Oh, he'd tell me. I could persuade him."

"Yes, I believe you could. Then when he was shot at, you'd be there too, is that right?"

"You take the bad with the good."

"Jess, I'm glad you didn't marry the Raider."

Jessica didn't answer.

Three days after the Montgomery wedding, nearly everyone in town was standing on the wharf, their eyes turned up toward the admiral and his soldiers, who were standing on the bow of a ship.

For a full minute after the announcement, no one could speak. Everyone just stood there, mouth open, and blinked in disbelief. The admiral had announced that three of Warbrooke's young men would be taken away to serve in His Majesty's honor. All three of the men were big, strapping, healthy young men, all three were intelligent and had an air of independence about them.

One of the young men was Ethan Ledbetter.

"He thinks he's sending the Raider away," Jessica said under her breath.

The next moment the air was split with Abigail's screams. Everyone turned to see Ethan put his strong arms around Abby and lead her away.

Jessica started to follow them, but Alex caught her arm.

"Leave them," Alex said, pulling her away.

She struggled to free herself, but Alex held her fast as he forcibly guided her away from the crowd and toward the forest.

"Alex, will you stop mothering me? I want to go to Abigail."

"For what reason? Jess, you're to keep your nose out of this. The admiral thinks he has the Raider or he's sure the Raider will try to rescue the men."

She jerked out of Alex's grip. "And the Raider *will* rescue the men. Everyone in town knows that."

Alex rolled his eyes, his hands in fists at his sides. "Jess, the admiral will have twenty soldiers guarding those three. Not even your Raider can attack against odds like that."

Jess smiled at him in a patronizing way. "Alex, cowardly men don't know what it's like to not be cowardly. The Raider will be bound by honor to save those three."

"Honor? What about blood? The red kind that gets spilled when a man's shot or stabbed."

Jess turned on her heel. "I have no time to talk to you. You'd never understand."

He grabbed her arm and spun her around to face him. "I understand more than you do. You're so overwhelmed by the romance of the Raider that you can't see the consequences. And as for being a coward, let me point out that *I* have repeatedly saved your hide."

Jessica leaned forward until she was nose to nose with Alex. He was actually several inches taller than she but he slouched so badly that they were usually about the same height. "The Raider will be there. I *know* he will. He could never allow such an injustice to be carried out. Twenty men, a hundred men, a thousand—they're all the same to him. He doesn't think about his own safety. He puts others before himself. He can dance before the enemy because he knows he has right on his side. Alex! Are you all right? Sit down here. You look a little pale."

Alex sat down on a tree stump, and Jess, worried about him, touched his cheek. He pulled her to him and placed his head on her breast. "Does he mean so much to you?"

"He means so much to the town. Without him we'd have no hope. Someday maybe all of us will have the courage to stand up against the English, but today there's just a select few of us." She was holding him to her, stroking his back as if he were a child.

"Us?" Alex asked. "I thought only your Raider was standing up for America, that *he* was the only one braving the English bullets."

"Alex, don't start getting jealous again."

"Jealous?" He moved his head so he could look at her but he kept her upper arms pinned down. "My *wife* rhapsodizes about another man, a man who is bigger than life, a man who makes the gods on Mount Olympus seem like cowards and you tell me not to be jealous."

"Alex, you're hurting me."

"Good!" He stood, still gripping her arms. "This little pain is nothing to what you'll feel if you expand on that 'we' and try to involve yourself in freeing those men."

"I never said I'd—ouch! Alex, let go of me."

"So help me, I'll have a leash forged for your neck if you do anything stupid."

She started to tell him she'd do as she pleased but the look in his eye stopped her. "Sometimes you're quite like Adam."

Immediately, Alex slumped down to the stump again and pulled her to him, hiding his blazing eyes from her view. "Swear to me, Jessica. Swear you won't involve yourself."

"Alex, I can't—"

She stopped because he was squeezing her so hard she couldn't breathe.

"Jess, I couldn't bear for anything to happen to you."

Jess was completely surprised by this and she lifted his face to look at him. "Alex, why did you ask me to marry you?"

"Because I love you," he said simply.

"Oh." She let him put his head back on her breast. Two men loved her, one a virile, handsome devil who refused to marry her, and now Alex said he loved her, and Alex was everything the Raider was not: where the Raider used brawn, Alex used brains.

"Alex," she said softly, "I won't do anything foolish. I won't get hurt. The Raider will—"

"Hell!" Alex stood, again glaring at her. "He'll not be able to help you. He's going to be shot to death by the hundred soldiers guarding the draftees. Who's going to save your precious town if the Raider is full of holes?"

She stepped away from him. "Alex, your love for me doesn't excuse this disgusting display of jealousy.

At least *I* can think of something grander and bigger than a single life. America needs—release me."

Alex was pulling her out of the forest and back to the road. "You're not leaving my sight until your precious Ethan is out of town."

"Ethan! You're jealous of him too? *Still?* After what you did to that poor man? Alex, I think you have an odd idea of what constitutes love."

"And you don't know anything about death. I'm going to save you no matter how hard you work to thwart me. Now come along and we'll find you something to keep you busy."

"Jessica, are you listening?" Abigail Wentworth asked, her voice angry, her eyes sunken and dark from worry.

Jess straightened in her chair. It had been two days since the admiral's announcement of the draft and during that time, she had worked about twenty hours each day. Alex had suddenly become very ill and she'd had to tend to his needs as well as run the disorganized Montgomery household. Plus, Alex had given her household accounts from the years he'd been at sea to verify. She'd run from fetching a book for Alex to directing a bondswoman in scouring a floor, to climbing onto the roof because Alex was sure there was a leaky place, to trying to add columns of fifty numbers while Alex talked to her.

When the invitation to tea had come from Mrs. Wentworth, there had been words. Alex's health had immediately returned in such vigorous form that Eleanor had come to tell them their shouting was drawing a crowd outside.

After she'd threatened to run away in the middle of the night, Alex had relented and let Jess visit Mrs.

Wentworth. After all, the old lady was highly respectable, wasn't she? And what trouble could Jess get into attending a tea party?

"There he is again," Abigail said, looking out the window.

Jess looked out to see Alex walking past—for the fourth time in the last thirty minutes. She held up her teacup and waved to him.

"How can you bear it?" Abigail said in a melodramatic tone. "How can you bear to be married to that . . . that glittering, lazy—"

"Leave Alex out of this!" Jess snapped. "He may not be much to look at but he's a good man. And now he's only concerned about my safety. Ethan may have the muscle, but Alex's little finger is smarter than—"

"Are we going to waste time while you two compare husbands?" Mrs. Wentworth snapped. "We have work to do and not much time. Jess, I like your idea of the gypsies."

"Women can always distract men, especially soldiers a long way from home."

"The Raider will save him," Abigail said.

"And get himself shot," Jessica said. "There'll be many men guarding Ethan and the others and they'll be on the lookout for the Raider. You two need to distract the soldiers while I release the men."

Abigail smiled. "Oh, I can distract them all right. Mother has made me a delightful costume. When Ethan sees it, he'll—"

Jessica could not tolerate one more reference to Ethan's virility. It had been much too long since she'd been alone with the Raider. She set her cup down with a click. "Let's just hope the soldiers are interested." She couldn't help giving a glance toward Abby's thickening waist. Married so recently and already with child. Jess refused to let herself think that she'd probably never have a child. At least not Alex's child. No! She wasn't going to think about the way he'd told her to get out of his bed. He had said he couldn't sleep with her near him and he wanted her as far away as possible. Alex's idea of love was quite different from hers.

"I'd better go," Jess said as she stood. "Alex will be in here in another couple of minutes. You'll have everything sewn by tomorrow night?"

Mrs. Wentworth put her hand on Jess's arm. "I knew we could count on you, Jessica. The rest of this town may be willing to sit back and wait for the Raider to save them, but I knew I had to do something."

"And, too, we knew you had to hate the admiral as much as we do since he'd made you marry Alexander," Abigail said.

Jessica clamped her jaws together over a nasty retort. "Do you hate Alex because he tricked Ethan into marrying you?"

Abigail's face changed to an expression of love. "I guess I owe Alex a favor."

"Will you be able to get away?" Mrs. Wentworth asked Jess.

"That's going to be the hardest part. I might get Alex's father to help."

"Sayer? He wouldn't go behind his own son's back, would he?"

Jessica frowned. "Mr. Montgomery is . . . disappointed in his youngest son and he's very interested in what is being done to us by the English."

Mrs. Wentworth nodded. "Go on now, there's Alexander again. You know, dear, there's more to marriage than what happens at night. Alex seems to care very much about your welfare."

Jess looked out the window to see a scowling Alex

starting up the porch steps. "Yes, he does. I'll meet you tomorrow night at ten o'clock. Have everything ready." She left the house, opening the door just as Alex raised his hand to the door knocker.

"What did you talk about?" Alex demanded.

"Good afternoon, Jessica," Jess mocked. "Did you have a good time? Were the cakes fresh?" She looked at him. "We're planning to single-handedly overthrow the English government and start our own rule. What do you *think* someone talks to Mrs. Wentworth about? She showed me some silk she'd bought, she complained about the servants and told me what a delightful houseguest the admiral is." Jessica was amazed at how easy the lie was. Probably because it was for a good cause, she decided.

Alex squinted his eyes at her, as if he were trying to decide whether or not to believe her. He pulled her arm through his. "Come on, let's get home. There's work to be done."

Jessica groaned. "Alex, couldn't we take a walk together? Down to Farrier's Cove maybe."

Alex looked at her hair, her face, held her fingers against his arm and thought of the secluded, private little cove. "I'd never survive that," he said and started toward the house.

Jessica went with him, wondering how bad his health really was. She was becoming rather attached to this man. In fact, there were times when she thought he was handsome.

Alex removed the heavy satin coat and hung it on a peg on his bedroom wall. He glanced at his watch before putting it on the chest by the window. Three minutes after midnight. His father had insisted he play chess with him until this hour, ignoring Alex's many hints that he'd like to go to bed. The past few days of following Jessica had nearly exhausted him. He was constantly on the alert, sure that she was going to do something utterly foolish, and he'd not been able to slip away to Ghost Island for some exercise. Also, being around Jessica so much, the way she constantly touched him, the way she bent and moved, all of it so unconscious on her part but so very exciting to him, was wrecking his health. He'd had to throw her out of his bed just so he could get some sleep.

All in all, he didn't know how much longer he could withstand his agony. But every time he decided he had to tell her he was the Raider, something would happen, like Ethan Ledbetter being sent off to serve in the King's Navy. Then Alex saw the light in Jess's eyes, that light of the crusader, and knew that if she knew she was so close to—and had so much power over—the Raider, he'd never be able to deny her anything. He had a sickening vision of Jessica tearing across the countryside wearing black, her hair flowing behind her. The English would arrest her within minutes.

So for days since the announcement of the conscription, he'd not let her out of his sight except to comfort Mrs. Wentworth and Abigail. He'd not wanted to do that, but Jess had asked so nicely and had leaned forward so far that her scarf had gaped open. He'd said yes before he had known what he was doing.

With a grimace, he remembered her saying that she could persuade the Raider to do whatever she wanted. Alex didn't like to think of what Jess would try to get away with if she knew she were married to the Raider.

He removed his vest and started to unbutton his shirt when he thought he'd better check on Jessica. She'd been asleep when his father had asked to see him. This morning Jess and Sayer had spent two hours closeted together and, twice, the household had heard Sayer's voice raised in protest.

When Jessica had left the room, she'd looked somewhat subdued but with a light of triumph in her eyes. Later, Alex had been asked to play chess with his father. Alex had been angered at the invitation. Jess, it seemed, had spent two hours trying to persuade a father to spend time with his own son.

Alex had wanted to refuse the invitation, but instead he'd worn his biggest wig, his pink satin coat and an emerald ring on his little finger. Just before entering his father's room, Alex had borrowed a heart-shaped patch from Marianna and stuck it on his chin just to the left of his mouth. Marianna had looked ready to cry when Alex had turned toward her.

Alex had had new resolve when he'd entered his father's room. For the four hours he had been in there, he hadn't spoken much, just won game after game from his father. His father might have thought he wasn't manly, but he now had no doubt as to his son's intelligence.

He put his hand on the connecting door leading to Jessica's room and found it locked. Immediately, he knew something was wrong. He was out his window in a minute and found the window to her room standing open. It took only seconds to see that her room was empty.

For a moment he cursed his father for inadvertently allowing Jess to escape; he cursed the Raider; he cursed Nick for bringing him back to America; he cursed Jessica; he cursed himself; he cursed the importers of black cloth. And when he was only halfway through, he began to run. He had to row to Ghost Island, change, and then the Raider had to save Jessica.

Chapter Seventeen

"G ET that relic out of here," the young soldier yelled. Behind him, half a dozen men began to wake.

The old woman, lines on her face, her once-gaudy clothes smelling of long-dead fish, climbed down from the wagon, her hand to her back as if in pain. "You wouldn't deny an old woman a little warmth, would you?"

"You can't stay here. We're under orders of His Majesty the king."

The old woman pushed the barrel of the man's gun out of the way and walked toward the fire, her hands stretched out toward its warmth.

The young man opened his mouth to protest, but just then, stepping down from the wagon, was a heavenly vision of a creature: a buxom beauty whose breasts were tumbling out of a loosely cut blouse.

"My goodness," said the young woman, clutching her breasts and pushing them up while she adjusted the front of her garment.

By now all the men in the camp were awake and most of them on their feet.

The young woman tried to climb out of the wagon but her skirt caught and, to free herself, she had to lift the hem above her knees. By the time she was ready to get out of the wagon, every man except the two on guard duty was standing beneath her, arms raised to help her down.

"How kind you are," the young woman said modestly, looking down at her audience. "But I believe you said my mother and I must leave."

With a loud wail of protest, the men looked toward the young captain who was their commanding officer. But the light in the captain's eyes was as bright as in his men's. He stepped forward.

"We have meager warmth and coarse food, but it is yours."

Abigail allowed herself to be helped down by the young officer, her breasts just grazing his face as she slid down his body until her feet touched the ground.

Jessica stood in the shadows and watched the little drama, played in the center of the glow of the firelight. For a few moments she was as fascinated as the men by the performance. Abigail genuinely loved her role.

As Jessica watched, Abby leaned forward at every opportunity, her loose blouse gaping, the men stupefied in their positions, unable to move a muscle. Jess had never realized a woman could have such power over men.

Jessica, fading into the shadows in the black garment Mrs. Wentworth had made her, waited until she heard the first strains of music. Mrs. Wentworth had loaded several musical instruments inside the old wagon. Her plan was to get the men involved as thoroughly as possible so Jessica could free the prisoners.

"I'll kill her," Jess heard a man to her left say. It was Ethan's voice and he was watching his wife's first undulations as she started to dance.

"Quiet!" the guard commanded Ethan.

Jess prayed Ethan wouldn't give the game away. It was too early yet, before the men were absorbed in Abby's dance, but Jess slipped through the shadows behind the three men staked by the big oak tree. Easily, she made it safely to the oak tree and the first man whose ropes she touched had sense enough to keep his eyes on Abigail's lascivious dance. The only sign he gave that he was free was a brief nod of his head. The second man was just as easy to untie.

But Ethan was another matter. He was straining against the ropes so hard as he watched his wife dance that the ropes were tightly knotted. Jessica removed a knife from her boot and began sawing.

Perhaps it was a movement from Ethan or maybe she moved too quickly, but something alerted a guard. The soldier turned and saw a flash of moonlight on the knife blade. The two men who were free moved quickly, one of them using his doubled fists to hit the soldier's head. One man caught him before he hit the ground.

"I knew you'd come," one of the men whispered. The music and the soldiers' cheering were getting louder.

Jessica stayed in the shadow of the tree, still sawing at Ethan's ropes. The men thought she was the Raider. "Go," she said in her deepest voice.

Eagerly, the men slipped away into the darkness.

"Jessica Taggert!" Ethan whispered over his shoulder. "I should have known it was you. You're the instigator of this, aren't you?"

She paused in surprise.

"Don't stop, cut them!" Ethan hissed. "I can tell a woman from a man any day." He looked back at Abigail jumping over flaming sticks a couple of men were holding. "I'm going to kill her."

"She's doing this for you," Jess hissed back. "There!"

The moment he was free, Ethan slipped away into the darkness. Jess stayed where she was, ready if she were needed to stop Ethan from doing something foolish.

Her attention was on Abigail and she didn't see the soldier on the ground. He was on her, pinning her body down before she was aware that he was awake. She rolled away from the knife he held but not before it had grazed her side. As she rolled, the man's hand came in contact with her breast.

"A woman," he gasped and the next moment he had his legs between hers and his hot, wet mouth on hers.

Jessica struggled but the man was too strong for her. He pinned her hands while he fumbled with his pants.

Then, suddenly, he was still.

Jessica was still struggling when she felt the man roll off of her—or, more correctly, being pushed off of her. She blinked in the darkness to see the Raider standing over her, sword drawn.

He didn't say a word as he offered her his hand and pulled her to stand before him. She could see the hard glitter of his eyes behind his mask.

"I . . . we . . ." she began.

He caught her hand and began pulling her toward his horse.

Jess put her hand to her side and felt the bleeding but she wasn't going to complain to him.

He half helped, half shoved her onto his horse, then mounted behind her and started galloping.

As they rode, the cool wind in her face began to revive her. Here she was, riding in the moonlight, the man she loved seated behind her, his strong arms surrounding hers. It was an exhilarating moment—yet she felt strangely unsettled. Something was worrying her and she wasn't sure what. It had been a successful raid, that is, if Abby and Mrs. Wentworth got home, but still something was wrong.

She twisted in the saddle, gasping at the pain in her side. "Stop!" she demanded. "You have to stop."

The Raider looked at her face in the dim light and pulled his horse to a halt. Immediately, his lips were on hers, kissing her face, her eyes.

"No, please," she whispered, all the while leaning her head back to give him access to her neck. "Where are you taking me?"

"Home. To our home. To Farrier's Cove, where we can make love all night long. And then I plan to tan your hide for doing such a damn fool thing as—"

"No, please, I don't want to fight with you."

"I don't plan to fight, Jessie, my love."

"You have to take me home."

"I *am* taking you home."

"No, I mean home to Alexander."

As she held him, the Raider felt as if a piece of steel had just shot through his spine, and his voice was as rigid as his body. "Alexander? You want to go home to that lace-encrusted, whining, cowardly ass after I just saved your life?"

Jessica felt as if she were being torn in half. She wanted to go with the Raider, even though she knew it would be an argument whether or not she slept with him, and, heaven help her, she wanted to lose the argument, but at the same time she knew she needed to go home to Alex.

"He's not been well and if he finds that I'm gone, he'll be upset."

The Raider's eyes bore into hers. "Jess, are you in love with this man?"

"Alexander? I should think not. It's just that he gets upset and his heart isn't what it should be. Please take me to him." Jess could feel the blood trickling down her side. Maybe it was her wound that was making her do this strange thing. Right now, the last thing she wanted was to wrestle with the Raider. What she wanted was Alexander to take care of her.

The Raider dismounted behind her, then lifted her to the ground. "I believe you know your way back," he said coolly. "I pray no one encounters you in that disguise." With that, he turned his horse and left her.

Jess caught her breath against the pain in her side. It was a two mile walk to the Montgomery house and she dreaded it. Each movement opened the wound again, and she could feel blood slowly flowing down her side.

The Raider had let her down at the head of an old Indian path that would lead her to the back of the Montgomery house. She walked and stumbled, rested against a tree, then walked some more.

There were tears of relief in her eyes when she saw the Montgomery house, and the window to her bedroom standing open.

It was difficult for her to enter and she was only halfway in when she saw Alex sitting there, his eyes on fire with rage.

"You'll never leave this room again, so help me God," he began. "I'll chain you, I'll starve you, I'll—"

"Alex, help me, I'm hurt," she managed to say and then fell forward into the room.

He caught her before she hit the floor and carried her to the bed.

"Alex," she whispered.

Alex didn't respond, as he was tearing the clothes off her.

"Just like the Raider," she said, smiling and at last feeling safe.

He left her, bare from the waist up, went to his room and returned with a lantern, clean bandages and a water basin. He'd removed his coat. Tenderly, he began to clean the wound at her side.

"Are you mad at me, Alex?" she asked, wincing at the pain.

He moved her to her side and washed blood from her back, her ribs, her hip.

"Alex, we *had* to do it. We couldn't let those men be taken. The admiral'd start taking *all* the men. He'd probably want Nathaniel next."

Alex just kept cleaning and didn't answer her.

"You do see, don't you? It went just as we planned. We had no problems at all." She halted at a sound outside. "What was that?"

"A shot," Alex said curtly, then pushed her on her back. For all his obvious anger, he was very gentle. He lifted her upper body and began wrapping her ribs.

"Alex, at least you can admire our plan. Mrs. Wentworth was dressed—" She stopped when Alex turned away from her to fetch a clean nightgown from a chest.

"Alex, at least say *something*. You certainly seemed to have a lot to say when I first came in."

He pulled the nightgown down over her head, laid her back on the bed, picked up her feet and began to undress the lower half of her.

"Alex, I don't think it's very kind of you to not speak to me. The Raider came at the very end of our raid and he wanted me to go away with him, but I wanted to come back here to you."

He gave her a look she didn't understand at all, pulled the blanket over her, picked up the lantern and bloody basin, then left the room. He shut the door behind him.

Jessica lay in the dark a moment, too astonished to think. Her first thought was, What does it matter if Alexander is angry with me? She had done something that would help a whole town.

She thought back over how well the plan had gone. Then she remembered the way she'd lied to Alex about what she'd been talking about to Abby and Mrs. Wentworth.

She remembered freeing the three men, men who'd been imprisoned by the tyranny of the English. Then she thought of Alex saying that he loved her and cared about her.

She thought of the way the Raider had saved her.

But she remembered it was Alexander who she knew would take care of her wound. There were some men who were full of passion and excitement, but there were other men who took care of you when you were sick.

Holding her side stiffly so it wouldn't bleed again, she went to the connecting door and opened it. Her hand was trembling.

Alex, his sleeves rolled to the elbows, was sitting in a chair set before a window, smoking a long cigar, his eyes fixed straight ahead. He didn't turn when Jess entered. Even when she placed herself between him and the window, he didn't look at her.

"Alex, I really am sorry," she said softly. "It was something I felt had to be done. Can't you understand that? Sometimes a person can't think of anything except what needs to be done. I didn't mean to get hurt. I didn't want to disobey you and make you worry. Your father tried to talk me out of going but I had to do it. Can't you understand?" She was pleading with him to understand. He was like Eleanor, so hurt because she hadn't done what was expected of her.

"Please, Alex," she whispered.

At long last, he looked up at her.

Jessica saw the pain in his eyes and the hurt she'd caused him. This man's feelings were as delicate as his body.

"Alex." She held out her hands to him.

With a look of resignation—and what Jess recognized as forgiveness—he held out his arms to her.

She climbed into his lap as if she were a little girl. Somewhere along the way, Alex had become her friend. He wasn't her lover, wasn't actually her husband, but he was her friend. For all his blustering and shouting at her, she'd known he would take care of her. "It was awful, Alex. I was so scared. My hands were shaking so badly I could hardly cut Ethan's ropes. Have you heard anything? What about Abigail and Mrs. Wentworth? You should have seen Abby dance!"

Alex was holding her as tightly as he could without reinjuring her wound. "Eleanor went to the Wentworth house. The admiral pounded on Mrs. Wentworth's bedroom door and Eleanor answered."

"Eleanor?" Jess gasped. "But I didn't tell her what I was planning to do. I didn't dare since she's bossier than you are."

"She is a woman of intelligence and common sense, which is more than I can say for you."

"I came home to you, didn't I? I knew the Raider couldn't help me, so I came home to you."

"So I could patch you back together," Alex said softly.

"Oh, Alex, don't get your feelings hurt. The Raider wanted me to go with him but I turned him down."

Alex's mouth drew into a line. "You turned him down because he doesn't carry a ready supply of bandages for when you do something as stupidly foolish as tonight. Do you have any idea how the admiral is retaliating?"

"No," she said hesitantly.

"One of the soldiers was killed, by your Raider I presume, so he's determined to find the killer. He said the dead man had a bloody knife in his hand. He thinks the blood is from the Raider, while I foolishly assumed it was Ethan's. To find the killer, he's marching all the young men of town to city hall and forcing them to undress. He'll kill any man who has a fresh knife wound."

"And the women?" Jess asked.

"All the English soldiers swear they can identify the gypsy women."

Jessica began to stiffen. "Alex, if they find out about Abigail and Mrs. Wentworth . . ."

"Perhaps you should have thought of that before you foolishly ran off into the woods and nearly got yourself killed. Now, as much as I love holding you, I want you to sleep."

"Where are you going?"

"To see what I can do to help."

Jessica got off his lap. "Alex, you should rest. Your health—"

He didn't allow her to finish as he leaned forward, and nose to nose, spoke to her through teeth clamped shut. *"Now* you worry about my health? You talk my own father into plotting against me, you put me through hell as I sit here all night waiting for you, and then you come home with an open, bleeding wound and now you tell me someone *else* might endanger my health? The English army is nothing compared to the misery you cause me, Jessica Taggert."

"Montgomery," she said softly. "You married me, remember?"

Alex leaned away from her. "I may have married you, but I didn't change you. Now, I want you to listen to me. I want you to climb into bed and get some sleep. I'll tell the household you're ill and Eleanor is to take care of you."

"Alex, wait. Won't the admiral want to speak to me? I know he thinks whoever freed the men was a man, but he might think I was the dancer."

Alex gave the front of her nightgown a pointed look. "There are some things a woman can't fake. You'll not be questioned." With that, he left the room.

Jess looked down at the front of her gown and realized that, compared to Abigail, she was flat-chested. With a frown, she climbed into Alex's bed. What did it matter what Alex thought of her physically? He couldn't do anything anyway.

Chapter Eighteen

J ESSIE."

Jessica refused to listen to the calls around her. She was sure they were her imagination. She was sure because no one in the world seemed to be still speaking to her after the raid two days ago. Alex was so angry he just looked at her from under black brows drawn together in a scowl. Eleanor lectured her without pause and Nathaniel crawled into her lap and begged her not to get killed. Jess didn't know how Nate knew about her escapade but he did.

So, once again, Eleanor had sent her out to do children's chores—and to think about what she'd done to her family.

Also, Eleanor wanted to keep Jess from hearing the anger of the people of Warbrooke. The admiral was taking his fury out on the shipmasters. He'd already confiscated two shiploads of goods.

Today Jessica had stolen a few minutes to visit Mrs. Wentworth. The admiral had refused to allow Abigail to be interrogated. "Abby's told him she's glad Ethan is gone, that she was made to marry the man, and that she actually prefers older men," Mrs. Wentworth said. "The old walrus believes every word she says and as long as Ethan stays hidden in the forests, Abby can keep up the charade."

"At least it's keeping her skin intact. How is Mr. Wentworth?"

Mrs. Wentworth turned pale.

"It's that way at my house, too. Oh, no, here comes Alex."

The two women parted quickly.

Jessica had nearly run to Farrier's Cove. Eleanor had thought that a day of fishing might clear her head and keep her out of trouble.

"Jessie."

She spun about on her heel to see the Raider standing in the shadows near the steep bank.

She held her clam shovel out toward him as if it were a weapon. "Don't you come near me. This is all your fault. If you hadn't come to Warbrooke, none of this would have happened."

"Oh?" the Raider asked, lounging against the bank. "You don't think that by now John Pitman wouldn't have stolen everything in town?"

"Hallelujah, you've replaced Pitman with Admiral Westmoreland. That's like replacing a naughty boy with the devil."

"Jessie, you really can't believe I'm completely to blame. If you hadn't interfered, I'd have been hanged by the British weeks ago. And releasing Ethan had nothing to do with me. I wasn't planning to try to save those men."

"That's what Alex said," she said with some bitterness in her voice. "He said you wouldn't interfere."

"Coward, am I?" the Raider asked, his fine lips slightly smiling.

She turned her attention to the beach, looking for clams' air holes. "I never thought you were a coward, but rescuing Ethan and the others had to be done."

"Did it? Abigail couldn't go without her virile young man for a few months? Ethan couldn't have stood a little time in the navy?"

"We had to show the admiral that we won't be taken advantage of. We're not children of the English. We're—"

"You're not using your brain, that's what. Now the admiral is very angry and he plans to punish Warbrooke any way he can."

"Brain! What do you know of brains? Alex said—"

"*Damn* that husband of yours." He took a few steps closer to her and pulled her into his arms, then kissed her until she felt her body weaken. "Does he make you feel like that? Does he make you cry out in passion?"

"Please leave me alone," she said, turning her head away. "Please don't torture me like this."

"I don't torture you any more than you torture me," he said with feeling. "You haunt my every moment, you fill my every—"

She pushed away from him. "Yet you let me marry another man," she spat at him.

"Not an actual man, but a—"

"You leave Alexander out of this."

The Raider's eyes, glittering behind his mask, showed his surprise. "You had me take you home to him. I'm losing you to a rainbow—all color and no substance."

"Alexander has more substance than you know about. He took on me and the kids. He never loses patience with them, he reads to them, sings to them, bandages their wounds and mine. He gets mad at me when I nearly get killed. He—"

"Does he sleep with you?"

"Heavens no!" she gasped before thinking. "I mean, Alex is my friend."

The Raider took her arms, his fingers caressing her skin. "But you sound as if you want to sleep with him."

"Please let me go," she said pleadingly, not knowing if she could continue resisting. "I'm a married woman."

"Yes." His lips were a breath away from hers. "But you're married to a man who can't give you what I can. Let me make love to you, Jessie. Let me make you feel like the woman you are. Forget that peacock you married."

She tried to push away from him. "You're jealous of Alexander."

"Of course I am. He has you all day, while I only have you for minutes at a time. How do his kisses compare to mine?"

"Alexander doesn't kiss me," she murmured. "Only you do."

He pulled away from her, his eyes open wide in surprise. "He doesn't kiss you? But you want to kiss him, don't you? You *want* to go to bed with him, don't you?"

Jess straightened the front of her dress. "You are losing your mind. Alexander is my friend. I'd as soon let Eleanor make love to me. I'd get about as much pleasure from a woman as from Alexander," she muttered. "Please go away and leave me alone. I don't want to see you anymore."

The Raider stood there, hands at his side, his mouth slightly open, as if he'd heard some horrible news.

Jess looked toward the bank. "Go! Someone's coming. It may be Alex."

The Raider seemed to recover himself. "Maybe your husband has been meeting another woman."

"Now I know your brain is addled. He couldn't even get a woman to *marry* him, much less go to bed with him. Go! Or do you want to be caught?"

The Raider was over the side of the bank within seconds.

It was only a deer on the side of the cove, but Jessica was glad that something had made the Raider leave. She knew she wasn't going to be able to resist him much longer. Just the sight of him made her body start to vibrate. It had been so very long since a man had held her.

She jabbed at a clam hole. A real man, that is, one who was capable of pleasing her body as well as her mind. She felt a little guilty having told the Raider about Alex but she felt torn between the two men. She was physically faithful to both of them. She wasn't an adulteress and betraying Alex, nor was she sleeping with her husband and thereby betraying the Raider.

"I'm without," she said aloud. "Without either man." She jabbed harder at the clam hole.

"Will you stop shouting at me?" Jessica yelled at Eleanor. "I told you. I haven't done anything to Alexander. At least not anything new. I took him his food, I even cut it up for him. I don't know how to be nicer to him. I even told him he looked very nice, that his coat made his cheeks pink and pretty. What else can I do for him?"

"Why is he brooding, then?"

"I don't know. He won't talk to me about his health. Do you think he's in pain?"

"Only what pain you've caused him."

"Me? I haven't done—"

They were interrupted by the door bursting open and Marianna entering, her face flushed, her eyes alight. "Have you heard? There's an Italian ship docking and someone said Adam might be on it."

"Adam?" Jessica gasped.

"Oh yes," Marianna sighed, her eyes closed in ecstasy for a moment. "My eldest brother. Adam the fighter. Adam the handsome. Adam who has come to save us."

"The English will burn our town to the ground if anyone else 'saves' us," Eleanor said.

Jessica looked down at her old, worn dress. "I can't meet Adam looking like this. I wish I had a dress as beautiful as Alex's red coat. Don't just stand there, Marianna, your hair is a mess."

"Yes, yes, of course." She started down the hall.

"Don't tell Alex you're dressing up for—" Eleanor called, but Jessica was already gone. "Adam," she finished and then put her hand to her own head. Perhaps she should have a look at herself before the famous Adam returned.

Jessica opened the door to Alex's room with eagerness on her face.

Alex shut his book. "What's happened?"

"Nothing." Jess was digging in a trunk in a corner of the room. "Oh, Alex, I wish you'd bought me a red dress like you promised."

Alex was out of the chair in seconds and grabbed

her arms. "Are you meeting the Raider?" he asked, his eyes hard.

"I don't have time for your jealousy now. Marianna says a ship has come from Italy and Adam might be on it."

"Adam? My brother Adam?"

"Yes, of course that Adam. Alex, go tell your father."

"Tell him that Adam the perfect will be here soon?"

She shut the trunk. "Alexander, would you please tell me what is wrong with you? You've been biting my head off for days."

"But that's the only thing of yours I bite, isn't it, my chaste little wife?"

Her face softened. "So that's it. You're remembering when you were a man. Alex, I swear to you that I won't sleep with the Raider or Adam or anyone else. There's no reason for you to be jealous. Have you seen that blue fan that belonged to your mother?"

"You're wearing *satin* to meet my brother? You're going down to the dirty, smelly wharf wearing a satin dress?"

She counted to ten to calm herself. "Alex, you wear satin each and every day. Now, will you help me dress?"

"Like hell I will," he said and stormed out of the room.

"Men!" Jessica said with contempt and left the room to search for a sister to help her dress.

By the time the ship docked, most of Warbrooke was there to greet the oldest Montgomery son— but he wasn't on board. The captain had never heard of Adam Montgomery and had no news of him.

As a group, the faces of the crowd fell.

Jessica moved away from Alex three times because she couldn't bear his jealous mutterings. Of course, she did feel sorry for Alex because his brother would get the attention Alex should have received. No one was going to laugh at Adam. A disappointed Jess watched as the sailors brought twenty-three leather-bound trunks down the gangplank, followed by three maids.

"Perhaps I should go back so my father can cry on my shoulder," Alex was saying in her ear. "Or maybe you feel like crying."

Jessica was about to say something to her husband when they heard a woman's pretty voice call.

"Alexander? Is that you?"

Alex looked past Jess, then his lips curved into a smile of delight. "Sophy," he whispered.

"Alexander, it is you."

Jess turned to see a tiny, exquisite, dark-haired woman with a pretty face shaded under a pink, frilled bonnet. She was looking at Alex with anticipation, laughter on her pretty lips.

"Alex, I barely recognized you. Whatever are you doing wearing that wig? And why are standing that way? And that coat—"

She didn't finish because Alex took her in his arms and kissed her to silence.

That effectively brought the crowd to a halt.

"What a welcome," Sophy murmured.

"Play along with me. Whatever happens, play along with me," Alex whispered. He pulled away from her.

Jessica was looking at the two of them with great curiosity. Alex had certainly never kissed her like that. Not that she'd ever wanted him to, but she'd never tried to stop him either.

"Jessica," Alex said, "this is the Countess Tatalini and, Sophy, this is my wife. Sophy and I knew each other before my fever."

"Fever? Alex are you ill? Is that why you're dressed—"

Alex put his arm around her waist and squeezed hard. "I'm no longer ill but I have been. Jess, could you get some of these layabouts to carry the countess's luggage? You are staying with us, aren't you?"

"Why, no, I'm on my way to—"

"We won't hear of it, will we, Jess?"

Jessica didn't say a word but looked from one to the other.

"Jess?" Alex asked. "We would love to have the countess as our guest, wouldn't we?"

Jess still didn't answer but kept looking at the way the countess was curving her body into Alex's. She didn't seem to mind at all that he was fat, that he slouched, that the color in his cheeks was probably rouge.

"Jessica," Alex said in a familiar whine, "you have to help me. I feel my strength going. Could you help with the baggage while the countess supports me?"

"It's nice to meet you," Jessica said at last. "And we have plenty of room for you. I'll get the luggage."

Alex leaned heavily on Sophy and she didn't say a word until they were in a room in the Montgomery house. Then she turned on him.

"I demand that you tell me what is going on." She reached forward and snatched the wig off his head. "I thought for a moment you'd shaved it. Alex, whatever have you gotten yourself into now?"

Smiling, running his hands through his hair, Alex sat down in a chair. "Sophy, you don't know how good it is to hear that question. You can't imagine how wonderful it is to hear a woman accuse me of not being what I appear."

"I'm glad you're happy." The countess was tapping

her small foot impatiently. "Alex, you may be receiving pleasure, but I am not. I am supposed to be in Boston in two weeks to see my husband and our children. He will be very angry if I am not there."

"Like the last time, when I climbed out on the balcony?"

Sophy smiled. "In the rain with not a stitch on. And when he was gone you were nowhere to be found. I was frantic. I thought the dogs had you. Instead—"

"A housemaid had. Could I help it if she felt pity for me? And then I had to show her my gratitude. Of course, since I had no clothes on, I fear my gratitude was self-evident."

"You!" she said but she was laughing. "My husband will never believe what I say if he finds out I've been here with you."

"With me and my wife and a house full of the nosiest people on earth."

"That wife of yours is a beauty, a little slow perhaps, but what does that matter in a woman? Her beauty is what counts. Is she why you're dressed like that? Alex, that disgusting thing isn't actually your belly is it?"

Alex stroked the protuberance fondly. "It's cotton, a little string, a pistol and knife and not much me." He glanced at the door as he heard a sound. "It's Jess." He grabbed the wig, slammed it on his head in a practiced gesture, then slumped until he was S-shaped.

"In here," Jess said, directing men in stacking the countess's many trunks. "I thought you'd put her in your mother's room." Jess kept standing there after the trunks were stacked.

"Jessica," Alex said in a voice of great tiredness, "could you leave us? We are old friends and have so much to talk of. Perhaps you could finish the accounts of four years ago. Or see to Sophy's maids' comfort."

Jess looked from one to the other, then nodded and left the room.

Sophy turned on Alex. "Of all the—! If my husband ever spoke to me that way, I'd remove his ears and his—"

Alex bent and kissed her. "Yes, you would and so would Jess if she thought I was a man."

"A man? What does she expect from a man if *you* can't fulfill it?"

Alex kissed her again. "Sophy, you are making me feel better by the minute. Did you see the way Jessica looked at you? If you don't have to be in Boston for two weeks, then you have a few days. I'd like to ask a favor of you. I'd like you to stay here and make my wife jealous."

"You do not *try* to make a husband or wife jealous, you try to prevent it."

"But you don't know the whole story."

Sophy sat in a chair, arranging her skirts about her. "I'm an excellent listener."

"What an absolutely vile, despicable trick, Alexander Montgomery," Sophy said with passion. "That poor woman has two men after her but she doesn't have one whole one."

"She plays her own tricks. She tells the Raider she wishes he'd never come to Warbrooke and then she tells Alex the Raider is the town's only hope. She doesn't know what she wants."

"It sounds to me like she knows exactly. She loves her country, so she helps the Raider; she loves her family, so she marries a man who she thinks can help them, a man who can never make love to her. She took a vow of chastity to save her family. And you have condemned her to this. That poor, poor girl."

"She was the one who started it. I never meant to play the Raider here, but Jessica laughed at me and made everyone believe I was fat and effeminate."

"I don't blame them. You look dreadful. No wonder no woman wanted to marry you."

"You didn't believe me."

"Yes, but it wasn't long ago that you and I—" She stopped and glared at him. "What is it that you want from this girl?"

Alex took her hands. "Sophy, I love her. Maybe I've loved her forever. I know I used to see her following one of my older brothers when she was a child, then I'd play some prank on her. Everything she did enraged me. My mother thought Jessica was wonderful. She constantly told us that Jess was the strength in the Taggert family. I wanted them to know that if I were faced with a similar situation, I'd be the family's strength. But I was the baby, with a father and two older brothers. Jessica never even looked at me—no matter what I did to get her attention."

Sophy touched his cheek.

"I can't tell her I'm the Raider. She'll do something utterly stupid, I know she will."

"It seems to me she's doing that already." Sophy squinted her eyes at Alex. "What's your *real* reason for not telling her you are the Raider?"

Alex smiled and kissed her hands. "I want her to love me. Me, Alexander. I want her to love me for myself, not because I wear a black mask and ride a black horse. Jessica's love is very important to me and I want to know that it's mine. I want to know that she'll love me even when I'm too old to mount a horse. If I end up like my father, I don't want to think that my beautiful Jessica is going to go running off with the next dashing figure."

"Alex, you're asking her to love only half the man."

"I guess I am, but she did leave the Raider and come to me. Of course she was bleeding and had to get help, but it was better than nothing. But then she told the Raider she'd as soon go to bed with a woman as with me."

"Alex, you ask so much of a woman. First of your Jessica and now of me. If you want Jessica to love something other than the physical side of you, how will jealousy help?"

"Spend some time with me. Jess only comes near me when there's a child that needs attention or when she's hurt. Maybe if she saw another woman, a beautiful, intelligent, wise woman who liked to spend time with me, perhaps she'd be curious."

Sophy laughed. "I think I might love Alexander, even if she doesn't. Of course I haven't seen you as the Raider. Are you terribly dashing and romantic?"

"And fearless. There is no danger too great for the Raider to face. Except Jessica, of course. Say you'll stay and help me."

"All right." Sophy sighed. "Perhaps I feel the woman should sense that her husband is also her lover. I'll help you make your wife jealous."

Chapter Nineteen

J ESSICA," Eleanor was saying, her voice straining to remain calm, "that woman is making a fool of you."

"She's making Alex happy."

"*Very* happy. Don't you care that they spend hours locked together in his room?"

"*Our* room," Jessica snapped. "The room belonging to Alexander and me."

"Ah, then, so you *do* care."

"Eleanor, what would you do if a woman flirted with that big Russian of yours?"

"Remove any part of her body that I could reach."

Jessica played with the food on her plate. "But the countess is really such a nice lady. Yesterday she took care of Samuel all afternoon."

"And thus freed Nathaniel to get into mischief. Do you know where he got that dory?"

"What dory?" Jess asked listlessly.

Eleanor took a seat across from her sister at the table. "You *are* concerned about that woman, aren't you?"

"Absolutely not. You know Alex and I don't have a real marriage. He said he . . ."

"What?"

"He said he loved me, but I guess that was before he remembered his love for the countess."

"Jess, why don't you fight her? Why don't you go to Alex and tell him you love him and that you'll set fire to that woman's hair if she isn't out of your house in thirty seconds."

Jessica stood. "Me in love with Alex? What a preposterous idea. He whines and complains and he—"

"Saves your life and waits up for you and takes care of you and—"

"Yells at me all the time. Where's the countess now? Maybe I can get rid of her another way."

"Sitting by the kitchen garden, the last I saw. Jessica, what are you planning?"

"To help my country," she said before leaving the house.

Jessica wasn't about to let Eleanor or anyone else see how the countess's presence bothered her. When in the world had she fallen in love with Alexander? She thought love was that wild beating of the heart. Love was closer to what she felt for the Raider—or at least once she'd thought so. But lately she'd been much happier to see Alex than she'd been to see the Raider.

Twice the Raider had come to her window since the night she'd been wounded, but each time she'd felt less inclined to leave with him. She knew she'd have a wonderful night in his arms but that was all. In the morning she'd wonder what had overtaken her and she'd look forward to Alex's company.

Since Alex had returned to Warbrooke, they had spent a great deal of time together, and it seemed to Jess that she'd never cared much about Alex. At first she'd resented the way he always wanted her near him, but gradually she'd come to enjoy him. And, now that she wanted to be with him, he wasn't there.

Jess couldn't blame the countess for wanting to be with Alex—after all, he could be charming. He could read sea stories with such gusto that you felt the wind on your face, and he could read romances in a way that made you blush.

Slowly, he was repairing the damage Pitman had done to the Montgomery fortunes. In the few weeks of their marriage, she and Alex had been able to put the Montgomery household in order. Together, they'd been a good team.

But now here was this countess, hanging on Alex's every word, looking up at him with big eyes that told him how strong and wonderful he was. And Alex acted as if all the Taggerts had disappeared. His attention was now solely on the beautiful Italian woman.

Jess stood at one end of the kitchen garden and watched. The countess was sitting under a tree, a thick shawl about her shoulders, a book open before her. Jess wanted to tell her to get out of Warbrooke and to leave her husband alone, but she couldn't do that. First of all, Alex would laugh himself to death if she did something that foolish. And later, he'd never let her live her jealousy down. He'd gloat and brag and do all the obnoxious things men do when they think they've won.

No, she had to be more clever than that. There had to be a better way to get rid of the countess.

"Hello," Jess said and the woman lifted her pretty face. "I hope you're enjoying your stay in Warbrooke. I haven't had much time to look after you, but perhaps Alex has been caring for you."

"Yes," the countess said cautiously. "He has been caring for me quite well, thank you."

Jess smiled and sat down on a low wall near the countess's chair. "Has Alex told you about what is going on in Warbrooke? About the opression we're under?"

The countess's eyes widened. "No, not really. I'm sure he mentioned it but . . ."

Jess leaned forward and the countess moved back sharply, as if she thought Jess might strike her. "I wondered if you might help me," Jess said. "You're so very pretty and I need help from a pretty woman."

"Oh?" the countess asked, obviously interested. "Help doing what?"

"You've heard of Admiral Westmoreland? He was sent here by the English to stop the Raider, but so far he hasn't succeeded." Jess smiled. "The Raider's had some help from a few of us."

"Alexander told me about your participation in what he called a raid. The English soldiers—" She halted at the look on Jess's face. "He didn't tell me much."

So! Jess thought, Alex told you about that night, did he? She kept smiling. "Yes, we do what we can to help the Raider. Since that raid the admiral has been punishing Warbrooke by seizing cargo. Once, a man's ship was taken and I'm afraid that's about to happen again. I need your help to find out."

"Me?" Sophy asked. "What can I possibly do?"

"The admiral is boarding with Mrs. Wentworth and she has invited me to tea. Yesterday the admiral received a sealed document from England and I'd like to see what's in that document."

"But where do I fit in?"

"The admiral likes pretty women and you are beautiful. I want you to keep his attention on you while I search his office."

Sophy smiled at Jess's flattery, then her face changed. "What if you're caught? What if this man realizes I was helping you?"

"We get hanged."

"Oh." Sophy took time to digest this.

"Sophy, if I may call you that, you can do it. Look at what you're doing with Alex."

"What could you possibly mean by that? Alex and I are old friends."

"Yes, and I'm so glad he has you. Alex is my friend, too, and I like my friends to be happy."

"You aren't, perhaps, jealous?"

"Not at all. He deserves any happiness he can get. He has so little."

"Maybe there's another man you'd be jealous of," Sophy said. This time, she was the one leaning forward.

"Alex is my husband."

Sophy smiled. "What of this Raider I hear so much of? Is he really so virile and handsome as people say?"

"More so." Jessica grinned. "Would you be willing to help us with the admiral?"

"The Raider isn't at all like Alexander?"

"Not even remotely. If you're frightened, say so. I'll understand. If I'm caught, I'd never tell on you."

"Mmmm. Wouldn't it be nice if you could combine Alexander's intelligence with the Raider's virility? You'd have yourself quite a man."

"There is no such human. You either get brains or beauty. Not both. Do you want to help or not?"

Sophy gave Jess a critical look. "Only if we have a suitable gown made for you. What must that husband of yours be thinking? Haven't you a single decent dress?"

"Alex gave me all his mother's clothes."

The countess said something emphatic in Italian.

"Alex did once promise me a red dress."

"Did he? And you never got it? Come along, Jessica, we have work to do. We must find the six best seamstresses this town has to offer."

"Six?"

"The better to get the work done quickly. When do we go to tea to meet this admiral of yours?"

"At four tomorrow afternoon."

"Difficult, but not impossible."

As Jessica and Sophy went through the common room, the countess chattering a mile a minute, Jess winked at her sister.

"What have you done to Sophy?" Alexander demanded of Jessica.

"I have no idea what you mean, Alex," Jess said innocently. "I merely invited her to tea at Mrs. Wentworth's. I know you don't trust me, so I thought your pretty lady could act as a chaperone."

"No, I don't trust you and with good reason. And I don't think Sophy should be allowed out under your care. There's no telling what will happen."

Jess widened her eyes. "I have no idea what you mean. I merely invited your guest to a social event, nothing more."

Alex squinted his eyes at her. "I don't trust you."

"What a terrible thing to say to your own wife. Have you seen the dress Sophy's having made for me? It's red silk."

Alex was rubbing the back of his neck where, as

usual, sweat and powder were making an itchy paste. "I'm going with you."

"What!?" Jessica gasped. "I mean, how good of you."

"You're up to something, Jess, and I'm going to be there to prevent your participating."

Thirty minutes later, Jess was asking Sophy, "Can you keep both the admiral *and* Alex occupied?"

"Of course," the countess said with confidence. "I can sustain a roomful of men."

"Good," Jessica said, breathing a sigh of relief.

But the countess had not bargained on Jessica. After Sophy's maids finished arranging Jess's thick hair and dressing her in the low-cut red dress, there was the possibility that no other woman would be noticed.

Jess went to show herself to Alex. "Do you like it?"

Alex didn't say a word.

"Alexander?" Jess said. "Are you feeling all right?"

Alex sat down.

"Come along, Jessica, we'll be late." Sophy pushed Jessica toward the door, then turned and hissed at Alex. "Control yourself and don't act like a fool. She is your tiresome wife, remember?" Sophy looked at Jess standing in profile just outside the door. "Beauty like hers could inspire hatred. I will *never* allow my husband to meet your wife. Come on, now, control yourself. Celibacy is your choice. No wonder you have no strength in your legs."

Jess had some difficulty at Mrs. Wentworth's tea. For days, Alex had hung on every breath Sophy had taken but now he didn't seem aware that she existed. He watched his wife's every movement with a glazed expression that she found quite annoying. Sophy was telling one amusing story after another, but Alex seemed oblivious to her presence or anyone else's—he just kept staring at Jess.

Jessica gave Sophy a look of exasperation, nodding her head toward Alex.

"Alexander!" Sophy said sharply. "Why don't you tell the story about fishing in the canals in Venice?"

Alex was reluctant, but Sophy leaned forward toward the admiral, showing off her cleavage, and the admiral asked Alex to tell his story. As soon as Alex began, Jess excused herself to Mrs. Wentworth and headed in the general direction of the outhouse.

Once she was out of sight of the guests, she went upstairs and into the admiral's room. She knew she had only minutes to search, so she tried to be as thorough as possible. She was about to give up when she saw a corner of white protruding from between books on a shelf. She pulled it out, glanced at it, and started to open it when a voice sounded behind her.

"I knew I would find you."

Jess whirled to see one of the admiral's lieutenants standing in the doorway.

"When you took so long to return, I knew you were waiting for me."

Jess held the paper in her hand, concealing it in the folds of her dress. She didn't remember having seen this man before, but he seemed to be convinced she desired him. Jess bit her tongue on a sharp comment about the vanity of men and, instead, smiled at him.

"I was on the way to the necessary and saw this window was open. It looked like it might rain, so I came in here to close the window."

The lieutenant was across the room in seconds. "We need have no secrets between us. You have wanted me for a long time. I've seen the way you look at me when we meet on the street. I've seen the longing in your eyes. You must hunger for a man after being married to that weakling husband of yours."

Jessica moved away from him, backing around the desk, the lieutenant getting closer by the second.

"Tell me where I can meet you."

Jess's hand fumbled for and found a letter opener on the desk. She wasn't going to let this man touch her.

"I will make you the happiest woman on earth. I will give you what that husband of yours cannot."

"I will do my own giving, thank you," came a voice from the doorway.

They turned to see Alex leaning against the door-jamb. He was wearing a pink coat and his wig that went down to his shoulders, but for all his soft appearance, his eyes were hard.

The lieutenant backed away from Jessica. "Sir, I meant no disrespect to the lady."

The expression in Alex's eyes didn't change and Jess could see sweat beginning to trickle down the side of the lieutenant's face.

"I should get back," the lieutenant murmured, edging around the desk and toward the door.

Alex stepped aside to let the young man pass, all the while never taking his eyes off him.

Jess was across the room in seconds. "You sure scared him, Alex," she said. She tried to get past him and into the hallway, but he put his arm out and halted her.

"What are you doing in here?" There was no humor in Alex's face.

"The window was open and I—"

Alex grabbed her arm, lifted it and removed the letter opener she still held. "Don't lie to me, Jessica. Were you in here to meet that man?"

Part of her was startled, but part of her was relieved. "He's handsome, isn't he?"

Alex put his hand on her upper arm and squeezed. "If I ever catch you with another man I'll—"

"You'll what? Spend more time with the countess? Would you mind removing that?" she asked, looking down at his belly blocking her way. How dare he suggest she was doing what he'd been doing all week?

"Jessica," Alex said, but she pushed past him and left the room. When she got to the foot of the stairs, she stuffed the document she held crumpled in her hand into the bosom of her dress and then went back to Mrs. Wentworth's tea party.

That evening, at the Montgomery house, Sophy cornered Jessica while she was doing the accounts. "Whatever did you say to Alex? He's been a regular bear all evening."

"While I was in the admiral's office, some fresh young lieutenant came in the room and tried to arrange a meeting with me. Alex arrived before it went too far, but then Alex accused me of encouraging the man. As if I didn't have better things to do than run off with some silly English soldier."

"Jealousy is good in a man," Sophy said. "You should dress like that every day."

"Dig clams in a red dress? The clams would laugh at me."

"There are other things a lady can do besides dig clams."

"Such as sew and flirt with handsome young men and scheme behind her husband's back?"

"I'm glad you don't scheme," Sophy said sarcastically. "Jess, may I borrow your black cloak? I must make a trip outside."

"Of course," Jess said, not looking up from her ledger.

Sophy slipped the cloak over her shoulders, pulling the hood up over her head. She was halfway to the necessary when, out of the darkness, came a shadowy figure. An oddly accented voice she didn't recognize said, "I have waited for you." Immediately, Sophy knew this was the notorious Raider and she knew he'd mistaken her for Jessica. Even though she knew this man was actually Alexander in disguise, it was difficult to remember. His eyes, hidden in the depths of the black mask, sparkled at her in dangerous glints.

She opened her mouth to explain the mistake but then felt a sword point at her throat.

"Not a word," he said, his voice rumbling and sending chills through her body. "Remove your clothing."

Sophy started to protest, but he pressed the sword deeper into her skin.

"Don't fight me tonight, Jessica. Tonight I take what is mine."

The way he said it made Sophy eager to obey him. She looked into his eyes and she knew she wanted this man.

With trembling hands, she began to untie the laces of her dress. She had forgotten that she was not the woman he wanted. Her dress was unfastened to her waist before Alex realized his mistake.

"Sophy!" he gasped, taking his sword away from her throat.

The countess didn't know when such an overwhelming anger had flooded her before. Here this fabulous man was one second making delicious demands of her and the next he was sounding as if he were a naughty boy caught by his mother.

"Alexander!" she said in the same tone. "Whatever are you doing out there, skulking about in the dark?"

He grinned at her and Sophy felt herself succumbing to his charm. He was frightfully appealing in that black mask.

"I was waiting for Jessie."

"Alexander, remove that mask." She might deal with him better if he were familiar-looking.

"No," he said, still smiling. "Is Jess inside?"

"What are you planning to do to her? What you just did to me? Alex, this has to stop. First you make her jealous of you as Alex, then you . . . you attack her dressed as something out of a play. You *have* to tell her the truth."

"You like her, too, don't you?"

"Yes, I do and I'm sorry I ever conspired with you against her. I have to leave day after tomorrow and if you haven't told her by then, I will."

The Raider, his sword lowered, leaned against a tree. "She's going to be angry with me."

"And well she should be."

The Raider stood up straighter. "But the rewards if I don't have to be secret with her anymore are staggering," he said in a faraway voice, as if contemplating those rewards. "I can be Alex during the day but at night, alone with Jessica, I can be the Raider."

"I envy her," Sophy sighed, then came back to the problem. "You'll tell her?"

"Yes, I think it's time. Tomorrow I will take her out and *show* her who the Raider is."

"Good," Sophy said. "Now go before someone sees you."

He kissed her mouth sweetly and then melted into the forest.

When Sophy returned to the small parlor where Jessica had been working on account ledgers, the room was empty. She found Jess in the little room off Alex's bedroom, everything a shambles about her.

"It's gone," Jess said.

"What is?"

"The paper I found in the admiral's room. I wanted to wait until Alex was out of the house before I read it, but it's not here."

"You lost it somewhere?"

Jessica looked up, her eyes wide. "No, I hid it."

It took Sophy a moment to understand. "Then someone has stolen it. Someone knows what the admiral plans. I don't guess you had time to read it?"

"Not with Alex hovering over me. If Pitman found it and knew I was the one who'd taken it—"

"We will know very soon. Sit down and let's make plans. For all we know, one of the children found it and used it to make paper dolls, but if your Mr. Pitman does have it we'll have to get you out of Warbrooke before they try to hang you."

"Yes," Jess whispered and sat down.

Chapter Twenty

Alex, isn't it rather late to be out? I think, with your health, you should be home resting. Sophy says—"

"I don't want to hear what she has to say."

Jess smiled in the darkness as she held onto the wagon seat. For a while he'd had his pretty countess all to himself, but now Sophy was spending more of her time with Jessica and the children than with Alex. The countess had planned to leave before now but this morning she had announced her intention of staying another couple of days. "Just until I see what happens," she said but wouldn't explain her meaning.

"Are you warm enough?" Alex asked.

Jess pulled the long, hooded cloak about her more securely. "I'm not the one who's ill, Alex. I think we should go back."

"Whoa," Alex called to the two horses, pulling back on the reins. "Here we are." He got down and went to Jess's side of the wagon to help her down, but she was already on the ground. "You can see all of Warbrooke from here," Alex said as he began to unhitch the horses.

"Alex, it's ten o'clock at night. I think we ought to return home. Don't unhitch the horses."

Alex continued what he was doing. He thought that Jess might be a little, well, perhaps just a shade angry when she heard that her husband and the Raider were one and the same. Of course, there was no reason for her to be angry, but who knew about women? There was always the possibility that she'd be sensible and realize that what he'd done, he'd done for his country and to protect her.

He attached an iron hobble to each horse. No, there was no remote possibility that she'd be sensible. It was much more likely that she'd be as unreasonable and difficult as she usually was.

He grinned in the moonlight. Of course he'd be able to calm her down. He'd stroke her and caress her and—

"Alex, what an odd little smile. Would you please tell me what it is that you came here to tell me, so we can get you home? This wet grass is going to ruin those new shoes of yours."

He slipped his arm about her shoulders. "Come over to the ridge and we'll look at the view."

Jess was impatient. "Alex, I have seen Warbrooke at night all my life. I have seen it from this view hundreds of times. Wait! Alex, have you bought a new ship? Is that what you want to tell me?"

He turned her toward him, his back to the village below. "Jessica, I came up here to tell you something much more important than that I bought a new ship."

"There's a lugger for sale that we could use to—"

He put his finger to her lips. "Just listen to me, Jessica. Let's sit down here, so I can talk to you about men and women and trust and duty and honor."

"All right, but if your feet or anything else freezes—"

"Sometimes people do things that they must. Perhaps to another person it may not seem to be something they *had* to do but—"

Jessica's mind began to wander, and as she half listened to Alex, she looked at the scene of the town below them. As she watched she saw moving torches. Someone must be unloading a ship at night, she thought.

". . . and we learn to forgive each other and accept each other in spite of what we might consider flaws and we . . ."

Jess kept watching the scene below. The group of torches was moving faster now, away from the wharf. Frowning, she began to study the group harder. More torches were coming from down the streets.

". . . of course, you did start this, Jessica, and if it hadn't been for you, much of this wouldn't have happened. I'm not really angry with you, but I do want you to remember that when I tell you . . ."

In the moonlight, Jessica began to see a moving form. She couldn't at first make out who it was, but as it came in their direction, she saw it more clearly.

Abruptly, she stood. "It's him," she gasped.

Alex, still sitting, looked up at her. "Who is?"

"The Raider. That crowd down there is chasing him!"

With a knowing smile, Alex rose. "Jess, let me assure you that whoever they are chasing is not the Raider. It's probably a stowaway who just came in or some other such—"

"There!" she yelled, pointing into the trees. "There by the courthouse. It's him I tell you and—oh, God—look, they have him blocked off." She lifted her skirts and began running toward the horses. "I have to help him."

She'd never seen Alex move so quickly or even dreamed that he was capable of moving so fast. He ran up behind her, practically tore the black cape from her body, slung it over his own shoulders, then ran to the horses. He'd unhobbled a horse and mounted it bareback all in a split second, while Jess was still standing where she was.

"Get back to the house," Alex yelled at her as he galloped away, forcing the wagon horse to move faster than it ever had.

Jessica was speechless. For a moment she couldn't comprehend what had just happened. One moment Alex had been whining about love and patriotism and the next he had galloped away while wearing a black cape.

Jess walked back to the ridge slowly, as if in a dream, and watched what was going on. She saw Alex tearing down the hillside and heading straight toward the crowd of torches, but then she lost him in the darkness. To her left she could barely see the movement of the Raider.

"My two men," she said with a sharply drawn breath. Both her men being pursued by an army of English soldiers.

She caught sight of Alex again when the light of the torches briefly illuminated him. There was a moment of confusion while the men turned and started after Alex, leaving the Raider a way to escape the second group of soldiers.

All of them disappeared from her view.

Jess sat down on the ground, her face in her hands.

Why is Alex doing such a foolish thing, she wondered. Why is he risking his health to help a man he considers an idiot?

Jess stayed on the ridge for an hour. She saw the torches reappear then disappear again into the forest. She saw pairs of them move down streets and alleyways and then back to the wharf.

"They've lost them," she whispered and started toward the horse. She had to get home to help Alex. The Raider would disappear to wherever he lived—maybe into the arms of his loving wife—but Alex would need her.

It wasn't easy driving the wagon with a single horse in a two-horse harness down the steep hill, but Jessica didn't notice the difficulty. Her only concern was being there when Alex returned.

Since she'd been watching the searchers from the hillside, she had an idea where they might be, and avoided those places. She didn't want to meet soldiers and have to explain why her husband had taken the other wagon horse.

She made it back to the Montgomery house without seeing too many people or any English soldiers. After leaving the wagon to the bondsman who worked in the stables, Jess started back to their room.

But Sayer called to her, and before she knew what was happening, she was crying on the old man's shoulder and telling him what had happened.

"You love him, don't you?" Sayer said, stroking her hair. "You love my son more than you love your handsome, virile Raider?"

"Yes," Jessica sniffed. "Alex whines and complains and he's an awful lot of trouble, but he really is a good man. He helps as much as he can, considering his state of health. But tonight was too much. He can't go riding like that. His health won't stand it."

Sayer held her closer. "It's *your* health I'm worried about. I think it's time this charade ended." He pulled her from him. "Go to your room and wait for Alex and tomorrow I want you both in here for four o'clock tea. Don't let Alex make excuses, but bring him here."

"If he's well," Jess sniffed. "I'd better heat some water. He'll need to soak his cold feet."

Sayer smoothed his daughter-in-law's hair back. "Yes, pamper him tonight, because after tomorrow you may not feel so inclined."

"What do you mean?"

"I'll tell you tomorrow. Now go and see to your husband. I'll see you at tea."

"Yes, sir," Jess said, kissed his cheek and then left the room.

"Who was it?" Alex asked Nick. Alex had barely escaped the king's soldiers and made it back to the Montgomery house, where he and Nick now stood in the dark, behind the stables.

"I have no idea," Nick said, yawning. "As far as anyone has told me, your admiral had been told a ship carrying contraband was arriving. He planned to search the ship at night."

"But someone dressed as the Raider led the soldiers away," Alex stated flatly, concealing his anger. "Someone pretending to be me."

"Where was your Jessica? She seems to—"

"With me," Alex snapped. "I took her to Mc-Gammon Peak to tell her I was the Raider, but then she looked down and *there's* the Raider riding across the town, soldiers in back of him, soldiers in front of him. I barely got there in time before they closed in on the fool. I would never have done something so stupid."

"Going to tell Jessica you're the Raider, eh?" Nick

gave Alex a lopsided grin. "That little filly is going to let you know what she thinks of you."

"Why do you think I took her so far out of town to tell her? I don't want Pitman hearing what she says to me." In spite of his words of dread, Alex was smiling. "Truthfully, I'll be glad when she knows. There'll be no more secrets between us."

"And no more separate beds."

"Come on, let's get home," Alex said, adjusting his wig. "I'll take Jess out tomorrow and tell her. Meanwhile, I plan to find out who this imposter is."

Jessica had to wait a couple of hours before Alex returned, climbing in through the window. He looked awful. His clothes were wet and muddy, his wig askew, his face drawn and tired.

"Jess!" he gasped when he saw her. "You should be in bed."

"So should you." She helped him through the window, then led him to the bed and pushed him to sit. Instantly, she was at his feet, removing his wet shoes and hose and then wrapping his cold feet in a warmed towel.

"Jess," Alex said, amusement in his voice. "What's this about? What are you doing?"

"Alex," she said, looking up at him with pleading eyes, "you shouldn't run off like that. You could hurt yourself. Your heart can't withstand escapades like tonight."

He was watching her. "You were worried about me?"

"Of course. Here, take off those clothes—all right, I won't look—and get into bed. And here's a dry wig if you think I can't bear the sight of a bald scalp. And I have soup for you. I'll feed you as soon as you're in bed."

Alex stripped off his clothes in record time, pulled on the dry nightgown and wig and got under the covers. He slumped into an invalid-looking pose and called to Jess that he was ready.

She brought a bowl of hot soup to the bed, put a napkin under his chin and began to feed him. "Whatever made you run off like that?" she chided.

He looked at her over the spoon. "I didn't want your Raider caught. He means so much to you."

Jess's eyes got watery for a moment. "Alex, you risked your life merely to save a man because I like him?"

Alex gave a shrug that said there was nothing else he could have done.

With a smile she leaned forward and kissed his forehead, then resumed feeding him. "That was very good of you, but your health means more to me than the Raider's. He can get himself out of trouble, he doesn't need—Alex! Are you all right?"

He caught her arm and pulled her back down to sit on the bed. "Repeat what you said."

"I said the Raider seemed quite capable of getting himself in and out of trouble. I don't want you to risk—"

"No, tell me how my health means so much to you."

He was holding her hands in his, his eyes like a hawk's.

Jess looked at her hands and blushed. "Well, Alex, maybe I've said a few things in the past, about your clothes and how you're so lazy and such, but I really do like you a great deal."

"How much?"

Jess didn't look up.

"You like me enough to love me?"

Jess climbed into bed with him, wrapped her arms

and legs about him, and put her head on his shoulder. "Alex, the Raider isn't real. He's just physical. I like you better, which is why I was so scared tonight. I may not have you for long, but I'm going to do everything I can to keep you alive as long as I can. Swear to me you won't go off chasing the Raider again."

"I think I can do that," Alex said, nestling Jess next to him.

"What was it you wanted to tell me tonight?" she asked sleepily.

"I don't think now is a good time," he said, holding her. "I don't want anything to ruin this moment. I'll tell you tomorrow."

"After tea with your father," Jess murmured.

Alex stroked her hair and held her as he sat up in bed, not sleeping but watching the sun come up, and thinking how good life could be. Right now he had what he wanted most: Jessica's love. He knew that she'd love him no matter what, through sickness, through full-bottomed wigs, even through a few little white lies about the actual shape of his body and what he did in the evenings. Not many men had the opportunity to verify their wife's love as Alex had done.

He smiled and pulled her closer. Tomorrow night he'd tell her everything and she'd understand. If she was woman enough to love him in spite of his unappealing physique, then she was certainly woman enough to understand.

But just in case, he thought with a smile, he'd better remove the breakables from his room. Jess might not understand immediately. But he'd tame her, oh yes, he would.

"You look lovely, Jessica," Sayer Montgomery said. "Is that the red dress the countess had made for you? Alex, don't you think she looks lovely?"

Alex didn't answer.

Jess laughed. "I think he does like the dress."

Sayer looked from one to the other. "You both look especially happy today. Did something happen?"

Jess put down her tea cup. "I'm glad the Raider wasn't caught last night. Did you hear any news?"

"Only that he got away and they got the contraband out in time."

Jessica was filling Alex's teacup while he lounged in his seat. She knew he liked to annoy his father.

"I wonder how the Raider knew about the ship?" Sayer asked.

"I'd like to know that, too. I'm assuming that was the message the admiral received, but I didn't give it to the Raider. I didn't even have time to read it before it was stolen."

"Do you think the Raider took it from your room?" Sayer asked.

"In broad daylight? I doubt—"

"What?" Alex shouted, coming out of his euphoria. "Did *you* take a message from the admiral? Is *that* what you were doing in his room?"

"Alex, please calm down."

Alex jumped up, overturned his chair and nearly upset the tea table. "Did Sophy know about this? Did she help you? I'll wring *both* your necks. You and that damned red dress, if it hadn't been for that, I'd have realized what you were up to. So help me, Jessica—"

"Sit down," Sayer bellowed, effectively stopping Alex's tirade. "I'll not allow a lady to be spoken to like that in my presence."

Alex slumped in the chair and sulked. His eyes told Jess he'd get her later.

"I want you to kiss your wife and tell her you're

sorry for your bad temper. It's from his mother's side of the family. No Montgomery man before him *ever* screeched at a woman."

Alex sat there, his jaw set.

"I like that idea," Jess said, not at all disturbed by Alex's outburst. Her only concern was the stress his anger put on his weak heart.

Sayer glared at his son until Alex grabbed Jess's hand, kissed the back of it and mumbled some incoherent words.

"Oh," Jess said, obviously disappointed.

"Goddamn you!" Sayer bellowed, ignoring Jess. "I've bred no son like you. I've seen you kiss that little Italian flirt and she's not half the woman Jess is. Aren't you man enough to kiss your own wife?"

Alex exchanged a look of rage with his father, then he grabbed Jess and pulled her into his arms. In spite of the fact that the tea table was between them and cakes and teacups went rolling, Alex kissed Jessica with all the passion he'd been storing inside himself for weeks.

"There!" Alex yelled back at his father as he shoved Jessica back down to her chair. "I may not be able to please you any other way but I *can* kiss my wife." With that, he angrily left the room.

Sayer was watching Jessica as she sat there, utterly dazed.

"Go on, go to him," Sayer said gently.

Slowly, Jessica got up and went to the door. Her eyes didn't focus as she made her way down the hall and stopped when she heard voices.

Eleanor and Sophy were sitting in Sophy's room.

Jess closed the door, leaned against it, and took a moment to recover herself. "Alexander is the Raider," she said in a voice of great strain.

"Yes, dear, he is," Eleanor said.

Jess sat down. So many thoughts were going through her mind. She was *married* to the Raider. Slow, weak Alexander was the Raider. "Am I the last one to know?"

"Not the *last,* I'm sure," Sophy said.

Jess took a deep breath. "Who else knows?"

Eleanor looked up from her sewing. "Let's see, there's Nicholas, Nathaniel, probably Sayer, Sam and—"

"Sam! But he's only two years old. Why am *I* the last to know?"

"Alex probably thought you'd harm yourself."

Jessica sat still for a moment, trying to let this news sink in. How had he managed to keep such a secret? Why hadn't she guessed? "How did you find out?"

Eleanor smiled. "You can't keep a secret from a woman who does your laundry. Men seem to think little green elves wash their clothes and put them away. Alex's never even noticed that I've twice washed his Raider clothes and rehid them. I had to dry them hanging inside my night clothes."

Jess blinked at her sister then turned to Sophy. "And you?"

"I knew him in Italy. He never had a fever."

"And Nate?" Jess asked Eleanor.

"As far as I can piece together, Sayer sent Nate out to find out who the Raider was. Nate followed Alex—you know how he always manages to be where he's not supposed to be."

"I guess that's why Nate and Sam adore Alex," Jess said. She had never felt so stupid in her life. "But Sayer always sneers at Alex," she said, hoping it wasn't true that she was the *only* one who didn't know.

"Alex doesn't know his father knows, and Mr. Montgomery has never informed him otherwise. I guess he feels that if Alex doesn't trust him, he doesn't trust Alex. At least the Montgomery men can keep secrets from each other—if not from their women," Eleanor laughed.

Trust, Jess thought. That's what it all came down to: trust.

Her mind was beginning to function once again. She began to remember things.

There had been their wedding night with Alex telling her to get out of his room, then the Raider climbing in her window. There had been Alex telling her the Raider was incompetent, and the Raider getting angry with her for repeating what Alex said. And when the gunpowder had exploded, she had worried about the Raider's blood on her hands, yet it had been Alex who came to her rescue, an Alex who'd seen her fears and let her suffer rather than tell her the truth. And Alex had arranged for Ethan to marry Abigail.

"How did it begin?" Jess asked. How could Alex have put her through this? The Raider said he loved her; Alex said he loved her; yet both men—no, this one man—had put her through hell.

Sophy and Eleanor together told all they knew about Alex, how he'd become the Raider, how he'd managed to hide it from the town.

"The Raider wouldn't marry me," Jess whispered. "I begged him but he refused me. He said Alex 'couldn't' make love to me."

"What?" Eleanor asked. "I didn't hear you."

"Who was the Raider last night when Alex and I were on the hill?" Why hadn't she seen how strong he was when he'd mounted that wagon horse? All she had done was think how he was endangering his health. *"I'll* endanger his health," she muttered.

"No one knows who it was," Sophy said. "I would imagine it's making Alex a little crazy."

Jess stood. *"I* am going to make Alexander more than a little crazy." She left the room.

Chapter Twenty-one

It was late when Jess burst into the room she shared with Alex. Her heart was pounding and her breath was coming in short gasps.

Immediately, the smug, knowing look Alex was wearing left his face. "What's happened?"

"I can't tell you. It'd be too much for your weak heart."

"Damn my heart!" he said, grabbing her arms. "Jessica, what has happened?"

She took a deep breath before answering. "It's the Raider."

The smug look returned to Alex's handsome face. "Yes, my darling, I know you know."

Jess put her wrist to her forehead. She was the epitome of distressed womanhood. "Can a woman love two men at the same time? You for your intelligence and the Raider for kisses like tonight in the forest?"

Alex smiled in the way of a man with superior knowledge. "Of course you can, darling, if his kisses are— Forest? Tonight? When?"

"Just now. I was in his arms moments ago. Oh, Alex, you're such a friend to me. I *can* tell you my innermost thoughts, can't I? I do so hate secrets, don't you?"

"What secrets? Our kiss tonight? Jess, I can explain. I have reasons for what I did." He looked at her with pleading eyes.

"No, no, *his* kisses," Jess said, hugging herself. *"His* arms. *His* body. Tonight when he touched me, I—"

"Who touched you?"

She looked at him in surprise. "Why, Alexander, you're not usually so slow to understand. The *Raider's* kisses, of course. Tonight when he touched me I—"

"The *Raider* kissed you tonight? Someone besides me in my father's room kissed you?"

"I knew you'd understand. What the Raider and I have goes beyond mere passion; it's a meeting of the minds. Oh, Alex, I wish I could forget him. Would you kiss me again? Try to make me forget."

After a moment's pause, Alex took her in his arms, and kissed her with passion.

Jessica's eyes were closed as she lay in his arms a moment. Then, briskly, she got up. "Could you try harder please?" she asked with some exasperation in her voice. "This is *important,* Alex."

He blinked a few times, then he kissed her face, her neck and her ears while his hands feverishly roamed over her body.

Jess pushed away from him and sighed. "It's just

not the same. I think I'm a one man woman. Alex, we'll always be friends, but, physically, it's not the same."

Alex didn't seem capable of speech.

Jess yawned. "I think I'll go to bed," she said and turned away.

Alex grabbed her arm and turned her to face him. He tore off his wig, revealing a thick head of dark hair. "Jess, *I* am the Raider," he said solemnly.

Jess opened her eyes wide in surprise. "Why, Alex, your hair grew back."

"It didn't grow back, it's always been there."

"Let me see." He bent his head and she inspected his hair. "It's still a little thin in places, but, don't worry, it will all probably return soon. I'm sure it's the good care I've been taking of you. Now, excuse me, I'd like to get some rest." She turned toward her bedroom.

"Jess, didn't you hear me? *I* am the Raider."

"Yes, of course you are, dear, and, Alex, I can't tell you how much your jealousy pleases me." She smiled fondly at him.

"Jealous of myself? I *am—*"

She put her fingers to his lips. "Alex, remember your health. Don't strain. It's kind of you to want to please me, but remember that you can't fool a woman who has kissed both men. Tonight I've kissed the Raider and you, and, believe me, the kisses are different."

Once again he kissed her fervently. "The Raider kisses better than that?"

Jess took a moment to recover. "Yes," she said at last. "Goodnight, Alex." She turned and shut the door in his face.

Once inside her room she poured a glass of water, started to drink it, then, on second thought, threw it in her face. "This is going to be more difficult than I thought," she muttered.

She was still shaking as she climbed into bed and, as she made her nightly prayers, she said, "Dear Lord, forgive me for lying but if ever a man deserved what he's going to get, Alexander Montgomery does."

It took her a long time to fall asleep and twice she woke to hear Alex pacing in the next room. She smiled, thought, I'm married to the Raider, turned over and went back to sleep.

When morning came, she stretched happily and thought of what she'd learned the day before. She couldn't quite believe that both her men were actually the same one, but she was certainly happy to contemplate the idea.

Of course, she wasn't about to allow Alex to share her happiness—at least not yet. He'd not let her know he was the Raider because he thought her too stupid to keep the secret—or too flighty or too whatever he thought was wrong with her.

When she remembered all the times Alex had made her defend the Raider and how the Raider had said terrible things about Alex . . .

She heard the latch between their rooms move and she snuggled under the covers, pretending to be asleep.

"Jessie."

Sleepily, she rolled over to look at him. He wasn't wearing his wig but he did have on his padding. His eyes were red from lack of sleep and he looked devastated. Never had a devil looked more angelic. Jessica gave him her sweetest smile. "Did you sleep well, Alex?" She almost purred, remembering the times the Raider had made her cry.

"I'd like to talk to you."

She sat up in bed. "Why of course, Alex. I'm always ready to listen, no matter what you have to tell me."

He sat on a stool beside the bed so his arms rested on the mattress. He studied his hands.

"Alex," she said softly, "I understand about last night. I'm sure it was brought on by your father's disappointment in you, but I've been telling him of the good you do around here. Don't worry, eventually, he'll begin to believe that you're worth something. You don't have to pretend to be the Raider to get either his love or mine."

Alex didn't look up. "Jess, how would you feel if you found out I *was* the Raider?"

She waited until he was looking at her, then answered as simply and as innocently as she could.

"Why, Alex, I'd hate you. I'd never be able to speak to you again, much less live with you. That's just too awful to contemplate. That would mean *you* were the one who told me the Raider was incompetent, yet when I repeated that to the Raider—you—you got angry with me and made me miserable. And that would mean it was you I begged to marry me—oh! that was humiliating!—yet you knew that I was marrying you. No, Alex, I can't believe a single man would be capable of being such a low-living, lying, sneaky, deceitful, cowardly bastard. I would deeply, sincerely *hate* any man who could play such a hideous game. Play with *my* feelings, with *my* life."

She stopped and smiled. "No, Alex, you're a *good* man and that's why I love you. I know that, had circumstances been different and you been physically able, you would have been as manly as the Raider, but I don't think you could be so dishonest as to be both Alexander Montgomery and the Raider."

She blinked, wide-eyed. "Does that answer you?"

Alex's face was white as he nodded.

"Are you planning to continue wearing your wig now that your hair is growing back?"

"I . . . I hadn't thought about it." His voice was hoarse.

She leaned forward and whispered against his cheek. "It *is* a little thin yet, perhaps you should hide it and pray that it grows back somewhat thicker. At this point the wig really is better-looking."

For three days, Jessica did everything she could to make Alexander's life miserable, and she did it in such a way that no one—with the exception of Eleanor—could fault her. She waited on him as if he were an infant, talked to him as if he were a wayward child—and did everything she could to sexually entice him.

She had another dress made, this one in emerald green satin, and she filled the low neckline with a piece of lace that had belonged to his mother. Once they were alone in his room, Jess removed the lace and bent over in front of him so often that her back began to ache. But it was worth any amount of pain to see him sweat.

At dinner she cut his meat for him, chided him to eat his vegetables, refused to allow the children to jump on him and, in general, let it be known how much of a weakling he was.

Eleanor watched her with angry eyes while Sophy's eyes sparkled in delight. Sophy even announced she was staying a few days longer.

Neither Marianna nor Pitman seemed to sense anything out of the ordinary in Jessica's behavior.

And Jess never missed an opportunity to tell Alex how she was so glad he wasn't the Raider. Then the next minute she'd tell him how, if he were the Raider, she could borrow his black costume and ride with him. She made up long fantasies of how romantic a couple they'd be, a Mr. and Mrs. Raider. And if they were hanged, they'd have adjoining nooses.

Each time she talked of this, Alex turned paler and Jess grew angrier at him. Why did he think she was so stupid?

On the afternoon of the third day she pointedly told Alex she was going to Farrier's Cove. His spirits were so glum that she had to say it three times before he lifted his head and heard her.

She went to the common room where Eleanor was bending over the fire.

"You'd better stop this," Eleanor hissed. "That man adores you and you're hurting him badly."

"I've shed a few tears over him, too." She stuck a sumac root onto a skewer and began to roast it.

"What are you doing now?"

"Making a little 'medicine' for my husband." Jess smiled at her sister and dropped the charred root into a mug of boiling water. She skimmed the nastiest bits off the top, then took it in to Alex.

"Here you are, my darling," she said in a tone one would use to talk to an elderly, invalid person. "This will make you feel better." She handed him the warmed mug.

Alex smelled of it and grimaced.

"Now, now, you must take your medicine. Drink up like Mama's good little boy." She turned her back enough so she could still see Alex out of the corner of her eye. She saw him toss the vile liquid out the window.

When she turned back around, she took the mug. "That's a good boy, now you just rest. Mama has an errand or two to do."

Jessica was out of the Montgomery house in no

time at all and running toward Farrier's Cove. She figured Alex would have to row to Ghost Island, then dress and come to her. She knew as well as anything that the Raider would appear to her. And she was ready for him.

Jess was so glad to see him that she didn't know if she could do what she'd planned. As he was running toward her she saw how like Alexander he was. Their hands were the same, the Raider had that Montgomery walk, his shoulders thrown back and walking lightly on his feet, and their lips were alike.

Jess opened her arms to the Raider. How could she not have seen that Alex's lips and the Raider's were the same? How could she have desired one pair and not the other?

The Raider was all over her at once and Jess knew she'd better say what she had to or she'd lose her resolve.

"His hair's grown back some but it's so thin it's pathetic and his breath smells terrible, as if he's decaying inside." The Raider's teeth were on her neck.

"What?" he murmured.

She had some trouble thinking. "I'm afraid my husband is dying. Please hold me. It's so good to feel *strong* arms about me. Alex is so weak I have to hold his arms in place. Oh, please make love to me."

He stopped untying the front laces of her dress. "Make love to you? But you're a married woman. Married to someone else." He was pulling away from her.

"I think Alex would understand." She clutched at him.

"Understand another man making love to his wife? *No* man understands that." He stepped away from her.

"It's not as if he were actually a man. Not a complete, whole one." She put her arms about his neck.

The Raider pulled her arms away. "He may come looking for you."

"No, I gave him a sleeping potion. He'll be out all night. He won't be here."

"You *drugged* him?" He was aghast.

"I wanted time alone with you. I knew you'd come tonight. I felt it. Come back to me. We have all night to make love."

"I thought you were an honorable woman, Jessica Taggert, but I can see you aren't."

"And who are you to talk of honor? You who encouraged me to marry another man. You who slipped into my room on my wedding night with my poor, broken husband only feet away."

"It's different for a man."

"Like hell it is," she snapped, further shocking him. "Go on, get out of here. I'd rather have my stinking, balding, poor-kissing husband than you any day. At least he has brains." She left the cove.

By the time she got back to the Montgomery house, Jessica was feeling a little guilty. After all, Alex was suffering because he loved her. He was afraid to reveal himself as the Raider for fear she'd hate him.

But then she remembered some of the many underhanded things he'd done to her as either the Raider or as Alex and her resolve hardened.

Eleanor waylaid her the next morning.

"Jessica, whatever you're doing to Alexander has to stop. He looks worse each day. And why does he keep breathing into his hand and sniffing? And this morning he asked me what wearing a wig does to a person's hair."

Jess smiled. "I'm not doing anything he doesn't

311

deserve. When I think of what he's put me through . . ."

"Yes, what you've put each other through. I think you should tell him you know."

"Not yet."

"Jessica, if you don't tell him soon, there won't be much of him left. He's refusing to eat anything you've touched."

Jessica laughed.

"Did you tell the Raider you were poisoning Alex?"

"Close enough."

She was still smiling when John Pitman halted her. She generally did her best to avoid him and she was grateful the Montgomery house was large enough to do so.

"I want to buy that cove you own."

"What?" Jess asked, not sure she had heard correctly. The cove where the dilapidated Taggert house stood was worth next to nothing.

Pitman spoke again and this time he offered her a healthy sum of gold.

If you've ever had any brains, now's the time to use them, Jess thought. "Sold," she said, smiling. "It's yours." And I'll do what I can to find out why you want it, she told herself.

Chapter Twenty-two

JESSICA surreptitiously watched Pitman for two days and nights before she was able to follow him. She'd been very careful not to say anything to Alex about what she was planning so he wouldn't feel it was his duty to "save" her.

She climbed out the window and began to follow the man. She kept well behind him because she knew where he was going.

At the old Taggert house, he stopped, looked around him, then pulled a light net from under his coat and cast it into the waters at the edge of the cove.

Fishing at night? Jess thought. Whatever for?

The next minute a heavy weight landed on top of her and a hand engulfed her mouth.

"Keep quiet," came Alex's voice in her ear.

She struggled a bit, then gasped when he released

313

her. "You nearly smothered me! What are you doing here?"

He moved to lay beside her. He was wearing his smallest wig and a plain brown coat. "I heard you thrashing about and went to investigate."

"Why weren't you asleep?"

His face was very close to hers and he gave her such a hot look that Jess could feel her skin warming. "I haven't been sleeping much lately."

Jess tried to recover herself. "Alex, your health can't stand this dampness. I insist you——"

"Quiet!" he commanded as he looked through the trees toward Pitman. "Tell me what's going on—and I want no lies, Jessica."

She smiled in the darkness. It amazed her that she'd not realized Alex and the Raider were one and the same. "Pitman offered me a purseful of gold for my land."

"For *that* land?" Alex gasped.

Jess gave him a look of disgust.

"What's he doing?"

Jess strained upward to see. "He's just pulled in a net of oysters, he's opening them and now he's throwing them away."

Alex raised himself. "Is he putting that oyster in his pocket?"

Jess grinned. "Oysters in lint sauce."

Alex grimaced.

Jess sat back down. Alex was hovering over her and she looked at him. The cotton padding in his breeches was lumpy and concealed his muscular thighs but there was no padding in his big calves. They came from years of walking on a swaying deck.

"If only the Raider were here," Jess sighed wistfully. "He'd know what to do."

Alex sat down beside her, keeping Pitman in view. "I thought you said his brawn was more than his brains."

"When it comes to acts of courage, he intuits what needs to be done. Animal instinct."

Alex's eyelids lowered. "Jess, are you seeing him again?"

"Not like you mean. He tries to persuade me to come to his bed, but I resist. I am your faithful wife."

"Why you little—"

"He's leaving," Jess said and rolled under Alex's body, snuggling against his warmth. If there was one thing she knew how to do, it was silence Alexander.

Alex seemed to forget Pitman as he slid down beside Jess and began kissing her.

Jess was losing her resolve. "Alex, don't you think we should see what Pitman was doing?"

"In a minute," he murmured, seeking her lips again.

"Alex!" She pushed at him with all her might. "At first I can't get you to kiss me and now you won't stop. Let's get out of here, I'm getting cold," she lied. The truth was, the small of her back was beginning to sweat. I'll have to stop this soon, she thought, because I'll not be able to last.

She managed to roll out from under Alex and stand, her breasts heaving, her face flushed, her body yearning for his. She lifted her skirts, turned on her heel and started running toward the water.

Once she was away from Alex, she could think more clearly. She knew some rotting nets had been left at the back of the house and she retrieved the best one now. When she returned, Alex was standing at the edge of the water.

She refused to look at him. A couple more of those

hot, longing glances of his and they'd be tumbling about on the sand.

"Jessie."

"Stand over there, Alex, and find some flint. I'm going to haul up some oysters and you're going to open them. And don't you dare touch me. Go!"

Alex smiled slightly and left her as she tossed him the first couple of oysters. "You know, Jess, I'm not really as ill as you think. In fact, in this moonlight with you looking so lovely I just might be able to—"

"To what?" she said impatiently. Maybe he'd been punished enough. Maybe *she'd* been punished enough. Maybe she ought to tell him that she knew.

Alex walked to her. "Look at this." Up to the moonlight, he held between his fingers a fat, perfect pearl.

"Pearls?" Jess gasped. "In these waters? No wonder Pitman wants to buy my cove. Alex, he'll be rich."

Alex kept looking at the pearl. "I wondered what had happened to it."

"To what? Here, let's open these oysters."

"My mother's pearl necklace."

"Your mother's . . . Alex, are you saying these pearls were planted?"

"Think Pitman will notice the holes drilled in the pearls? I can't see in this light, but the hole seems to have been filled with a paste."

"Filled? Seeded?" Jess asked. "Nathàniel. He did this. Wait until I get him."

Alex caught her arm before she could move. "I'm sure Nate did do this but he didn't make the plan."

Alex put the pearl in his pocket. "My brother-in-law embezzles Montgomery funds, then uses that money to buy your land, thereby keeping the money in the family."

"Your father," Jess said.

"Exactly. My father. That crafty old devil. I had no idea he knew what his son-in-law was doing."

"He'll go a long way to protect his children," Jess said, but Alex didn't seem to be listening. "Maybe he didn't want to hurt your sister."

Alex started walking. "Let's get back."

"Yes, you need your sleep."

Alex just kept walking, Jess having to run to keep up with him. At the house, he left her in her room and gave her orders not to leave. Jess started talking about his poor health, but the look he gave her made her sit down on the bed.

"I swear I won't leave," she said and meant it.

Alex nodded and left the room. He went down the hall to the boys' room, picked up a sleeping Nathaniel and carried him to his father's room. He dropped Nate into the feather mattress beside Sayer.

"What the hell!" the old man yelped.

Alex lit a lantern.

Nate sat up in the bed while Sayer floundered about, trying to right himself. "Hello, Mr. Alex," Nate said. "Did something happen?"

Alex pulled the pearl from his pocket and tossed it to his father. "Familiar?"

Sayer looked at Nate, then back at his son. "Possibly."

"How many did you put in the oysters, Nate?"

Nathaniel looked like he wanted to run away. He didn't like being caught between the two men.

"I think we've been found out," Sayer said. "Took you long enough," he said, looking at Alex.

It took Alex a moment to comprehend just what his father was saying. "What do you know?" he asked in a low voice.

Sayer locked eyes with his son. "I breed no cowards."

Alex didn't know whether to laugh or be enraged. He'd been hating his father these many weeks, yet his father had known all along. "You kept your secret well."

"Can't say the same for you. If it hadn't been for some of us in this house protecting you, you'd have been long dead."

"Jess helped me a few times, but she was helping a man other than her husband. She has no idea I'm the Raider."

"She does, too!" Nate said, then subsided under Sayer's glare.

"What?" Alex gasped. "Nathaniel, I'll raise blisters on you if you don't tell me the truth. Does Jessica know I'm the Raider?"

Sayer put his hand out to his son. "Of course she does. She's known since you kissed her in this room. I thought you'd been tormenting her long enough and I wanted an end to it. Jess is a good girl and she didn't deserve what you were doing to her."

"But she said my kisses weren't—And that my hair—" He stopped and shook his head. "I'll get her for this."

"She was prepaid," Sayer snorted. "Can you forget your bride for a moment and concentrate on the pearls? You think Pitman believes the cove is full of pearl-bearing oysters?"

Alex told of seeing Pitman. "He's offered Jess four times what the cove is worth."

"My money," Sayer muttered. "Tell Jess to hold out for more money. I'll get all the Montgomery money back yet."

"I didn't know you knew of his embezzling."

Sayer gave his son a cold look. "What was I to do? Accuse my own son-in-law? Haul him before the courts? *You* may have no loyalty to your family, but I do."

Alex just smiled. He was so pleased that his father didn't believe he was a weakling and a coward, that nothing could make him angry. He toyed with the lace at his sleeve. "How many pearls did you plant and how many have been found?"

"With this one and the one Pitman found tonight, I'd say there are three left. If Jess waits, he'll raise his offer."

"And what happens if he finds out he's being played for a fool?"

"He's too greedy to see that. Now, the two of you may be young enough to do without sleep, but I'm not. Go on and go to bed. And you, boy," he said to Alex, "go in to your wife and stop this charade. You can trust her."

"Yes, probably," Alex said noncommittally. "To bed, Nate," he ordered and followed the boy to the door. Then, on impulse, he turned, hugged his father and kissed his cheek. "Thank you for believing in me."

"Humph!" Sayer snorted. "When *I* make a son, he stays a son and doesn't change."

Alex smiled. "I'm as good as Adam and Kit?"

Sayer looked as if Alex had lost his mind. "When I see those two I'll let them know what I think about their not coming to help us when we needed them. I'll tell them about leaving you here all alone to save an entire town." Sayer took Alex's hand. "And I'll tell them what a goddamn fine job you've done of it, too." Sayer chuckled. "Even won the hand of a beauty like Jessica without so much as removing your wig. You're

319

a Montgomery all right, boy, and one of the finest."

Alex left his father's room feeling twenty feet tall.

Eleanor was laughing at Jessica as her sister struggled under the weight of two buckets of hot water.

Jess gave her sister a malevolent look.

"It's your own fault," Eleanor hissed at her. "You're the one who continues playing the game. Tell Alex you know he isn't ill."

Jess shifted the buckets. "He thinks I think he's dying. Until he trusts me enough to tell me the truth, I cannot tell him what I know."

Eleanor threw up her hands in despair. "You've made it nearly impossible for him to tell the truth. All right, have it your way. Wait on him until your fingers fall off, for all I care."

"Thank you," Jess said and started down the hall with the hot water.

"He knows," Sophy said. "Alexander knows she knows he's the Raider."

"Of course he does," Eleanor said. "But let them play their lovers' games."

"Speaking of lovers' games, where were you and that handsome Russian last night?"

Eleanor blushed.

"Mmmm," Sophy said. "I think I'll postpone my journey south another day. I couldn't bear not seeing how all of this turns out."

"Here you are, Alex," Jess said tenderly, setting down the basins of hot water for his feet. It had been two days since they'd seen Pitman at the Taggert cove, and since then Jess was beginning to doubt that Alex really was the Raider. He looked awful, he seemed to be too weak to move, he wouldn't eat, he just lay in bed, his eyes only half open. Jessica was beginning to think she'd been wrong. How could this sick man be the Raider?

Just before sundown, Alex went to sleep and Jessica left the room. She went outside, enjoying the cool air, and began to walk. Before she knew what she was doing, she was at Farrier's Cove.

She watched the sunset and tears began to trickle down her face. She knew she was feeling sorry for herself but she couldn't help it. She didn't seem to have either of the men she loved anymore.

"Jessie."

She turned to see the Raider standing there in the fading light. She took a step toward him but he stepped back. She stopped.

"I've been waiting for you to come here for days. I have something important to tell you."

Jess wiped away her tears. Now he'd tell her that Alexander and the Raider were one and the same person. Now he'd eliminate her fears that it wasn't the truth. Now he'd relieve her worries about Alex's health. Now he'd at long last trust her.

"I've been thinking about what has happened between us and I've decided that you're right."

"Yes," Jess said, smiling. She *was* right. She was trustworthy, she wasn't foolish as he thought and she deserved to be told the truth.

The Raider looked at the ground, as if what he had to say was very difficult for him. Jess felt sympathy for him.

"This isn't easy for me to say, but I've finally listened to you." His head came up. "You *are* a married woman and I've decided to respect that. Cynthia Coffin has let me know that she'd be delighted to receive my attentions. Therefore, I'll be seeing her from now on and leaving you to your husband." He turned away from her.

Anger rushed through Jessica's veins. With one great leap, she jumped onto his back, hanging on with one hand and beating whatever of his body she could reach with the other hand. "I'll *kill* you, Alexander Montgomery. You touch another woman and I'll attach a live clam in its shell to your—"

He pulled her around to the front of him and kissed her.

She pulled the mask off his face as they kissed. "It *is* you," she whispered.

"The one with the cruel mouth," he said. "The weak-spined piece of seaweed you married."

He was holding her off the ground and she began to kick.

"You made me miserable! Our wedding night! I cried all night. And there you were, sneaking in the window."

"What about Ethan Ledbetter? What about the way you told me no woman would have me? You said a woman'd only want my money and that the *good* Montgomerys hadn't answered the distress call. And you made everyone laugh at me. I was shot and bleeding and you called me a drunk."

She was kissing his face, her hands running through his hair. "What about when I saved you from the gunpowder? I had your blood on my hands and there you sat—alive and well—yet you let me worry myself sick over him—you."

"And remember when I saw you after that? You cried on my back."

She hugged him. "Oh, Alex, how could you be so completely different? Alex is so delicate and soft, while the Raider is . . ." She stopped and looked at him. "It's a good thing that mask covered that big nose of yours or everybody in the county would have known who you were."

"Big nose?" he said threateningly. "Let's see what my big nose can get into."

Jessica squealed with delight as Alex began untying her dress, then followed his fingers with his face, nuzzling her breasts. He tossed her onto his hip as if she were a child and continued undressing her while he kissed her. "Not sorry you didn't get Adam?" he asked as his lips moved down to her breasts.

"Alex, you're the only man I love. No matter how many people you are, you're the one I love."

He lowered her to the ground after that, his mouth making hot little circles on her breasts, her stomach, her thighs. Her hands searched for him and she was impatient when she touched fabric.

Alex removed his clothing quickly and lay beside her.

Jess pushed him off the top of her. "I want to see all of you. I want to see that you really are Alexander."

Chuckling, Alex lay still as she inspected him in the fading light.

For the first time Jess could see his face and his body. She knew both of them well, but Alex's face had always been atop a grotesque body. She ran her hand over his flat, smooth belly, then looked at his face. It was indeed Alex's face.

"Satisfied?" he asked.

"Not by a long way," she said, moving her hand down until she grasped his manhood.

Alex was no longer laughing as he pulled her to him. "It's been such a very long time, Jess."

"Yes," was all she could murmur as he moved on top of her.

His hands caressed the inside of her thighs, then the

outside, until she was impatient for him. "Alex," she whispered and he entered her as smoothly as water lapping at a ship's bottom.

He made love to her slowly, gently, until the passion began to rise in both of them. Eagerly, Jess pushed him onto his back and climbed on top. She opened her eyes for a moment, then smiled at her sense of confusion. The only man who'd ever made love to her before wore a mask, and the only way she'd seen an adult Alexander was as a fat invalid.

But she thought no more as Alex pulled her to him and caressed her buttocks as she moved up and down.

At the last, when they could no longer stand their torment, Alex pushed her beneath him, Jessica's legs locked about his waist, and finished.

Jess clung to him for a long moment, not wanting to release him, afraid he'd disappear again.

He seemed to understand what she was feeling and pulled away from her to smile. "Who do I become now? The Raider or Alexander?"

She was suddenly serious. "You have to continue to be Alexander in public. People will guess you're the Raider if you change now."

"You mind if I'm the Raider at night?" he asked, nuzzling her neck.

"Feel free to raid whatever you find in your bed."

"Oh?" Alex said, laughing. "Think you'll sleep with me now?"

"I've *always* wanted to sleep with you," she protested, then laughed. "Oh, Alex, so *that's* why you didn't want me in your bed. You knew I'd know if you—"

He kissed her. "I thought you might guess. And you learned after I kissed you at my father's request, didn't you?"

"Mmmm, maybe," she said.

He began to tickle her. "'Why, I'd *hate* you, Alexander,'" he mocked in a falsetto voice. "What did you call me? Lying, sneaky, deceitful? *You* could have written the book. And my hair!"

"It *is* a little thin, Alex."

He rubbed his hair and his face on her bare breasts. "You have a lot to answer for."

"Maybe it will take me a lifetime."

"At least," he said, his eyes glowing. "Let's get back. I have to become Alex again for dinner, then I can raid you tonight."

Jessica giggled.

One minute they were laughing and the next all hell broke loose. They had been so enraptured with each other that they hadn't heard the six men sneaking into the cove, their lanterns covered with black cloth.

At a command from someone, the cloths were removed, the lantern doors opened and Jess and Alex were lying in a pool of light, surrounded by six leering men.

Alex used his body to cover Jess as best he could while grabbing her dress and draping it about her. Before them stood the admiral, Pitman behind him.

"I arrest you, Alexander Montgomery, in the name of the king," the admiral's voice boomed, "for treason."

Pitman rushed forward, grabbed Alex's Raider mask carelessly tossed onto the rocky beach and looked at Alex. "This'll teach you to play with me. Did you think I wouldn't know about those pearls?"

"But Alex—" Jess began but Alex stopped her.

"Take your lanterns away and let her dress," Alex said. "I'll go with you."

"Alex, no!" Jess cried.

The admiral motioned the lanterns away as Alex stood, as proud nude as at any other time.

She dressed in the darkness as she watched Alex, in the circle of light, pull on his clothes. The black silk, the way he stood, his broad shoulders, his flat stomach no longer concealed by padding, proclaimed who he was.

He never looked back as he walked away with the soldiers.

"I found him and lost him all in one night," Jess said, then began running.

Chapter Twenty-three

"ALEX has been arrested," Jessica said, slamming the door to the dining room of the Montgomery house behind her.

"Oh my God!" Eleanor began to cry, her body shaking.

"Whatever for?" Marianna said. "Did his clothes frighten the sun away?"

Jessica gave vent to her anger and fear. "For being the Raider," she screamed. "And *your* husband betrayed him."

Nicholas entered the room before Marianna could speak. Immediately, he went to Eleanor and pulled her into his arms. "Alex?"

Eleanor nodded against his shoulder.

"This is ridiculous," Marianna said. "Alexander is as likely as I am to be the Raider. He'd starve to death if Jessica didn't cut his food for him. They'll release him when they see the size of his belly."

There were hot tears beginning to roll down Jess's face. "He doesn't *have* a fat belly. He doesn't have anything wrong with him. He's perfect, he's . . ." She was crying too hard to finish.

"Perfect?" Marianna said. "Alexander? But he's fat and—" She halted, then her eyes widened. "You mean Alex *is* the Raider?"

No one bothered to answer her.

"I have to tell his father," Jess said, trying to control herself. She ran down the hall and burst into Sayer's room.

His face changed when he saw her. "Alex," he gasped.

Jess did what she often did when she was upset and ran into his arms. "Pitman told. He found out about the pearls and was angry. It would be easy to spy in this house. The admiral took Alex."

Sayer stroked her back and let her cry for a while, then pushed her away from him and said, "We have to make a plan."

"They're going to hang him. My Alex."

"Stop that!" Sayer commanded. "Nobody hangs Montgomerys. We get shot or die of sword wounds or get crushed under barrels, but we *don't* get hanged. You understand me? Now stop that sniveling and let's figure out what to do. First, get Eleanor and Alex's Russian in here, then that Italian woman and young Nathaniel. Give Marianna a glass of whiskey and tell her to go to bed. We'll try to make some plans tonight."

It was Sophy who was able to think most rationally. Eleanor, Jessica and Nathaniel were every minute on the verge of tears, while Sayer and Nicholas were enraged.

"What proof do they have that Alex is the Raider?" Sophy asked.

"He's my son," Sayer bellowed. "Of course my son would—"

Sophy kissed the old man's forehead and winked at Jess. She tried again. "It's my guess that we have time. I don't think the admiral will hang Alex tomorrow." She put up her hand to stop the protests. "I think the admiral will want to gloat. He'll send for more Englishmen to come observe him. At least, I think he's a man of vanity."

"Mrs. Wentworth had to give him her pier glass so he could see himself in his uniform," Eleanor said.

"Yes, I thought so," Sophy said. "I wish we had someone else to play the Raider. If more raids were made while Alex was in prison . . ." She looked at Nicholas.

"He's taller than Alex. People would see at a glance he wasn't the Raider," Jess said.

"That didn't matter when *I* was the Raider," Eleanor snapped.

Everyone turned to her until she fidgeted in her chair. "I found the message Jess had taken from the admiral. It had fallen to the floor and been blown under a cabinet. So I knew the English were planning to search the *Poinciana* when most of the crew was gone. Alex and Jess were gone, so I borrowed Alex's Raider clothes and led the soldiers away from the ship."

"And almost got yourself killed," Jess yelled. "If I hadn't seen you from the top of the hill, you'd have been trapped. Alex saved your neck."

"Yes, but if you—"

Sophy stepped between the two quarreling sisters. "I think I have a plan. First of all, we need to find out what's going on. Jess, do you think your Wentworth ladies would help Alex?"

Jess was solemn. "This town would die to save him. He has done much to help them."

"I think I have an idea."

"I knew I would catch him," the admiral was saying while sitting at the Wentworth dining table. "He never fooled me with that fat belly and that wig. I suspected him all along."

Mrs. Wentworth slammed her glass down and her husband kicked her ankle under the table.

"Good work," Mrs. Wentworth mumbled.

Abigail was still too stunned by the news to speak. Jessica Taggert had won after all. She'd won the man with the money, as well as the most desirable man in this decade. While she, Abigail, had to make do with weekly visits to where Ethan was hiding in the forest. He wasn't in the English army; now he was a fugitive.

"Yes, and I'll hang him for what he's done. Just as soon as the other officers get here, I'll hang him," the admiral said.

"Here, Admiral," Mrs. Wentworth said, "have another muffin. I made them especially for you. Do you have any idea when the officers will be here?"

"End of the week. Come Saturday morning I'll hang that traitor."

Abigail blinked back a few tears, then hid her face so the admiral wouldn't see. She wondered what Jessica was doing right now. Her head came up and she looked at her mother. Jessica was making plans. She knew that as well as she knew the curls in her own hair.

"We must console the Montgomerys," Abigail murmured. "They must be devastated."

"I'll hang anybody that interferes in this," the

admiral bragged. "I hear old man Sayer Montgomery used to rule this town. Well, Warbrooke has a new master now."

Mrs. Wentworth looked down at her plate.

Eleanor met Jessica and Nicholas at the wharf at one in the morning when Nick's ship returned. "Well?" she said as loudly as she dared when Nick came down the gangplank. "Did you get it?"

"No kiss?" he teased.

Eleanor gave a pointed look to a tired Jessica following him. "You had no problem with the ship's master?"

"They treated Nick as if he were the master," Jess said.

"All Russians treat each other with great respect."

"It's just us you treat like rubbish, is it?" Eleanor asked.

"Here, take this," Jess commanded her sister, handing her a canvas bag.

"You *did* get it."

"We bought every pot of black dye Boston had to sell. Is everyone ready to start distributing it? We don't have much time."

"We're ready." She put her hand on Jess's arm. "The admiral moved the trial to tomorrow. The winds were good and his officers arrived a day earlier than expected."

"Then the people of Warbrooke will have to work tonight," Jess said firmly.

"But nothing will be dry," Eleanor began, then stopped. "They'll wear them wet, then. Jess, have you slept?"

"No! She paced the deck over my head all night so I, too, did not sleep," Nick moaned.

"You look healthy to me," Eleanor said.

Nick grabbed her waist and pulled her to him. "Come, we have work to do."

All night the Taggert children ran from one house to another, slipping through the shadows, whispering directions and plans.

The Wentworths did their job of entertaining the admiral and his officer friends with a noisy party that distracted the men from anything going on outside.

Jessica had given Marianna orders to keep her husband busy. "Even if you have to sleep with him," she'd said.

Marianna had paled. "I guess I owe Alex that much. I wish I'd believed in him."

"I wish I had, too," Jess murmured.

Eleanor had tried to get in to see Alex while Jess was gone, but the guards had refused to let her see him. There was a double row of guards surrounding the building where he was held and she couldn't sneak past them.

By dawn, Eleanor had the children in bed, their faces showing their exhaustion. On impulse, she pushed Jess, fully clothed, in with them. "Be still or you'll wake them."

Jess was too weary to protest. She slept.

Alexander's trial before the English judges was a farce. They knew he was guilty before a word had been spoken. He was still wearing his black silk clothes, his hands tied behind his back, as he stood in the prisoners' box.

There were very few people from Warbrooke at the trial, only a few girls whose sighs were audible as Alex stood with his shoulders back, chest out, legs apart and black whisker stubble on his sharply cut cheeks.

"Quiet them," a judge commanded.

A bailiff brought forth Alex's Raider mask and tied it in place while Alex stood impassively.

The girls in the gallery gave a swooning sigh.

"It looks to me that he's this Raider," a judge said and the others nodded.

The admiral nodded smugly toward the men surrounding him. It was essential to him that he impress these men.

"Hang him."

The bailiff grabbed Alex's arm and was about to lead him away when a man came flying through the window, glass going everywhere. He was dressed entirely in black with a mask just like the Raider's.

"So! You think you caught me, do you?" the masked man yelled delightedly.

"What's the meaning of this?" a judge roared. He pointed at the admiral. "I thought you'd caught the scoundrel."

"I did," the admiral yelled. "This is an imposter."

Chaos and noise reigned in the courtroom as English soldiers began chasing this new Raider, who was now on the balcony. The pretty young girls in their frilly dresses kept getting in the way though, and the young soldiers quite often tripped over a dainty foot. Then they had to comfort the girls because a few skirts were torn.

"Seize him!"

Through the opposite window of the courthouse came charging another Raider.

"So! You think you caught me, do you?" the new Raider said.

Everyone halted for a moment, even the two young men who were rolling on the floor with pretty girls.

"Seize him!"

"Which one, sir?"

"Either of them, *both* of them," the admiral shouted.

One Raider made it out the broken window while the first one—or was it the second one—was caught.

"Unmask him!" the admiral ordered. The judges had sat back down, as had the admiral's officer friends whom he'd invited to Warbrooke at his expense to witness his triumph. They were beginning to look amused.

The soldiers pulled off the Raider's mask.

"Abigail Wentworth!" the admiral gasped.

The judges snickered and the officers laughed while the soldiers holding Abby let their hands slip over her body.

The north doors of the courtroom burst open. "We caught him, sir." Four soldiers held another Raider. They stopped when they saw Alex, still wearing his mask, still standing in the witness box and Abigail wearing men's trousers. They unmasked their Raider.

"Ezra Coffin," someone said.

The south doors opened.

"We caught him, sir."

By now the officers were howling with laughter, glad to witness the pompous admiral's humiliation. The judges were trying to keep their dignity.

"Shall we release them all or hang them all?" a judge asked solemnly.

"Look out the window," someone called.

Within minutes, only the judges, the admiral and Alex were left in the courtroom because everyone else had rushed outside to see the excitement.

Warbrooke was awash with Raiders. They were on rooftops, in the church steeple, upon damp-looking black horses. Two well-upholstered Raiders were on a porch, each churning butter, and one Raider about five feet tall was holding the hand of a three-foot-tall

Raider and carrying on his hip a two-foot-tall Raider who was trying to remove his mask. Four English soldiers started chasing a Raider who had what looked to be a twenty-inch waist and thirty-seven-inch hips. One limping, suspiciously old-looking Raider was leading a cow wearing a black mask.

The judges, after a few minutes at the window, returned to their seats.

"Release him," they said tiredly and since there was no one else to do it, the last judge in line lifted his robe, took out a knife and cut Alex's bindings.

"But he's the Raider," the admiral said. "You're releasing him to defy me again. You can't let him go."

Alex pulled the mask from his face and walked out of the courtroom. Jess was waiting for him, wearing her red dress, just outside.

He smiled at her and put his arm about her waist. "Let's go home."

"Yes," she said and clung to him.

Epilogue

AND did you see Mrs. Farnsworth?" Jess laughed. "Ninety if she's a day. She had all four of her cats wearing masks."

It was the next day and Jessica and Alex and Eleanor were sitting alone in the common room. The town had declared it a holiday and Eleanor had banked the cooking fire. She said everyone would be drinking the wagonloads of beer Sayer had ordered and no one would need food.

After the ending of the trial, the admiral had been ordered back to England, his record forever blemished. The admiral, never one to suffer alone, had blamed everything on John Pitman. As a result, Pitman had been relieved of his post as customs officer and sent back to England. Marianna had refused to accompany him.

"So it's ended," Jess said, holding Alex's hand. She couldn't stop looking at him. No more wigs, no more peacock coats—no more putting his life in danger. And he was all hers.

"Did Jess tell you?" Eleanor asked.

"Eleanor, I'm sorry, I forgot."

"Nicholas has asked me to marry him and I've accepted," Eleanor said. "I know he's only a bondsman, but we'll manage. Maybe your father would help us. Alexander! I see no reason for your laughter."

Alex couldn't contain himself. He was laughing hard and pointing out the window behind Eleanor.

"Now what?" Jess asked.

They heard the sound of trumpets and then the door was thrown open. As the three watched in silence, a thick red carpet was rolled down on the floor by handsome young men in beautifully tailored military uniforms. A man, resplendent in a dark uniform with braid on his shoulders and sleeves, stepped forward.

In a deafening voice he said, "Presenting His Imperial Highness, the Grand Duke Nicholas Ivanovitch, twelfth in line of succession to Tzarina Catherine of all the Russias."

"Not another customs officer already," Jess groaned.

In walked Nicholas wearing a red uniform encrusted with so much gold it put Alex's coats to shame. His sword hilt glistened with jewels.

"Good heavens, it's—" Jessica began, but she stopped because Eleanor had just fainted and fallen off her chair.

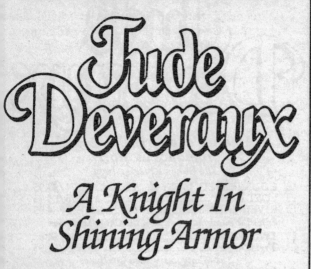